The fourth installment of this award-winning mystery series draws actor-turned-supersleuth Tennyson Hardwick into his most challenging case.

Tennyson and his family are in South Beach, Florida, where he landed a role in an upcoming horror movie by celebrated director Gustavo Escobar. Ten's soon-to-be-adopted daughter, Chela, runs into an old friend, Maria, from her earlier days as a prostitute in Los Angeles. The pair dive into the South Beach scene, but Maria mysteriously goes missing.

When Maria's body washes ashore, Chela and the authorities fear that her suspicious death is connected to a serial killer. When it's believed the suspected killer may have committed suicide, things return to normal for Ten and his family. But the respite doesn't last long, and Tennyson discovers someone is after him, his girlfriend, and Chela.

In a pulse-pounding thriller that could be described as Walter Mosley's Easy Rawlins meets *Miami Vice*, Tennyson Hardwick is back big time with his trademark sexiness, sizzle, and James Bond-like sophistications.

OTHER WORKS IN THE TENNYSON HARDWICK SERIES

Casanegra

In the Night of the Heat

From Cape Town with Love

BLAIR UNDERWOOD PRESENTS

SOUTH BY SOUTHEAST

A Tennyson Hardwick Novel

TANANARIVE DUE AND STEVEN BARNES

ATRIA PAPERBACK
New York London Toronto Sydney New Delhi

ATRIA PAPERBACK
A Division of Simon & Schuster, Inc.
1230 Avenue of the Americas
New York, NY 10020

First Atria Paperback edition September 2012

ATRIA PAPERBACK and colophon are trademarks of Simon & Schuster, Inc.

For information about special discounts for bulk purchases,
please contact Simon & Schuster Special Sales at 1-866-506-1949
or business@simonandschuster.com.

The Simon & Schuster Speakers Bureau can bring authors to your live event. For more information or to book an event, contact the Simon & Schuster Speakers Bureau at 1-866-248-3049 or visit our website at www.simonspeakers.com.

Manufactured in the United States of America

10   9   8   7   6   5   4   3   2   1

Library of Congress Cataloging-in-Publication Data

Underwood, Blair.
    South by southeast: a Tennyson Hardwick novel / Blair Underwood; Tananarive Due and Steven Barnes. — 1st Atria paperback ed.
        p. cm.
    At head of title: Blair Underwood presents
    1. Murder—Investigation—Fiction. 2. Miami (Fla.)—Fiction. I. Due, Tananarive, 1966– II. Barnes, Steven, 1952– III. Title. IV. Title: Blair Underwood presents.
    PS3621.N383S68 2012
    813'.6—dc23   2012014242

ISBN 978-1-4516-5063-1
ISBN 978-1-4516-5065-5 (ebook)

For our mothers,

Eva Reeves Barnes
1928–1981

Patricia Stephens Due
1939–2012

in loving memory

"The very least I can do is afford you the opportunity of surviving the evening."

—*North by Northwest*

"It's so horribly sad. How is it I feel like laughing?"

—*North by Northwest*

Suggested MP3 Soundtrack

"Represent" (Orishas)
"El Cantante" (Héctor Lavoe)
"Night Life" (Aretha Franklin)
"In the Air Tonight" (Phil Collins)
"Conga" (Gloria Estefan)
"Somos Latinos" (Adalberto Alvarez y Su Son)
"Quimbara" (Celia Cruz & Willie Pacheco)
"Give It Up" (The Goodmen)
"Freak" (LFO)
"Culo" (Pitbull, featuring Lil Jon)
"SOS" (Rihanna)
Gasolina (DJ Buddha Remix) (Daddy Yankee, featuring Lil Jon,
Noriega, and Pitbull)
"Gun Music" (Talib Kweli)
"Tha Crossroads" (Bone Thugs-n-Harmony)
"Can't Let Go" (Anthony Hamilton)
"Shhh" (The Artist Formerly Known as Prince)
"Fame" (David Bowie)
"Dirty Laundry" (Don Henley)
"The Collector" (Nine Inch Nails)
"Welcome to the Terrordome" (Public Enemy)
"Tightrope" (Janelle Monáe featuring Big Boi)
"If This World Were Mine" (Luther Vandross, featuring Cheryl Lynn)
"A Lo Cubano" (Orishas)

PROLOGUE

ALL ACTORS DREAM of a meeting that will change our lives forever, but I didn't dare hope that Gustavo Escobar would be mine. Even my agent had no idea why Escobar had called me. Escobar was an Oscar-nominated director on a hot streak, and I was lucky to have a job playing a corrupt lawyer on one of the last surviving soap operas.

After twenty years in the industry, I no longer believed in the Big Bang. My microscopic part in a respected film set during the Harlem Renaissance, *Lenox Avenue*, hadn't done much for my career. And the last two Hollywood heavy hitters who had contacted me—both women—craved skills that had nothing to do with my acting. Let's just say I was wary of calls from powerful strangers.

So when Escobar hadn't shown up by nine o'clock for our eight thirty dinner meeting, I was sorry I had agreed to meet him without more questions. Once again, the joke was on me.

But it was hard to nurse a bad mood inside La Habana.

La Habana was L.A.'s new ethnic restaurant du jour, modeled after a 1930s Cuban supper club. That night, a full orchestra played a rousing rumba against colorful walls splashed with artificially aged murals of palm trees and revelers in old-fashioned Cuban dress. Black-and-white footage of bandleaders Beny Moré and Arsenio

Rodríguez flickered on overhead screens. At least I would have an excuse to call my former girlfriend, April; I was glad for any novelties to bring us together.

I was pulling out my phone to give my agent the bad news when a hand rested on my shoulder. *"Lo siento,"* a man said. "Sorry, I'm on Cuban Time. Gus Escobar."

I started to stand, but his firm hand on my shoulder told me not to bother. Instead, Escobar sat across from me with a wide smile, sweeping off his white fedora.

I was surprised to note from his short-trimmed graying hair that Escobar was probably in his fifties, long past the norm for an overnight success in Hollywood. He had a slightly rounded midsection, but he carried himself fluidly, like a man who was fit and comfortable in his own skin. His round, thick-framed black eyeglasses were prominent, more fashion than function. His skin had only a whisper of a suntan, so I wouldn't have guessed his Latino heritage if I hadn't known. His accent was as much Brooklyn as Havana.

"I lived in New York too long," he said. "I never get used to the traffic."

"No problem," I said with my trademark grin. "Just glad to meet you, Mr. Escobar."

"No, no, please, it's Gus. You have to try the Bucanero beer. They keep extras on ice for me. *Oye,* Ramon!" He signaled for the waiter with two fingers.

Like a lot of Hollywood types, Escobar was broadcasting himself at full wattage, creating a character, but I liked him. Rather than focusing on himself, he pulled his chair closer and gave me his attention, as if I had summoned him. "You're kind to make time for me on short notice," he said. "I'm such an admirer. I saw *Lenox Avenue,* and you stole the scene. But Sofia Maitlin and I are distant cousins, did you know? She's told me so many good things. She said you've never gotten full credit, but you're a hero."

Here it comes, I thought, my grin turning to concrete. A year before, I'd helped an A-list actress save her adopted South African daughter from a kidnapping ring. I'd forgotten that Maitlin shared Escobar's Cuban lineage on her mother's side. I was sure Escobar was about to offer me a job as a bodyguard, and I wasn't interested.

But I was wrong. Escobar reached into his aged leather satchel and pulled out a script, which he nudged my way on the table. The title showed through the plastic sleeve: *Freaknik.*

"For your eyes only," Escobar said. "I have a beautiful part for you. We start shooting in Miami this fall." Then he waited for my response as if his livelihood depended on my answer.

The floor seemed to shift beneath my feet. I was glad the beer had arrived, because I needed a swig of moisture against my dry throat. I didn't want to look as shocked as I felt.

"Good, no?" Escobar said, meaning the beer.

I wouldn't know. I hadn't tasted anything. My mind was still stuck on Escobar saying he had a part for me.

Three months before, Escobar had been featured on the cover of *Entertainment Weekly* during the Oscar campaign for his last film, *Nuestro Tío Fidel,* his arty biopic of Fidel Castro. He had lost the Best Director Oscar to Martin Scorsese, but barely. Len Shemin, my agent, had told me that his entire client list would kill to be in Gustavo Escobar's next film.

"Why me?" Len would have kicked me under the table if he'd been there, but I asked.

"*Lenox Avenue,*" he said. "The fire in you. I want that fire for *Freaknik.*"

I wanted to hear more, but a respected young actor passing our table—I won't say who—did a Scooby-Doo double take when he saw Escobar. He barely hid the *who the hell are you* glance he shot my way before he stretched out his hand to the director. He gushed at Escobar like a college coed meeting the team quarterback. Escobar was polite and patient while the actor angled for a meeting, but Escobar's eyes frequently apologized to me for the intrusion.

"Thank you so much, but I . . ." Escobar began, hinting for privacy.

"Man, I've wanted to tell you," the actor went on. "I'm blown away by your human portrait of Fidel. Our government talks shit about him, but you weren't afraid to show the good he's done. You didn't take the easy road."

Escobar shrugged. "Truth is in the eye of the beholder, but *gracias*."

The actor excused himself reluctantly, his last gaze toward me full of burning envy. I gave him a mock salute before he walked away. *Adios*, asshole.

I'd watched *Nuestro Tío Fidel* to prepare for the meeting, but Fidel hadn't seemed sympathetic to me in the film, which chronicled his transformation from a young revolutionary to a frail, paranoid dictator. Reviewers had compared Fidel's depiction to Michael Corleone's journey in *The Godfather* and *The Godfather Part II*. From what I'd heard, the Cuban exile community in Miami had practically proclaimed Escobar a patron saint.

"Fidel's good side?" I said. "Was that what you were trying to show?"

"No man is only one thing." Escobar winked, and I was sure he wasn't talking about Fidel anymore. "The good and the bad are always at war."

My father often told me how his pastor could stare at any congregant and see his story. That was how I felt sitting across from Escboar that night in La Habana, watching the glow of insight in his eyes. If he'd talked to Sofia Maitlin about me, he had doubtless spoken to others. He knew details about my history that I'd tried to bury in a deep hole. He seemed to know I was broken, afraid to dream, that I'd almost talked myself out of meeting him.

He might even know I had killed a man. Had Maitlin guessed and told him?

I wanted to say more. To confide. To confess. To explain.

Escobar nodded, as if I had spoken aloud. He sighed, and tears suddenly shone in his eyes, erased when he blinked. "Let me tell you something," he began. "I lost everything and everyone as a boy. People ask why I would follow *Fidel* with a horror movie. I ask, why not? Loss is one of the true universal experiences. Our walking dead follow us. They know us as their own."

For the next two hours, while patrons came and went and the orchestra packed up its music, Escobar talked to me about his project. *Freaknik* was a zombie movie only on the surface, he said. "This film, at its heart, is about love and redemption in the face of unspeakable evil," Escobar said, tapping the script. "The ultimate trial. Like me, Tennyson, you've known trials. That's why my vision won't be complete without you."

April and my father often said everything happens for a reason, but I never believed it until that moment. My worst experiences had led me to a table with a stranger who was willing to help me build a future in Hollywood. It wasn't just the best night of my career; it was one of the best of my life.

If only I had known what real horror would be waiting in Miami.

All of us are the walking dead.

ONE

SALSA IS THE sound of Miami, and Miami changed everything. The Magic City's betrayal follows me with music.

Salsa was blaring the night of Marcela's birthday, when I was showing off the fruits of the dance skills that had once been a part of my trade. Dancing comes easily to me, so I was delighting Marcela's sisters and girlfriends by twirling them two at a time—one in front, one in back—spinning and weaving through the intricate beat like a black Fred Astaire. Anybody watching me would have thought I'd been raised in the heart of Havana or San Juan. *Baile!*

I hate to brag, but this brother can dance his ass off in any language.

That night, my life's pieces were still in place. When I have trouble sleeping, I hold that snapshot in my head, every detail close enough to touch. My patio was packed with Marcela Ruiz's relatives, aunts and cousins and half-siblings of all ages and sizes, dancing with equal fervor. Up and down the street, the night was lit by candy-store colors.

I didn't know anyone at the party. I didn't even have a date. Didn't matter.

Marcela was my father's girlfriend, although *girlfriend* is a funny word for a woman in her fifties whose boyfriend is pushing eighty. Marcela coaxed my father back from the dead. She had become his "special friend" when he had his stroke and ended up in a nursing home years before. Marcela was an RN, and she'd taken a liking to Dad before he could speak or move, appreciating what was left. At the time, I saw nothing but a husk. Marcela gave me my father back, and Dad and I were doing better the second time around. LAPD Captain (Ret.) Richard Allen Hardwick was a cool-ass guy.

With each passing month, a part of me braced for the next time Dad would go to a hospital. I'd believed he was as good as gone at the nursing home, and I'd never been so wrong. When the time came, it would be the worst day of my life. I could tell already.

Dad couldn't dance the way he used to—he could barely walk—but he was dressed for the dance floor in white linen slacks and matching guayabara. He bobbed his head to the salsa beat, walking with the polished wooden Ethiopian cane my ex had given him as a gift. Dad worked his cane like a fashion statement. Somehow Dad had found peace with his limitations. When I doubted miracles, I remembered Dad rising from his body's ashes.

Dad hovered over his party like a movie director. "Hey!" he barked at a middle-aged man near the serving cart. "Get that damn pig away from the dance floor."

A wide-hipped woman turned, shooting him a nasty look over her shoulder. While her hips rocked with exuberant worship to Rubén Blades, she'd nearly sent the serving cart and its whole roasted *cerdo* flying to the floor. The pig was a traditional Cuban meal Dad had ordered for Marcela, and the skewer was rammed through the porcine mouth, emerging on the other end. Made me want to swear off pork. Dad had ordered enough food to feed a village.

"Mister, do you speak *inglés*?" Dad said, raising his voice. "Move it, *por favor*."

After two years of speech therapy, people could understand almost everything Dad said. Marcela's cousin Fernando, a neurosurgeon from West Palm Beach I'd introduced to Dad an hour before, didn't appreciate being mistaken for the help. He stared at Dad with a combination of pity and loathing.

I gently led Dad away from Marcela's cousin. "Sorry, man," I whispered to Fernando. "You know how it is."

"No," Fernando said, and sipped from his mojito. "I don't know how it is. In fact, I'd very much like to understand, but . . ." He shrugged, leaving the thought hanging.

Like everyone in Marcela's family, he wondered why she was wasting her last hunting years with an old man on a cop's pension. Dad was old enough to be her father. If I hadn't been so confused about it myself, Fernando's attitude might have pissed me off. Dad was seventy-six, and he didn't even have charm on his side.

"*El corazón quiere lo que quiere,*" I said, repeating the phrase Marcela had spoken when I'd finally gotten up the nerve to ask her. *The heart wants what it wants.*

Fernando huffed a curse in Spanish and moved away, tired of conversation. I couldn't blame him. That single phrase had justified endless reckless behavior and heartaches. A copout. Maybe Marcela had daddy issues. Maybe she had a fetish for wrinkles. Maybe she only felt safe when she was in control. Or maybe . . .

Or hell, maybe she was in love with him. I tried to count Dad's good qualities from Marcela's point of view: He stayed home, never running the streets. He didn't talk much, so he was a good listener. And he threw a hell of a birthday party, apparently—even if the best he'd done for me was bringing cupcakes to day care.

Dad had created a Cubana's wonderland for Marcela, with white Christmas lights strung across my South Beach hotel's patio and balcony like stars hanging above the beachfront. Her favorite restaurant had catered a feast, with roast pig, black beans and rice, fried plantains, and fried yucca. A five-member salsa band was working the crowd of fifty into a sweat. Dad had even sprung for a butterfly-shaped ice sculpture, although the painstaking creation wasn't faring well in the warm, humid fall night.

Marcela had been slimming down for the trip to Miami for weeks. She'd squeezed into a short silver glitter dress that was snug in all the right places and showed off the calves she'd won in her new morning jogging regimen. Marcela Ruiz had seemed plain when I met her, but under my father's care, she had blossomed. Dad stared at her as if she were perfection in female form.

But what happens in five years? Or one or two? Six months? I didn't like those thoughts, but it was hard to avoid them when Dad's prescription bottles could fill a Hefty bag. Nothing in his body worked without jumper cables. Marcela understood that better than anyone.

"How much did all this cost, anyway?" I asked Dad. Until he'd met Marcela, he'd been the most frugal man I'd ever known. Even my fifth-grade cupcakes had been on sale, two days past fresh.

"None of your business," Dad said. He looked nervous, fumbling in the pocket of his slacks as if he'd misplaced something. A medicine bottle? He took nitroglycerine tablets for his painful angina, which mimicked heart-attack symptoms. Perspiration beaded his forehead.

"You all right?"

His least favorite question. "I'm no damn child," Dad said. He nearly tripped over his feet as he pivoted away from the catering table, but I didn't move to steady him.

I wandered to the balcony with my bottle of Red Stripe and stared out at Ocean Drive's collection of art deco hotels lit up in candy-shop neon. I'd spent too much money renting the two-bedroom suite for my shoot, even at the "friend" price from a woman I knew who'd made a fortune when South Beach flipped from Retirement City to Vacation Haven in the nineties, But what the hell? My family was celebrating my casting in a horror film as if they thought I was headed for the A list. Chela, the teenager I'd rescued from my former madam, had graduated from high school and would be going to college . . . eventually. We were on our first family vacation—maybe our last. I wanted it to count. I had money sitting in my bank account after winning a sexual harassment settlement against producing powerhouse Lynda Jewell. Long story, and it was far behind me.

Neon. South Beach. The salty-sweet ocean air. *Perfecto.*

Beyond the neon's glare, my beachfront perch was close enough for me to make out the moonlit Atlantic, as still as a sheet of black glass. Pinpricks of lights from distant cruise ships or cargo vessels twinkled in the distance, but the water was undisturbed.

Even on the hottest summer days, Southern California's ocean seems immune from the sun. Now it was fall, and I went swimming practically every day in Miami, often after dark, when the beaches emptied. Heaven. I didn't need a wild ride; a calm, warm bath felt just fine.

Watching the ocean made me think of my ex, April. I almost reached for my cell phone, until I remembered that April was still at work for another hour on the West Coast. I felt itchy if I didn't talk to her every night. How had I let myself end up in a long-distance relationship? *Only you're not in a relationship anymore—remember?*

One day, April and I would have to put a name to what we had. Friends with Fringe? Lovers Lite? We'd collected enough pain over four years to make us both wary of labels, but we couldn't keep hiding from each other forever. *You're the one who's hiding,* I corrected myself. We both knew the next move was up to me. If April nudged me and I pulled back, we would never have another chance to salvage whatever we were trying to build.

"Isn't true love beautiful?" Chela said, startling me from behind. I thought she'd taken up mind reading, until I saw her gazing toward Dad and Marcela. They both stood close to the martyred pig, swaying gently to the band's *bolero*. Dad wobbled, but he didn't fall.

Chela had just turned eighteen, nearly as tall as I was, with a swimsuit model's lithe curves, a scalp full of wild corkscrew ringlets, and a sun-browned complexion that kept observers guessing about her ethnicity. In Miami, most people assumed she was Cuban. Modeling scouts had approached Chela as she strolled South Beach's streets with me, but so far, I'd managed to talk her out of taking any meetings. I'd argued that the scouts weren't from Elite or Ford, so why settle for anything less than the best? In truth, as a college dropout who'd left school to pursue acting, I knew that if she put school off to do modeling shoots, she would never bother to go to class.

But I felt guilty discouraging her. She wasn't avoiding the scouts because of any advice from me; she just didn't see the same beautiful face in the mirror that the scouts did. Chela was slowly emerging from the cocoon of drab, bulky clothes where she'd been hiding. Ocean Drive Chela wore bikinis and sheer fabrics, but not the girl I knew at home.

"So, what's true love?" I said. "Drop some wisdom on me."

"You're asking me?" Chela said. "Please."

"You're the one who said it."

Chela shrugged. Instead of looking at me, she stared toward the ocean. "Loving someone no matter how scary it is," she said. "No matter what anybody says."

After Chela's adolescent liaisons with johns twice her age, her definition of true love could excuse almost any toxic behavior. I used to live by the same credo, and my old life had nothing to do with love. She saw the skepticism in my face.

Chela gave me a cutting look. "Hey, you asked. Not my fault if you can't deal with the answer."

She started to walk away but stopped in her tracks when Dad

rang his martini glass with a knife. The patio slowly hushed except for the slow-moving traffic on Ocean Drive below us, laughter, bicycle bells, and revving motors.

Chela grabbed my arm, excited. "It's time," she whispered, grinning.

Once again, I was the last to hear almost everything under my roof. I'd been invisible to Dad when I was Chela's age, and she was his new BFF. Call me childish, but I felt a sting of annoyance.

Then I was captivated by the sound of Dad's voice; he spoke slowly, careful to enunciate, all evidence of his stroke gone as he rediscovered the basso voice that had made him a coveted public speaker. "Marcela's the birthday girl today, but I'm hoping she'll be good enough to give me the gift of a lifetime," he said.

Dad sounded like himself again for the first time in years. He suddenly clasped Marcela's hands and stared into her eyes. I suspected what was coming, and I doubted the night's fairy tale would have a happy ending.

"Marcela Consuela Ruiz . . ." Dad said, "Will you marry me?"

The gasps that followed were more shock than delight. I think I gasped, too, at least to myself. The night froze. Marcela's face was slack. When I'd once joked to Marcela that she would be my Evil Stepmother one day, she'd looked me dead in the eye and said, "I'm a romantic, Tennyson, but I'm also a realist."

Chela grinned widely and grabbed my elbow, clinging tightly, as if we riding a roller coaster together.

Marcela blinked, and her eyes pooled with tears. She looked confused. "Captain?"

That was what she called my father—Captain Hardwick. At first, the formality had seemed like a ruse to hide their relationship, but the pet name had stuck. It was only one of the unconventional aspects of their union.

Dad reached into his pocket and brought out a felt ring case. After a couple of tries, he flipped it open: my inheritance sparkled inside. The ring was big enough to see from a distance. Marcela gaped at the engagement ring, her face flaring bright red.

"I know . . . it's a surprise," Dad said, more quietly this time. If not for the patio's hush, I wouldn't have heard him. But we spectators didn't want to miss a word. A woman close to me was tossing yucca fries into her mouth like popcorn as she watched.

This conversation was none of our business.

"*Dios mío,*" Marcela said, flustered. She hid half her face with her hand, as if to shield herself from the crowd. Marcela's voice trembled. "You said—"

"I know what I said." Dad cut her off. "What you said. What . . . we said. Let sleeping dogs lie. Face facts. No need to be . . . foolish." For the first time, he hesitated as if he were struggling for words, because of either emotion or his lingering disability. "But I was still hanging on to . . . the past. When I buried Eva, I swore I'd never take another wife."

Marcela blinked, and a single tear made a snail's slow journey across her cheek.

"It's time, Marcy," Dad said. "If not now, when? I can't promise you forever. But I can promise to love you every day. And I'll do whatever it takes to stay by your side as many years as I can."

Dad looked exhausted, his last words mere breath. Beside him, Marcela seemed younger and more vibrant than ever, the sun eclipsing a fading star. She shook her head back and forth, almost imperceptibly, maybe a reflex. *Damn.* My mother had died when I was a baby, and I'd never known Dad to be interested in any woman before Marcela. When had he ever taken a woman out, except to a meeting? Stubborn fool! Why had he waited until it was too—

"Yes!" Marcela said, wrapping her arms around him. When Dad swayed beneath her weight, she steadied him. "I'll marry you. It is my honor, Captain Hardwick!"

More gasps came, louder than before. Chela applauded loudly, and I shook myself from my shock to clap along. A few other people clapped, too, but I think they were the caterers and maybe the scattered children, who loved any excuse to make loud noises.

Most of Marcela's family just stared, never waking from their stunned silence.

"Oh, that's just *wrong*," April said.

I laughed grimly. "Which part?"

I'd finally caught April for our nightly phone date at about eleven—eight o'clock Cali time—when she got back to her apartment after shopping at Whole Foods. I knew her routine, could practically see her opening her whitewashed kitchen cabinets and metallic fridge with her long pianist's fingers while she put her food away. She'd been a reporter for the *L.A. Times* when I met her, but since her layoff a year ago, she was blogging and working publicity for an entertainment PR firm. Whenever I asked how work was going, she said she didn't want to talk about it. Her newshound's soul hadn't adjusted to babysitting celebrities, but the job market was brutal.

I'd closed my bedroom door to mute the party noise from revelers who hadn't gotten the hint when Marcela and Dad went to bed at ten. The band had left, and the food was gone, but Marcela's kin were determined to dance to the mix blaring from her nephew's speakers. The party had started at five in the afternoon, and some folks were still showing up—on Cuban Time, as Marcela had complained. No one group can claim exclusive rights to tardiness.

I would have a hell of a mess to clean up in the morning, but morning was a world away, and I was alone with April's voice. We'd tried keeping out of each other's way after she dumped me, but somehow we'd gotten tangled up again. Before the shoot, we'd been seeing each other two or three times a week, more than we had when we were officially dating.

April's laugh was music. "What kind of son are you?"

"You know I love Dad, but this isn't like May-December. It's like June-December 31st. At eleven fifty-six."

"It's not like they'll want to have kids."

I tried not to feel the prick. During a fateful dinner in Cape Town, April had given me a last chance to win her back, a Get Out of Jail Free card, and I'd blown it with my shock when she mentioned the idea of raising a family together. I'd practically raised a kid already, so why had I nearly choked on my food when April brought up wanting to have children?

Instinct made me change the subject fast. "What about a honeymoon?"

"What about it?" April said. "Don't you think you're confusing sex with intimacy? Besides, you don't know what they do behind closed doors."

A sour mixture of garlic and something tangy played at the base of my throat, and I had to work to flush away the image of Dad and Marcela in bed together. Besides, what had possessed me to bring up Dad's proposal? April never made it a secret when she had a date, and the sole reason we weren't officially together anymore was that April believed she was too old to have a "boyfriend" at nearly thirty. She wanted a family. If I didn't ask her to marry me, I would lose her. It wasn't a threat; it was prophecy.

"Well, I think it's beautiful," April said primly.

"No, you're right—it was," I said. "I was just scared for him, thinking she would back off . . . but she didn't. She'll be with him at the end. What's more beautiful than that?"

Our silence stretched the length of Ocean Drive.

"Let me fly you down this weekend," I said. She'd been promising to visit the set.

"Can't," she said. "Award season. How do women walk in ten-foot shoes? I'm too much of a tomboy to wear dresses every night. I feel like a transvestite."

Good. Between the Golden Globes, the People's Choice Awards, the NAACP Image Awards, and every honor until the Oscars, April wouldn't have much time to meet new men. *Except the rich and famous ones*, my Evil Voice reminded me.

"Cutest tomboy on stilettos I ever saw," I said. "Anyway, I'll make a visit worth your while. I can get you a sit-down with Gustavo."

April could always be lured closer with the right carrot, and my film's director, Gustavo Escobar, was the whole *ensalada*. Escobar was a near-recluse who was impossible to reach when he was working on a project. April supplemented her publicity work with freelance journalism, and an interview with him might be the coup she was looking for to help her land a job on the staff of *Entertainment Weekly*. Even if not, she might impress her bosses by convincing him to sign with her agency. April was looking for any break she could get.

Gustavo Escobar's enlistment to helm a horror movie was the fanboy coup of the year, evidence that horror and prestige weren't mutually exclusive. He'd won Sundance and been nominated for an Oscar for *Nuestro Tío Fidel*, which he'd shot guerrilla-style in his homeland of Cuba. Our current project, *Freaknik*, was more blood and guts than heart and soul, but he was a meticulous craftsman.

As always, I wished my part were bigger, but my agent thought it was the right move for me on the heels of art-house juggernaut *Lenox Avenue*, which had just been released to slobbering reviews. My slim part in *Lenox Avenue* had barely survived the editing booth, but it was still listed on my IMDb page for the film world to see.

"Play your cards right, Ten, and this could be a new beginning for you," my agent had lectured me at our last lunch before I left for Miami. He knew I chased trouble like a junkie. A year before, I'd been a household name for all the wrong reasons. Unless you live in a cave, you know about my brush with actress Sofia Maitlin.

Even that wasn't enough for me. In the past six months, I'd allowed a bad influence in my life to get me into new trouble I hadn't told my agent about—or April. Just as April had once told me, maybe on some sick level, I *needed* to ride the tiger.

I hoped I was ready for a new beginning, free of trouble. But I couldn't lie to myself about the biggest secret I still harbored: I would never propose to April Forrest. It would be cruel to inflict someone like me on a nice girl like her.

"I want to see you," my mouth said, ignoring my conviction. "I miss you."

This time, the silence was barely noticeable. "I know," she said. "I miss you, too."

TWO

I WAS LESS impressed by *Freaknik* after I read the script. Even if you haven't seen it, you've seen it: Teenagers in bathing suits on spring break on an island paradise contract a venereal virus that turns them into pustuled, sex-crazed killer zombies. Despite Escobar's reputation, any aspirations toward art were only in his press releases. Len Shemin, my agent, told me that *Freaknik* was a script Escobar had been shopping for quite a while, based on a series of novels by a bestselling husband-wife team I'd once encountered at the NAACP Image Awards. His new name recognition had finally won him $25 million to bring his vision to life.

Picture a standard zombie movie with a bit of political philosophy sandwiched between bloody orgies. The disease had originated in Project Coast, the real-world South African attempt to create a race-specific disease back in the seventies. Look it up.

Escobar hadn't cast me as one of the leads, since they're both twenty-somethings meant to lure in Hollywood's Golden Demographic: white boys between the ages of fourteen and twenty-one. The female lead, Brittany Summers, had leveraged her implants into a role on a struggling cable series, and the unknown male lead had been hired because of ripped abs and his ability to command a Jet Ski. I was the only real actor on the payroll.

Escobar had offered me the part of the brilliant black marine biologist who happens to be staying at the resort when the infection breaks out. Since my character makes the mistake of hooking up with one of the white girls, I'm one of the first to get infected, and I'm the face of Evil who, at the climax, must die so that the nice white couple can survive.

There won't be a dry seat in the house.

Even after shooting began, I still wasn't sure why Escobar had handpicked me for his movie, but I wrote it off as micro-management. My past as a male escort to Hollywood's desperate housewives had leaked out—although I still denied the rumors to my father—and I figured Escobar thought my name would add salacious *sazón* to his project.

Whatever. Work is work. As my contact in the spy business— let's call her Marsha—liked to remind me, I was still a whore. Longer story.

I finally had a mid-morning set call late enough to accommodate Chela's schedule, so she agreed to come to work with me at the Star Island mansion that doubled as a resort on the fictitious Isla del Sueño, the outbreak's Ground Zero.

It was Chela's second or third visit to a set since she'd been living with me, but this was the first time she'd dressed as if she had an actor's chair waiting with her name on it. Her faux-designer sunglasses covered half her face. She wore white short-shorts, a white tank top with spaghetti straps, and a bare midriff barely covered by a sheer beach wrap. Chela had mastered stilettos in a way April never might. She'd lathered herself in glistening baby oil.

Now I understood why fathers are afraid to let their daughters out of the house.

"What?" she said, pretending she didn't understand my scowl. "Maybe he'll offer me a part."

A part of his what? Escobar's eyes were feasting on the young women on his set, and I'd heard rumors that he and Brittany had late-night rehearsals. Call me a hypocrite, but Chela's past made me want to keep her far away from show business. I knew how easy it would be for her to slip into her old habits. "It's cold in that house," I said. "Put on some jeans."

"You said everybody's wearing bikinis."

"I hear them complaining. The AC's too high." I was lying, and poorly.

Chela ignored me, climbing into my rented red Grand Prix. She'd barely listened to me before she was eighteen, but now she'd dropped the charade entirely. It was hard for me to get indignant over a story I'd spun out of thin air.

"Okay," I said. "Just don't run shivering to me."

I was already sorry I'd brought Chela to Miami.

But not as sorry as I would be.

I would never let anyone shoot a movie in my house, period. Every day on the set, I wondered what the owners had been thinking when they said, "Sure, come trash my mansion."

A cracked floor tile here. A crushed flower bed there. No one went out of their way to be destructive, but it just takes too many people and cameras and generators and miles of cable to make a movie. The wide circular cobbled driveway glistened with at least fifty cars parked around the fountain. A crushed Coke can carelessly kicked into the rock garden was only the day's first offense. I picked up the can to dispose of properly. Some people have no respect.

The house was like an Italian palace, with a stately 1920s quality that Escobar was in love with. The patio, overlooking the bay, had fans with blades as wide as palm fronds, spinning lazily above the cast and crew as they finished the last of their muffins, bagels, and fruit cups from catering and prepared to shoot the morning's scene.

Chela's eyes were wide and excited at the sheer number of hard-bodied extras assembled before enough cameras to shoot the moon launch. It takes a village, all right.

"Who's starring in this?" Chela asked me.

"Trust me, nobody you'd know."

Chela grinned. "Good. You never want big stars in a horror movie. No offense."

"Why not?"

Chela looked up at me as if I was crazy. "Hel-lo? 'Cause they suck, that's why."

"Johnny Depp was in the original *Nightmare on Elm Street*. Kevin Bacon was in *Friday the Thirteenth*."

"Don't count. At the time, they were nobodies."

I chuckled, sipping from my latte. "You sound like you've got it all mapped out."

"B and I came up with Horror Movie Rules."

Poor Bernard had been left behind in L.A., and I was afraid he'd been forgotten. The boy had transformed Chela from street to geek. "Let's hear them," I said.

"One, no big stars. Two, it has to be rated R. PG-13 horror is a waste of film."

"Not a problem in this one." *Freaknik* would be lucky to get past the MPAA, considering the nudity and incest themes between the leads, who played a brother and sister. Just the thought of their scenes together made my skin crawl.

"Three, absolutely no CGI monsters. CGI's great for talking animals, but it isn't scary. Too fake. You always know the monster isn't real."

A laugh rumbled behind us. I knew the voice, but his laughter was rare.

"*Fantástico*," Gustavo Escobar said. "A visionary. Where was she when I was fighting the studio suits? Who is this thoughtful young lady, Tennyson?" Escobar took off his round-framed black sunglasses to peer at Chela more closely.

Chela's face turned deep crimson, and she moved closer to me, nearly hiding. Her shyness pleased me; once upon a time, Chela had been anything but shy.

"Gus, this is my daughter, Chela," I said before she could speak. "She's in high school."

The word *daughter* was fudging. I'd been raising Chela since she was fourteen, but her birth mother had refused to sign the adoption paperwork when I tracked her down, and we'd never made it official after Chela's eighteenth birthday. As a recent graduate, Chela probably wanted to stomp on my foot for saying she was in high school, but Escobar's presence mesmerized her. His aura made both men and women stare. Escobar carried himself as if he harbored the wisdom of the world.

He leaned close to Chela's face and spoke to her with a storyteller's voice. "No big stars, *sí*. The bigger they are, the fewer chances they take. A PG-13 rating only announces to the world that you won't make them uncomfortable. CGI monsters? As the lovely one says, they're merely shadows on the wall. No substance. Only makeup and prosthetics will frighten us. But you forgot one rule."

"What?" Chela said.

Escobar winked at me. "A black man must die, preferably first," he said. "Preferably to save a white female of child-bearing age—the most valued member of our society. This sacrifice gives viewers a pang of loss and foreboding. Politically incorrect for a time, yes, but an important statement in our culture. Remember what Kubrick did in *The Shining*."

How could I forget? I'd read Stephen King's novel, so I was surprised when poor Scatman Crothers caught an ax in his chest as soon as he walked through the door. Didn't happen that way in the book. Kubrick and Escobar apparently shared the same philosophy.

"The Sacrificial Negro," I said blandly.

Escobar's eyes lit up. "*Exactamente!* Rule Number Four."

While Chela giggled, I almost missed Escobar's gaze flickering to her chest. At least he had the courtesy to pretend he wasn't checking her out in front of me.

"Kubrick broke the first rule," I corrected him. "Jack Nicholson. A-list star."

"Everyone knew Nicholson was crazy, so it worked, *mijo*," Escobar said, shrugging. Then he pinched my cheek like a child's before walking away.

Escobar's novelty had worn off. Good thing he moved on, because my muscles were stone. I have little tolerance for a man putting his hands on me, and he was too close to my age to use the Spanish term for "my son," *mijo*. I almost told Escobar that *Freaknik* wouldn't shine *The Shining*'s shoes.

"Ten?" Chela whispered. "That was the coolest effing conversation I've ever had in my life." *Effing* was her boyfriend's contribution to Chela's vocabulary, since he rarely used profanity. She pulled out her cell phone. "I have to text B . . ."

I knew that feeling, having something to share and the right person to share it with. April was the first person I told anything I was willing to tell. April would hear about Escobar's little monologue, too. Later.

The pool churned with extras, and long rows of reclining beach loungers transformed the patio from a home to a hotel. I was costumed in Geek Chic: khaki shorts, leather sandals, and a loose short-sleeved, button-down shirt, with the requisite tortoiseshell glasses. My character is on a working vacation when the outbreak hits, conveniently in place to try to explain the epidemiology before he falls victim to an infected party girl's enhanced pheromones.

Four women lay in a row on loungers, all of them topless, but there was so much nudity on the set that most people walked past them without a glance. We had their chests memorized.

"Classy stuff, Ten," Chela said, gazing at the display.

"Told you it was nothing to get excited about. Just a paycheck."

Gustavo was in his director's perch inside the car of the crane that would help him oversee the high shot he wanted, as if he were shooting *Citizen Kane*. I could have made three movies for what the studio had given Escobar. The crane was still on ground level as Escobar huddled close to Brittany, ostensibly with last-minute instructions as he swept his arm across the crowd scene to illustrate his vision.

"Gus, what's the holdup?" a woman said, elbowing her way past the huddled crew to the crane car. "Do you want to get stuck with noon lighting again?"

Louise Cannon, Escobar's technical adviser, was also a producer and one of the few people on the set who talked to him with no fear of consequences. She was slightly younger than Escobar, probably in her mid-thirties. She had raven hair and dark eyes, but she was a *gringa* from Fort Lauderdale who had met Escobar in film school after a stint as a cop. I research the folks I work with, since it pays to know about the people who know you. She'd parlayed her forensics work into a steady stream of film and TV consulting gigs.

"Why don't you do your job and leave me to mine?" Escobar snapped.

"These girls are waiting out here naked while you're taking your time," she said.

An uneasy hush came over the set, and Chela gawked at Cannon. Escobar had a temper. I'd seen it on display in his shouting matches with his assistant director, but he only smirked at Louise with pursed lips and waved his hand to scatter the cast and crew to their posts.

"*Cuidate*," he told Brittany gently, kissing both of her cheeks. Escobar muttered a few unflattering things about Cannon beyond her hearing. Another gesture, and his crane whirred, rising high above the patio. Everyone assumed Escobar was screwing his lead, but I'd put my money on Cannon. There was more to them than their public arguments.

"I want to be *her*," Chela whispered to me, nodding toward Cannon.

"I'll introduce you," I said, distracted, as I ferried Chela off to the fence that separated onlookers from the cast. The crowd beyond the fence was mostly teenagers and service workers. Locals. I wanted Chela stashed somewhere safely in view while I was working. I didn't want to look up to find her sunbathing topless because she was invited to make her film debut.

"Behave yourself," I told Chela, wagging my finger.

"What am I, six years old? Bite me."

Strangers might not have understood what Chela and I meant to each other, but every barb from her concealed a history. As April reminded me, I'd rescued a precious soul from the edge of the world. We'd all been disappointed when her birth mother robbed me of my gift to Chela before her eighteenth birthday—"Told you she was a loser bitch," she had said with a shrug, hiding the depths of her true feelings—and I'd sacrificed a lot to track the woman down. But I could adopt Chela much more easily now, if she would let me.

"As soon as we get home, you're signing those papers," I told her.

"Not if you lie and tell anybody else I'm still in high school."

"Just do it for me. And Dad. He wants you to have his name."

Dad was her soft spot. Chela had been raised by an ailing grandmother until she was eleven, and she'd loved Dad when there'd hardly been anything left of him. Chela shrugged. "Maybe," she said, which we both knew meant yes.

The last thing I heard before the camera started rolling was Chela's excited squeal after a young woman called her name.

THREE

ONLY ONE PERSON called her "Che-LAAA," with the accent on the end, drawing her name out like a song a boy band would sing. Chela hadn't heard the voice in years, but she knew it like yesterday, out of time and place and yet so *right*. She turned around, wondering if Maria was only a ghost bumping around in her head, but then she saw Maria angling her bone-thin shoulders as she slipped toward her through the crowd like a fish. "I do not believe this shit," Maria was saying. "It's you!"

They both screamed so loudly that a guy from the movie crew glared and waved at them, but it was hard to be quiet as they hugged. Most of the memories they shared were bad, but once upon a time, she and Maria had been each other's only clean harbor in an ocean of filth. Maria no longer wore bubble-gum lip gloss or cheap knockoff Chanel swiped from Walgreens, one flirting with the cashier while the other stuffed her purse, but Chela could smell those old days on Maria.

They were Maria and the Kid again. Maria was the one who had given her the street name Chela, which she said was sexier than Lauren, a new beginning.

"What are you doing in Miami?" they said, and laughed when they both said, "Jinx!"

Chela was taller than Maria now, who seemed oddly petite beside her, no longer towering over her because she was two years older and had navigated the streets three years longer. Although she couldn't be older than twenty, Maria looked at least twenty-five, with lines framing her eyes that had been absent in L.A., making her look slightly sleepy in a way that rest wouldn't help. She was probably stoned, Chela remembered. Maria was dressed like a pop star in shredded jeans and a glitter bikini top, and she looked as if she lived a pop star's long hours.

But she was still gorgeous. Maria's hair shone like onyx against olive skin, hanging long across her bare shoulders. Maria had seemed so beautiful to Chela that she'd once been confused by her emotions, wondering if she liked girls. Later she'd realized that the floating sensation she felt around Maria only meant that she wanted to slip into Maria's skin and experience the world from behind her eyes, never missing a moment of her. Not a sex thing—more like a spirit thing. If that was a girl crush, so be it.

"I've been partying with a millionaire all week," Maria whispered in her ear. "He lives down the street, and he told me someone was shooting a movie. What are you doing here?"

"I'm here with my . . ." The word *Dad* had never seemed as wrong as now. "Friend," she finished carefully. "He's in the movie!"

They squealed and hugged again, the way Chela imagined two old friends might at their twenty-year high school reunion after they both learned they had married for love, had children they adored, held high-powered careers, and could still fit into their cheerleader skirts and sweaters.

The bald, fat guy on the crew who was closest to the fence glared again, his unappealing stomach jiggling beneath a tank top as he raised his finger to his lips to shush them. "Which one is your friend?" Maria said, scanning the crowded patio.

Ten was easy to spot, since he was wearing the most clothes.

"I'm not feeling the glasses," Maria said, and Chela's memory of Maria sharpened. Maria needed to be choosier, more discerning. She always found a defect to point out.

"That's just for the part. He doesn't really wear those."

Maria nodded, relieved. "Oh, okay. Definitely fine, though. Nice face under there." She nudged Chela. "Good body?"

Chela's throat tightened. *Ugh.* "He's not that kind of friend," she said. "Ten's more like a big brother. He looks out for me. I moved in with him and his dad a couple years back."

"For reals?" Maria said, her voice hushed. She seemed confused by the concept, and Chela suddenly felt so sorry for both of them that grief stabbed her. The idea of a family almost seemed like a betrayal, since they had given up on the idea by the time they met. Families were people they saw on TV on those old sitcoms like *The Cosby Show*. Families were a lie.

How would she explain that her boyfriend was president of the chess club ("Wait—there's a club at your school just for people who play chess?") or that she'd graduated with a 3.8 GPA and that her mailbox had been flooding with recruitment letters from places like UCLA and Spelman, falling over themselves to woo her ("You mean colleges are writing to *you*?").

And there was no way in hell Chela could explain that she and Bernard had never had sex—even though they were creative about their chastity—because he was born again, saving himself for marriage. She didn't think Bernard's resolve would last much longer, but she wasn't pushing, either. Sex was no mystery to her, but she preferred romance. She liked holding hands and falling asleep with her head on his shoulder at the movies. Besides, if she had sex with Bernard, it would only be fair to tell him about the revolving door in her panties, and wouldn't he run for the hills when he knew? Chela didn't keep the number in her head, afraid to do the calculations. Too many.

"Who's your millionaire friend?" Chela asked, deflecting.

Maria flipped her hair over her right shoulder the way she always had when she was about to tell a story she was proud of, true or not. "Twenty-six. Totally ripped. His father's company flies executive jets, so they're rolling. He says he's gonna fly me to Jamaica. And he never gets tired—I mean, he can go all night without stopping."

In another life, back when Chela had been working, Ten had rescued her from rapper M.C. Glazer, who'd put her up in his mansion and promised she could live with him forever. Now she understood how deluded she must have sounded to Ten. Maria's millionaire might not be paying her in cash, but he was a john.

Maria's eyes sparked as if she'd seen Chela's thoughts. "We're not exclusive or nothing," Maria said. "We just like to party. We met at Phoenixx." Maria suddenly grabbed Chela's wrist, her eyes wide with a revelation. "Maria and the Kid! We should party tonight. Have you been to Phoenixx? *Chica*, it's the best club on the East Coast, like the best clubs in Vegas. All the stars go there. You won't believe it."

Chela had been about to suggest that they should go to the beach or have lunch on Ocean Drive, where they could hear their conversation. Chela wanted to know where the lines radiating from the corners of Maria's eyes had come from. If she was still in the Life. Chela hadn't been to a club in years.

Her lame California driver's license, which clearly stated her age as eighteen, was the only ID she carried. The Kid was dead. Nothing about going to a club sounded like a good idea.

"I don't have a fake ID," Chela said in her *oh well, end of story* voice.

Maria laughed, giving her a playful push that nearly knocked her into the toddler-wrangling woman next to her. "You're kidding, right? Please. I can hook you up with an ID that could get you through an airport. Takes ten minutes. We'll pick it up on the way. Just bring an extra fifty bucks. Let's meet at ten thirty, okay?"

Chela's heart surged as she imagined a hypnotic bass beat and flashing lights, a dance floor writhing with bodies, and perfumed sweat fogging the air.

My, my. Seemed the Kid wasn't dead after all.

She hadn't been to a club in years! And hadn't she been meaning to get a fake ID so she could sip an appletini once in a while? If people could go to war at eighteen, they damn sure should be able to have a drink.

Maybe it was true that people could feel eyes when they were staring hard enough. Something made Chela look back toward the patio just as she heard the director yell, "Action!"

Ten was staring straight at her, as if he had heard every word.

FOUR

WHEN YOU'VE SPENT as much time as I have near trouble, you can smell it from a distance.

"An old friend and I are going to hang out tonight," Chela told me after dinner. The pitch of her voice rose slightly as she tried too hard to sound casual. Even Dad caught it, glancing away from our living room's fifty-inch flat-screen. "I'll be home late. Just letting you know."

My stomach gurgled, but not from the food. We'd just finished a boatload of raw fish from Sushi Rock down the street; even Dad had tried his first taste of raw fish. Any parent of a teenager knows you have to pick your battles, but it's more important to know how to pick.

This was a test I'd been dreading. I thought of all the times I'd postponed talks with Chela about making good decisions because she was doing so well. Stayed in school and graduated with good grades. Picked a nerdy boyfriend who, aside from wrestling meets, seemed to lack the slightest trace of testosterone. Save for a single internet incident I'd squashed by spying on her, Chela had stayed far away from her old life. Now I'd brought her old life back to her feet. I'd never met the girl Chela had been chumming with at the morning's shoot, but if she wasn't a prostitute, she'd missed her calling. Girls like that had supplied Mother, my old madam, with enough Stoli Elite vodka and real estate holdings to last two or three lifetimes. *Takes one to know one,* my Evil Voice taunted.

But that wasn't quite true. An escort in my price range would have been tougher to spot. Chela's friend might be a streetwalker, or she might be working the clubs or hotel bars. A worker bee, not a Queen Bee. It's a designation that has nothing to do with her looks, because I could see that the girl was a beauty, or had been, even if life had trod on her hard. Cute is only part of the story for girls like her.

"An old friend from where?" I said, nailing the casual tone she'd been striving for.

Chela wasn't fooled. She raised her eyebrow, defiant. "Catholic school," she said. "Our Lady of Mind Your Own Damn Business."

Marcela clucked disapprovingly from the kitchenette as she threw away our takeout containers. This was not going to be a conversation for witnesses.

I whistled softly to Chela, nodding toward the dining area's balcony behind a glass sliding door. "Let's check out the sunset," I said.

"The sun sets in the west," Chela said.

"Humor me."

It was a little after six. Below us, families of sun-reddened beachgoers were streaming back to their cars, and the dating set was just beginning to arrive in heels and pressed shirts. In a few hours, the after-dark hordes would take over Ocean Drive.

Chela was silent, staring at me as if she didn't know what I wanted to talk about.

"Is she one of Mother's?" I said.

Her mouth dropped open before she caught herself. "Who?"

Now I stared. Waiting.

Flustered, Chela flipped her hair away from her cheeks while the breeze tried to wrestle it back. "You're such a jerk sometimes," she said.

"Why? Because I'm right?"

"You're not," Chela said. "Sorry, detective. I knew her before I knew Mother. She did her own thing. An independent operator." She didn't conceal the pride in her voice.

If I remember the story right, Chela had fallen into the company of streetwalkers who taught her the trade when she was at an age too young for me to ponder without a stomachache. Mother had been a major step up for Chela. Mother had let Chela go only reluctantly, when I threatened to take the old bat to jail if she stood in my way of giving her underage novelty a shot at some kind of life. I have a flinch response on the subject, seeing the aged madam beneath every rock and behind every bush, even on the other side of the country. But even if the girl didn't know Mother, she was no one I wanted back in Chela's world.

A small flock of seagulls rose skyward north of us, six birds veering in perfect formation. Dad used to say that a flock of seagulls meant a storm was coming. No clouds marred the fuchsia sky yet, but South Florida thunderstorms don't give much notice.

"I know you don't want to hear me . . ." I began.

"True."

"But this is a bad idea, Chela."

"You don't even know her!"

I nodded. "What's her name?"

Chela paused, sensing a trap, as if I were a cop. "Maria."

"You're right, I don't know Maria. But I know what she represents. And I think you do, too. So even though you're eighteen now, which makes you a grown-ass woman, I hope you'll remember that sometimes old habits don't die—they just go to sleep for a while."

Chela was so angry her face colored red. "Thanks a lot for the trust, Ten. If I come home late, just check out the alleys to see if I'm sleepwalking in kneepads."

She headed back for the glass door, where I could see Dad and Marcela on the sofa pretending they weren't wondering what we were talking about.

"I'm not just making this up to hurt your feelings, Chela," I called after her. "Ask me what I was doing on those trips six months ago."

Chela stopped cold.

I wasn't supposed to talk about those trips; my lady friend with ties to the Cowboys In Action had told me that the people I'd been working with would disappear me if I did. Last I heard, there's a price on my head in Hong Kong, and I don't plan to visit to verify it. Some people might say I'd been working for a patriotic cause, but despite the labels and justifications, I'd seduced a woman under false pretenses. Even back when I'd worked for Mother, I'd never had to lie my way into anyone's bed; my clients did the lying to their husbands and boyfriends. Mother had given me all the training I needed. It was piss-poor consolation that I'd almost died for my sins.

Chela whipped around, lovely mouth twisted in a sneer. "Well, listen to Mr. Hypocrite."

The word *hypocrite* cut me; it fit my size just right. "I just want you to know how easy it is, Chela," I said. "Wrong people. Wrong place. Wrong time. The next thing you know . . ."

"Did you ever even find my mother, or was that just another cover story?"

My tongue froze. I don't think any question has ever hurt me so much. I had crossed new moral lines to find Chela's birth mother—information about Patrice Sheryl McLawhorn had been the bait to lure me into a job I hadn't wanted. My ethical sacrifice felt empty.

"You think I'd lie about something like that?" I said.

"Guess I don't know what you would do," Chela said. "You tell me."

I could barely keep my voice steady. "She's living in Toronto." I gave Chela both the home and work addresses, which I had memorized. "I've got no reason in the world to lie about one of the worst disappointments of my life. And if you're gonna go that deep with it, what are your plans with Maria tonight? A cup of coffee? Catch a movie?"

Chela's eyes fell away. She'd never learned how to back down with grace. "No," she said quietly. "She's helping me get a fake ID. We're going dancing at a club called Phoenixx. Sorry if you don't approve, but it's the truth. I'll be fine."

The truth was Chela's peace offering. At least I knew where she was going; half the cast lived at Phoenixx after hours, and I'd turned down invitations to hang out in the VIP room. I probably wouldn't even go to spy on her. Probably.

"If you even think you have a reason, call me," I said. "And have the bartender open the bottle in front of you. Don't even *think* about drinking anything that's been out of your sight. Drinks get drugged." I knew that from experience. A couple of years back, a drugged drink had nearly gotten me killed in a Florida swamp.

"Thanks . . . *Dad*," she said, lighter on the sarcasm than usual.

I wanted to tell her that her mother couldn't stand in our way unless we let her. And that I knew how much it had hurt when Chela had gotten her hopes up, only to let the mother who split and left Chela to be her grandmother's nursemaid close enough to damage her again. And that I understood why she couldn't flush Maria away, and maybe it was wrong to ask her to.

But I didn't say any of those things.

My heart was still ringing from the word *Dad*. Any man who has answered to that name knows why a nest of wasps was stinging my stomach as Chela walked straight toward trouble.

While Marcela and Chela rifled through her suitcase in Marcela's room, I told Dad everything, even the part about the fake ID. Then I waited for his lecture.

"Nothin' you can do," he said.

"Like hell. And she's living under my roof?" I sounded like Dad, circa 1980. We had switched scripts. "I'll go in there and tell her she's staying home tonight. Period."

"Better lock the doors and windows to keep her in," Dad said, and flipped from the news to *Judge Joe Brown*.

Chela had run away from every home she'd ever known, even Mother's, so we were still surprised she had stayed with us so long. You lose the moral high ground when you spend years dodging the system, harboring a juvenile fugitive living under an alias. Chela was only a street name; none of us had gotten in the habit of calling her Lauren, the name her mother had given her. I suddenly wished we had. Instead, we'd kept her street name alive and well.

The wasps stung my stomach again.

Through the closed door, I heard Chela's cell phone ring with the screech of metallic rock. "She's already here!" Chela yelled from the bedroom, panicked. "She's downstairs."

"Tell her to come on up and wait," I said.

Much to my surprise, I heard Chela pass the message on.

"She said thanks anyway, but she'll wait outside."

Of course. I went back to the balcony and peered down until I saw Maria in the neon glow. She was smoking a cigarette beside a parking meter in a low-cut gold dress that looked spray-painted on. Her barely harnessed cleavage made men stare as they walked past her. If Maria had been anywhere except Ocean Drive, she might as well have been wearing a sign for the cops. Would she be working at Phoenixx?

"Oh, hell no," I muttered when I came back in.

Within a minute or two, Marcela and Chela emerged. Marcela's lips were tight with concern, but she fussed over Chela at the front door as if it was prom night. Compared with her club date, Chela looked like a prep-school student in leather pants, heels, and a conservative black blouse that could be office attire. Marcela buttoned the blouse nearly to her chin and helped her adorn it with a string of faux black pearls. Not an inch of Chela's skin showed, but that wasn't much comfort. With dark mascara and blown-out hair, Chela didn't need a fake ID to look twenty-one and luscious as a sugar-frosted Fudgsicle. The girl needed a bodyguard.

"I'm gonna go down and introduce myself," I said, and Chela gave me a look that said, *Don't you dare*. I sighed and pulled out a couple of bills and pressed them into Chela's palm. "Cab money. Don't get drunk, and don't get in anybody's car, hear?"

My wild imagination veered from date rape to international sex-slavery rings. I could barely keep a tally of everything I thought could go wrong.

Watching my worry, Chela's face melted into a soft smile. "Thanks, Ten. I'll be fine," she said, and kissed my cheek before she slipped out the door.

I'll have the rest of my life to wish I'd found a way to keep her at home.

THIS CHICK LOOKS nothing like me," Chela said, examining the ID she'd rented from a guy working out of his minivan below Fifth Street. She'd left fifty dollars and her own license behind as collateral. The woman in the photo was about twenty-five, with a narrow face and curly blond hair. "Isn't this a white girl? Five foot four? Come on."

Maria was undulating snakelike to the throb of the bass that seeped through Phoenixx's brick façade, leading Chela to the front of the line. Leggy women dressed in Cleopatra costumes strolled up and down the lines with drink shots on golden trays. Chela wondered how much waitresses at Phoenixx made a night in tips.

"Relax," Maria said. "That's a Florida driver's license with a hologram. That's all they care about. He'll barely glance at your face. You're hot, so you're in."

Chela was pleasantly stoned from the joint she and Maria had shared walking on the beach toward Fifth Street, and she remembered what she'd always liked about weed. Everything slowed down. Lights and colors were brighter. Music was crisper. The only drawback was the paranoia that made her keep staring at the photo, more and more convinced that she was about to get arrested. Signs outside the club warned about prosecution for using a fake ID. Her heart raced as they got closer to the velvet rope.

"Are you sure?" Chela said.

"*Dios*, who *are* you?" Maria said. "You were never such a baby."

Lillian Holly Jasper. Lillian Holly Jasper. Lillian Holly Jasper. The name printed on Chela's ID tumbled through her memory. D.O.B. January 5, 1987. The signature was a mess. What if she had to give a writing sample?

Chela wanted to tell Maria to forget it. She'd been bold in the old days, but Maria was right, easy living had dulled her edge. What kind of shit had Maria given her, anyway? A couple of hits, and she was losing it. Any door host would see how nervous she was.

Maria suddenly held her hand. "It's okay, *chica*," she said. "I got you."

Chela's head stopped spinning just as they reached the head of the line, where waiting customers glared at their brazenness.

The door host was a pro in black slacks and a black sports jacket and white shirt, as if he was in the Secret Service. He had an earpiece like in the L.A. clubs. His pen flashlight made Chela's heart sink. If he thought she was cute, nothing showed in his stern, bearded face.

"Back of the line, ladies," he said.

"Can you call Hector?" Maria said.

Chela tugged back, still holding Maria's hand. "Why can't we just wait?" she whispered. Why was Maria drawing attention to them and her lame fake ID?

The door host sighed and peered back over his shoulder. He tapped at the window behind him, where a beefy Latino man was on a phone. The man's face lit up when he saw Maria. He grinned and gestured to the door host: *Let her in.*

The door host unhooked the velvet rope, the path to freedom, and Chela thought she might be spared the humiliation of arrest after all. But before either of them could pass, the host held out his palm. "IDs," he said.

Maria went first. She was only twenty, so she had a fake ID, too, but the woman on her ID was her cousin. Maria breezed by.

Chela tried to summon her acting skills from drama class, but her hand still trembled when she handed over her license. The door host spent much longer on hers, studying it closely with his light, holding it near his face. Turning it over. Feeling for imperfections. Chela tried to keep a smile on her face, but maybe she was only gritting her teeth as if she was in pain. She wanted to hide herself when he turned his flashlight on her face. *I'm so busted.*

"My hair's dyed in that picture," she said. The lie itched in her dry throat. "Obviously."

He stared at her with steel-blue eyes. Laser eyes. "You look way better as a brunette," he said, and waved her in.

Something happened then. The tension uncoiled, and Chela suddenly felt as loose as the Kid again, *catch me if you can.* She winked at the poor moron. "I'll remember that advice, gorgeous," she said, and followed Maria with the Kid's walk, swinging her hips, riding her high heels. Someone from the line whistled.

"Save some for me, baby!" a man called out.

When Chela turned around to blow him a kiss, three or four guys cheered.

Maria's eyes danced. "That's more like it!" she said. "Where you been, girl?"

Chela wasn't sure where she'd been, but she was glad to be back.

The club's foyer was a dark tunnel painted in Day-Glo streaks, lit up like Picasso's untamed dreams in the bluish glow of a black light. Overhead, nearly microscopic bulbs blinked secrets in Morse code. The driving bass beat shivered the floor. A steady breeze of chilled, purified air from the heart of the club greeted her with scents of life and motion.

Chela's heart and spirit galloped. She'd asked Bernard to take her clubbing at one of L.A.'s under-twenty-one clubs, but it was hard to explain a dance club to someone who had never been to one. Besides, no lame teen club could recreate the sound.

"It's so alive in here!" Chela blurted, too close to Maria's ear. "I've missed you!" She hadn't known that she had missed anything or anyone from her old life, but the realization dizzied her. She and Maria were survivors on an epic scale.

Maria hugged her with one arm, and they walked like Siamese twins. "I've missed you, too, Chela! There's so much to tell you . . ."

The music swallowed their words. Maria opened her thin purse and pulled out a laminated photograph from the L.A. County Fair. A brown-haired princess, about two years old, stared back at Chela with big dark eyes. It might be Maria's baby picture, except for the photo's stamp from that same year.

"That's Esperanza!" Maria said.

"Wait . . . she's yours?"

Maria nodded, face beaming. "My life! She's with my aunt for now, but I'm gonna get a nice place soon, make her a home. Isn't she amazing?"

The dizzy feeling intensified. Maria had a daughter? The idea brought back the image of the shell of a Chevy Impala with dark windows and a stained old quilt draped over the backseat, stinking of pine-scented air freshener. Maria had hosted her parade of thirty-dollar johns in the Impala before it got towed from behind the little pastry shop off Sunset, which had the best powdered doughnut holes Chela had ever tasted. After Chela's first time alone with a man in the Impala—ten minutes with her eyes closed—she'd gone straight to the Sugar Shack and washed away the taste of him with crullers and coffee with too much sugar. That became her ritual. "See how easy that was?" Maria had said. Chela thought about the old-fashioned sugar server her grandmother kept on the kitchen table, the one with patterns of linked strawberries, where Gramma treated herself to one teaspoon in her tea every morning—only one, because of her diabetes. Chela remembered the table for two she and her grandmother had shared, waiting for her mother to come home as she kept promising. Chela had waited for her mother until her grandmother died. And a few long, lonely, terrifying days after that.

"How old is she?" Chela said.

"What?" Maria said, because the music was howling in a gale around them. Cologne, perfume, sweat, and sweet alcohol danced in Chela's nostrils.

Chela bent closer to Maria's ear. "How old is your daughter?"

"She just turned three," Maria said with the same proud smile, as if birthdays were all Esperanza needed from her.

"When do you see her?"

"What?"

Chela wondered if Maria really couldn't hear her or only didn't want to.

She cupped her palm against Maria's ear. "How often do you see her? Your daughter?"

Maria cast her eyes away. "It's been six months," she said. "I know, it's too long. I'm saving my money. Flying is so expensive now!"

Her millionaire could promise to fly her to Jamaica, but he had never offered to fly her to see her daughter? Did Maria say "Mommy will see you soon" when she talked to her on the phone? Or maybe she was more like That Bitch and hardly bothered. Chela felt her cheeks heating up despite the club's cool interior.

Maria grabbed Chela's shoulders, staring her in the eye. "I know what you're thinking. I'm scared of being a mom, Chela. I don't know shit about that. But what keeps me going is, I remember how you hated your mother. You talked about that all the time, how she was selfish and never gave a shit. I'm not going to be like that for Esperanza. I have a plan—New Year's! I almost have enough for my security deposit and plane tickets. Scared or not, I've already told Tía Rosa I'm bringing my baby to Miami."

"Really?" Chela said.

"Damn right, baby!" Maria said, grinning. She was nearly hoarse from shouting.

Chela shrieked, and Maria joined her, dancing with her in a giddy circle. Chela was glad she had ignored her doubts and come to Phoenixx. A reunion with Maria on the heels of her latest encounter with That Bitch, both of them woven together in a karmic knot? B would say God was sending her a message. Now she just had to figure out what the message was.

"Let's dance!" Chela said, pulling Maria toward the throb of bodies congealing in the center of the massive dance floor. The cavernous club was far from full at only eleven o'clock, but the crowd was growing like a living organism, spilling into empty spaces as confetti rained.

"I want a drink first."

Chela didn't like to drink before dancing. She was still flying from her puffs on the beach, and alcohol dehydrated her, slowing her down. The deejay was rocking "Gasolina," one of her favorite reggaeton jams, and her hips were answering the energetic crescendo, left and right, forward and back. "Please?" Chela said. "I'll get you a drink after this song."

"Okay, but I can't get sweaty," Maria said. "This dress stains like crazy."

Dancing was bliss. Every man in their radius stared with open hunger, but Chela gave herself only to the music. Maria turned their dance into a show, draping her arms over Chela's shoulders, gyrating close, flinging her hair with sensual abandon. When Chela peeked through slitted eyes, she saw that men had forgotten their dates, practically forgotten to dance except in shuffles, hypnotized by longing for Maria and the Kid. *If we were working tonight, we would clean up in this place*, she thought.

The powerful, unexpected thought popped Chela from the music's spell. She floated above the room, her mind noticing the glimmer of Rolex wristwatches, the designer shoes on the feet of the men. Scouting for marks. The club was full of rich guys looking for a good time. Such easy money. Warm arousal flushed Chela's face.

"Drink time," Maria said as soon as the song slipped to another. Maria hadn't come to Phoenixx to dance.

"Let me buy you a drink, *linda*," said the nerviest man in their audience, who was only as tall as Chela's shoulder and looked as if he'd bought his shirt at Walmart. Maria gave him a pitying smile and pulled Chela toward the bar.

A huddle of a half-dozen women made room for them at the end of the bar, greeting Maria in a cloud of perfume. Kisses on both cheeks all around. Maria's dress looked conservative compared with the other women's, and Chela felt draped in a nun's habit. She unbuttoned her blouse three buttons, undoing Marcela's careful work so she could let her modest cleavage breathe. A sheet of blue light from behind the bar made her skin glow purple. The music pounded her heart.

Chela raised her hand for the bartender, but Maria pulled her arm down. "Don't waste your money. Don't worry, Raphael will hook us up. You won't go thirsty."

Chela wondered who Raphael was, but not enough to ask. *Know who you owe*, as Mother used to say; her voice was as crisp as a broadcast in Chela's memory, down to the Serbian accent. The crowd looked like working girls, all under twenty-five. They were dressed up in a place to party, but they only smiled in view of witnesses. In their huddle, their faces were sober.

Chela computed the math. She'd been spared a cover charge, but after fifty bucks to rent the ID, another forty on drinks would leave her barely enough for a cab back to her hotel. What had she been thinking? She'd forgotten how expensive clubbing could be. She vowed not to spend Ten's cab money, but she could afford two drinks.

"I'll get the first round for you and me," Chela told Maria, and waved to the bartender. The other girls groaned at the tragedy of wasted cash.

While she waited for the bartender, Chela counted three American Express black cards in the hands of men waiting to pay their tabs. She hadn't seen a black card since M.C. Glazer's.

"She your buddy?" a girl with horridly dyed blond hair asked Maria.

Maria giggled, nudging Chela. "Sure was, back in the day." Chela's stomach clenched. A few johns had paid to spend time with them together, a blur of skin.

"No, I mean here and now," the blonde said. Her hair color was nearly lost against her deeply olive skin. Her eyebrows were jet black. "We're all doing buddies tonight. The girls on Collins and Washington Ave started a week ago."

"Daytime, too, not just at night," said a woman whose voice reminded Chela of a mouse. She introduced herself as Solana, but Chela just silently called her "Mouse Girl." Mouse Girl was in her mid-twenties but sounded much younger. Chela wondered if that was her real voice or a voice she put on for men who only liked teenagers.

"Those meth heads need a buddy just to walk straight," Maria said. She always had been a snob, but at least she had made Chela swear to stay away from pimps and hard drugs, which might have saved her life.

"It's not just meth heads," the blonde said, and whispered in Maria's ear.

Maria's face changed as she listened, her jowls dropping until she looked as if she'd aged ten years. "What?" Maria mouthed.

The blond girl nodded. "It was on the news tonight. She washed up on a beach." The other girls nodded confirmation. "No clothes on."

"Who?" Chela said. Again, she wasn't sure she wanted to know. It already sounded like bad luck waiting to rub off on her.

The girls looked at her with baleful eyes full of disdain. Her ignorance irritated them.

"A girl we know," Maria said, waving Chela silent. "Lupe. She was, like . . . I can't believe I'm saying *was*. She's the queen of South Beach."

"No way she went skinny dipping," the blonde said. "She hated getting her hair wet."

"She could barely swim, like me," Maria said. "Got scared in the pool that time."

"Washed up on a beach like that?" another woman said. "I couldn't stand her, but I wouldn't wish that on nobody."

"You're jealous," said Mouse Girl. "That's why you can't stand her."

"We were all jealous," Maria said, wiping the corners of her eyes. "And she was all about herself, treating everyone like shit. But that's not the point. Somebody killed her."

"Used to be just the street hos, but not anymore," Mouse Girl said. "Lupe's the second drowned girl in two weeks. So that's the new rule: buddies."

Just as Chela was wondering whose rule, the bartender finally made his way to her, gazing at her with raised *can I help you* eyebrows. Was that a condescending smirk?

"What'll you have?" Chela asked Maria.

"Nonsense," a man's voice said. All of the women's eyes went up to him, so Chela looked up, too. The man was at least six foot five, as wiry as a praying mantis. His tailored Italian suit was his most attractive feature, but he carried himself with a princely aspect. He was handsome despite a severe brow and pockmarked skin. "A beautiful woman should never buy her own drink. Bring the ladies a bottle of Cristal and whatever else they desire."

The other women tittered thanks. His eyes were fixed on Chela, waiting for an introduction. He spoke with a light, elegant accent.

"Raffi, this is my girl Chela," Maria said. "I knew her in L.A."

"Well," Raphael said. "Very nice." Maria hadn't said they'd *worked* together in L.A., but she didn't have to. He knew. Chela saw the spark in his eyes.

He glanced away from her, down the length of the bar, and Chela thought he made eye contact with a hefty, long-haired man with a monstrous nose. The man gave a vague nod, looking their way. The man's eyes were hidden behind sunglasses, but his stare cooled her blood. She reached up to button her blouse, glancing away.

"Is Miami fortunate enough to have wooed you here, too, Chela?" Raffi said. He was careful to remember her name, bringing his eyes back to hers, as if he were immersed in her. But Chela knew a mask when she saw one; his interest was only surface, not personal. Business.

"Just on vacation," she said. She almost said *with my family,* wondered why she didn't.

"You'll find that our fair city has much to offer," he said. "Much more than palm trees."

"That's for sure," Maria said, an amen corner. "Much more."

Chela counted down in her head: *five . . . four . . . three . . . two . . .*

The man brought his face closer to Chela's, as if leaning casually across the bar to rest. "The gentleman down the bar would like to buy you a drink. In the sunglasses."

Chela pretended to look to see which man he meant, and she found his nose again. He looked like a Before picture in a plastic surgeon's office. Truly repulsive. Chela was glad she didn't have to wonder what she would have thought about a man who looked better.

"That's sweet," she said, mustering a smile. "But I have a boyfriend."

The other girls, including Maria, looked at her as if she were crazy. But Raphael kept any surprise or disappointment from his face. "I'm sure of that," he said. "But Miami is especially kind to young ladies receptive to generosity. A man like this, a business traveler, is shy and grateful for company."

"Awww," Chela said with exaggerated concern. She shrugged. "Wish I could help."

Raphael blinked and nodded, deciding not to press her. He abruptly walked away just as the champagne bottle and six glasses were arriving.

The man with the nose was staring at Chela. Raphael walked up to him and spoke to him privately. It was hard to tell in the dark, but the nose guy's face seemed to turn to stone as he kept staring. Chela wished she had brought a coat to wear over her blouse. Or Harry Potter's invisibility cloak.

"You're out of your mind!" Maria said too close to Chela's ear in a pretend whisper. "Do you know who Raphael is? Only millionaires go to him. So what if you have a boyfriend? If you feel guilty, give him a Beemer and a blow job."

"Is that how you met your friend?" Chela said.

"Of course! Raphael is like gold. I hope you didn't piss him off."

The pieces didn't fit right. If Maria was doing so well with her introductions from Raphael, why hadn't she been able to afford to see her daughter in six months? Was Raphael the only reason Maria had invited her out? Would Maria have gotten a percentage if Raphael made a deal with her?

And those eyes were still on her from across the bar. She could tell without looking.

"I need to get out of here," Chela said. She didn't wait for Maria to answer, walking in the opposite direction, away from the nose guy. Even if she had to walk all the way around the dance floor to get to the exit, she didn't want him to be able to see her.

"Stuck-up bitch," the blond girl muttered behind her.

"What?" Maria said, following Chela. "What's wrong?"

The music was so loud it vibrated to Chela's bone marrow. She practically had to shout. "I thought you knew, Maria," she said. "I don't do that anymore."

"Do what?" Maria said. "You don't make friends? Let people buy drinks?"

"Don't be cute."

"Can't help it. But it's not what you're thinking," Maria said. "Raphael is—"

"I don't care what he calls himself, or what you call him. You know what he is."

"You're wrong, Chela," Maria said. "Seriously, who turned you into such a little princess? The Chela I knew would have been all over that shit."

The strobe lights blinded Chela, the music's blasting siren gearing up as if in urgent warning. She blinked and realized she was close to tears. Maria was right. The old Chela wouldn't have cared how he looked or how old he was. The old Chela would have hidden her heart and greeted that hideous man with a smile.

Chela hid her face. "I have to go," she said.

"Honey, we ain't all got somebody acting like a daddy at home," Maria said. "What does he do, creep into your room when Grandpa's asleep? Or maybe you do both of them?"

Chela couldn't stop the tears. She couldn't tell whether Maria was trying to hurt her, or if she just couldn't imagine two men who wouldn't try to screw her. Either way, her stomach felt queasy. Maria was wrong, but she wasn't exactly lying. Maria knew Chela's truth better than Ten ever would.

Maria followed Chela as she walked away. Maria gently took her arm. "Wait, baby, don't trip. Don't be mad at me."

"I'm not mad," Chela managed to whimper.

"I thought you were down with everything. Everybody knows this is the place to hook up with rich guys. I don't want you to leave by yourself, but I'm not ready to go yet. Now I gotta stay and kiss Raphael's ass, make an excuse for you."

"I'll be okay," Chela said. "I'll take a cab."

"Don't forget to go get your real ID from Julio."

Damn, she *had* almost forgotten. That would add more money to the cab ride. She hoped she wouldn't get to Julio's designated corner and find he'd left with her license. A hassle with the DMV would be poetic justice. She hated filling out forms and having her picture taken, a remnant from her time in the system.

"I won't forget."

"You sure you're okay?" She sounded like the old Maria again, a big sister.

Chela nodded but couldn't speak. Her sob was buried in the shallowest space in her throat, stinging to be free.

Maria grinned, and her face lit up. "Maybe Raffi's friend will get over you and give me a chance, right? But did you see the nose on that guy?"

Chela let out a small laugh, and Maria hugged her until they were laughing together. Maria had once given her the advice to pretend ugly guys were Brad Pitt, but the latest Brad had just looked like another old guy she would never be interested in. In those days, she hadn't had anybody in her head she wanted to have sex with. Before her grandmother died and she ran away from home, she'd never kissed a boy, or even thought about it. When her friends had been out having a life, she'd been helping Gramma manage her bedpan and refilling her meds.

Laughing brought real tears to Chela's eyes. The club was too hot, too crowded. If she didn't get outside, she would scream. But it was hard to let go of Maria, who was twirling her around to the endless beat, trying to cheer her up and make up for letting her claws out. It was hard to walk away from the *boom-boom* on the speakers that mirrored her heartbeat, the sheen of Maria's sweet-smelling dark hair, and the knowledge that Raphael thought she was beautiful. Chela had not felt powerful in years. Beauty was the only power that mattered here.

Phoenixx was a trap, and Chela had been fortunate to escape. This time.

SIX

I DIDN'T HAVE a good reason to be worried only a few minutes after midnight—still early by club standards—but I was worried plenty. I'd hoped Chela would take one look at Club Phoenixx, size up her friend's world, and realize she had made a mistake. I thought I heard the doorknob rattling a dozen times, expecting to see Chela's sheepish face, and I was always wrong. I'm not the nervous type, but her absence wore on me as if part of me knew our future.

Why hadn't I tried to bribe her with hard cash? That had worked in the past. Although I was already tired, I found myself pulling on a rumpled black T-shirt and my snakeskin boots. Underdressed, maybe, but I'd have no trouble getting into the club. The name Tennyson Hardwick mattered in shallow circles, even if it was for all the wrong reasons.

When I opened the door, Chela was standing in the hall, searching her purse for her key.

We were equally surprised to see each other, but she recovered first. "Going for a walk?" Chela said. "Oh, wait—swimming, right?"

"Busted," I said. "I was about to go to Phoenixx and get all Double-O-Seven on you."

Instead of complaining, Chela gave me one of the shocks of my life: she hugged me right there in the hall. A tight, needy hug. I pulled away to give Chela a closer look. Her clothes weren't disheveled, but Chela's eyes were red-rimmed behind her mascara's mask. *I hope I don't have to go out there and hurt somebody,* I thought.

"Nothing," Chela said, before I could open my mouth to ask what had happened. "It's just . . ." She wiped the side of her eye. "Have you ever wished you were somebody else?"

I'd been hoping for this kind of frank conversation with Chela since the day we'd met. Somehow, my wish for her evening had come true, but it carried pain I wouldn't have wished on an enemy. I guided her into the empty living room, and we sat on the sofa. Dad and Marcela had been in bed since Chela left, so we wouldn't have to censor our words.

"Have I wished I could change my past?" I said. "Hell yeah. But I don't dwell there, Chela. Yesterday is gone. Instead, I live my life new every day."

"Usually, it doesn't seem real," Chela confessed in a whisper. "Those days."

"But it got real tonight?"

Chela nodded. She crumpled, resting her head on my shoulder. "How can I ever tell B, Ten?" she said. "*Not* telling feels like lying, but . . ." A sob raked its way from her throat. "I'm so disgusting. No matter what, it's always there. I ruined my whole life . . ."

"That's not true. Don't believe that for a minute."

"Every new guy I meet, I'll be afraid he'll find out."

"April knows about me," I said. "She knows about Mother. All of it."

Chela's sobs went silent as she gazed up at me, her nose red. "Really?"

"From day one," I said. "A cop source told her. Trying to scare her off. It didn't work."

As soon as I said it, I realized April wasn't a good example of hope.

"Is that why she dumped you?" Chela said.

My throat tightened as I shook my head. *Yes,* a voice whispered. "No," I said. "She was ready to be married, and I wasn't. She wasn't rejecting who I was—it's who I *am.*"

"Maybe we're always the same person," Chela said. "Deep down. Like you said."

"That's not exactly it," I said, wishing I'd chosen my words more carefully on the balcony. "The more we can look at where we've been . . . it's easier to stay on the path to where we're going."

I was talking to myself as much as Chela. Hell, I needed to write that down.

"I want what you had," Chela said. "Somebody I can tell. Should I tell B?"

I sighed, stroking the tangles out of Chela's hair. Bernard Faison, Chess Genius, didn't seem a likely candidate for a cold dose of History 101.

"It's beautiful that you want to tell him," I said. "And maybe you will, one day. But B's just a kid, Chela. Two parents. Million-dollar house in the Valley. There's no way he could see where you came from. I'll be the one you can say anything to. Deal?"

In Chela's silence, she didn't seem satisfied. I could almost hear April's voice warning me not to try to be a substitute for a man in Chela's life, even if I was only trying to protect her. April never forgot that Chela had tried to climb into bed with me the first time I brought her to my house. That was all she'd known. Instinct made me stop stroking Chela's hair.

"If it's right to tell Bernard, you'll know," I said. "Only you. I can't tell you when."

"I will," she said, her voice brightening. "I want to. As soon as I get back."

Good luck with that, kid, I thought. Disaster might be on

Chela's horizon, but how could I blame her for wanting someone who could accept her blemishes? The truth is powerful enough to change everything, and nothing is harder than change.

I just hoped Chela would be ready.

I woke up in a cold sweat that night, but it had nothing to do with Chela.

The dream was so vivid that I checked my face and skin for wounds. I'd been fighting for my life. I could almost smell Spider's cigarette smoke and adrenalized sweat in my room.

My nightmare gallery has a colorful cast of characters. Sometimes it was the corrupt LAPD cops who nearly killed Chela and tried to end my life in the desert. Or the bear of a man I wrestled in the Florida swamp. More and more, Dad showed up in my dreams: a husk confined to a hospital bed in the nursing home he had been lucky to escape.

In Miami, my dreams were about Spider. I only met Spider a couple of times, but I might have known him better than anyone. He was a South African drummer extraordinaire, and the fiercest knife fighter I'd ever seen. We weren't on good terms the last time we met, which is a kind of tragedy; under different circumstances, I would have liked to share a beer with Spider. Sweated together with him in a dojo. Instead, I'd had to kill him.

Maybe the dreams of Spider came back to ask me if the right man had been left standing. He was the better fighter; I was just nastier. I had justice on my side, but I'm the last person who could define that word.

I wasn't due on the set until noon, so I'd planned to sleep in like Chela; but my dream woke me before daylight. I'd lost interest in sleeping, so I threw on some sweatpants and went to the kitchenette to fix the morning's first coffee.

Dad had beaten me there, with the pot already brewing and the news playing low on the living-room TV. CNN was Dad's true religion. Dad had always been an early riser, but five thirty was pushing it even for him. He was in the hotel's terry cloth robe he wore most of the day when he wasn't going out. He grunted a greeting, and I grunted back. While he pulled out a coffee mug for me, I checked the mini-fridge to see if we had any eggs left. Dad and I might not talk much, but we liked to cook together. We hadn't had many chances since Marcela moved in.

As I studied Dad's profile, I noticed that his cheeks had hollowed in the past year. Even while he'd taught himself to walk and speak again, time was a thief. I knew exactly how he would look in his casket.

"What?" Dad said.

I shrugged. "Life," I said, although I was thinking about just the opposite.

Dad nodded. "I . . . thank the Lord every time I open my eyes."

I dumped three sugars into my coffee and so much milk that it turned cold. I wondered what it felt like to know, really *know*, that the next five years, or two years, aren't promised to you. I'd had that realization when I fought Spider and expected to die at his hands. But if I lived long enough, what kind of old man would I be?

"Never told you . . ." Dad began. "Saw Shapiro before I left."

Dr. Joel Shapiro was Dad's cardiologist, an office I'd visited often. Shapiro's name made my heart skip. Dad would have reported good news right away.

Dad's pause was endless, so I prodded. "And?"

He shrugged and did something rare: he looked me dead in the eye. "And whatchu think? Bad heart's a bad heart. He says . . . I need surgery."

The kitchen's fluorescent light seemed to dim. Suddenly, I wanted to go back to bed. The last time Dad was in a hospital was because he'd suffered chest pains after helping me investigate a case, and we'd both breathed a sigh of relief when the doctors sent him home.

"What kind of surgery?"

"Don't matter, Ten. Won't do it. Chances are fifty-fifty for . . . complications. We don't think it's worth it."

"Marcela knows? Since when?"

"She was there."

I wanted to escape back to my dream with Spider. Marcela had accepted Dad's proposal at the party even knowing about his bad prognosis? Marcela was an RN, so a cardiologist probably couldn't tell her anything she hadn't guessed. Why had he waited so long to tell me?

"What does it mean if you don't get the surgery?" I said.

Instead of answering, he looked at me as if I were a toddler. Dumb question.

"Well . . . what do we do?" I said.

Dad shook his head. "What do we do? Eat. Sleep. Wake up. What we always do."

I didn't feel anything, just as I hadn't when I'd felt Spider's neck break. The past year had flown by, as would the next. And the next, and the one after that, until one day a doctor with sad eyes would say to me what one had said to Dad.

My coffee tasted like milky chalk, so I put the mug down. "Shit."

Dad patted my back. "Is what it is," he said. "Least . . . you gave me a grandchild." He smiled for the first time all morning. Thoughts of Chela always had that effect on him.

I chuckled. "Never saw that one coming, did you?"

"Damn right."

We laughed, but the laughter didn't last. I remembered breakfast and found a pan to cook the eggs. I didn't have an appetite, but I needed the ritual.

"You did . . . good with that girl, Ten. Real good. That was

God's work. We started rough, but . . . glad to see how you turned out."

I wanted to reject the admiration in his voice. "If you say so."

April was on the tip of my tongue. Maybe his, too. But neither of us spoke her name.

"Why you up so early?" Dad said.

"Bad dreams. Spider."

Dad sighed, nodding. I'd told him all about my encounter with the knife man in graphic detail, as if it were an action scene from some damn movie.

"Not surprised," Dad said.

"Hell, that was a long time ago. Didn't bother me before."

"Dead's dead forever," Dad said. "He'll stay with you. Sneak up . . . on you."

I felt a surge of anger, remembering. "The bastard had it coming. I'd do it again."

"Sure," Dad said. "Don't mean . . . you don't wish it hadn't come to that."

I'd expected to be arrested. To see my name in the headlines as a killer. But my Double-O-Marsha had wiped Spider away as if he'd never existed, and no one knew my sins but me and Dad. Nothing about it seemed right.

"Ten, you 'member me tellin' you 'bout back when . . . I was in patrol? That crash?"

I'd expected a Vietnam story, but Dad rarely talked about the war. This was a cop story Dad had shared with me only in the past three years, since he left the nursing home. He'd been alone in his patrol car, on his way home, when he'd seen a Buick weaving in and out of the lanes, the driver drunk or high. He'd flipped on his flashers to pull the car over, but the driver had panicked and sped away. Bad move.

"That drunk who wrapped himself around a pole off La Cienega?" I said. "I remember."

"More to it," Dad said. He handed me a can of nonstick cooking spray, and I greased the pan. He waited a moment, and I realized that Dad's clipped words and growing pauses were allowing him catch his breath. Dad went on. "See . . . he was headed for that intersection . . . no sign of slowing. I knew . . . he was gonna plow over someone, or broadside 'em. He didn't care. Wasn't just . . . running. He was . . . ready. Didn't care who else he took with him."

Dad took a breath. "You don't have time . . . to think. You just are . . . who you are. So I sped up . . . saw the pole. Saw my chance." Dad gestured with his hands, a sharply turning steering wheel. He had deliberately side-swiped the driver into a pole. "I . . . coulda died, too. But only one of us did."

He'd never told me that part of the story.

"What'd your bosses say?"

Dad shrugged. "Went through the motions. Then it was over. I was promoted."

I wanted Dad's story to solve my uneasiness after dreaming about Spider, but it didn't.

"Like you always say, Dad, you reap what you sow."

"One thing . . . kept bothering me," Dad said. "Why? Why not stop and take the ticket? Turned out . . ."

"He was a fugitive," I finished, guessing.

Dad nodded. "Warrants on a double. Would've got the gas. Life at least."

"So it was suicide by cop instead."

"He chose . . . his time and place." Dad sounded as if he respected the notion.

A long silence followed, and I wanted it to last. I already knew I wasn't going to like anything either of us might say next.

"We're . . . selfish," Dad said. "When people die . . . we really don't think about them. It's only about us. Makes death real. Too real. Death . . . might let you wander away. But never far. Never . . . long."

My heart sped as I cracked the eggs and heard the sizzle. I'd planned to scramble them, but I'd forgotten to get a spoon.

"My whole adult life . . . only three things mattered," Dad said, and I noticed he had slipped into past tense. "God first. You know that. My . . . family. And . . . my work. Maybe not even . . . in that order. Trying to fix the world . . . make it right."

"That's a big job."

Dad nodded. "It's God's charge to us. And when I can't work . . . at least there's family. Sometimes that's enough. But when I was in that place . . . staring at those walls . . ." He shook his head. He didn't have to finish. I'd hated putting Dad in a nursing facility, but I hadn't had a choice. Even with a full-time staff to treat him, he'd developed a bedsore on his lower back like a winking, weeping eye. It had healed, but I'd never seen a wound yawn open that way in anyone's flesh. A horror.

"You won't go to a place like that again," I said. "You'll be at home."

Dad shook his head. "Same thing, Ten. Doing . . . nothing. Being . . . no one. Can't do that again. If it comes to that . . ."

I needed a spatula to make some kind of effort with the eggs, but I didn't move to get one. Breakfast was burning.

"I get it, Dad," I said. "No machines. No feeding tube." We might have been discussing the day's weather forecast. *Next subject, please.*

"Not just that, Ten," Dad said.

I prayed that my father wasn't about to ask me to shoot him before he got sick again.

"Then what?" I said.

Dad fell silent, deep in thought. He patted my back again. "You'll know," he said.

"Maybe it won't be like you think," I said. "You might just fall asleep one night."

"Maybe," Dad said. "Or I'd want to be doing something that mattered. Making the world right. God's work."

Once April had accused me of riding the chaos. I'd inherited the urge honestly.

I nodded. "Me, too."

Dad reached for his cane. He'd been leaning on the countertop, but he used his cane to turn around and walk away. "Better flip those eggs . . . 'fore they turn brown."

"Yessir."

Halfway to the living room, Dad stopped and turned. "Free tomorrow? 'Bout noon?"

"I think so. Why?"

"Was talking . . . to Marcela last night. We're goin' to the courthouse today, sign the papers and whatnot. Decided not to wait. Tomorrow, we're getting married."

SEVEN

I WAS ON the phone with April at ten thirty telling her about the wedding when Chela burst into my room without knocking.

The frantic look on her face scared me. When I'd seen her only fifteen minutes earlier, she'd listened to Dad's news with dreamy teenage bliss.

"What is it?" April's voice said in my ear.

"I'll call you back," I said. "Chela just came into my room."

April gave a short, hot sigh. Our relationship had been dancing around Chela from the beginning, with Chela trying to block her at every turn. "Ten, you need to teach her boundaries."

"I know. I will," I said, my familiar promise. Wishful thinking. I hung up.

Chela held her iPhone out toward me, and I noticed her hand trembling. "Maria's missing," she said.

"Who?"

After Dad's talk, I had forgotten who Maria was.

"My friend!" Chela said. "I just got a call from a girl I met at the club. They found Maria's purse and her phone. I was one of the last numbers on her phone, so a girl with a voice like a mouse called me to ask if I know where Maria is. They have her picture of her daughter."

I stared at Chela blankly. "Maybe . . . she dropped her purse?"

"That's not like her," Chela said, certain. "Maria is too to-gether for that. She wouldn't drop her purse."

"Everybody makes mistakes."

Like me, letting you go to that damn club with her. People like Maria are present even when they're gone. My covert lady friend was like that, and there is no such thing as an easy escape. I won-dered if I had underestimated Maria; she might have orchestrated her "lost purse" to keep her hooks in Chela. Good one. My own Lady M could do no better.

"Take a deep breath," I said. "Why are you so worried?"

Chela pursed her lips and glanced behind her, closing my room door. Her face looked gray. "I didn't tell you everything the other night," she said, and cold foreknowledge stole over me again. Of course she hadn't told me everything. "Maria's friends said some freak is out there killing working girls, so everyone was on the buddy system. A girl named Lupe washed up on a beach. They say she hated the water. I was supposed to be Maria's buddy, but I left early. Nobody's seen her since then. It's all my fault, Ten!"

I felt my eardrums pop, as if I were in an airplane racing to thirty thousand feet. My fist curled with anger I could direct only at myself. "What are you talking about?"

She repeated what she'd said almost word for word. The im-plied agreements and associations made me wonder what she'd been doing for the few hours she was gone.

"Tell me everything," I said. "Right now."

My phone vibrated as April called back, but I ignored it.

"Nothing happened while I was there. We got the IDs and went to Phoenixx, just like I said. We danced, and this guy Ra-phael bought us drinks. He tried to play me, but I blew him off. That's when I decided to leave. But Maria's friends told me about this killer guy. They were all freaked out about this dead girl. They think a murderer is out there faking drownings. I have to find Maria and make sure she's okay."

Slowly, relief unclenched my fist. Chela had run into a gaggle of hookers with overactive imaginations. Someone was watching too much *Dexter*.

"If they think she's missing, they should go to the police," I said.

Chela planted a hand on her hip and gave me a poisonous look. *Right.*

"What do you want from me, Chela?" I said

"That's the best you can do?" Chela said. "I thought you were a detective."

She was wrong. I'd pretended to be a detective for a while, but I'd had the urge beaten out of me. I didn't have time to indulge panicky streetwalkers or Chela's guilt for finding a different life. I summoned my acting abilities to assure Chela that everything was fine, that Maria's friends were probably imagining things.

I don't think I calmed Chela down much, but she finally left my room.

"Why is everything the end of the world?" April said when I finally called her back and explained that Chela had manufactured another teenage crisis.

Why, indeed?

The *Freaknik* cast and crew partied harder than any I'd ever worked with—including my costars in a *Beverly Hills 90210* rip-off called *Malibu High* a million years ago. My costars back then had played their roles as if they were perpetually sixteen, but they were all older than twenty-one and determined to prove it. Sometimes I'd hung out with them just to get my face exposed to the hordes of paparazzi who trailed them, but bars have never been my scene. *Freaknik* had them beat, as if we'd gotten a memo warning us to squeeze in every ounce of living before the Zombie Apocalypse.

Louise Cannon, the producer, was Mommy over a cast gone wild. I tried not to be one of her problems, but she treated me as if I were a lawsuit waiting in the wings.

My sexual harassment settlement from Lynda Jewell was never made public, but Louise Cannon always kept me at such a distance that I wondered if Jewell had told her about it at a Pilates class or a Hollywood party. Small town. Cannon took a step back when I approached her, averting her eyes and folding her arms the way the girls had in junior high school when they were trying to hide a crush on me. I violated her *do not approach* force field to corner her at the catering table, where workers were laying out seafood from Crab Shack.

Storm clouds on the horizon had brought a breeze with them to the beach, churning the waves in a pale imitation of the Pacific. Cannon was no doubt terrified that it might rain.

"Any news?" I said.

"You'll know when I know," she said curtly. The wind was blowing east, so we had decent odds, but she was still nervous and needed someone to take it out on.

I was in full makeup, which would make it hard to eat, but I piled a few overpriced crab legs on my plate. If I smudged any of the simulated rot covering my face, Elliot would fix it later. Makeup effects were Escobar's trademark. In *Nuestro Tío Fidel*, the actor playing Castro had aged fifty years onscreen, and Escobar maintained he'd used zero computer effects. After working with Escobar on *Freaknik*, I believed him. The beautiful hardbodies who'd been sunning themselves in previous scenes were a shambling horde of zombies. Some of them were lurching. Hungover, not acting.

Since no one could go swimming in costume, our only diversion at the beach was the overcrowded cantina a stone's throw from the set. The Jamaican proprietor was doing brisk business selling beer and tropical drinks while the local television news played on the mounted flat-screen. Tourists snapped photos and posed with their favorite walking corpses. Cannon would have been wise to break up the party, but it wasn't up to me. I glanced back at her pacing the shoreline on her cell phone, her shouts obscured in the wind.

I don't know what made me look up at the television screen. The volume was so low that I could barely hear it, aided by a stream of rapid closed captioning.

. . . *found dead this morning in Biscayne Bay* . . .

The words caught my eyes first. The face came next, and I almost dropped my plate.

A sketch artist's rendering of a woman's face. Dark hair. Olive skin. Dark eyes. Attractive. *In her early to mid-twenties*, the streaming explanation said. The face could have belonged to any one of tens of thousands of young Latina women in South Florida.

But it was Maria. The sketch didn't do her justice, but I didn't need a photo to know.

The food's smell of steamy garlic and butter twisted my stomach. *Presumed drowning . . . As yet unidentified . . .* the streaming said. Drowned! Ice cooled my blood. Chela had accurately predicted her friend's fate, down to how she would die.

I was about to ask the bartender to turn up the TV's volume, but my phone vibrated in my pocket. Chela. I didn't want to take the call until I knew more, but I didn't have a choice.

Chela didn't say anything, but she was breathing so fast that I was afraid she would hyperventilate.

"Shhh," I said. "I just saw it, too. Calm down, honey. We don't know it's her."

But that was a lie. She knew, and I knew.

"That's her haircut *exactly*," Chela said. "Her eyebrows. Ten, it's her!"

The face lingered on the screen. The artist's rendering was so detailed that it looked like a loving gesture, an homage. It was Maria.

I'm usually a quick thinker, so I didn't like the numbness clogging my mind. The implications grew with each breath. "Ten, Maria couldn't swim," Chela told me. "There's no way she paddled out into the waves or whatever and got in trouble. It's so not her."

I didn't have a comeback. This might become a homicide investigation, and Chela was tangled in it somehow. She might not have told me everything that had happened at Phoenixx. The dead girl on TV could have been her.

"Ten, we have to do something!" Chela said. "I'm calling the police—"

"Wait," I said. Despite Dad's status as a retired LAPD captain, the police weren't usually my friends. Chela didn't even really exist—she was living under an alias, a runaway I'd raised as a secret. We might be wrong, but being right might hold grave consequences, especially if Chela were right about a killer targeting prostitutes. Before Chela brought her name into a police investigation or left an anonymous tip, I needed to know more.

"Wait for what?" Chela said.

"For me. I'm coming home."

Louise Cannon's eyes widened when I told her as much of my story as I dared. She was so absorbed she forgot to step away from me, her blue eyes falling into mine.

"My daughter has a friend who might have died, and she's very upset," I said. "It might turn out to be nothing, but we just saw it on the news. Body pulled out of the water. I need to run home and hold her hand. When you need me, just text me."

"Oh my God," Cannon said. Her face paled to milk before my eyes. For the first time, I noticed how tiny she was, barely five-two and built like a sparrow. Fragile. I put a reassuring hand on her shoulder. She tried to hide her flinch; she nearly pulled away but stopped herself. I made a mental note that Louise Cannon didn't like to be touched.

"It just happened, so she's in shock," I said.

Cannon nodded. "Of course she is. Yes, go. Do whatever you need."

But her eyes said something different. I'd just been transformed into the kind of producer's problem she had feared. Her mind was a flurry of curses.

"I'll stay in makeup," I said. "I can be back a half hour after I get the word."

"Take your time," she said. "Really. I understand. I'm so sorry. It's fine."

Louise Cannon was a first-class liar, but on that day I appreciated the fantasy.

Showing up on South Beach in full zombie regalia doesn't turn as many heads as it used to. I scared a couple of young children before I got to the hotel, but most of the adults either ignored me or gave me mildly bemused grins. Jaded, just like L.A.

Chela, however, shrieked when I walked through the door. She'd never seen the costume.

"Freak!" she said. "Ten, you scared the effing crap out of me."

At least she sounded like Chela again.

While Marcela was out shopping for her last-minute wedding, Chela, Dad, and I had a conference. As I had done with Cannon, Chela left out strategic parts of the story—namely the prostitution—but Dad gave me glances that told me he knew full well that something was missing. While Chela dabbed her eyes with tissue, we worked out a plan.

Chela would contact the girl who had called her about Maria's purse and tell her what she'd learned on the news. She would urge

her to go to the police with the purse in case Maria could be identified. If Maria had an arrest history, I pointed out, identification
would only be a matter of time. But the police needed to know that
local clubgoers suspected a pattern of drowning simulations, and
that might not show up on a database.

Chela stared down at the tabletop with red-rimmed eyes. "I've
known her longer than any of those girls," Chela said. "I should be
the one to tell the cops."

I hoped Dad wouldn't weigh in on Chela's side, but he
shrugged. "Don't see . . . the point," he said. "You don't have the
purse. Other girls . . . were with her last, not you. You heard the
drowning theory second-hand. See how . . . it plays out."

Chela pondered his logic in silence. I wondered how much of
Dad's pragmatism was fueled by his desire to preserve peace for
his wedding. My fears were far worse: headlines and publicity
dragging Chela's name, and history, into the public eye. Her story
might not matter on its own, but I'd just been granted a respite from
tabloid headlines after my last public case—and as my "daughter,"
Chela would be fair game, especially since she was older than eighteen. The *Enquirer* would have a field day with this story's lurid
combination of sex and death. Chela deserved her privacy.

"We still don't know if it's Maria, Chela," I said.

Reluctantly, Chela nodded. She probably knew full well what
Dad and I were thinking. Dad reached for Chela's delicate hand
across the table, and then mine, scabbed with movie gore.

"Let's say . . . a prayer," he said. "Hope it's not your friend. But
pray for whoever she is."

We should have been praying for ourselves.

EIGHT

THE SKY TURNED gunmetal gray for Dad's wedding.

But Dad and Marcela didn't mind or notice. They sat holding hands inside the art deco courthouse, posed beneath framed photographs of the Miami Beach mayor and President Barack Obama. Dad and Marcela were the only couple in wedding attire in the waiting area for the wedding room. Marcela had settled on wearing the same sparkling, clingy dress from her birthday party; the only addition was a partial veil pinned across her hair. The rest of the couples wore uniforms, jeans, shorts, or skirts and slacks from work, probably on their lunch hour. The younger couples had small children with them, fussing with sippy cups. Together they were fugitives from tradition, a portrait of collective courage.

"Smile," Chela sad, snapping photos with her iPhone.

Marcela beamed. The women stared at her veil as if they wished they'd thought of wearing one, but without envy. *Good for her*, their gazes said.

A lady friend of mine, Alice, would have pointed out how the tacky wood paneling and too-bright fluorescent light overhead killed some of the romance. A golden urn displayed outside the wedding-room door was full of dust-gray plastic flowers. We might as well have been waiting for traffic court.

I hadn't thought about Alice in a long time. She was an actress of advanced years who had been one of my first and most reliable paying clients. Travel companion, Scrabble player extraordinaire, unmatched storyteller. She never stopped paying me, but our client-customer relationship had ended almost from the start. When she died, she left me her house in her will, and now my family shared her space. Our space.

As I stared at Marcela and Dad, I remembered how Alice and I had sometimes stopped laughing mid-joke to catch each other's eyes. She'd kept her affection for me hidden in her checkbook. A beautiful woman almost forty years my senior was the closest thing I'd had to a girlfriend before April. We'd swapped secrets; I'd told her about the mother I'd lost as a baby, and she'd revealed her body's slow transformation to time as my fingers traced her soft, loose skin. We had decided from the start that she was too old for me, so it had never mattered that I might be in love with her. Or to think that loving her mattered.

Dad and Marcela deserved better than a crowded waiting room at a courthouse. Why hadn't I insisted that they get married in a church? That was what Dad must have really wanted. He and I didn't have friends or family in Florida, but why hadn't someone from Marcela's family come to celebrate with her? I checked my watch. We'd been waiting an hour, and we might be there another hour if the line didn't pick up. Four couples were ahead of us.

"You sure there isn't anybody else you want to invite?" I asked Marcela.

Marcela shook her head, and I saw the spark of sadness she tried to hide in her eyes. "There's such a thing as too much family."

"Got that right," Dad said.

Marcela knew how her family felt about Dad. I wondered if her relatives had declined outright or simply made up excuses. Hell, I was lucky to be on the guest list myself, since I'd been wary of Marcela for so long. But she was a good woman. Even back at the nursing home, she'd never fed me lies about my father. She'd always told me what she thought, even when the news was bad. She'd reported every improvement Dad made to help me find hope I couldn't have found on my own. "Always believe," she'd said.

"How do you have so much family here?" Chela said. "Weren't you born in Cuba?"

Marcela nodded. "Yes, but so many of my relatives fled here in 1959, while they could," she said. "Then Operation Pedro Pan brought me here, too. And my cousins."

"Pedro Pan?" I said.

"Like the story of Peter Pan and the Lost Boys," she said. "Lost girls, too. Thousands of us. Our parents didn't want us indoctrinated in Fidel's schools, so even if they couldn't get out themselves, they sent us here through Operation Pedro Pan. A boat ride to America. Thousands! It's history—the largest exodus of unaccompanied children in the western hemisphere. I was one of the younger ones. I went to live with my aunt and uncle in Hialeah. My mother is gone now, but she came here five years later. I never saw my father again. I was always waiting."

The way her voice broke at the end, the loss fresh, gave me unwelcome insight into Marcela's attraction to Dad. It was hard to imagine parents being desperate enough to send their children off to a new country, but my long relationship with Miami had taught me that Fidel was a dirty word to the 1960s generation of Cubans. Miami had been the only American city to picket Nelson Mandela when he arrived after his release from a South African prison in the 1990s—because he had refused to renounce Fidel as a friend. Alice, who had met Mandela, had ranted about it for days.

Alice again. Why did she keep popping into my head?

"Anyway," Marcela went on, her tone lighter, "I was one of the lucky ones. I got to stay in Miami, where it was warm, because I had blood relations here. My friends Isabel and Pilar were sent to New Jersey to strangers. We were scattered everywhere."

"Weren't you scared?" Chela said to Marcela. "All alone on the boat?"

Marcela closed her eyes for an instant, transported back in time. "My older cousin, Maria, looked out for me. Without her, I don't know how I would have survived."

Chela's face froze, and her eyes darted away from Marcela's. I don't think Marcela noticed, but I wished her friend's name hadn't been Maria. I tried to put my arm around Chela, but she wriggled away and pretended to study the graffiti etched on the wooden bench.

Chela had made contact with the girl who called her about Maria's disappearance, extracting a promise that she would report everything she knew to the police, but Chela wasn't satisfied. I was committed to a late afternoon and evening on the set, mostly because of my director's tardiness the day before, but I'd promised Chela I would help her follow up the next day. I'd said I would go to Club Phoenixx with her, if it came to that. All I needed was a day.

The door to the wedding room opened, and two happy teenagers bounded out. The wispy-haired girl was clearly pregnant, but her new husband looked buoyant instead of trapped. They wore matching Metallica concert T-shirts. They might be as young as Chela. *Good luck with that,* I thought.

The couple next in line stood up, both in beachwear. Instead of following the clerk into their waiting future, they walked to Dad and Marcela.

"*Perdoname,*" the man said to Marcela, hushed. "I couldn't help overhearing. My father's a Pedro Pan kid, too. He's a county school administrator. He talks about it all the time."

Marcela's face lit up, but she glanced nervously at the waiting clerk. "*Fantástico,* but you don't want to miss your turn."

The woman rested her hand on Dad's shoulder. "We think

you're the cutest couple," she said. "We'd like to give you our place in line."

Dad and Marcela tried to refuse, but the whole waiting room insisted. The other couples applauded as Marcela and Dad made their way carefully across the room to the open door; the woman standing proud in her glitter dress and veil, her beau walking with a cane.

Romance wasn't dead after all.

Dad shoved the ring case into my hand as an afterthought on the way in, his way of asking me to be his best man. Dad and Marcela hadn't written special vows, so the ceremony was brief and unremarkable, the clerk reading from an index card with a bent head. He recited the vows in English and Spanish. He sounded like a bureaucrat.

Finally, the clerk looked up to meet their eyes with a grin. "And nowwww . . ." he said like a game-show announcer. "You may kiss the bride!"

I swear the clouds broke when their lips touched.

Suddenly, the windows flooded the room with light.

CHELA HAD DISCOVERED the art of telling lies early in life, having been raised by a grandmother whose hearing and eyesight were poor, and from time to time by her mother, an addict who knew no other means of communication. She most often lied about her age, adjusting up or down according to her needs, but even her name was a lie. Maria's lie. Gramma had always said that lies would catch up to her, and Chela liked lying less and less.

Especially to Ten.

"You doing okay?" he said during his third call to check on her.

Hell no, she wasn't okay. If she hadn't ducked into the gas station's bathroom, she wouldn't have been able to answer the phone, because Ten would have heard the traffic noise from Fifth Street. She'd hoped he would stop calling after nine, but he wanted to make sure she was at home. Ten always tried to keep one step ahead of her. But not this time.

Like most gas-station bathrooms, the floor stank of piss. Maybe vomit. *Great.*

"Everything's fine," she said, breathing through her mouth. "Get to work and stop worrying about me."

"Dad in bed?"

Marcela and Captain Hardwick had been in their room by nine thirty. Some honeymoon. Giddy from the wedding, they had talked and laughed longer than usual. God help her, they might have been having sex. Chela had waited an hour before slipping out.

But Ten didn't want to talk to his father; he wanted to make sure she was where she said she was. A woman outside the restroom door yelled at someone in Spanish, and Chela's heart skipped.

"Who's that?" Ten said, missing nothing.

"Some soap-opera crap on Telemundo," she said. "That'll show you how desperate I am to find something good on TV." Quickly, she muted her phone to block the woman's voice.

"You should go to sleep, Chela," Ten said. "We'll get on this tomorrow—I promise."

The shout vanished, but someone rattled the doorknob so hard Chela thought it would break. "Hello—I'm busy in here!" she snapped, and the rattling abruptly stopped.

"Hello?" Ten's voice said.

Deftly, she unmuted the phone. "Yeah, Ten, I'm trying to dry my hair," she said, another easy lie. "Like I said, I'm fine. Don't keep calling me, okay? Or I'll turn off my phone."

"Promise you'll hang tight and wait for me," Ten said.

Chela sighed, exasperated with herself because her mouth wouldn't say the words. "Promise me you'll stop treating me like a baby," she said instead.

Ten laughed. "Okay," he said. "Deal."

Chela blinked, her eyes stinging with tears. Lying had never been so hard. Ten's laugh had done it; he believed her, and it made her sad. He thought she was in her room toweling off her hair and watching Telemundo, and Chela wished her lie were real. If she waited for Ten, he'd see so many things she wouldn't. He knew how to run a real investigation.

But Ten was too cautious. He wasn't moving fast enough. He

was afraid of bad publicity. A dozen things were more important to him than Maria, especially since she was a working girl. Ten had walked away from that life, and he didn't like to get close to the memory.

But someone needed to pay for what had happened to Maria. Someone needed to stop her killer before he stole someone else's life. Someone else's mother.

The odor in the bathroom was suddenly overwhelming. Chela felt her stomach heave. "Ten, I have to go," she said.

"Yeah, me, too," Ten said. "I'll be home as soon as I can?"

His tone said, *Don't even try it.*

Maybe he knew he was already too late.

The familiar white van finally showed up at 10:33, pulling into the same gravel lot beside a construction site, an old hotel being rehabbed, where Maria had brought her only two nights before. Chela could almost smell Maria's perfume and her weed-scented hair. Her mind swam with the differences between then and now.

Now, as always, Chela noticed more shadows when Maria wasn't with her. She was wearing a beach wrap to cover her provocative clubbing costume and its plunging neckline. She felt exposed. She wanted to run to the van but walked slowly both because of her stilettos and because she wanted to be cautious. What if it wasn't the right van? And even if it were, a single past transaction didn't mean she could trust this guy. Hell, he was a suspect! Like her, he'd been one of the last people to see Maria alive.

Salsa played softly through his open driver's-side window, the old-school sound Marcela liked to play. She saw him bobbing his head to the beat. She tried to remember his name. Julio?

Five yards away from him, Chela hesitated when she heard his voice speaking in low Spanish. Was someone else with him, or was he just talking on the phone? Chela's heart pounded. Maria's ghost whispered to her: *You were never such a princess.*

Chela jumped when the driver whistled to get her attention. He waved to her. "*Oye*, what are you doing? You'll attract attention standing out there like that."

Chela remembered the routine from when she'd come with Maria. They'd climbed into the van through the passenger-side door, where there was an easy path to the rear of the van and its well-lighted array of fake IDs, condoms, and knockoff perfumes and colognes—a convenience store on wheels. Now the idea of climbing inside his van felt crazy.

"I'm staying outside," Chela said firmly, avoiding his eyes. "I want an ID."

The man grunted and spoke in Spanish again, wrapping up his call. He peered out of his window to get a better look at Chela. "Ahhh . . ." he said. "Maria's friend."

From his voice, she could tell he knew Maria was dead. For an instant, neither of them spoke again. His sigh seemed so heartfelt that Chela wanted to tell him about her suspicions and her search.

"Please," he said gently. "If you stand by my window, you know what it looks like. Cops cruise up and down pretending to be cabbies."

Chela's face flushed with embarrassment. She would look like a prostitute if she climbed inside, too, but if she moved to the passenger side, at least she would be out of view from the street. When she stood at the closed passenger window, he whirred the window down and leaned over.

"Cops looking for me?" he said.

The question jarred Chela so much that she took a step back. "Why? Should they be?"

Instead of answering, he said, "Did you know her a long time?"

"Yes." Chela couldn't bring out more than one word.

He sighed again. "I only knew her a short time, but she was like sunshine, you know? Always smiling."

Chela didn't ask if he had identified Maria to the police. A guy who sold fake IDs out of his van on South Beach wasn't a candidate for citizen of the year. *Like you're any better*, Chela thought, remembering how she'd let Ten talk her out of going to the police.

"So you were very close?" he said.

"Like sisters."

He nodded thoughtfully. When he reached under his seat, Chela wondered if he was about to pull out a gun. Instead, he showed her a California driver's license. Chela's eyes went wide when she saw the jet cascade of hair in the photo: Maria!

"She asked me to hang on to this, remember?" he said. "The other night?"

Chela's heart slowed, and her veins stopped racing with electrified blood. Memories beat back her mind's haze. Maria had brought her own fake ID to go clubbing, her cousin's license, but she *had* asked Julio to hold her license for her when she brought Chela. Maybe she hadn't wanted to have two licenses in case she was questioned by police. Chela remembered how he'd slipped it into his pocket. But even after she remembered, Chela's knees trembled from the shock of seeing Maria's smiling face.

"I wondered why she wasn't with you that night, why she never came back for it," he said. "Then I turned on the news. Take it. You should have it, not me."

So there's no evidence of Maria near you. Chela took the license, but she held it carefully, her fingertips touching only the razor-thin edges. This guy's fingerprints were all over the license, if he hadn't wiped it clean. Evidence. Hell, she watched *Criminal Minds* and *CSI*. She wished she had a baggie, but the empty change compartment in her purse would have to do.

"So you believe the story going around?" he said. "Someone drowning girls?"

"Like I said, I knew Maria a long time. She couldn't swim."
Maria was afraid of water. She'd said it a million times. No way she
had accidentally drowned.

He shook his head and crossed himself listlessly, a tired old
habit.

"I need an ID," Chela said again.

He looked at her with mournful eyes. "How old are you?" he
said. "Seventeen? Eighteen?"

"Is this the part where you change my life?" Chela said. Lec-
tures from lowlifes who needed to straighten up their own shit got
on her nerves. She was already in character, barely trying. Why had
she been so timid last time?

"Hey, *amor*, I'm just tryin' to look out for you. With all the stories going around . . ."

"Just make sure the girl looks like me. Like, brown? A suntan,
maybe?"

His eyes glinted in a way that made Chela think he might turn
her away, but he gave her a smile that was half a sneer and vaulted
himself to the back of his van. "*Quien hace lo que quiere, no hace
lo que debe*," he said. "My grandmother used to tell me that. You
know what that means? 'He who does what he wants doesn't do
what he ought to do.'"

Chela curbed the barb forming on her lips about what his
grandmother would think about his illegal enterprise selling fake
IDs to college kids. She needed to get back into Club Phonenixx.
She needed to find Maria's friends, or Raphael, or preferably
both.

She especially needed to find the man with the big nose. Maria
had talked about making a play for him after Chela had turned
him down—and what if he was the one who had killed her? The
memory of that hideous face made Chela shiver in the warm beach
breeze.

"Your grandmother sounds like a wise woman," Chela said

diplomatically. "I'm not like Maria. I'm here on vacation with my family, and I want to get what happened out of my head."

Julio nodded, satisfied. "Here ya go." With his pen flashlight, he showed her a license picturing a girl slightly darker than her, short hair in tight curls. "This one's brand new."

Ana Montes. Perfect. Chela wondered who she was, what her life was like. Her smile had never seen a day's trouble.

"Where do you get these licenses?" Chela asked him. It seemed far-fetched to imagine Julio killing women to steal their driver's licenses, but she'd seen stranger things on TV.

He clucked. "You'd be surprised at what people lose in the sand."

Yeah, right. Chela had more questions, but she didn't want to make him suspicious. Besides, her answers were at Club Phoenixx.

She reached into her purse to get the cash she'd liberated from her savings account, the getaway first-last-security-deposit stash Ten called her college fund.

"Keep that one—my gift," he said, and crossed himself again. "I'm sorry for your friend. No matter what happened, at least you know she's with God now."

Sermon by streetlamp. Chela tried not to smirk as she thanked him and turned to find her way back to the club where her oldest friend had spent her last night.

This time, the throbbing music and fevered lights flashing inside Club Phoenixx gave Chela a headache. Every whiff of cologne or perfume was too strong, the air hot and heavy, every face a menace. The club was also more crowded, a maze of bodies. She finally waded her way to the end of the blue-lighted bar where she'd hung out with Maria and her friends, but of course none of them was in sight.

Eerily, Maria herself seemed to be standing only a few feet from her, her face speckled with floating, glittering white spots from the disco ball overhead. No, it was only a woman who could have been Maria's sister, taller and chunkier. A lot of people would look like Maria tonight.

Where were those damn girls?

Chela's phone vibrated in her hand, and she hoped it was Maria's friend Mouse Girl returning her text. But it was only Ten calling. Again.

"Will you leave me alone?" she muttered, annoyed, although she didn't dare pick it up. It was 10:45. Now he would be suspicious; she hadn't turned her phone off the way she'd threatened, so it would ring several times before it went to voice mail. He might have called Marcela and asked her to look in on her, so she might already be busted. Ten's lack of trust might as well be a sixth sense. She had to hurry and get home.

The nightclub reminded Chela of a busy street scene from the movie *Casablanca*, which Ten had made her watch with him while he rambled on about how it was the best movie ever made. The clubgoers who weren't sacrificing themselves to the dancing gods were making their way through the crowd like schools of fish, holding their drinks above their heads to avoid spilling them in the endless traffic streams.

Impossibly tall, busty women danced on mounted platforms near columns strategically placed in every corner, balancing Egyptian-style headdresses as they swayed and gyrated like pole dancers, their bodies wrapped in flesh-colored Lycra that made them look topless. The flashing lights transformed them into mascara-smeared ghouls. Their dance held no joy or any real sensuality, and the choreographed gyrations resurrected painful memories. Chela had never been a stripper—she'd been too young to get hired anywhere, and she'd skipped straight to the streets—but she'd always seen her work as a kind of dance, too. *Hey, baby, what's your name? Looking for a party? You here all alone?*

And men's eyes followed her, just as they always had, even before she had understood the meaning behind the stares. Even here, swallowed inside a crowd, eyes tracked her movement with restlessness and false promises. "Your innocence, your freshness, is a treasure," Mother used to say. "You remind us all of when we were young. Give them your body, your skill, your smile. But never, ever, what lies behind it. That is yours alone."

Ten was wrong about some things. Mother *did* care. She was the only mother who did.

Chela's phone buzzed again. Her moan of frustration was cut short when she realized it was a text this time—from a Miami number. Maria's friend Mouse Girl. But her relief was cut short when she read the message: SEE U AT P @12.

Midnight! Chela's fingers flew across her phone's display as she asked where she was, where the other girls were. WHERE'S THE PARTY?

Chela waited, frozen in place. No answer. Bad texting etiquette. *Bitches.* Mouse Girl was always cagey with calls and texts, revealing as little as possible.

Chela was alone in this damn club with no leads and no one to talk to. She remembered her lies to Ten again and felt shame. *But he lied to you, didn't he? That whole Hong Kong thing?* She still had no idea where he had been, and she didn't want to know what he had done. But a lie for a lie didn't make her feel any better.

Chela realized that the oppressive weight in her chest was sadness. Tears. Who was she fooling? She wasn't a detective; she might never know what had happened to Maria. Cops didn't care about working girls. Maria had a daughter, and she'd been saving money to finally be a mother to her. What would happen to her daughter now?

It was just then, when Chela felt the most hopeless, that she saw Raphael, like a mirage floating in the crowd.

He was almost exactly where he'd been when she'd first seen him, midway down the bar, a head taller than everyone else, scanning the room while he nursed a drink. She blinked to be sure, but she recognized his face, his height, his curly hair, even his style— loosely fitting Italian suit, dark blue this time, and an expensive one. Open shirt. Nearly hairless chest.

He was looking away from her, so Chela didn't think he had seen her yet. Good. That would give her time to plot her move. She hadn't expected to find Raphael on her own, alone. She couldn't just go up to him asking questions about Maria. Maybe she could get him to come to her instead.

Heart pounding, Chela ducked out of his sight, trying to think past her adrenaline surge.

She found her mark: a young guy with two buddies at the bar counter near her, all of them ruddy-faced from the sun. Maybe college kids. Two were too husky for her tastes, but the lanky one looked harmless. As soon as Chela spotted him, her stare made him look up at her as if she'd tapped him on the shoulder.

Chela smiled. She almost laughed when he glanced over his shoulder, convinced she must be smiling at someone else, but he recovered quickly and smiled back. She could have stayed planted and drawn him to her with smiles, but she didn't have time to waste, so she beckoned him with a bent finger. This time, he pointed at his chest: *Me?*

Chela nodded and slipped her fingertip into her mouth.

When he approached her, Chela realized how well she had chosen. His gold chain wasn't gaudy, but it had easily cost a grand, and she couldn't mistake the scent of his AQVA Pour Homme Marine, which went for seventy-five bucks a pop. She hadn't smelled it in at least two years, but she would know it anywhere. Manicured fingernails. Well-kept shoes. The kid had money, or at least his family did. Damn, she was good.

He grinned. "Hi," he said, and flicked loose strands of gelled dark hair from his eyes. He looked Latino, like more than half the guys in the room. "Can I buy you a drink?"

"Before you do that, I want to tell you a secret . . ." she said, and leaned closer to him, sure to keep her profile in Raphael's view if he turned her way. The kid's neck turned bright red. Excited body heat radiated from him.

"Sure," he said. "I like secrets."

"You might not like this one," she said. "The truth is, you're really cute, but I'm only trying to make my boyfriend jealous. And he's sort of not a nice guy, so it wouldn't be good for either one of us if I take it too far. But if he sees me talking to you like this, he's sure to notice—and he'll remember what a good thing he has. It also doesn't hurt you for your buddies to see you making moves on me." Carefully, she draped one arm across his shoulder. "Right?"

His grin melted. He gave a start, as if to move away . . . but he didn't.

"Which one's your boyfriend?" he said, recovering.

"Blue suit? A little down the bar?" This guy could scout him for her.

He made a face. "Dude's a little old for you, isn't he?"

Chela shrugged. "Maybe I like experience. Still want to buy me a drink?"

"I'd love to," he said. "But I can't."

"Why not?"

Wistfully, the guy brushed his finger across her chin. "Because he's coming over here. *Felicidades.* Your plan worked. Can I at least ask your name?"

"Chela."

"I'm Enrique. I live in Coral Gables. I'm a law student at UM. When you're ready for a nice guy, let me know." And he stepped away from her, vanishing into the crowd.

Enrique's tone hadn't been chiding, but his words stung. Hard.

She *was* ready for a nice guy. She already had one. What the hell was she doing here?

A tall figure, silhouetted, blocked the flashing lights from the dance floor. *Raphael.* He moved like a vampire, floating rather than walking.

Chela's mind went blank in his shadow.

STILL ON HOLIDAY?" Raphael said.

The odd phrase confused Chela. With his accent, maybe she'd misunderstood him. She'd assumed he was Latino, but his accent seemed different now that she was paying closer attention. What kind of holiday? She didn't answer.

"*Vacanza,*" he said. "Vacation. You said you were here on vacation."

Italian, she realized. Raphael was European. *Duh.*

Chela tried to wipe the confusion from her face. He was standing as close to her as Enrique had been, and her heart was pounding so hard she wondered how he couldn't feel the vibration. She fought the urge to bring up Maria.

"You could say that," she said blandly. She looked away from him as if he were crowding her. Their avoidance of Maria was excruciating.

"Don't you remember me?" he said. "I met you the other night. With your friend."

"I remember you." Thank goodness he had finally brought up Maria. Chela stared at the floor, allowing sadness into her face. "I guess you heard."

He clucked. "She was a lovely girl. But I don't think she was careful."

If Raphael were a doctor, he would have terrible bedside manner. He barely sounded sympathetic. All of the lights and sounds in the room sharpened as Chela's heart sped.

"No one is careful all the time," Chela said.

He winked at her. "But you are. I saw that from the start. Maria took too many chances, but not you. You would never swim alone at night."

Whether or not Raphael was a suspect, he was pissing her off. He had a lot of balls, considering that he might have introduced Maria to the man who'd killed her—if he hadn't killed her himself. "So that's still the story? She went swimming and drowned?"

She couldn't swim, jerkwad. You didn't know that?

He conceded by canting his head. "Whether it is literally or not. My only point is this: I admire your . . ." He paused, searching for a word. "Discretion? I share it, in fact. I apologize if I've spoken too harshly of your friend. I did not mean to offend. And I apologize for my behavior when we met. It is not my nature to approach a stranger that way. Who can blame you for not wishing to speak to a stranger?"

His jade eyes bored into her. Chela looked away and noticed Enrique staring at her from the huddle with his friends. Enrique shook his head slowly back and forth, like a disappointed older brother. The way Ten would have.

Chela didn't look away quickly enough, and Raphael followed her gaze.

He smiled gently. "That one is a schoolboy," he said. "Spending Papa's money. A waste of your time."

"I think I should go," Chela said. She blurted the words so unexpectedly that she wondered if she meant it. Her proximity to Raphael warmed her skin in a way she didn't like. His scent was pleasant bath soap, more intimate than cologne.

Raphael held up a hand as if to stop her in her path. "Again, I apologize. I am too blunt. But Maria was an associate of mine, and I know she cared for you . . . so I can't help the urge to give you advice. While you are enjoying yourself on holiday, be careful while you make friends. Many of the friendliest men in here carry badges and handcuffs."

"And you're my friend?"

His smile radiated kindness. He leaned close, as if to combat the throbbing music, but in reality to create a false intimacy. "I could be, if you were receptive to friendship."

"No offense, but Maria was your friend, too." Chela held her breath, waiting for his reaction. Maybe she shouldn't have said it, but it was a fair observation.

Raphael didn't blink. "True—and I will forever be haunted by my last words to Maria," he said. "I asked her to stay here with us. With the other girls. I asked her not to go out alone."

Bull, Chela thought. Why would Maria have left the gold mine inside Club Phoenixx? Maria's last conversation with Chela had been all about what a great connection Raphael was and how she'd hoped to make a play for that horrible guy with the big nose.

A more terrible thought came. What if Raphael was telling the truth? Maria might have left Club Phoenixx to go look for her or to make sure she made it to Julio's van. Mouse Girl had told her that Maria had hung out with them to drink champagne for a while, and then she had disappeared, leaving her phone and purse behind. Maria's death might have nothing to do with Raphael and the man he'd tried to set her up with.

Chela needed more information, and she could only play hard to get for so long.

Raphael leaned forward with both of his elbows across the bar, staring straight ahead as if he weren't talking to her. "An intelligent girl like you will want to weigh her options, of course, but I would like to make an invitation, Chela."

She hadn't reminded him of her name, so he had remembered. Raphael was probably a genius with names. "Freedom of speech," Chela said. "Go on."

Almost imperceptibly, he brushed a single fingertip across her knuckle, and her hand was aflame. The effect surprised Chela so much that she stared at her hand. Raphael's sensuality was so quiet she hadn't noticed it until he touched her.

"You are very beautiful, and I like to spend time with beautiful women," he said. "It is, in fact, my greatest weakness. I have friends who share my weakness. You are free to take your chances with schoolboys and undercover police here at Club Phoenixx . . . or you may accompany me to a private party with my friends who have too much money in their pockets, and join some other girls. These are girls you have met—girls, like you, who cared very much for Maria. We can all drink a toast to her. And then, I hope, we will no longer be strangers."

Chela's pounding heart shook her toes. The scenario he'd described was so perfect that it seemed too good to be true. Now she would have no reason to wait around the club until Mouse Girl arrived at midnight—if she really was planning to come meet her. Chela clasped her hands behind her back, both to prevent more touching and to keep Raphael from seeing her fingers trembling. She was more frightened of herself than she was of Raphael.

"But you're still a stranger," Chela said.

"This is true," Raphael said. "But we would never be alone— not for an instant."

"Where's the party?" Chela said.

"Not ten minutes from here. At a very nice luxury hotel friendly to me and my girls."

"Tell me the address," Chela said. "I'll meet you there."

Raphael's smile grew. *Gotcha*, his eyes said.

"Nonsense," Raphael said. "My driver will take us."

✦ ✦ ✦

Although it was parked in a row of stretches, Chela had no trouble finding the black Mercedes limo across the street from Club Phoenixx with the sign taped to the windshield she'd been told to look for: *M. GARCIA.* In Miami, that was like saying the car was for J. Smith.

Raphael must have phoned ahead to his driver, because a white-haired, white-bearded man in a formal black uniform appeared as soon as she saw the vehicle, opening the rear door with a grin. His face was so wide and jolly that if his beard had been longer, he'd have been a ringer for Santa Claus. She'd wanted to take a photo of the license tag, but she couldn't now.

"Evenin', miss," the driver said. "My name's Ian. Pleasure."

He even had a British accent. Not English, though. Ireland or Wales or Scotland. His attention awakened a familiar feeling in her, the notion that she'd earned her membership in a special, secret society. Only suckers took cabs or paid for their own drinks or meals, or lived life any other way.

The limo was an older model, probably Raphael's personal property; it was immaculately kept, the seats as soft as baby skin. She guessed that it might seat eight people with room to spare. An open bottle of Cristal cooled in the gleaming silver ice bucket, so she helped herself to a glass for the sake of appearances, only filling it halfway. No way was she getting buzzed tonight. A tentative sip told her it had been freshly uncorked. She'd always liked champagne, since it reminded her of soda pop.

"Forgive me," the driver said, "but I'll need to drive you around the block. Traffic is a nuisance, but I can't stay parked now you're here, or I'll get a ticket."

Chela knew that Raphael had sent her out first so he wouldn't be seen leaving the club with her—a precaution that probably helped him stay in business—but in the ten minutes Ian took her in a circuit around the block, she forgot her anxiety and made herself at home. She turned off her phone, since she didn't need Mouse Girl anymore. When she noticed a television monitor, she found the remote beside the champagne tray and flipped the channels until she found BET, a rerun of *Black Girls Rock*. She stretched out her legs and watched the blur of neon lighting up the crowded streets of the Magic City. She remembered M.C. Glazer and the parade of celebrities who had treated her like a queen. Until now, it had all seemed like a faraway dream—but the dream had been waiting for her in Miami.

Then the limo pulled up in front of the club, and the dream ended.

Raphael opened the door and climbed in beside her. He didn't speak to the driver, only gesturing, and the limo took off again as quickly as it had stopped. Chela muted the TV so she wouldn't miss a word he said.

Raphael's features were more severe in the light from the TV monitor, his pockmarks like craters, and he seemed taller in the car beside her. Chela felt self-conscious at how high her black mini-dress was riding on her thighs now that she was sitting down, but she couldn't show modesty now. Her beach wrap was crumpled on the seat beside her, useless.

"Good, you found the champagne," Raphael said. He poured himself a glass. "Let's have our first toast, then—to new friendship."

She pasted on a smile and clinked her glass with his. "To new friendship."

She was glad when she saw Raphael take a thirsty sip. She'd sipped twice already during the drive, forgetting Ten's warning not to take drinks from anyone. And from an open bottle! This time, she kept her lips pursed, only pretending to drink. She promised herself that she wouldn't make any more stupid mistakes.

"You look like an angel, Chela," Raphael said. "You can be roy-alty here. So . . . untouched. So . . ."

"Fresh," she said, Mother's word for her.

Raphael's smile became a grin. "Yes," he said. "A fresh flower."

Slowly, he took off his jacket and laid it on the empty seat an arm's length from him. He moved with grace. From habit, Chela sought out things to like about him: his fluidity, his manners, his swirling curls, his Italian accent. There was nothing wrong with Raphael. Yet.

"I intend to show you that I do not make empty promises," he said. "I am a man of my word." He gestured toward the side pocket of the door closest to her.

The limo was so old-school that Chela could see that her door was still unlocked, a silver pin standing at attention. With traffic crawling so slowly, she could open her door and jump out at almost any time. They hadn't left Ocean Drive. She could find her way home. Reassured by her escape plan, Chela reached into the pocket and found a sealed white envelope. It was thick. Chela recognized the weight and shape of its contents.

"Go on," Raphael said. "For you, my flower. Open it."

With the envelope in her lap to disguise her unsteady hands, Chela tugged at the seal, which gave easily. She knew the scent before she saw the crisp stack; the visible bill pictured Benjamin Franklin, and she guessed he had twenty twins. At least. It had been years since Chela had held two thousand dollars in her hands.

"Before you accompany me to my party," he said, "I would like to know you are someone who keeps her word as well. Who is what she seems to be."

The door remained unlocked, but Raphael pushed a button, and a dark panel began its silent, seasoned slide across the front seat to give them privacy from the driver. Ian was only a few yards away, but now a gulf separated them. Chela's heart clogged her throat, but the tightness went away when she stared at the carnival of muted lights through the tinted window.

Raphael had promised they would never be alone, after all. He was a man of his word.

Chela closed the envelope without counting the bills. Her purse was small, but the bulk fit inside when she folded it, nestled outside the compartment where she'd stashed Maria's license. She tried to think of a plan, but some part of her had known the plan from the start.

When Raphael's smooth hand found her thigh, Chela did not flinch away.

She smiled.

Chela never allowed her mind to go quiet, concentrating on her performance, the caress of the leather seat against the side of her face. She had begun her trade in cars, long ago. Her mind knew where to go without prompting. For one horrible instant, she thought about Bernard, but she banished him by clenching her body so tightly that Raphael forgot his English and hissed Italian words she did not know.

She touched the right places and made the right sounds, whispered the right words, and Raphael's grunts were a scorekeeper's tally. He knew better than to kiss her on the mouth but welcomed her mouth upon him. He produced a condom before she had to insist. No big deal. He was pleased with her. That was the important thing. How else could she win Raphael's trust? Now she could send the money to Maria's daughter.

Their clothes were back on, perfectly in place, by the time they pulled up in front of the Swordfish Hotel, coasting to a stop in the gilded motor lobby.

Raphael kissed her forehead. "You will find a makeup tray beneath your seat," he said. "A brush, mints, perfume, whatever you like. Take all the time you need."

And he climbed out of the limousine to wait for her. Such a gentleman.

Chela wished she could shower, but baby wipes and a swish of mouthwash made her feel clean enough. She forgot about the silent driver behind the panel, and she hoped he had forgotten her. With every passing moment, her time beneath Raphael felt less real. Old memories tried to surface and blend with the sharp scent of Raphael's soap coating her nasal passages, but she buried them while she applied new lipstick in the lighted mirror, refusing to meet her own eyes.

She had made two grand in ten minutes, and she had done it for Maria. Soon this night would be over, and she could go home. It was only a big deal if she made it one.

Raphael was waiting outside the limo, and he extended his hand like Prince Charming ready to escort her to the ball. Strangers admired them as the doormen held open the doors and they graced the hotel lobby, walking hand in hand.

She could feel observers wondering who she was. An actress? A model? A singer? Watching eyes no longer bothered her; they gave her the power to silence her memories.

Chela noticed Raphael's protectiveness, how he kept her near him, angling his body between hers and any man who walked too close to her. Chela had never known Maria to work with a pimp, but she understood why she had chosen Raphael. He wasn't like the men who ran the streets, wrangling women like circus animals who needed whips to perform. He felt more like a manager, or even a date, opening every door, warning her to watch her step, protecting her like china. Her palm felt damp and moist nestled in his; nervousness she could pretend was attraction, fooling them both for a time.

"We'll visit a suite with a private party upstairs," he said, "but first, if you don't mind, I would like to take you to the bar. A new face is a welcome novelty."

Chela spoke for the first time since they had left the limousine. "No one else tonight," she said. That was her old rule from her time with Mother, who had insisted upon nightly exclusivity no matter how much money she was offered. "Never treat yourself like a garbage bin with endless deposits," Mother used to say. "Professionals don't play the street whore's game."

Raphael's smile looked genuine. "I would not have it any other way. Tonight, you are with me, and I am with you. These are introductions only. You have no reason to be nervous."

Obviously, he could feel her palm and her quickened pulse. Chela drew in a deep breath, willing herself to be calm, and returned Raphael's smile. "Good," she said. "I have rules."

"Hear me, my angel . . ." He leaned close to her ear for dramatic effect, and she caught herself before she flinched away and destroyed her night's work. "My only fear is that I will grow possessive and want to keep you for myself—always."

Chela's fixed smile turned to steel. That was a pimp's line, all right. Pimps, at heart, were shrinks gone to the dark side. *It's all for you, Raphael. Anything for you, Raphael. Am I your main girl, Raphael? Do you love me, Raphael?* Raphael might have been the last person Maria ever saw. Was drowning his idea of "keeping" someone for himself? Chela's stomach grew taut as the memory of the back of his limousine tried to break free.

They passed a wall-sized aquarium display teeming with tropical fish, and Chela recognized the tetras Ten kept replacing in their home tank when older ones died. Thoughts of Ten turned her stomach to stone. Was he trying to call her now? Was Bernard? To Chela's horror, her eyes suddenly stung her fiercely. She kept them open wide, afraid to blink, trying to remember Mother's Rules for keeping her thoughts controlled. "Think of parts, not the whole. What you are doing, not what is being done to you. The mask, not the heart it protects."

She imagined her hand in Raphael's slowly turning to ice, going numb, and willed the numbness to travel throughout her body, to her face, until the stinging was gone. She spotted a pudgy middle-aged woman in a ridiculous leopard-pattern dress across the room, and a laugh rose in her throat.

"This will be fun," she said, capitalizing on her unexpected laugh.

Raphael squeezed her hand, approving. He didn't notice when she flicked at her eye to dry it.

The bar was populated with businessmen, an older crowd than at Club Phoenixx, with wider paunches and grayer hair. Still, none looked as bad as the man with the big nose. Even while she searched, she wondered what she would do if she faced him again. Would she have to flirt? Let him touch her thigh? Gooseflesh flared on her bare arms.

The men at the bar did everything but applaud when Raphael arrived with her on his arm. Their admiration was open, like patrons at an art auction viewing a surprise masterpiece. But Raphael kept her at a distance from them even while he paraded her.

"I'm flying to Dubai tomorrow!" complained a squat man in a white guayabera like the ones Captain Hardwick often wore. "Only two weeks, Raffi. Will she travel?"

Hell no, Chela thought.

Raphael batted away the notion. He didn't glance at Chela to consult with her. "Call me when you return," he said, leaving it at that.

At the bar, all pretense of glamour fell away. Chela had studied slave auctions in her AP history class, when she'd felt the urge to raise her hand and share comparisons to her old life. Unlike a slave, an escort would be paid well, but she was not a person to these men, or to Raphael. Sex workers, maybe most women, were rented property to them, the way the johns were like children to her. How hard would it be for any of them to murder an object? A toy?

Chela saw a row of suspects on bar stools, all of them drinking her in with eager eyes. Hopelessness swamped her again. Had she expected to detect Maria's killer on sight?

As Chela lost her will to flirt, she glanced toward the bartender, who was a woman in her late twenties, pretty despite the way she'd pulled her hair into a businesslike bun. She avoided looking at Chela. The bartender worked with her clothes on and probably thought Chela was a sellout to all womankind.

Chela gave Raphael's hand a soft tug. "I'm ready to go upstairs," she whispered.

"My lady knows what she wants!" Raphael said, kissing her cheek as if she were his girlfriend. Again, she fought not to flinch. "*Ciao* for now, gentlemen. Now you have met Chela. She is with me tonight. But tomorrow . . . ?" He left the future to their imaginations.

A couple of the men scribbled down her name on bar napkins, tucking them into their pockets for safekeeping. One snapped a photo of her with his cell phone. Christmas shopping.

"I'm sorry," Raphael said as they walked toward the golden elevators. "Some of my friends need a lecture on manners. But you were perfect. The way you pretend shyness—I love it! Now, to the other girls . . ."

Thirty more minutes, Chela promised herself. *Then you can leave and take a shower.* Maybe she would get a memory wash, too, like in a novel she'd read about a girl her age with telepathic powers. How could she face Bernard now?

Raphael took her to the penthouse level, swiping a key card for access. Suite 800. Again, his key let him inside.

Chela braced for deception. The room would be empty, and Raphael would expect her to sleep with him again. Shower with him. Let him tie her in handcuffs. And then what? Take her to the beach and drown her?

Chela felt rocked with relief when she heard a din of voices inside the room. About fifteen people were having drinks, all of them dressed, most of them men, but Chela spotted three women she recognized swaying in a loose dance circle to low music that sounded like Brazilian percussion. Mouse Girl was there! The petite bleached blonde stood beside her and recognized Chela, too, but nothing friendly showed in their eyes. All of the girls suddenly stared at her with an intensity Chela recognized as envy.

Right. Once upon a time, *they* had been the one Raphael seemed smitten with, his fresh meat. Other girls had been jealous of the way she'd lived in Mother's house, with Mother doting on her, so Chela knew how envy looked.

But she had to win these girls over to get information about Maria.

Raphael had his own agenda, so his grasp on Chela's hand felt persistent as he led her to man after man to introduce her and ignite fire in their eyes. It wasn't hard to play the shyness card, since she barely wanted to glance at the men. But she did—searching for the one she and Maria had seen at Club Phoenixx.

Too thin. Too tall. Too bald. Nose after nose was too small. A few of the younger men looked like actors, the kind she would have targeted in the old days. Handsome was always a plus. She might leave with nothing tonight except a secret.

"Go with the other girls for a while now," Raphael said finally. "I know you want to remember your friend. But come right back to me."

His true nature was bubbling out, already giving her instructions.

"Of course, Raffi," she said obediently, and pecked his lips.

By the time Chela joined the three working girls, they had lost their pretend smiles.

"You work fast," Mouse Girl said. "I thought you had a boyfriend."

The room flared red. All of Chela's fingers curled as she pondered how satisfying it would feel to smack Mouse Girl across her cheaply painted face. She closed her eyes, trying to remember why she shouldn't, finding her breath the way Ten tried to teach her to meditate. What was the best response? She could break Mouse Girl in half, no problem. Would have been able to even before Ten's patient, vicious lessons. But that wasn't the right play. Dominating Mouse Girl would just mean having to climb over another alpha bitch in the room. And she could do that, too, but it wasn't necessary, and felt distasteful to her. The opposite approach, then: roll over and expose her tummy, triggering a maternal response.

"Uh . . . hello?" Mouse Girl said, unaware of how close she'd come to loose teeth.

"I do have a boyfriend," Chela said, allowing her voice to crack as she opened her eyes. She summoned the tears she'd fought earlier, her eyes pooling with moisture. "But he's in Cali, and I need the cash. Maria told me Raffi's good to know. So I'm sorry if I'm stepping on anybody's toes."

Her tears embarrassed the other girls, who shifted uncomfortably away from her, as if tears might be contagious.

"Whatevs." Mouse Girl shrugged. She gave Chela's shoulder a pat that felt more like a shove. "Keep your problems outside when you're at a party. You know better."

Good. If Mouse Girl and the others behaved like big sisters, they might not feel threatened. Chela nodded, quickly wiping her eyes. "Sorry. I'm in shock about Maria. We were all just talking . . . and now . . ."

Silence stole over them. The music played on, but none of them danced.

"She said good things about you," the third girl said. She was thin, sweet, a lollipop in a skirt. "Told us stories."

Good-natured laughter passed between them. Chela didn't want to know what stories they had heard. Maria could have chosen from dozens.

"Did you tell the police about Maria?" Chela asked Mouse Girl. "Like you said?"

Mouse Girl's eyes flicked around the room. The other girls gave Chela disapproving gazes, and Mouse Girl sighed. "Bathroom," she said.

The suite's bathroom was nearly as big as a studio apartment, with a telephone and a mounted TV alongside the massive shower and marble Roman bathtub. Mouse Girl went straight to the mirror, running her fingers through her hair to spike it.

"First of all," she said, "if you're gonna hang with Raffi, you don't talk about cops near him—ever. Are you stupid?"

"Sorry," she said. "I just—"

"Second of all, I called without leaving my name just like anybody could've. Like you could've."

Chela hushed her voice. "Did you talk about the drowning part?"

"Sure I did. Told them about Lupe, too. And now they're not gonna do shit, which is what cops always do. Everybody's happier if she drowned. Murder's bad for tourism."

Chela wasn't sure she could believe her. She'd been crazy not to call the police herself.

"What about Raffi?" Chela said. "Could it be him?"

Mouse Girl met Chela's eyes in the mirror, unblinking. "So, what? You're Sherlock Ho, now? Is that what you're doing? Better watch your ass. Raffi don't like games."

"Fine," Chela said. "But could he do something like that?"

"Raffi ain't like that. Would I be here if he was psycho? He's all about the *moneda*. Most of the girls call him El Santo. Never even raises his voice."

"What about that guy at the bar he tried to set me up with? Did Maria go with him?"

Mouse Girl's attention went back to her hair. "I never saw him after you blew him off. Maria asked Raffi about him, but Raffi said he only wanted you."

"Do you think Maria went looking for him?"

Mouse Girl sighed impatiently. They had already discussed this on the phone, with Mouse Girl giving clipped answers, but Chela wanted to pull more out of her or see if she would change her story. "Maybe. She said she was gonna look for him, I dunno. She had a couple drinks with us, danced with a few guys, and then she was gone. A bartender brought her purse to us. He said he found it under a seat cushion, and he thought it might be Maria's. She always had the same one."

"Where'd he find it?"

"The VIP room. We can go in and out of there. The bouncer knows us."

Damn. That was new! She'd never seen the VIP room at Club Phoenixx. She would have to go back.

"Do you know who else was in there?"

This time, Mouse Girl spun around to study Chela's eyes. "You sound like a cop."

"Yeah, right," Chela said. "You know how far back I went with Maria. If the cops don't give a shit what happened, somebody has to."

Mouse Girl gazed at her a moment longer, then blinked and turned to the mirror again. "I don't know who was there that night," she said. "But lately, it's a lot of movie people. Sometimes they show up dressed like zombies or whatever. They think it's funny."

Zombies!

"You mean that movie *Freaknik*?"

"I don't know what it's called," Mouse Girl said. "Yeah, *Freak* something. Raffi knows all about it. He hooks those guys up."

Chela felt her mind whirring to put pieces together, but too many were missing. "How long ago did that other girl drown? Lupe?"

"Two weeks. And another girl the week before that, but she worked Biscayne, not the beach. I didn't know her. Just heard about it."

Ten had reported to his set two weeks before, the same time Lupe had died. Was there a connection? Chela wasn't sure if Ten had arrived at the start of the shoot or not; some of the cast and crew might have been in Miami longer. The man with the big nose might have been just another tourist having nothing to do with Maria's death.

Maria had been watching the movie shoot the day they had seen each other! Why hadn't she considered that connection before?

Before Chela could ask the next question, a knock came at the door.

"Shit," Mouse Girl said, alarmed. "Probably Raffi."

She was right. Raphael didn't look angry, but his presence was significant. He was keeping a close eye on his new investment. He ignored Mouse Girl.

"Chela," he said, glad to see her. "I thought you had vanished into the air."

Chela gave him her brightest smile, apologizing. She took his hand and allowed him to introduce her to the party's newcomers. Chela hoped to recognize people she had seen on the movie set with Ten, but the new men were from Latin America, dressed sharply in business attire, probably fresh from the airport. Like the others, they beheld her like a prize.

It was almost midnight, and Chela was ready to go home. She wasn't sure what she had gained for the price she had paid, but she hoped it was worth something. She might have earned one answer about Maria from Raphael, but she wanted to choose her question carefully. Should she ask about the man with the big nose? Or maybe the guy Maria had been hanging out with, the one she'd said was a pilot who would fly her to Jamaica?

But instinct told her not to ask him anything about Maria. She kept thinking about the VIP room and *Freaknik*.

"How will I find you tomorrow?" Chela said, signaling that she was ready to leave.

Raphael glanced at his watch, irritation shadowing his face. "It's early yet."

"I'll be back. No worries."

Raphael gave her specific instructions, the way Mother used to. He dialed a number into her phone and let it ring once so it would register in both of their phones' memories, explaining that it was an answering service. She was to call that number the next night at eight precisely and wait for a return call. He warned her not to go back to Club Phoenixx or the hotel on her own, meaning that she shouldn't try to capitalize on her introductions without him.

Was that what Maria had done? Had her independence gotten her killed?

"Do you have any questions for me?" he said, walking her toward the door. She guessed that he would walk her downstairs and all the way to a cab, or his driver, just to make sure she didn't double back without his knowledge. And his percentage. They had yet to negotiate, but he'd hinted she would make two thousand per client—which meant he would charge much more.

"What if there's a guy I want to pick?" she said.

"Name him," Raphael said. "Anyone you saw tonight?"

She pretended to consider the question, scanning the room. "Well . . . not anyone right now. But I hear there's lots of movie people around. From that zombie movie?"

Chela realized she might have made a mistake to sound so star-struck. She'd told Maria that Ten was working on the movie, and Maria might have mentioned it to Raphael and the other girls. She didn't care if she burned her bridge with Raphael—she had no intention of calling him again—but lies might tip off the killer to her first, especially if Raphael was involved. Wasn't it possible, even likely, that Mouse Girl would tell Raphael everything they had talked about to win favor with him?

But Raphael's brow, which had been tightly knitted since she said she wanted to go, loosened again. His smile returned, amused. "Everyone loves movie people," he said. "Is that what you want, my angel? Your big break?"

Chela pursed her lips, glancing at the carpeted floor. "Not exactly . . . I just . . ."

Gently, Raphael pinched her cheek. "I'm teasing. You deserve that and more. Call me tomorrow night. I am the one who will make you a star."

ELEVEN

BY MIDNIGHT, I was in a bad mood.

Gustavo Escobar had sent most of the cast home and insisted on reshooting my sex scene with Brittany Summers, which I'd thought was already in the can. I'd spent an hour in the makeup chair being reverted back to my normal face, and instead of going home as I'd planned, I'd been asked to spend another two hours half-naked on the set.

My contract had stipulated a single sex scene. Len and I had negotiated carefully to avoid exploiting any rumors about me circulating in Hollywood. By now, I was sure Escobar had already broken half a dozen provisions of our agreement, which had called for "a standard of tastefulness." Like hell.

Usually, it's actresses who worry more about their sexuality onscreen. Some actresses refuse to shoot sex scenes unless they're wearing a bra, and others, such as Angela Bassett, outright refuse. Whatever Halle had made for *Monster's Ball* wasn't nearly enough, Oscar or not. But my situation was unique. I'd begun to suspect that Escobar had only cast me to fulfill some kind of *Mandingo* imagery he believed would horrify the movie's viewers, a brutish black man violating his lead actress's milky blond treasures. That night, I believed I had my proof.

My ego was at stake, too. I didn't have a body double, and I hadn't expected to shoot any scenes with my shirt off that week. Last time, I'd gone on a juice fast and doubled up on my crunches two days beforehand as usual, which helped define my abs. Movie standards for bare skin are much higher than in life. If Escobar had wanted to reshoot the sex scenes, he should have given me more notice.

I know some actors who get off on building chemistry during sex scenes, rehearsing for real-life playtime later, but to me, there's nothing sexy about it. Between the lights and the crew, it's impossible to forget I'm at work. Sex, real or imaginary, didn't have special allure to me anymore, unless I was with April.

Yes, even with Brittany Summers. She's a beautiful lady with a body she works hard to maintain, but I don't have any particular taste for the Nordic look. And at twenty-three, Brittany was closer to Chela's age than mine, so she was a kid to me. It also seemed likely that Brittany and the director were sleeping together—or they had—so I had nothing to gain from fanning any flames of lust for her. We were doing our jobs.

And I was exhausted. The perspiration Brittany and I were drenched in was real, and I was more annoyed for Brittany's sake than my own.

Despite limited acting talent and implants more suitable for a porn star, she'd been an island of professionalism. She covered her chest with a hand towel between takes and shifts for new camera angles, and we negotiated every touch. I always try to follow a director's wishes, but when it comes to scenes involving intimacy or nudity, the actress has final say. I might look as if I'm rubbing an actress between her legs under the covers, but I'm probably just mimicking the motion or kneading her stomach or thigh. If the scene calls for a breast in my mouth, I keep my tongue far away if I can. I may look naked but am actually wearing a flesh-colored "modesty pouch" and my partner a flesh-colored latex pubic wig.

The scene we were shooting seemed endless, and Escobar was pushing his R rating. The bed's covers were thrown aside, leaving only our nudity, and I was miming thrusts while she wrapped her legs around me, arching her back. Was I aroused? Not even slightly, although our lower torsos couldn't avoid contact. I worried that her pelvic bone might be getting sore. So sue me.

Instead of clearing the set of all but himself and a cameraman, Escobar had a dozen sweaty guys standing around handling lights and sound. Escobar was practically standing over us, almost in the camera's frame. I felt more self-conscious than I had ever been on a set. Black men don't get much experience doing love scenes in Hollywood, so at first, I'd blamed my discomfort on inexperience. But as Escobar called for take after take, my hindbrain started tingling. Something didn't feel right; he seemed more like a voyeur than a director.

"No, no, *no!*" Escobar said, and moved closer to ruin yet another take. I heard the cinematographer sigh. "I said passion, Tennyson—animal passion. What is this choirboy nonsense? You're taking her. You've lost control. Grab her. Hold her in place."

The word *animal* clenched my teeth. I might lose control, but not on camera. I climbed away from Brittany, coming to my feet, and a male intern immediately flung a robe over my shoulders so I could cover myself while Brittany's assistant draped a blanket over her.

"Gus . . ." Louise Cannon warned. "Look at the clock. They nailed this a week ago."

Sometimes Cannon could bring Escobar back down to planet Earth, but not that night. He was obsessed with the scene. I've never walked off a set, but I could feel the moment coming. I glanced at glassy-eyed Brittany, who looked resigned to Escobar's whims.

Escobar brought his face far too close to mine. "You're supposed to know women, no? You're the expert? Where are you hiding it? Do I have to show you?"

I was glad he stepped away from me, or I might have broken his nose. No, you can't actually drive a man's nose bone into his brain regardless of what your ex-Marine neighbor told you. But it might have been fun to pretend I could.

He sat on the bed beside Brittany and grabbed a handful of hair from the back of her scalp, yanking her face close to his. One of the female interns gasped audibly from the back of the room, but the rest of the set was stone silent. "You see?" Escobar said to me, as if Brittany were a rag doll. "This is how you master a woman. You take control."

Still tugging her hair by the roots, Escobar pulled Brittany's face closer and mashed his mouth to hers. Unconsciously, she lightly touched his chest as if to push him away but reconsidered and let her hand fall to the mattress. In the script, Brittany's character was infected and had seduced *me*, not the other way around; but the more footage we shot, the more the director was pushing the scene toward visual rape. I never would have agreed to the oldest stereotype in American history for the sake of a horror movie. No thanks.

I still don't know how I resisted laying my hands on Escobar. I loathe men who mistreat women, no matter what their pretense.

"We're done tonight," I said, my voice thick with gravel.

Escobar released Brittany and shot to his feet. "What did you say?"

"Ten, it's all right," Brittany said, sitting upright. "He has his vision for it, what he sees in his head, and it's not a problem. Seriously, I'm fine with anything he wants."

I felt like the only sane man in a mental ward, but no one crosses the director on a shoot unless he can afford to lose his job. Mine might be lost already, but my dignity matters more than my work. It would cost him a fortune to replace me this late, so I had power, too.

"Sorry, Brit, this scene is over," I said. "You can put your clothes back on, darlin'."

Cannon's feet pattered as she ran from her chair to try to stand between me and Escobar, who was staring at me as if I'd round-house-kicked him in the back of the skull. Visions of mayhem danced in my head. "Gus, it's late," Cannon said. "He's tired. Everyone's tired."

She reasoned with gentle, pleading tones. An observer might have thought she was worried he was about to pull out a gun.

I had nothing left to do but turn and walk toward the dressing room, where my clothes were waiting. I remembered how strange Chela's voice had sounded when I'd last spoken to her two hours ago. She'd been lying to me. I was furious with myself for the way I'd been wasting my time instead of taking care of my family.

Escobar followed me step for step. "You!" he said. "Get back to the bed."

I stopped and turned so Escobar could see my eyes. "You," I said, "are an asshole."

Cannon moaned, watching her movie unravel.

Escobar's face wore a tight smile, but his eyes gathered information from mine. Maybe he saw Spider lurking there. Whatever he learned only made his anger glitter with an unspoken, terrible promise. His smile strained but never faltered.

"Yes. I am," he whispered. He extended his arm toward the exit, in invitation. "Then go, *cómo no*. Good night, Tennyson."

The sound of the calm before the storm.

I tried to call Chela as soon as I was in my car, but her phone was off. *Please let her be home in bed*, I thought, although I knew I couldn't count on any miracles.

Since L.A. is three hours behind Miami, I decided to call my agent, Len Shemin, while I drove back to my hotel. I wanted him to hear the story from me. I felt guilty for how glad he sounded to talk to me. He said he was driving home from the office, too.

Our pleasantries didn't last long.

"Jesus," Len said, his one-word response to every sentence I told him about my night on the set—my last night, I assumed.

"So then I called him an asshole and left."

"Jesus, Ten." Len sounded as if he might cry. I almost asked if he needed to pull over. Maybe both of us should have; I almost clipped a midnight Rollerblader wearing glowing bands around his neck as he dashed across the intersection at the yellow light.

"He's lucky I didn't knock his teeth out," I said.

"So you could go to jail instead of just getting fired?" Len said. "You're the lucky one."

So much for wondering if Len would share my outrage. Len and I have had difficult moments during our agent-client marriage—through my sex work, two murder investigations, and a kidnapping debacle—and he'd rarely sounded so grave. Now that Len was on the phone and my clothes were back on, the second-guessing began. Had I overreacted?

I hated to care whether or not I was fired, but I did. Asshole or not, Gustavo Escobar was one of the few players in Hollywood who had been willing to work with me. Len had warned me for years that I was trashing my career. Maybe I'd finally managed to do it.

"You had to be there, man. Something about Escobar wasn't right."

"You're telling me you put it all on the line to defend the honor of Brittany 'Look at My Tits' Summers? Who, by the way, everyone knows has been vaginal bungee jumping with Escobar from day one. She's tweeting about it! Is that what you're telling me?" He was nearly shouting by the end.

Again, I was silent. My anger was burning off, dampened with doubt. I didn't want to get into a shouting match with Len.

"Ten, I have a migraine, so I blew off Scott Rudin's premiere party to go straight home. But now, instead of closing my eyes in a dark room, I'll be on the phone with my buddies at CAA begging to kiss Escobar's ass so I can make sure you still have a job in the morning."

"You don't have to do that." I wanted to say, *Forget it, I quit.* But I didn't.

"Yes, I do have to do that," Len said, "because I put *myself* on the line for you. I'm one headline away from being a laughingstock because I didn't cut you loose a year ago."

Len wasn't just my agent; he might have been my best friend. That's how much that hurt. I wouldn't have minded his bad mood, or his candor, but he'd snapped to judgment without respecting my opinion.

"Don't do me any favors, man. If I'm that much trouble, don't represent me."

I was trying to give him an escape hatch, just as I had with April. Neither of us spoke for the next half a block. A full moon hung over the Atlantic, painting the flat ocean in a sheet of golden white. A beautiful lie.

Finally, Len sighed. "Goddammit, Ten. Get some help."

My phone beeped to let me know he had hung up. If iPhones weren't so expensive, I would have thrown it out my window.

I almost called Louise Cannon to try to fix it myself—I wasn't the first actor who'd called his director an asshole and stormed off the set, and I wouldn't be the last—but I put my phone away when I remembered what I had seen roiling in Gustavo Escobar's eyes.

Please let Chela be home, I thought. I needed some light to sleep by.

But her room was empty.

Chela was gone.

TWELVE

SOMETIMES IGNORANCE IS bliss.

If I'd stayed at the shoot or come home fifteen minutes later, I might never have known that Chela went out. Not knowing might not have changed anything to follow—or might have made what happened worse—but I still dream about coming home that night and finding Chela asleep where she belonged, the events of the real world forever undone.

She had lied to me, but after my episode with Escobar and my conversation with Len, I was drained of anger. I felt a sense of calm reflection as I waited in the uncomfortable art deco lounge chair in Chela's room for her to come home. I'd decided that Dad was dead wrong. I wasn't going to allow Chela to run wild on South Beach with a fake ID, no matter what her reasons. No more nightclubs and no more staying out till the cows wandered home. If she didn't like my rules, she could either pay for her own hotel room or go back home.

That was what I'd planned to tell her.

Our suite's front door opened quietly at 12:45, and I heard Chela slipping into her room. Her breathing was shallow, relieved, when she closed her door.

When she flipped on her light, she found me waiting. Her party dress barely qualified as clothing.

She didn't start, or scream, or even blink. She stood frozen, staring at me with wide eyes that told me more than I wanted to know before she said a word. Chela looked smaller, as if her insides had shriveled while she was gone. I forgot my speech and my ultimatum.

"What happened, Chela?"

At first, she shook her head as if to say *nothing*. But her eyes said something else.

Before she spoke, Chela opened her drawer, found a gray UCLA sweatshirt she often wore at home in L.A., and pulled it on over her mini-dress. It hung to her thighs, nearly as long as the dress. Next, she tied on her robe, covering herself. I told myself she was being modest because she was embarrassed that her dress was so skimpy, but it might be worse than that. When she sat on her bed across from me, she gathered a rumpled bath towel into her lap, playing with the edges. She wanted to bathe.

"I went to Club Phoenixx . . ." she began.

While I was at work, Chela had been conducting an investigation. Her report was so detailed that I asked her to wait while I grabbed a pen and hotel stationery to take notes. She produced Maria's driver's license and showed me a photo on her cell phone with the license tag of the van of the man who had given it to her, a fake ID vendor known as Julio. Impressive.

She told me about the escort operation at the Swordfish Hotel and the kinds of men Maria might have been working for. She told me her pimp's name was Raphael, a.k.a. Raffi, a.k.a. El Santo, and apologized because she hadn't had a chance to snap a photo of his license plate. But the older-model black Mercedes limousine she described wouldn't be hard to spot.

Her voice grew soft when she talked about the limousine, so I underlined Raphael's name twice. My fingertips felt cold as I held tightly to the pen, grinding the tip into the paper almost hard enough to tear it. I had questions, but I kept them to myself.

"Go on," I said.

She matched my measured tone. "Still nothing on the big-nosed guy I saw that night, but her friend thought she went after him. Maybe Raffi didn't like her chasing a john on her own. Maybe Maria found the guy in the VIP room and left with him. Maria's friend said movie people hang out up there, by the way. From *Freaknik*."

My eardrums seemed to foam, so I gave my head a firm shake. I hadn't expected my bad night to converge with Chela's. Could someone from my movie be connected to a pimp whose girls were turning up dead?

Chela went on. "The first girl disappeared about three weeks ago, and another one, Lupe, two weeks ago. Were any of the movie people around at the beginning of the month?"

The shoot had started two weeks before, but plenty of crew had been there before the cast arrived. "They think someone connected to the film is killing the girls?"

"I didn't say that," Chela repeated patiently. "It's just an interesting coincidence."

I could be talking to a homicide detective; she sounded as if she had aged a decade. Chela's work was stunning. The driver's license alone would have been a coup for a cop.

"Chela . . ." My questions tried to form but got caught in my throat. I couldn't bring the thoughts to my mind's surface, much less into the quiet room. Chela's eyes retreated far into her head as she stared at me. I had seen that mask dozens of times. I'd worn it, maybe. *Don't ask me,* it said.

But I didn't have to ask. A high-end pimp like Raphael would not give his trust away easily, especially when a dead prostitute was involved. Chela had told me plenty, but information like hers never came free.

"I wish you'd let me come with you," I said, my voice hollow. "That you'd waited."

Chela shrugged. "You weren't here. You were working. But it's okay. Now you have something to go on, right? I'd start with the VIP room at Phoenixx. I'm going to sleep now."

I'd barely had a chance to close her door before I heard Chela's shower go on. She must have run to her bathroom as fast as she could.

In the dark living room, I counted twenty long minutes before she turned the water off.

Sometimes a night goes so wrong that you can only ponder the immensity of it, your mistakes laid bare beneath a magnifying glass. In one night, I had lost my job, probably my agent, and maybe four years of work with Chela. I felt gut-punched. I'd had a similar feeling before, usually related to my cases, when the wrong move convinced me that I had failed, leaving a murderer to go free or a kidnapping victim to die. But that night, it was my own home, my own world. A dozen razors were slashing my insides to the bone.

I wished Chela had screamed curses at me, calling me a coward for avoiding the police after Maria died. But instead, her calm sweetness, the way she'd reassured me and sent me on my way, was ripping me apart. I was no longer the father figure, nor she the child. We had become something else. *She* had become something else. And it was my fault.

And I felt exiled from my one place of rest—April. Yes, she would listen and give me good advice, but every word I spoke would only reinforce her worst fears about me. I wanted to put off that final day of reckoning as long as I could. How could I tell her I was being drawn into another murder case? Or that she'd been right all along when she warned me that I couldn't save Chela from her damaged past by hiding her and pretending we were a family?

If I'd been a crying man, I'd have spent my night in tears.

My first impulse in the face of catastrophe is to find a way to fix it, but no ideas came. I didn't have any cop sources in Miami. I couldn't let Chela stay in Miami now, much less use her as a tour guide through Maria's world. And any connection to *Freaknik*, no matter how far-fetched, was beside the point; I would be banned from the set unless I crawled back to Escobar. I could humiliate myself if I knew it would lead somewhere, but over wild speculation?

"This ends tonight," I said to the empty room. I didn't recognize my own voice.

First thing in the morning, I would send Chela back to L.A. Dad and Marcela could keep the suite through the end of the week for a honeymoon, but my business in Miami was finished. I would try to find a police source to use Chela's hard-won information, but from a healthy distance. Maria had created enough destruction in my life. I wanted to raise that girl from the dead just to slap her face.

I thought I felt better by two in the morning, when I made my decision, but instead of going to bed, I went to the kitchen and opened the cabinet where we'd stashed the leftover booze from Marcela's party. I drink beer or a few glasses of wine now and then, but I'm not a drinking man. I don't like the headaches, dehydration, and judgment lapses alcohol brings. I couldn't remember the last time I'd been anything close to drunk.

But that night, I poured a glass of rum and splashed it with stale Coke. When that one was finished, I poured another. Maybe I wanted to make sure I slept, but I was wide awake. The walls of the hotel suite seemed to close in on me, blurry blandness, so I decided to go outside.

I needed a swim. In my hurry, I didn't bring bathing trunks or a towel. I was so drunk that I would have been weaving if I'd climbed into my car. But I could walk to the beach.

South Beach never truly shuts down for the night, but by two, it had gone from a boil to a simmer. Traffic on Ocean Drive was at a steady pace, no longer clogged, so I dodged honking drivers while I reeled toward the sand. Saltwater perfumed the night air. Wind whipped sand granules across my cheeks as storm clouds hid the fat moon.

On the beach, the precious solitude of a night swim. Not a single person was in sight. Despite whatever hazards lay in the dark—beached jellyfish balloons, broken glass, even a shark fin gliding in the distance—the peace was worth the risk.

One of my loafers came off in a clump of damp sand near the shoreline. I flung off the other without slowing my pace, too drunk to care if I found either later. I stumbled out of my pants next, racing the rainclouds. My abandoned T-shirt turned invisible on the sand behind me. I splashed into the water, wearing only my briefs.

Cool water embraced my bare ankles. The Pacific had taught me to expect a shock of cold every time I waded into water, but I could handle the Atlantic. I barely noticed the chill. I closed my eyes and sank to my knees, up to my neck in water.

I wouldn't call what I did swimming. It was more some groggy kind of surrender. I floated on my back, only stroking when the waves upset my balance or plugged my nose. For all I know, I might have dozed. Half-formed thoughts and images about Chela broke through, dogging me.

The wind picked up, matching my mood.

The ocean floor rose as I approached a sand bar concealed beneath the water to the right of me. I was ready to swim to the sand bar to give myself a rest when the rip current hit me.

Every time I get drunk, I remember why I don't like to drink.

If I'd been sober, I would have paid more attention to the wind conditions and noticed the telltale swirling of the current near the sand bar—the perfect recipe for rip currents. But I wasn't sober. I was so drunk that I'd barely been able to walk straight, and I was a long way from walking anywhere.

We forget how mighty nature can be. That current pulled me like a tractor towing a log.

Instead of snapping to alertness, my mind went blank with surprise. Instinct made me open my mouth wide and yell. Big mistake. I drank in so much saltwater that my throat and nose burned. The alcohol haze lifted, stripped.

Ten, you're in trouble, a calm voice inside me said. I'd heard that voice before, and that voice was always right.

Under the best of circumstances, I'm not a great swimmer, just a good one. Drunk, I wasn't even that. I flailed and splashed, making the classic swimmer's mistake in the face of a rip current. As the current swept me out to sea, I tried to swim against it, toward the lights of shore. A few useless strokes were enough to remind me that I was no match for the ocean. But instincts are strong, and my eyes told me I would be safe if I swam away from the void.

Parallel! the voice said, no longer calm. *Swim parallel to shore, across the rip!*

I tried to change direction, struggling to judge my bearings through stinging eyes. By then, I could barely swim at all. My arms were filled with lead, and a bear of a cramp seized my right leg. I was coughing instead of breathing, craning to keep my head above the water's surface, still being swept away from shore with horrifying speed.

A wave devoured me, stealing my light and air, and the world went black. The certainty that I was about to die wasn't new, but the feeling never got easier. The ocean wasn't Spider, whose arrogance had cost him his life; the ocean didn't get tired, feel pity, or make mistakes. Its size was incomprehensible, and I have never felt more alone.

But I kept up my strokes, kicking despite my cramp, praying

that I was swimming in the right direction even while my lungs were aflame, promising me a fiery death in the depths.

Then I popped free of the current, as if it had gotten bored and spat me away. In all, less than a minute had passed, the longest seconds of my life.

By the time I reached shore, I was so tired from my struggle that I let out a choked yell of frustration to the empty beach before my feet finally touched the ocean floor. I crawled to shore, coughing. I vomited brine. My arms and legs trembled from adrenaline. My heart thrashed, punishing me for my stupidity. I hadn't been that scared in a long time.

I imagined what Maria's last moments had been like, her lungs afire, a terrified young woman at the ocean's mercy. Anyone could drown—anyone. Like me, she could have been drunk and foolish.

But what if her death had been worse than that? What if someone had held her in the water while she struggled for life? The idea of it made me vomit again.

The clouds broke, and the moon lit up the sand in ghostly blue-gray as far as I could see in either direction. The current had swept me so far from my origin that I had no hope of finding my clothes and shoes, but I had my briefs. Ocean Drive's party was still under way to the west, but the beach was deserted. I could have yelled out at the top of my lungs all night, and no one would have heard me.

The beach didn't fit the story. Maria hadn't survived the streets for years without wisdom. According to Chela, she didn't swim. Was afraid of water. Maybe Chela was right: the police just didn't give a shit, were ignoring evidence. *Hell, they're just strolling sperm banks.* Suddenly, it seemed obvious.

Chela's friend hadn't drowned accidentally; someone had killed her.

The killer might be someone Chela had met. Someone hiding in plain sight.

That dark knowledge weighed down my weary bones as I trudged barefoot on the sand back toward the lights.

Walking barefoot on Ocean Drive for three blocks in soggy underwear in the middle of the night doesn't turn as many heads as one might think.

Luckily, I'd had the sense to leave my phone waiting on the kitchen counter. I'd missed three calls and a text while I'd been gone. Once I'd rinsed the sand out of my hair in the kitchen sink and wrapped myself in a robe, I checked the screen. The message was from Len:

REPORT TO SET A.M.

GUS SEZ HE WAS A PRICK,

& HE'S NOT THE ONLY ONE.

FORGIVE ME?

Even if I'd been holding a grudge, the ocean had reminded me not to be petty. Len should have stood up for me, taking my side until he had evidence that he shouldn't, but I could understand why Len's trust in me was frayed. His message on my phone lightened my heart, almost making me smile.

I would be staying in Miami after all.

THIRTEEN

USUALLY, I PASSED the hours in the makeup chair listening to Walter Mosley or Michael Connelly audio books, but now I had a mission that couldn't wait for my hangover headache to subside. The search for Maria's killer would be the easy part. First, the hard part.

I caught April by phone at barely 7:00 A.M. her time, so she was still in bed. After I told April what I needed from her, the sleep shook from her voice. "You want me to *what*?"

"It's just for a few days, maybe till the end of the week. I have to keep working, and I can't leave her here. We had a breach of trust." I left it at that. I would tell April more if I needed to, but I knew Chela wouldn't want me to share too much. Besides, I didn't want to tell April I was working on another case. I'd almost been killed at least three times since we'd met, and she didn't want that life of worry.

"Did you get sunstroke?" April said. "Chela can't stand me."

"That's not true. She's warmed up to you. She'll do what I ask her to do."

"Since when?"

Touché. But I had leverage over Chela—she wanted me to look into her friend's death, and I wouldn't agree to do that unless she agreed to leave Miami and stay with April. Period.

"Since now, April."

April sighed. "She's eighteen, Ten. Can't she just stay at your house?"

I'd thought about that but decided against it. I didn't know what kind of emotional impact Chela's night out would have on her, and I didn't want her to be alone. April would give her someone to report to, at least in theory. "It's better if she's with you."

"Better for whom?" April said, irritated. "This isn't a fair position to put me in. You know how Chela feels about me, and now I'm supposed to be some kind of . . . den mother?"

"Chela told me she hopes she can find a relationship like ours."

April stopped in mid-rant. "She said that?"

"Yeah, I was telling her how honest I've been with you, how you've been there for me. She thinks you're good for me. And you don't have to watch over her every minute. She'll have her car, she'll hang out with her boyfriend. She's grown now. I just want her to have someone I trust to go home to."

I hadn't told April a thing, and I'd already said too much.

"Ten . . . is Chela in danger?" she said.

"She got mixed up with some bad elements down here, an old friend from the streets. I think it'll be fine, but I want her back in L.A."

"Chela knows we're not still . . . ?"

Invisible cymbals crashed against my temples. It was my fault for bringing up our relationship, but I hated the reminder. "She knows," I said. "We're just friends." Friends who slept together at every opportunity, but I didn't nitpick. I hadn't been able to give April what she wanted when I had my chance, and now I was stuck with her rules.

April sighed. She probably suspected I hadn't told her everything, or she'd heard enough. Either way, that sigh told me she would let Chela stay with her.

I told April that I would fly Chela home that day if I could, or by morning at the latest. I didn't want Chela to spend another night in Miami.

April's voice went soft. "You know what, Ten? You're a great dad. I hope Chela knows how lucky she is to have you."

April had never said that to me, and her words came at the moment they felt least true. The lump that rose in my throat tasted like saltwater.

"We'll see," I said.

When I hung up, I was staring at myself. The special-effects team had constructed a perfect likeness of me from the shoulders up, complete with eyeglasses, to be rigged for an explosion. The script called for my character to be blown away by a National Guard sniper once I was "cured," a twist stolen straight from Romero's *Night of the Living Dead*. The dummy head sat on the makeup table across from me, awaiting its close-up. The likeness was mesmerizing.

"Ten, meet twin," said Elliot, the makeup artist. "Props just dropped it off."

Elliot, like a good barber, had mastered the illusion that a wall of privacy separated us. The whole time I was on the phone with April, I'd forgotten that Elliot was hovering, applying sticky zombie prosthetics to my forehead.

I'd worked with Elliot before, during my short-lived stint on a TV show called *Homeland*. Most people pegged Elliot as a stuntman or bodyguard type rather than a makeup artist; his voice rumbled with bass, and he looked as if he could bench-press a Honda.

"Sounds like I missed the fireworks," Elliot said. "Bang, bang. Real gutsy, Tin Man. And everyone thought you were just a pretty face."

I wasn't surprised that word of last night's disagreement had made it to the crew. Movie sets, like churches, are gossip mills. Escobar hadn't made it to work yet when I arrived at 9:00 A.M., and I intended to avoid him as long as I could.

"I can't cave to bullshit, man," I said. "It's not in my DNA."

"My hero," Elliot said with a playful grin at me in the mirror. He flirted with men and women alike. Elliot had never made a play for me or touched me unnecessarily, so I ignored his crush. Hell, let him dream.

"Just so you know," Elliot went on, "Cannonball gave him an earful after you left."

"Nothing worse than a director on an ego trip. You should've heard him—"

But I stopped short when Elliot clicked his teeth and gave me a meaningful pat on the shoulder, a warning. Rapid footsteps approached Elliot's domain from the hall, and we both knew the sound. Escobar walked quickly, as if he were late to catch a train. He probably had been close enough to overhear us, but too bad.

Escobar was all smiles when he breezed into the makeup room, looking unusually refreshed for the early hour. He had a Starbucks grande coffee in one hand and a gift bag in the other; but unless there was more aspirin in the sack, I wasn't interested in anything from him.

"Tennyson, Tennyson . . ." he said, reciting my name like a nursery rhyme. He set his coffee on the counter and made a motion as if to pinch my cheek—but the horror on Elliot's face and something worse on mine made him stop an inch before he touched me. "I'm so embarrassed, *mijo*. You were right to object last night—absolutely right. My behavior was shameful. You must think me a monster."

I didn't see what I would gain by sharing my thoughts, so I shrugged. "We all have our bad days."

"Look at him," Escobar said to Elliot. "The consummate professional! I'm in your debt, Tennyson. Anything you need from me, only ask, and it's done."

His sudden change of demeanor stank of lawyering. I generated a smile, studying him. Up close, I saw a physical trait that had escaped my notice. His earlobes were attached to the sides of his head instead of hanging free, and starkly so. It would be noticeable enough for someone to remember, if it ever came to that.

But there's no law against being an asshole, at least so far. I keep waiting.

"*Pues*, I have to get to the set," Escobar said in Spanglish. "*Pero* I wanted to apologize personally. I hope this will help compensate for your aggravation." He offered me the gift bag.

I took the bag but didn't give him the satisfaction of watching me peek inside.

"Well?" Elliot said when Escobar was gone.

The strong scent betrayed the gift before I opened the wrapped box inside: Cuban cigars. Cohibas, according to the label. Very good, from what I'm told, and very illegal in the U.S. But even if I'd been a smoker, I wasn't interested in Escobar's offering. Elliot asked if he could hold a cigar beneath his nose, and he inhaled the aroma like a fat line of coke.

"Take them," I said, handing the box to him. "They're yours."

The big man's mouth dropped open. "Are you shitting me?"

"Nah," I said. "Share them with the rest of the crew, if you want. Half the people here deserve a box from that guy. Am I done in the chair?"

Elliot nodded. "I can always ugly you up a little more, but sure. Thanks for the Cohibas, Tin Man, you cruel SOB. That's a nasty trick, trying to make me fall for you."

Elliot hoped if he kept fishing, he might catch me.

"Get in line," I told Elliot.

At least one of us would feel like celebrating.

From our silence in the terminal, no one could have guessed about our screaming match in the car on the way to Miami International

Airport. Chela and I had both loaded plates with *arroz con pollo* and *tres leches* at La Carreta, one of the best airport restaurants in existence (modeled after the Mothership on Calle Ocho in Miami), but neither of us felt like eating.

Chela's redeye wasn't until nine thirty, so we had time to kill. I'd hoped she would be less angry by the time she left, so she might actually show up at April's house in the car I'd ordered for her, but I wasn't sure. For all I knew, Chela would vanish in L.A.

But at least she wouldn't be in Miami.

"This," Chela said, "is bullshit."

"It is what it is," I said, my voice distant. "But I'm not doing jack to investigate this case until I know you're on that plane."

"And you wonder why I never signed the paperwork?" she said. "Maybe because I don't want to spend the rest of my life legally stuck with you!"

The previous night's calm demeanor was gone. Chela's voice rose, drawing stares from the airport reunion at the next table, a boy who looked barely eighteen wearing Army fatigues, surrounded by proud and worried relatives. The oldest woman at the table, perhaps the boy's grandmother, looked aghast at Chela's insolence.

I only shrugged. Chela's words couldn't touch me. To me, Chela's explosive anger was only an indication that I was right to send her away. Whatever she'd done last night had unsettled her emotions, and I was the most convenient target. The dust would settle, and we would see where we stood on the other side.

I checked the time. Eight o'clock exactly.

"Call him," I said.

"Screw you."

"Call him," I said again, leaning closer, "or I'm out."

"I can't believe you're using my dead friend to blackmail me," Chela said.

"Believe it. Call him."

"Ten, if you show up instead of me, it'll ruin everything!"

Chela might be right, but I didn't care. If I needed Chela to snare Maria's pimp, it wasn't meant to be. My heavy stare was my only answer.

To my surprise, tears pooled in Chela's eyes. "It'll all be for nothing," she said, her true fears spoken aloud. "Everything."

Her tears were like acid. I blinked and reached to take her hand, but she pulled it away. I leaned closer to her, over my plate of steaming food. "Chela, I promise you . . . I can do this. I know you've made sacrifices, and you did amazing work, but it's time for me to take over. I *will* find out who killed Maria—just like with Serena and T. D. Jackson. I won't rest until he's paid for it, hear me? But you matter to me more than anyone in the world, and I want you far, far away from these guys. If anything happened to you . . ."

I couldn't finish the sentence. Even the thought.

"I'll be careful," Chela said, still not convinced, although her temper had calmed.

"You want to be careful? Get on that plane. But first, call Raphael. Get a meeting place. I'll figure it out from there."

I saw it in her eyes, then. Chela wanted to leave Miami even more than I wanted her to. She'd been fighting me because of a sense of obligation to Maria's ghost, but she didn't want to see Raphael. She didn't even want to hear his voice.

"Did he hurt you?" I asked gently. I realized that I probably should have taken Chela to the hospital the night before. It was obvious that she'd had sex with the pimp, but what if he'd hurt her? Or hadn't let her use a condom? My heart hammered with fury waiting to be unleashed.

Chela dried her eyes. "No, but shut up. I said I don't want to talk about it."

Then she steeled herself with a deep breath and dialed the number Raphael had given her.

Someone answered right away. A woman's voice? I wasn't close enough to tell.

"Chela," she said. "Okay." Then she hung up. Phone contact was clipped, just as it had been with Mother.

"Well?"

"She said I'll hear back in five minutes."

We ate in silence, waiting. I smothered my food in hot sauce; my taste buds were dead.

The call came in ten minutes, not five. Raphael, apparently, wasn't as prompt as Mother had been. From the look on Chela's face, he'd called her personally, so he wasn't too worried that his phone was under surveillance. Her voice was so chipper as she spoke to him that I realized she might be a far better actor than I was. She even smiled and twirled her hair with her finger, as if he could see her. I gave her a pen to scribble what he said on our restaurant receipt.

"Great! See you then," she said, and hung up. Her smile melted, gone, as she took notes. Chela pushed the receipt to me, not meeting my eyes. "He said he'll meet me there. Don't screw it up."

He'd given her a hotel name and room number, a different hotel from the previous night but still on Miami Beach. It was new, part of the development explosion that had remade the city in a five-year span. I didn't have contacts in the hotel or know my way around.

But that didn't matter.

It was time for Chela to go home.

FOURTEEN

I SETTLED ON white jeans, a white tank top, and new sneakers that I dirtied with soil from the potted palm on my balcony. I tried on my Lakers baseball cap, but a baseball cap at night looked phony. On my way to Chela's designated meeting place, I stopped at a local Chinese dive that was open late and grabbed a paper bag full of takeout.

Instant delivery man. I had an excuse to be anywhere.

I considered the scant danger that I might be recognized, but often people had trouble placing my face. I had a ready answer: "Yeah, people say I look like that bodyguard who screwed up Sofia Maitlin's daughter's kidnapping, Hardwick or whatever."

After twenty years in Hollywood, being a screw-up was my biggest claim to fame. The reputation wasn't fair, but I'd been buried by the FBI's need to take credit for my work—and more shadowy agencies' need to pretend I hadn't had help from a spy named Marsha. Most people still knew my name better than they knew my face, which was for the best.

The hotel was modestly sized, built to imitate the older art deco hotels that were blocks closer to the water, colored in bright peach.

I could have asked Dad's advice, but I had "gone dark," in Marsha's words. I wasn't just on my way to interview a person of interest in a potential murder case—I had a chance to beat the hell out of a scumbag who had put his hands on Chela. Lucky for me, my Glock was in its gun case back in my closet in California. I wanted my gun for all the wrong reasons.

A chorus of voices in my head told me to slow down and think it through—Dad, Chela, April, even my agent, Len—but I hadn't been thinking straight since I'd seen Chela's face when she came home.

I strode across the lobby to an open elevator door with such purpose that I was a shadow. A family of four crammed in behind me, but no one seemed to know I was there. The food in my grease-spotted bag made the elevator car smell like egg rolls.

A video monitor built into the wall streamed the next day's weather forecast in English and Spanish, against idyllic beach backdrops and ads for the hotel's lounges. Speakers played techno at a low volume while snippets of Chela's night with Raphael battered my memory. How many men had touched her? "Raffi, will she travel?" one had said. She'd left out the worst of it, but she'd told me enough.

Rational thought broke through only after I reached the fifth floor and began my walk toward room 515, where Chela had been told to meet the pimp. I followed arrows around corner after corner, making a plan.

I would listen at the door. If I heard a party, I would knock with my delivery routine, try to talk my way in, assess the situation. But if the room was quiet, if Raphael was alone . . .

My hand itched for his throat.

The hallway was as silent as a tomb. As I'd expected, room 515 was in the corner of the hotel reserved for suites, sharing a wing with suite 513. That side of the floor wasn't as crowded, but I would still have to be careful about loud noises. I glanced behind me; no one in the hall. Careful to keep away from the peephole, I pressed my ear to the door.

Nothing. I didn't hear music or a TV. I vaguely smelled marijuana despite the NO SMOKING sign displayed on the door.

I couldn't do my delivery routine if he was alone, I realized. He would know he hadn't ordered food, so he could send me away without opening the door. *So come up with something.*

I knocked.

He must have been near the door, because I didn't hear footsteps before I saw a shadow flicker across the peephole. I had ducked to the side of it.

"Hello?" he said. Was Maria's killer on the other side of that door?

I roughened my voice and tried a Latino accent. "Raffi!" I said, chiding. "Raffi, Raffi, where is she?"

Locks turned. "How did you—"

Raphael flung the door open, and we stared at each other.

"Hey, Raffi," I said with an easy grin. He was tall enough to make me look up.

Human nature made him mimic my smile, but it faded slightly. He thought he knew my face, because he never looked alarmed or concerned. His mistake.

He didn't see my elbow coming before it cracked him across his lower left jaw. I snagged my skin on one of his teeth, but he had the worst of it. He jaw might not be broken, but the night was young. Judging by his hairline, he could be as old as forty.

Raphael stumbled back two steps and tripped over his feet, landing flat on his ass. Maybe no one had ever hit him with bad intent. He was wiry, with thin limbs and a long neck. He reminded me of an insect on its back.

Before he could stand, I kicked the door closed behind us and straddled him in a chokehold. When he dug his nails into my skin to pull against my arm, I wrenched my grip more tightly. It was dangerous to have him in a chokehold. Killer or not, he had touched Chela.

His eyes widened, his face red from panic and oxygen loss. "Who . . . who . . ."

I leaned close to his ear, whispering. "I'm a father, asshole. One of your girls?" My voice almost cracked. I loosened my grip slightly so he wouldn't black out, and so I wouldn't accidentally twist the other way.

"*They* come to *me*," he said. "Ask her what she makes. It might be more than you!"

Arrogant sonofabitch. My eyesight faded, and the room seemed to wheel. Since I didn't want to go to prison, I released his neck.

Instead, I vaulted over him and sent my knee into his groin, hard. My palm pinned his mouth shut, barely muffling his yell. A second strike might have done permanent damage, but I couldn't do it, even as much as I wanted to make him hurt.

When I stood up, he didn't move from his fetal position on the floor. His eyes were glazed. He was dignified about his pain, but he would remember me.

I quickly surveyed the suite to make sure no one else was hiding in the wings. The upscale hotel suite had fur-lined scoop chairs and metallic cabinets. The array of liquor bottles on the bar indicated that Raphael was prepared for a party.

"We need to come to an understanding real fast," I said.

"Get out," Raffi said through gritted teeth. "I don't hold any-one. Take her home."

He didn't move, but his eyes darted toward the nightstand. I stepped over him to fling open the metal drawer, and something clanked inside.

A shiny .22 automatic lay beside the hotel's King James Bible. If Raffi had answered the door with his gun, the night would have been a different story. I grabbed the gun and noted from its weight that it was loaded. I was careful to keep it at my side, not trusting myself enough to point it in his direction.

"You want this?" I said. "Come get it."

"We are just talking. We don't need a gun."

"Oh, but I like the gun." My voice scared even me.

I knelt, keeping the gun's barrel pointed at the floor. I was well out of reach if he tried to surprise me with a sweep to take it. Only a fool gives up the advantage of a gun by moving too close to his prospective target. But I wanted him to see that I wasn't sweating, and if one of us was going to die today, it would more likely be him.

"You like running underage girls . . . Raffi?"

His face turned brighter red. "That's a lie," he whispered solemnly.

"My daughter's sixteen, dickwad."

Raphael seemed to realize that Chela was my daughter, but he kept his thoughts to himself. Chela was tall, but she still had a baby face. It was easy to believe my lie.

I pulled the slide back with a snick, jacking a round onto the floor but putting another in the chamber. I smiled. "Ooh. Boy Scout. Likes to be prepared."

Raphael licked his lips. His eyes dimmed with grim understanding. "*Signore,*" he said slowly, "you have some very wrong ideas about me."

"Tell me about Maria."

"Who?"

"Maria, my daughter's friend. I need to know why she's dead. The first lie that comes out of your mouth . . . in fact, since you've already lied, I'll show you."

This needed to be personal. I pocketed the gun and knelt down, smiling like a long-lost uncle. Grasped his left index finger with my right hand.

"Make a wish," I said, and pulled back until it broke.

He shrieked, and I muffled that scream with my left hand. "You have nine left. If you're gonna lie, make 'em good ones, because I promise you'll remember them. Nine fingers, Raffi. But only two testicles. Think of the testicles, Raffi. Think of them hard. Because by the twelfth lie? Only memories will remain." That sounded good. Almost a Hallmark moment.

For three long seconds, Raphael didn't speak. Then: "I knew her." Raphael tried to mask his pain, but I heard it in his voice.

"The night she vanished. What happened?"

"*Signore*, she is a streetwalker I did favors for. She came to me. They all come to me. I introduced her to a few men, mostly travelers. Lonely businessmen."

"What about the pilot?"

Chela had mentioned that Maria was seeing a pilot who had promised to fly her to Jamaica. Raphael's eyes narrowed, surprised at how much I knew. "Another lonely boy," he said. "He saw Maria. He saw many girls."

"Give me a name."

Raphael looked dismayed, but he didn't pause long. His eyes never left my face. "He could not have killed Maria. He is in Europe this week. He's my pilot, and he's made a run to Rome and Prague."

"To bring you girls?"

Raphael ignored my question. "You can look at the flight logs. Will that make you happy? He has not been in Miami all week."

If that was true, it explained why Chela had never seen or met Maria's mystery man.

"You wrapped that up neat and clean," I said. "Maybe too neat." I grasped his middle finger. "Odd how this finger doesn't really have a name. Thumb, index, ring, and little finger. But this one is just sort of the 'fuck you' finger. And you know what, Raffi?"

"Wh-what . . . ?" His eyes bulged from their sockets.

"Fuck you," I said, and wrenched.

He screamed, then began to babble. "Look, he is young. He still lives with his parents. You want a name? Oscar Reyes. They are a good family on Fisher Island. Anyone you talk to will tell you he's in Europe. He probably does not know Maria is dead—not yet. Their friendship was casual. He likes interesting girls, but he is not a killer."

"Who else was she with?"

Raphael bit at his lip. Blood drooled from his mouth, and he looked as if he might faint. I hoped he would. I know so many interesting ways to wake a man up, and I've always believed it good to polish one's skills. Perhaps he saw this in my eyes. "She is a street prostitute, *signore.*"

"*Was,*" I corrected him. "She's dead, remember?"

Raphael began to cry. The slightest tickle of sympathy scratched at the door of my control. "I . . . I need a doctor."

"I'd say so," I heard myself say. "Right now, an emergency room physician could handle it. Why not go for the gold?" My smile would have chilled dry ice. "Who else was Maria with?"

He spoke quickly. "I am not a pimp, a *magnaccia.* The street girls hound me for introductions. My own girls advertise on Craigslist. They see two or three men a week. That wasn't Maria. Maria was an alley cat. My clients come for film festivals, book fairs, international art festivals. They want a woman they might bring on their arm, who is not empty-headed, who will not steal from their wallets. Maria was beautiful, but . . ." His voice trailed off.

That was the same assessment I'd made of Maria from a distance. "I get it. Go on."

"Maria was not a match for my clients. Only Reyes, from time to time."

"But she had her eye on somebody that night. Give me his name."

Raphael tried to roll away from me, but I stopped him with my knee. "Alley cats watch anything that moves."

I almost broke another finger but stopped myself. *Variety is the spice of life,* I thought. Instead, I hit him squarely across the mouth with my bare knuckle, my left cross, the same spot I'd hit with my elbow. I wasn't surprised when I saw a thin smear of blood on his teeth. I hauled him to his feet as if he was weightless and hurled him into a chair. He landed with a thud, blinking, face gone pale with shock and fear. I shook my hand to get blood back in it.

"Give me a name," I said. "This is the last time I ask politely."

Raphael glared. "I do not know his name."

"Bullshit. Shall we try another finger? Personally, I can't wait to get to your balls."

Raphael stared at me as if wondering if I was insane. Hell, so did I. "I made a mistake with your daughter, *signore*. One mistake. You will maim me for that?"

"If you don't tell me his name, you'll be typing with your tongue."

Raphael raised his right hand to wipe his mouth and winced. The fingers were already swelling. "He calls himself Juan. Everyone is Juan or John, Mr. Garcia, Mr. Smith. Some clients give me real names if they use a credit card, but Juan uses cash. He has been coming to the clubs for a few weeks, almost every night. He is in Miami on business. The girl I introduced to him said he has a boat. She spends time with him there but comes home unharmed. I do not know where he docks."

A boat would be a good place to drown someone. And to let a victim drift.

"Which girl?"

Raphael closed his eyes, preparing to betray a confidence. "Her name is Victoria."

Still keeping him in my sights, I wrote down the telephone number he gave me for the escort who had spent time with the man Chela called Mr. Big Nose. Then I laid Raphael's phone back on the nightstand and punched the numbers without putting the call through, to see if the phone number was real.

His phone offered the owner's initial above the number I'd input: V.

"I'll talk to Victoria," I said.

"You are ruining me," Raphael murmured.

"What about Maria?" I said. "Did you introduce her to Juan?"

Raphael shook his head. "No. That night, he wanted another . . ." Raphael paused, and I could almost hear him thinking about Chela. "He wanted a more sophisticated girl, one who was much more beautiful, more refined. She was a very intelligent girl, with the best breeding."

"Move on," I said, my voice dead.

Raphael rushed on. "When this girl refused Juan, Maria asked me to introduce her. But I said no. Some of the street girls think she tried to talk to him anyway."

"Or maybe you saw her with him," I said. "Maybe you didn't like her trying to score your john behind your back." One of Chela's theories was that Raphael might have killed Maria for trying to cut him out of her deal.

Raphael looked baffled. "Why should it matter? I do not follow these girls. *Signore*, I am not a pimp. What she does, who she sees, this is not my concern. I do not have time enough in the day to count how many men a girl like Maria was with. Twenty a day!"

Raphael probably was exaggerating his lack of concern, but his words rang true. Chela told me he had warned her to stay out of the clubs, grooming her the way he'd described.

"Tell me what Juan looks like," I said.

Raphael's description matched the one Chela had given me, but it still wasn't nearly enough to help me recognize him. I also asked for more details about the girl who had been with him, which he gave even more reluctantly. He had known her for a year, a steady earner. She charged clients fifteen hundred dollars per night, and Juan was happy to pay her price.

A knock came at the door. Two knocks, a pause, and two more knocks. A code.

I raised my finger to my lips, warning Raphael not to speak. He squirmed, but he obeyed. Immediately, his cell phone vibrated on the nightstand where I'd found the gun. I shook my head no. I was glad the ringer was off, or the person at the door would have known Raphael was in his room.

Careful to keep an eye on my patient, I snatched up the phone and pushed the button to silence its vibrations. PRIVATE NUMBER, it read. After a moment, I heard footsteps retreat from the door.

"There will be others," Raphael whispered, hoping I would leave him. Praying, probably.

"Let's talk about Phoenixx," I said. "You're tight with the management. Who else besides Hector?" Chela had told me every name she could remember, and Hector was the guy at the door who had let her and Maria in.

"They are . . . friendly to me," Raphael said.

"I want security footage. I want to see who Maria was with and what she was doing at Phoenixx that night."

"That is not possible! They would never agree."

"Somebody better agree," I said. "*Tonight.* Or it'll be cops asking instead of me. You and your girls are the last people to see Maria alive, Raffi. I will wreck your world if you get in my way."

Raphael stared at the floor. "Let me make some calls," he said.

"No," I said. "You're coming with me."

FIFTEEN

RAPHAEL MOVED LIKE an old man, wincing and hissing. His bottom lip was swollen, starting to bruise bright red. We'd wrapped a torn pillowcase around his right hand, but those fingers would definitely need splints. He was lucky he could walk.

His limo driver kept his eyes on me in his rearview mirror. I don't think the driver believed Raphael's claim that I was a client, but he didn't ask questions. Raphael and I didn't speak during the ride. It took all of my concentration not to think about him touching Chela. With those hands. I wanted to break the rest of his filthy fingers. Maybe his neck.

Raphael was nervous and fretful. I'd confiscated his phone to keep leverage on him, and it vibrated constantly in my pocket. The sound of each missed call made him run his left hand's fingers through his hair and curse in Italian.

I'd kept the little .22 in my pants in case I would need it. I could get popped on a concealed weapons charge, but I didn't want to be unarmed if Raphael signaled for backup at Phoenixx. The first night I'd met Chela, I'd been jumped by a pack while I tried to investigate a murder, and I could feel history ripe to repeat itself. People get killed every day for less than I had done already.

It was only ten on a weeknight, so Club Phoenixx was barely awake. Raphael moved through the club like a dolphin at sea. I kept a step behind him. Nods and waves got him past the velvet rope, past the VIP lounge, and into the nightclub's bowels, where the sound of pounding techno was reduced to a low growl against the walls.

In the security booth, a bank of twenty LCD flat-panel monitors laid the club out for us in pieces. Cameras covered the front and rear entrances, the bars, the dance floors, and the VIP room we had just left. Maria's killer might be on video, but he would be hard to find.

"No chance in hell, Raffi," said the blond-haired woman behind the desk Raphael tried to negotiate with. She sounded like a Brooklyn transplant, in her thirties. She reminded me of Brittany Summers but without the implants. "I don't know this guy. It would be my ass if J.D. even knew I was in here talking to you, much less this guy."

"You said you have an hour," Raphael said.

"Maybe, I said. *Maybe* an hour. I'm gonna risk my job for a maybe?"

Raphael gave me a *well I tried* shrug, but my stare told him to try again.

"I double my offer," Raphael said to the woman. "Give us one hour. My friend is looking for his stepdaughter. He came a long way. One of my girls thought he saw her here."

The security woman, whose shiny name tag identified her as Joan, cast me a sidelong glance. She didn't believe the story. Most likely, she thought I was a cop.

"Joan," I said, "if she's not taking her medication, she might hurt herself or someone else. I just want to be able to call my wife and tell her I saw her, and she's okay."

The Liar's First Law: the more specific the details, the more convincing the story. We would never get access if she knew we were trying to view the tape as part of a murder investigation that might be linked to her club.

"We don't let in anyone underage," Joan said, a disclaimer.

"She's twenty-one," I said. "She just needs her meds."

"Yeah, well, you should be careful with the company she keeps," Joan said, glancing toward Raphael.

"No shit."

Joan studied Raphael and seemed to grasp the significance of his bruises. She gave me a small, approving smile.

"Enough talking," Raphael said, impatient. "Will you help us or not?"

"Fifteen hundred," Joan said. It was twice his last offer.

"Yes, yes, it's done. Hurry." As Raphael fumbled out his wallet and managed to extract neatly folded bills, an unwelcome thought came to mind: *Did Chela get paid?* If she had, she wouldn't have told me. My stomach filled with rocks. I would be as glad to be rid of Raphael as he would be to get away from me.

Joan popped her gum. "It's a lot easier to ignore people than it is to find them. I gotta get somebody to do the desk for me. Then we'll search on the laptop."

Joan asked us to wait in the hall while she called for a replacement. She didn't want her boss to find us loitering in his command center. I leaned against the corridor's exposed concrete wall, close enough to Raphael that he wouldn't try to take off.

"After this," Raphael said, "you walk away?"

"And leave your fingers in peace."

Raphael glared. "And give me my phone."

"Make me," I said.

We stopped talking.

In five minutes, a broad-shouldered, crew-cut man named Hector came in to relieve Joan, sipping a fountain drink from Pollo Tropical. He nodded a "whassup" at Raphael as he walked by. I wondered how much Raphael spent greasing Club Phoenixx and how many other clubs he had in his palm. Chela had told me that Hector was friendly with Maria, and probably the other girls, but I made a mental note to interview him later.

"Gimme fifteen," Joan told Hector, and we followed her down the hall with a laptop under her arm. She led us to a semi-furnished break room with a vending machine and microwave. She set up her laptop on the table, avoiding the food stains. Phoenixx's glamorous exterior hadn't penetrated the bouncers' break room.

"When am I looking for?" Joan said.

"Friday. Eleven o'clock," Raphael said efficiently. He remembered the exact time he'd last seen Maria. A businessman's mind at work, or maybe he had reason to remember.

"Our video's digitized," she said. "Where am I looking?"

"The VIP room?" I said.

"Rear bar," Raphael corrected. He knew better than I did. "North end. Near Xavier."

"Ho Central," Joan said. In other words, the usual spot.

Four screens emerged on Joan's laptop screen, and she focused on one, racing through time stamps. Raphael saw the women before I did, pointing his left index finger. "There," he said.

Joan enlarged the image to full screen. I followed Raphael's finger to the right side, where two or three women were gathered in a corner well lighted from the bar. Two more arrived—Maria and Chela. The images were slightly grainy in infrared black and white, but I knew Chela's hair. Her arrival in the circle looked like a homecoming.

My little girl was stunning. No wonder Raphael remembered exactly when he'd seen her.

But I pointed out Maria. "The one in the sparkles," I said. "That's her. I want to see everything she did."

"You're kidding, right?" Joan said.

On the video monitor, Raphael approached Chela and Maria. "Stop it there," I said. "Go slow."

I forced myself to let my emotions go dead as I watched Raphael propositioning Chela. I looked for signs that he was using intimidation on the girls, noting how they behaved in his presence. As soon as he'd shown up, all of the girls started smiling and posing, hoping to be noticed. But he had eyes only for Chela.

On the screen, Raphael pointed Chela's attention down the bar.

"Show me where he's looking," I said, hoping to find Mr. Big Nose. From Chela's description, he'd been sitting at the same bar but farther down.

"Thought you wanted to watch Maria," Joan said. I was surprised she knew Maria by name, but I tried not to show it.

"I do. But there's a guy she might have gone off with."

"Try the second register," Raphael said.

"There's some obstruction in that angle, but we'll try," Joan said.

I leaned in closer to the image Joan produced. Club Phoenixx was packed, and so was the bar. I'd hoped his face would stick out, but so far . . . nothing.

"Where was he?" I asked Raphael.

With a sigh, Raphael leaned closer to the screen. "There, I think. At the bar."

As soon as Raphael pointed him out, the man was obvious: wide build, wild hair, sunglasses. I couldn't see the monstrous nose Chela had talked about, but close enough. His back and profile faced the camera. While everyone around him was in motion, he stood stock still, staring toward the women. Staring toward Chela. He barely seemed to breathe.

"Closer on him," I said, pointing. "And slow."

Joan froze the footage and zoomed closer to the man, trying to bring his face into focus. The image blurred and sharpened as she worked the controller. "You're not paying me enough for this, Raffi," Joan murmured.

Frozen on his profile, I could see that his nose was bulbous, perhaps misshapen. Mr. Big Nose, indeed. Something about his profile jumped out at me.

"I want a copy of that image," I said. "That guy."

"Thought you were looking for your stepdaughter," Joan said, trusting me less and less.

"I am. Let's go back to the bar."

Chela chatted with the women for a while, but soon after her contact with Raphael, she looked nervous and eager to leave. What had he said to her? Chela and Maria seemed to argue, and Chela abruptly walked away. Maria followed.

"Can we keep them in view?" I said. "Maria and her friend?"

"Not the whole time, but if I know where they're going, I can try to follow them."

"The nearest exit," I said, guessing. "Her friend wanted to go."

Joan worked the footage like an air traffic controller. A camera caught Maria and Chela hugging right before Chela exited. Had Chela wiped away tears? Rage tightened in my chest; I wanted to knee Raphael in the groin again. I was glad when Chela vanished, safe at home.

For the next hour, Joan searched footage to track Maria's movements. Raphael helped her pinpoint the instant when Maria had come to him to ask for a meeting with Mr. Big Nose, and her disappointment in his answer was obvious despite her frozen smile.

Maria spent a bit more time with the women in the corner, but they dispersed when Raphael left. They had hoped to impress him, and their show was over when he was gone. He didn't seem like a strong-arm pimp, but it could be hard to tell.

Mr. Big Nose sat like a statue at the bar. He listened without moving when Raphael came and whispered to him and sat frozen for two long minutes after that until he stood up to walk away.

"Where's he headed?" I said.

"The VIP room," Joan said. "Same place I bet Maria's going."

The camera angles were much tighter in the VIP room, since there were fewer people to track. Mr. Big Nose's face was clear, and something about him was suddenly familiar. Had I seen him before?

"I want that image, too," I said.

The encounter came within twenty minutes of Chela's departure. Maria approached Mr. Big Nose in the VIP room at 11:33, girly and flirtatious, her shiny purse clutched under her arm. I glanced at Raphael: *Did you see this?* He only shrugged and shook his head.

This encounter might have gotten Maria killed, but I couldn't pinpoint why. Mr. Big Nose's familiarity gnawed at me. I might know him, but he felt all wrong.

A disguise, I realized.

On the video, Maria's smile lit up the room. Most of the men were staring at the way her dress clung to her ass, but her smile was her most memorable feature.

"Your daughter's pretty," Joan said. "Your stepdaughter, I mean."

At first, Mr. Big Nose seemed to dodge her, retreating to a plush chair with his drink. But Maria came at him again, and this time she ended up sitting on his armrest, crossing her legs at indelicate angles.

They exchanged a few words, and Mr. Big Nose's hand landed on Maria's thigh.

I couldn't see everything that happened between them because of obstructions when people entered or left the room, but at some point, Mr. Big Nose gave Maria a drink.

"Maybe I was wrong," Raphael said. "He likes her."

But in some ways, that didn't seem true. Big Nose's expression was sour, never cracking a smile. He seemed only to tolerate her, but he kept her close. Sometimes his lips curled when he looked at her. *She sickens him,* I thought. But why buy her a drink?

Maria and Big Nose were in the VIP room together for thirty-eight minutes. I only saw Maria take one drink, but she giggled over her wobbly legs when she tried to stand. Offering her an arm to lean on, Big Nose smiled for the first time.

"Does Maria get drunk?" I asked Raphael.

"This is an act. She likes champagne, but I have never seen her drunk."

If it was an act, it was a good one. Maria looked sluggish and confused as Mr. Big Nose led her toward the exit. But no one nearby noticed her face, only her dress.

He drugged her, I thought. I hadn't seen him touch her drink, but I felt certain. The confident Maria who had entered the room was nothing like the Maria who was leaving. She wasn't carrying her purse. She had left it behind.

"That one," I told Joan. "The two of them. Print me that one, too. With the time stamp."

"Hope that helps, cuz I'm done," Joan said.

I couldn't persuade Joan to try to find the footage of Maria leaving the club, but I thought I might have enough to go on. The only men I'd seen Maria talk to at Club Phoenixx were Raphael and Mr. Big Nose. I might be heading somewhere.

"We are finished," Raphael told me.

It was time to let him go. I was sick of the sight of him.

"For now," I said.

He held out his palm. "My phone."

I only stared at him.

"Hope you find out what happened to your daughter," Joan said.

"Me, too," Raphael said, returning my pointed stare. "Your daughter is one of the most promising call girls I have ever known. So seasoned and so young. I could make her rich."

Joan looked up suddenly, wondering what was about to play out between us, but Raphael had chosen that moment because we weren't alone. He didn't think I would hurt him in front of Joan, and he was right.

"Easy, boys," Joan said.

"I'll see you later, Raffi," I said. "Bet on it."

Raffi's lower jaw trembled as he brought his bandaged hand to his bruised face. "You are her father? Shame on you. I did not create her."

"Perhaps you're right, Raffi," I said. "Perhaps neither of us should be too quick to point fingers."

A swift flash of fear and pain and masked rage. Raphael opened the door and walked away. I was glad he was limping.

"He's not so bad, as asswads go," Joan said in his defense.

"Whatever you say."

"I hope you're not a problem for me," Joan said.

"I'm not a problem. I'm looking for my kid. I think she might be dead."

"Yeah, I didn't want to say anything, but . . ." She'd heard the rumor about Maria.

Without condolences, Joan handed me the photocopies from Maria's last night alive.

Just another lost girl.

SIXTEEN

APRIL, NOT CHELA, sent me a late-night text from L.A. to let me know the package had arrived safely. I held off on calling as soon as I woke up because of the three-hour time lag, but it was good to begin the day with a celebration.

Before I left for work, I laid out my case for Dad. With thirty years of LAPD experience, he would call me on my bullshit, and he always had good ideas. I wanted to make sure he thought I was following the right angles. Dad was grumpy because he was in his wheelchair, but he'd conceded that the chair was the easiest way for him to get around. I didn't like anything about pushing Dad in a wheelchair, but we put up with it.

Marcela dragged us to a popular South Beach breakfast restaurant, Lil Pink's, so Dad and I could barely hear each other over the noise. Lil Pink's was a huge diner-style restaurant, packed with families, tourists, and half the city's police force. I was paranoid we might be overheard, but the cops were there to eat.

"Going after the pimp?" Dad said. "That wasn't smart. Taking that gun, neither."

"Yessir," I said. "I won't be so reckless from now on."

"Forget him now. He'll be ready next time. Don't know what you were thinking. "

I wasn't thinking—I wanted to kick his ass. I hadn't hinted that Chela might have slept with Raphael, but I'd told Dad that Chela had learned about him through her investigation at the club. He was still annoyed that I'd rushed Chela to the airport without a proper good-bye.

"Why won't you talk to us about Chela?" Marcela said. She was my stepmother now, and sounded like it. "Everything's a secret. Maybe we can help."

I shook my head. "I gave her my word."

"But whatever happened was so bad that you sent her home in the middle of the night?" Marcela prodded.

Dad only sighed. As a police captain who had worked in Hollywood Division, he understood what Chela's life on the streets had been without me saying a word. "Leave it, Marcy," he said. "I'll talk to Chela when we go home."

Marcela clicked her teeth and signaled for a waiter. The waiters dressed like auto repairmen, part of the restaurant's shtick. "I'd like to know what's going on for a change."

Family politics were slowing us down, but I tried to be patient. Finally, Dad turned his attention back to the photocopied pictures I had from Club Phoenixx. He spent a long time staring at the photo of Maria and Mr. Big Nose.

"That's a disguise," Dad said. "Not his real hair. Sunglasses. He's hiding."

"I thought so, too."

While Marcela told the waitress our order, Dad and I slipped into a bubble where his wheelchair disappeared. Even after a stroke, there was nothing wrong with Dad's mind. He had forgetful moments, but I did, too. He was a smart cop.

"Got enough for South Beach Homicide now," Dad said.

Dad knew I had made a mistake by not going to the FBI in my previous case. Chela had wanted to bring in the police all along; instead, I'd made her feel obligated to go to Raphael. Even if Maria's killer confessed to me personally, the ending wasn't happy already.

"I hate calling cold," I said. "And I left handprints on that pimp."

"Think he's gonna press charges?" Dad said. "Just say what you know. In and out. I'll try to dig up somebody."

"I don't want Chela dragged into this," I said. "It might become public."

"Might not," Dad said. "Worth the chance, with what you have."

While the waitress set down our huge round waffles, I studied the picture of Mr. Big Nose sitting by himself in the VIP room, his clearest image. My eye went to his ear lobe, and my heart jogged. Mr. Big Nose had a prominently attached lobe.

Just like Gustavo Escobar.

I stared at the face again. Same complexion, potentially, but his nose was nothing like Escobar's. "Unless it's fake, too," I said, thinking aloud.

"What?" Dad said.

"Does that nose look fake to you? Another part of the disguise?"

Dad studied it and nodded. "Could be. Professional job, though."

I itched to call Chela to ask what she thought. She'd said that Raphael worked with cast and crew from *Freaknik*. But most of the crew members couldn't afford Raphael's prices, and the man's build didn't match any of the actors. I glanced from the attached lobe to the man's arms to his slight midsection paunch.

If I ignored the face, it could be Gustavo Escobar sitting at that bar stool. Was he really a suspect, or did I want him to be a suspect?

"Whatchu thinking?" Dad said.

"This guy could be the director of my film," I said. "If I take away the disguise."

"You think he was with Maria?" Dad said, to clarify. "Can you prove it?"

Even if the police watched the video footage, we both knew they weren't likely to question Escobar over such a flimsy resemblance, and Raphael might not tell the police about Mr. Big Nose at all. After last night, Raphael might have taken the first flight back to Italy.

"All I can do is try," I said.

Dad patted my hand with an approving smile I would have given anything to see from him as a kid, even if I couldn't have admitted it. "Tennyson," he said. "What did you do to that man?"

"Raphael?"

He nodded.

"Not much," I said. "Just gave him the finger."

Elliot stared at the photos, his face blank. "Too much of his face is covered," he said. "Nice prosthetic nose, though."

"You can tell the nose is fake?"

"Look at the size of that thing. I'm betting the mustache is fake, too. That's how he's masking the nose. A little crude, but not obvious. I give up. Am I supposed to know this guy?"

I hesitated. I didn't want to lead Elliot.

"Someone you've worked with," I said.

He flipped through the photos, staring without recognition. Then he leaned over to see more clearly, tracing the man's earlobe. "Wait a minute," he said, and grinned.

"You know him?"

"Where'd you take this? Are you spying on him? This is creepy, Tin Man."

"Who is it?"

Elliot gave me a skeptical look. "You're shitting me, right? It's Esocbar."

"You can tell under all that makeup?"

"Look at the ear. Most people don't think to cover that. Don't realize how distinctive it is. There are some things you can't hide without a plastic surgeon. What, are you following him around?"

Elliot was right; the longer I looked at the photo of Escobar in the VIP lounge, the more obvious his features. If I squinted and ignored his nose, I was staring at my director. But would anyone else see it besides a makeup artist and me?

I glanced at Elliot. "Would Escobar need help making that nose?"

"Like me, you mean?" Elliot said. "I would've done a better job, but anyone who knows a thing or two could put it together."

"What about Escobar? Could he do it himself?"

Elliot looked at me as if I were blind. "Ten, come on. Escobar's knee-deep in makeup and effects. *Fidel* wasn't an accident. Makeup nearly got him that Oscar. That's all anyone remembers. I'm lucky he doesn't have the time, or what would he need me for?"

Elliot's intel on Escobar was useful, but the worship in his voice worried me. When Escobar wasn't partying, he was being feted at dinners and book signings. *Nuestro Tío Fidel* had been a major event in Miami. And I was about to visit South Beach Police to name Escobar as a potential murder suspect? I didn't have a photograph of Escobar with Maria—I had a photo of a phantom. The most Elliot could say was that it *might* be him.

So far, Maria's death was still classified as a drowning, and no homicide department wanted to open a potentially difficult case, especially with political overtones. The police would need convincing just to open a murder investigation, never mind sniffing around Escobar. Dad was right when he said I was always looking for reasons not to trust the police, but I had good reasons.

"Nice life, huh?" Elliot said, gazing at the photos from the club. "Are you stalking him?"

I could confide in Elliot and try to enlist his help, or I could keep quiet. For the sake of my case, and maybe Elliot's sake, too, I chose the latter. "Just a bet with a friend," I said.

In between reciting lines, I had a few hours to try to build a case against Escobar that would at least make him sound plausible.

The police would have to catch up to me.

I cut my makeup session short to find a corner to work my cell phone while Escobar huddled with his lighting guys. The mansion's high ceilings were a lighting nightmare. Escobar told us not to wander far, always certain we would be rolling at any moment, but after fifteen minutes, I realized I might have an hour on my phone. Signs condemning cell phones were posted everywhere on the set, but I kept mine on vibrate and my conversations quiet.

I'd tried calling Victoria, the high-end escort Raphael had told me about, but she'd never answered her phone the night before. I wanted to find out about the time she'd spent with Mr. Big Nose, a.k.a. Juan. She might not talk to the police at all. I tried her number again.

"Who's this?" a woman's voice said.

"Raffi gave me your number," I said.

I apologized for bothering her and stuck with my story that I was looking for my daughter. I had no idea if Raphael had mentioned me to Victoria or what he had told her to say.

In the long silence, I wondered if she'd hung up on me. Finally, she sighed as if I were an annoying pollster. "Raffi told me I shouldn't talk to you. But you're not a cop, so go on."

Victoria told me she had "dated" Juan twice, and both times she had been to "his boat." She said he liked to sit and watch her touch herself, a sanitized story. A good lawyer could say she hadn't described an illegal act. In her place, I wouldn't have trusted me, either.

I glanced around to make sure I was out of anyone's hearing range, especially Escobar. I was in the archway leading to the patio, out of Escobar's earshot.

"Where's this boat? What does it look like?"

"It's not a yacht or anything, but it has a cabin."

"Cabin cruiser? How big?"

"Not too big. Maybe thirty feet. Nice, but it got cramped."

"Does his boat have a name?"

"Yeah." A pause while she thought about it. "*Rosa.*"

"That's it?" Boat owners didn't usually name their boats the way they would name a pet. The names were usually more elaborate. "That's not part of a longer name?"

"R-O-S-A, painted next to a picture of a red rose. I can spell."

The boat might be a rental, but I finally had a clue. "Where's it docked?"

"Once I boarded at Bayside, another time at Miami Beach Marina."

Details were precious, so I wrote them all. Escobar might rent slips all over town, a different dock each night. Neither marina she had mentioned was likely to let him live aboard, but I would check.

"He ever mention where he lives?" I asked her.

"No, but he's working, so maybe a hotel." She might know more, but she wouldn't say.

"What kind of work does he do?" A quick flick of my eyes again, and I saw Escobar staring up at a footlight's stream, preoccupied. "Is he in the film business?"

"I don't know. He's not the chatty type," Victoria said. I wondered if she was protecting him or if she really didn't know.

"Could he be wearing a disguise?" I said.

"Definitely a wig. I can tell. He never takes it off."

"Does he have an accent?"

"Maybe a little. Everyone in Miami has an accent. He might be Spanish." Spanish, to Victoria, probably meant Cuban or Nicaraguan or Puerto Rican or Panamanian. I didn't waste time pressing, since she wasn't likely to know his ethnicity. Escobar might still be my man.

I took a chance. "Have you ever heard of Gustavo Escobar?" My voice was so low I had to repeat his name twice. He was thirty feet from me, but I had nowhere else to go except the archway. Bored crewmen were smoking on the patio behind me.

Victoria said she hadn't heard of Escobar. Over the phone, I guided her to photos of him on Google Images on her iPad, but she didn't recognize his name or face. Obviously, she would have been more likely to see through the disguise if she'd met him beforehand. But then again, my Escobar theory might be wishful thinking.

"Did the guy ever hurt you in any way? Anything rough?"

"He's on an ego trip, so he's got a mean mouth. But he barely touches me."

"Has he ever drugged your drink?"

A pause. "How does this help you find your daughter, exactly?"

"Miss, I'm sorry, but she might have been with the same man. I'm trying to eliminate him as a suspect." I cringed at my wording; I sounded like a cop, not a father.

"I've never had blackouts with him, if that's what you mean. He's a business associate."

"No dizziness, then?" I said, remembering Maria from the surveillance tape.

Victoria sighed hotly. "You're way off base with this one. I have to get ready for class. Tell Raphael to go to hell for giving you my name and number. Good luck making your case." She hung up.

Damn. I'd pushed her Cop button, and I was back where I'd started. I didn't have evidence to make Escobar a real suspect to anyone but me, and I couldn't eliminate him, either. But at least I could start looking for his boat.

Gustavo suddenly snapped a finger at me, as if he'd heard my thoughts.

"Is that your daughter, Chela? Tell her hello for me," Escobar said.

He gave me a long gaze, and I doubt he missed how much he'd startled me. "I'm ready for you, *mijo*. Put the phone away." Escobar winked at me and flashed me a dolphin's smile before he walked off.

I felt sick when I remembered that I'd introduced Chela to Escobar on the set the same day she later went out with Maria. His careful eyes probably had spotted Chela at Club Phoenixx; maybe he'd chosen Chela *because* he recognized her.

If he was a killer, I had let a sociopath into my life. Close to my family.

Maybe he'd wanted to drown Chela, not Maria. Maybe he'd only settled on Maria when Chela backed away. How many others had he killed? For how long? Like any good director, Escobar might have had our story mapped out long before I arrived in Miami.

Why had Escobar chosen me to be in his movie? What did he want?

During that day's shoot, I could barely remember my lines.

SEVENTEEN

THE SOUTH BEACH Police station is dressed up in lights, blending into the art deco district like an attraction. It's one of the loveliest stations in the country, but nothing makes up for having to visit the police on a sunny day.

One of Dad's connections had led me to an appointment with Detective Lydia Hernandez, who hardly looked a day over twenty-five. I wondered how she'd had time to make detective, much less in homicide. In all likelihood, her boss had asked her to talk to me; most of the cops in LAPD who knew Dad held high positions.

She was tall, with wavy dark hair wrapped in a long ponytail. Miami's women are also among the finest in the country, and Lydia Hernandez could have let good looks carry her anywhere. I knew in a glance at her peach-colored tailored pants suit that she was a climber who wouldn't appreciate flirting. She dressed more like FBI than local police. The handcuffs on her belt reminded me to be cautious.

"So you're reporting a homicide?" Hernandez said once we were in an interview room. She flipped a tiny metal paper clip between her fingers.

"Your Jane Doe drowning victim is a prostitute who was working South Beach. Her name is Maria Dominguez. She's part of a suspicious pattern. I'm a private detective, and I've been asked to share my investigation." I'd given her the basics on the phone, but I summarized again.

"Tennyson Hardwick," she said. "I know who you are." To her credit, her tone was neutral. For whatever reason, she'd decided to hear me out—or pretend to.

I handed her my evidence packet, which included Maria's driver's license, Raphael's cell phone (I'd copied all of the incoming and collected numbers for my own use), and duplicates of my security photos.

Detective Hernandez registered surprise at the driver's license. She opened a file on her desk and compared it with the artist's sketch. "We got intel it might be her," she said. "Prints match, so we'll make her ID public today. You got this license how?"

She was taking notes, suddenly very interested in my opinions. I told her about Julio's fake ID enterprise below Fifth Street and the prostitution ring at Club Phoenixx.

"Excuse me," Detective Hernandez said primly. She stood up with my evidence and slipped the bag into her folder. "I'll be right back."

I wondered if she was having a rookie moment, unsure of how to proceed. Or maybe she was trying to sweat me to shake up my story. It could have been a little of both.

Fifteen minutes later, she came back with a silver-haired male detective whose name tag identified him as R. MCCLARY. His face was leathery from sun; I guessed he was in his early fifties. A third detective stood in the doorway, a brother in his thirties with bulky arms and a sour face. I'd wanted the police to take me seriously.

Be careful what you wish for.

"Go on," Detective Hernandez said. "You were saying?"

Hernandez and the brother took notes while I described Chela's encounter with Julio. I only called Chela "a witness" and didn't tell them she was my daughter; I would save that information for when it was absolutely necessary. I described Raphael's relationship with the girls and the nightclub's nonintervention policy.

"Sounds like SIU," Detective McClary told her, not sounding impressed. SIU was short for Strategic Investigations Unit, which included prostitution and drugs.

"What makes you think this was a homicide?" Hernandez asked me.

"Third suspicious drowning of a prostitute in three weeks?" I said. I looked at their faces, and they seemed surprised but engaged. "One in Miami, two on the beach. The girls are doing a 'buddy' system. Plus, our girl doesn't swim. Hated the water. She's last seen looking woozy leaving the club on this guy's arm. She was so out of it she left her purse and cell behind."

They passed the photocopy around.

"Another serial killer," the black detective said sarcastically, shaking his head.

"Who's this again?" McClary asked Hernandez, as if I weren't there.

"He's a PI," Hernandez said. "Hardwick. The Sofia Maitlin guy."

The black detective laughed. "Oh, shit! You're right. He is that guy."

"T. D. Jackson didn't look like a homicide, either—at first," I said, reminding them that I was still in the room. Before my reputation took its dive with Sofia Maitlin, I'd gained recognition for solving the murder of T.D. Jackson.

"A broken clock is right twice a day," Detective McClary said.

Same song, different city. I nearly graduated from the police academy, but cops and I have never gotten along.

I soldiered on with my story, summarizing my conversation with Victoria. I invited them to call her, as well as the woman Chela called Mouse Girl. I described the boat named *Rosa* and where it had been docked.

"The man in that photo is wearing a disguise, but I have a possible name," I said. "Gustavo Escobar."

Hernandez dropped her hand away from her pad in mid-sentence. "Gus?" she said. I didn't like the sound of *Gus*. She almost said more but stopped herself.

"Who?" McClary said.

"Gus Escobar," the black cop said. "You know, the Cuban film director."

"Why would I know that?" McClary said.

Hernandez ignored her colleague, staring heavily at me. "Do you have evidence against Gustavo Escobar?" Her voice had been placid, but now a razor was primed to slash at me.

"He's good with makeup," I said. "I believe he has a connection to Raphael. He frequents that nightclub. If you notice his earlobe—"

The brother gave Hernandez a look: *Are you kidding with this?*

Hernandez looked embarrassed. "Fine," she said, cutting me off. "Thank you for bringing this to us, Mr. Hardwick. Leave your cell number, please."

"Yeah, thanks for stopping by from Hollywood to visit us little people," McClary said.

I wanted to say a few things to McClary, but Hernandez steered me toward the elevator, giving me her business card. "There might be something here," she said. "But leave the police work to us. If you try to publicly link Gustavo Escobar to this drowning, you'll be opening yourself to legal retaliation like you've never seen."

"Excuse me?" I said. She was so polite I almost missed her threat.

"We don't like circus acts," she said. "You've got a dead hooker who might be a homicide, fine. I'll look into it—I promise. But I also promise that if you turn this into a circus with your Hollywood bullshit, you'll be sorry you came to us."

I was already sorry. So much for Hernandez being the Good Cop.

We had reached the elevator. "You called him Gus. You know him?"

"Sure, I know him like most people in Miami do—from the newspaper," she said. "I read the *Miami Herald*. He made *Nuestro Tío Fidel*, which my parents saw three times. He just gave a million dollars to Miami's performing arts school. The mayor of Miami hosted a private party for him last week. My lieutenant tells us, 'Remember, Gus is shooting on the beach today.' That's how I know him. If we find evidence he's a serial, I'll be the first to lock him up. But without evidence, you came to the wrong town to take his name in vain."

The elevator *dinged*, signaling the end of our conversation.

"You can't find evidence you're not looking for, Detective," I said.

"You've got nothing on Escobar," she said, making an O with her fingers. "*Nada*. If you've got any kind of real chops, you know I'm right. I can spend my time finding out what happened to Maria, or I can fuck you over all day and night. Your pick."

Call me old-fashioned, but profanity sounds wrong from the mouth of a pretty woman.

"I get it. No waves, right?"

"No press conferences, no circus—no jail. *Comprende?* Goodbye, Mr. Hardwick." Her ponytail lashed from side to side as she walked away.

I had never been shut out with such efficient grace.

And people wonder why I never want to go to the police.

When I didn't have any luck sniffing around Miami Beach Marina for Escobar's boat, escorted away by security, I decided to go back to the set. That was the one place I knew I wouldn't run into any cops.

My scene was over, but Escobar was scheduled to work until nightfall, and I wanted to try to learn by observing him. Maybe I could goad him into revealing something the police could use. I hoped he was arrogant enough to make a mistake.

Once I'd found my corner near the set, I checked out the newspaper archives on my phone, squinting at the small type as I scrolled. Gustavo Escobar was one of Miami's favorite sons. The love affair had begun two years before, when he shot some scenes from *Fidel* in Miami and drummed up support from local fundraisers. He'd visited frequently, appearing on local television and at the party scene throughout the film's release and Oscar campaign. And he had made contributions in the tens of thousands of dollars to various Cubano charities. One of the newspaper stories mentioned that he and his sister had fled the homeland on a raft in the early 1960s. His father, the story said, had been a political prisoner in one of Castro's jails, executed while his family watched.

The more I read, the more I understood Detective Hernandez. The police weren't in a position to casually question Gustavo Escobar about a prostitute's murder. I would have kicked my ass out, too. Worse, I had just crippled my own case, since the information flow would cease once the police started digging around Raphael and Club Phoenixx. I'd probably burned my sources before I went to the police, but now they were trashed for good.

Maybe the police would lift fingerprints from the driver's license. Their first suspect might be Julio, the fake-ID guy. I'd been so caught up with the Club Phoenixx angle that I hadn't tried to talk to him.

My earlier paranoia about Escobar seemed silly once I was back on the set, standing in the wings with the interns while we observed a master at work. On the surface, he was shooting a massive orgy scene, but as more cast members took their places under Escobar's careful hand, I noticed that their makeup and costumes were smaller pieces of a whole—an undulating design that would stretch from one end of the set to the other. Elliot looked exhausted but happy as he directed his three-person team to apply finishing touches. He and Escobar worked well together.

Gustavo Escobar was an artist, whether or not I wanted to admit it. Escobar was way beyond slasher territory with *Freaknik*. He was using sex and zombies as metaphors for isolation, collapse, chaos. And he would somehow weave it all together into the message of hope by the end, with his male and female leads sharing an untainted kiss.

My phone vibrated, and I ducked into the empty hall when I saw it was Chela calling. I hadn't talked to her all day.

"How's the case going?" she asked me. Not even a hello.

"I just left the police station. I broke it all down for them, so we'll see."

"And that's it?"

"You said you wished you'd gone to the police," I said. "Now you have."

"Sure, that's fine for backup. But you're the one who'll find her killer, Ten."

Chela's trust had boosted me up before, but trust could be tiresome. "I'm on it."

"Did you get any new leads?"

"Maybe." I glanced around to be sure no one could overhear me. "This guy you call Mr. Big Nose—had you ever seen him before? Think carefully. He probably was wearing a disguise at the club."

"Like a wig?"

"For instance."

"I wasn't that close to him, thank God. And he had sunglasses, too."

"Could it have been my director? Escobar?" Long silence. "Hello?"

"You think your director's a psycho? April says he's a big deal. And his nose is nothing like that guy's."

If Chela couldn't identify Escobar as Mr. Big Nose, I had even less to go on. "What if it's fake? Look, I'm going to send you a scanned photo later from a security camera at the club. Just take a look and see if it helps jog your memory."

"You're no slacker," Chela said, impressed.

"I made you a promise, didn't I?"

I didn't tell Chela that I thought Escobar might have recognized her. That was the last thing she needed to hear, even from nearly three thousand miles away.

"I'm keeping up my end, too," Chela said, her voice dropping into a sigh. "But Ten, she's trying to give me an eleven o'clock *curfew*. You need to talk to her."

Good for April. April had improvised the curfew without direction from me. Her house, her rules. "Just don't hurt her," I said, chuckling. "She means well."

"I'm not playing, Ten. She's acting like she thinks she's my mother."

Chela never made references to her mother lightly, and her words caught me so off guard that I forgot any snappy answers. If I'd proposed to April in Cape Town instead of backing away, April would have been Chela's stepmother by now, sort of. And Chela's damage from her birth mother's neglect was still multiplying, even years later. Chela needed a mother, and I needed April. Why had it seemed so complicated?

"I'll make sure everything works out fine, Chela," I said.

I wish I had known the magnitude of my lie.

"Tennyson!"

Escobar caught me at seven o'clock, just when I was ready to slip out to go home. How long had he known I was there? I hoped he wasn't about to try to enlist me in his orgy scene. I surveyed his masterpiece of makeup: a collection of two dozen nude extras with perfect painted bodies and misshapen faces lay arrayed on dark-colored pillows.

I turned warily, and he gestured for me to come to his high director's chair. Elliot, who was nearby, looked surprised to see me hanging around the set so late.

"I'm off the clock," I said to Elliot, but the message was meant for Escobar.

"You've been spying on me," Escobar said.

I glanced at Elliot, wondering if he'd told Escobar about the surveillance photos. I'd been foolish not to ask him to keep it to himself. Elliot shook his head: *Nope, not me.*

"What do you mean?" I asked Escobar.

"What do you think?" Escobar leaned closer to me so I couldn't miss his earnest expression. His chair was so tall that we were at eye level. "This moment. This is the crossroads, Tennyson. All is lost, or all is won. The killing is stopped, or it goes on unchecked. The forces of good marshal against the forces of evil. One is vanquished."

Elliot might have heard his director talking about his movie. Not me. My heart took a leap, turning cold. Escobar was toying with me.

"I already know how this story ends," I said.

Escobar's eyes flashed. "Do you?"

"It looks great, Gus," Elliot said. "It could be a painting by that Spanish artist who went crazy—Goya."

Escobar and I both ignored Elliot, intensifying our staring match. Finally, Escobar said, "Yes, Francisco Goya. His so-called black paintings, from his time of illness. He painted them directly on his own walls, so they always surrounded him. Do you think true art can only be inspired by madness?"

"You tell me," I said.

Escobar laughed, patting my shoulder. "This is what I like

about you, Tennyson. It's why I chose you. You're a truth seeker. A truth speaker."

Elliot, puzzled by our exchange, stepped away to give us privacy. Louise Cannon appeared in his place, flustered as always. "Gus, can we all maybe get some sleep tonight?"

Escobar stared on at me, not blinking. "I won't be sleeping tonight, *mijo*," he whispered. "I'll be dreaming. But you already know this, don't you, Tennyson?"

Gooseflesh crawled across my arms. It took all of my willpower not to shove him away.

EIGHTEEN

I SAT IN my car in the parking lot with the engine off, and I couldn't force myself to go home. Escobar had all but announced to me that he would be hunting that night, and if the police weren't going to tail him, I would. I needed to interrupt his plans. I didn't want to hear about another dead woman on the news.

I needed computer-savvy backup, which meant I couldn't rely on Dad, either. I dialed April's number and hoped she was in a good mood.

She wasn't. April had a litany of complaints about Chela, although everything she described sounded mild to me. Chela was apparently on her best behavior.

"Does she know how to pick up her clothes?" April said. "She dropped her jeans in the middle of the hallway! And when she took the milk carton out of the fridge this morning, she left it sitting on the counter. Do you play Jiffy-Maid at home, Ten?"

"I'll talk to her," I promised, although my thoughts were far away.

"Okay, well, I can see you didn't call for an update on Chela," April said. "What's up?"

"I'm working a case," I said, and bit by bit, I told her the real reason I had sent Chela to live with her, including my suspicions about

Escobar. I held back on some of the details about Chela's night with Raphael, but April probably knew. I braced for a lecture, but none came.

"Ten, that's awful," she said. "But I know you're only telling me this because you want something, so what is it?" The distance in her voice was like a slap.

I missed the version of April who would have reminded how much my investigations had already cost me. But she didn't have to. We both knew.

"Are you near your computer?" I said.

"Yeah, I'm at work. Trying to get out of here early."

I pretended to miss her hint. "See if you can tie Gustavo Escobar to a boat called *Rosa* that's docked somewhere down here. If it's his boat, maybe he's mentioned it or been photographed with it. I think he takes women to that boat before he drowns them."

"Based on what?"

I sighed. "Just a hunch, April. I told you, my case has nothing to stand on."

"If you find his boat, then what?"

"I don't know," I said. "I'm trying to pull together enough evidence for the cops."

That might have been partially true but not entirely. We both knew that, too.

"I'm only going to say one thing," April said. "I know you made Chela a promise, but it sounds like you're trying to sabotage your movie role. Just when things start moving ahead for you, all of a sudden your director is the bogeyman. Gustavo Escobar is eccentric, but that doesn't make him a serial killer."

Before my last exchange with Escobar, I might have agreed with her. "When it comes to my cases, when have my instincts ever been that wrong?"

April couldn't argue. Never.

"I hope this isn't the first time," April said finally. "I'll call you back. But under one condition. Don't shut me out. If I'm helping you, I know what you know. And if there's something to it, you won't talk to any reporters before you talk to me."

The *L.A. Times* may have laid her off, but April's reporter spirit was alive and well.

"Deal," I said. "Tell me anything you find, no matter how small."

"I'm on it," April said, and hung up.

For a short time, at least, April and I were a team again. It almost felt good.

April took twenty minutes to call me back. Escobar hadn't come out to his car yet, and neither of the security guards in the lot had noticed me sitting in my car waiting.

"I can't see a name on this boat, but I might have something," April said.

She had found a *Miami* magazine story online about Gustavo Escobar with a photograph of him at a dockside party after the release of his film. The only boat in view was white with a cherry-red stripe, a vessel small enough to match Victoria's description. The photo had been taken at the Fontainebleau marina a year earlier.

The Fontainebleau was one of Miami Beach's best-known hotels, on Collins Avenue and 44th Street. I had stayed there many times. It was an iconic hotel with a history, featured in *Goldfinger*, and had hosted Frank Sinatra, Jerry Lewis, Elvis Presley, and countless other celebrities over the years.

That seemed like a good fit for him.

"Okay, thanks."

"Hey, not so fast," she said. "What are you going to do with this information?"

"Think I'll do a little fishing. And find a way to keep him busy tonight."

Since April insisted on full disclosure, I worked out my plan with her. Escobar preferred to drive himself to and from the set in his bright white Hummer, which was easy to recognize from a distance. Still on the phone with April, I composed a note to stick beneath his windshield wiper. If he was my killer, the note would get his attention.

YOU AND ROSA ARE IN DEEP WATER. I HAVE ENOUGH EVIDENCE TO DROWN YOU, BUT I WOULD RATHER GET RICH. MEET MR. VANDAMM IN HIS ROOM AT THE FONTAINEBLEAU HOTEL AT 8 A.M., OR I WILL UNMASK YOU.

"He's going to laugh at that," April said.

"Unless he has reason not to."

If Escobar was my killer, the note might shake him up enough to keep him from hunting. He would have to assume he was being watched. And what if he actually came to the hotel? A killer would not politely wait until the assigned meeting time.

"If he doesn't show up, please try another angle," April said, her voice pleading. "I know you've been right before, but this sounds really far-fetched. It could blow up in your face. He tried to give you a break, Ten. If you mess this up . . ."

"I promise," I said. "If he doesn't bite when I go fishing, he's not my guy."

I have a dummy credit card under the name of Phillip Vandamm left over from my past year of secrets. I hadn't used that card since Hong Kong, but I kept it with me as a souvenir. There was a chance that the card had been deactivated, but I bet it still had a bit of juice left. Extra cash would be Marsha's way of inviting me to call her again anytime. I was her gambling addict in need of a fix.

I might accidentally invite my femme fatale back into my life if I put a charge on the card, but it was a chance I was willing to take. I didn't want my name anywhere near the hotel records.

Phillip Vandamm is the bad guy who chases hapless Cary Grant in Alfred Hitchcock's *North by Northwest* in a case of mistaken identity, and if I know Marsha, the name wasn't a coincidence. She could have named the card for Grant's good-guy character, Roger Thornhill, but that wasn't her style. I tried to forget what happens to the villain at the end of the movie.

I sat for a long time to give my plan thought. I didn't want a direct confrontation with Escobar. I only wanted to lure him into my trap so I would have evidence, however flawed, for the police. If I could, I wanted to avoid a face-to-face meeting. I would need time to set up my lair, and I couldn't let Escobar out of my sight.

This would be a two-person job.

The Fontainebleau had plenty of rooms available, so I made my reservation from the car, using the dummy credit card to hold two adjoining rooms. I also left instructions that a key to the first room only, room 1025, should be given to Gustavo Escobar at the front desk if he asked for Mr. Vandamm. He should be sent right up for immediate entry without a call.

My net was ready. Next, to bait the hook.

I scanned the sheet of paper where I'd written the note, searching for identifying characteristics—a stray phone number or information about me. I'd used the blank side of a WaveRunner rental receipt I'd gotten at the beach with Chela a week before. I'd paid cash, so it only mentioned the price, date, and company, South Beach Day Rentals. No names, no credit-card numbers. I would have preferred a blank sheet, but it would do. My note was written in carefully masked block letters on the blank side, the Sharpie's ink bleeding through.

I was parked near the gated exit. Escobar was parked with the other early arrivals near the mansion's garage door, which lay open as a makeshift rally point, equipment storehouse, and break area. The parking area was well lighted, but I was able to stick to the shadows as I made my way from one end of the driveway to the other on foot, walking casually. I had credentials to explain my presence if either of the guards saw me—hell, they knew me—but I didn't want Escobar to suspect I'd been sniffing around his car.

When I got to the Hummer, I slipped the paper firmly in place and hopped down in one smooth motion. The paper flapped a bit in the breeze, but it was secure. He couldn't miss it.

I slipped into the garage to make one more phone call.

He picked up his cell phone on the second ring. I'd finally trained him to keep it on.

"Yeah?" he answered, sounding grumpy because he was already sleepy.

"Hey, Dad," I said. "You busy tonight?"

I judged that the shoot had at least another hour left, so I made a quick run to the hotel.

The Fontainebleau is a spectacle as much as a hotel. When it opened in the mid-1950s, it was the luxury gem of Miami Beach, dreamed up by famed architect Morris Lapidus. Now it's listed on the U.S. Register of Historic Places, and the walls vibrate with stories. The rooms are arranged in a bow-tie shape, mirrored by the huge pool area, where a scene from *Scarface* was filmed.

The lobby was made famous in Jerry Lewis's 1960 movie *The Bell Hop*; the hotel was the real star of that film. I've visited a lot of luxury hotels, but the sheer size of the chandeliers and the expanse of the Fontainebleau's shiny lobby, bow-tie patterns on the floor, evoke an old-school glamour newer hotels can only dream of. Of course, there's a dark side to that history. During segregation, I wouldn't have been permitted to walk through the front door, much less reserve a room. And that was true for entertainers such as Sammy Davis Jr., who could perform at the hotel but couldn't stay there. Mind-boggling.

I was whistling Sammy Davis Jr.'s "Candy Man" when I went to the front desk to check in and claim my key. It was eight thirty when I walked into Mr. Vandamm's tenth-floor room.

The room was smallish, with only a partial ocean view, but I wasn't there to sightsee; at night, the ocean is just a dark hole in the air. A smaller space was better for my purposes, anyway. I surveyed the room and found a good home for the nanny-cam disguised as a clock radio I'd picked up at a cheap spy shop on my way. Spy shops don't rule every corner of Miami like they did in the eighties, at the height of the cocaine trade, but you can find the basics on short notice.

I set up the camera on the desk, angled between the bed and the doorway, and checked to make sure it would capture Escobar once he entered the room. My evidence might not hold up in court, but his presence alone would be incriminating.

I finished a few last touches to prepare the rooms according to the plan I'd mapped out with my father, and everything looked as perfect as a movie set.

"Gotcha, you sick freak," I whispered.

I had no idea how right—and wrong—I was.

I would have loved to see Gustavo Escobar's face when he found my note on his windshield, but I lacked equipment and prep time for that. Instead, I parked half a block down the quiet residential street outside the gate to wait for the end of the shoot.

After an hour of waiting, I was climbing out of my skin. Dad had always come home in a bad mood when he had to spend long hours on surveillance, and I understood why. At least fifteen cars streamed out before Escobar's. I was wondering if he'd decided to ditch the Hummer when it came racing around the corner, turning toward the stop sign with a screech of brakes. I'd kept my infrared binoculars trained on the gate, but he'd left so fast that I'd missed the driver's face. Was it a decoy, or was it Escobar himself?

Cursing to myself, I followed the Hummer.

At the stop sign, I got my positive ID. I could tell that Esocbar was driving the car by the shape of his head, but he wasn't alone. Louise Cannon was sitting beside him, talking in an animated way. Escobar kept his eyes straight ahead. Had he shared the note with her? If so, it wasn't likely he was the killer.

"He's out," I said after I got Dad on the phone. "Heading for the causeway."

"Remember—two or three car lengths," Dad said. "Don't get antsy."

Dad sounded more alert than he had in months. Gleeful, really. He'd given me a lecture on exercising caution, but he loved the chase as much as I did. Maybe more. He knew I'd had surveillance training, but he couldn't help acting like my CO.

"Yessir," I said, just to give him the thrill. "I've got him."

Because there was so little traffic, I stayed far behind him. Star Island is tiny, so Escobar only had to turn twice before he reached the guard gate leading to the MacArthur Causeway. We were all familiar faces by now, so the guard waved us past, Escobar first and then me a safe distance later. On the causeway over Biscayne Bay, I drifted back eight or ten car lengths.

I expected Escobar to keep driving east toward the hotel-laden shoreline, maybe even to the Fontainebleau, but instead, he turned north on Alton Road, away from the tourist district, into a neighborhood of modest homes under canopies of coconut palms and shady ficus trees. Six-foot bougainvillea hedges flamed in hot pink and orange under the streetlamps, both street décor and privacy fencing. The quiet area nudged a memory free: I'd heard that reclusive novelist Thomas Harris had a house somewhere on Miami Beach, a thought that brought unwelcome visions of Hannibal Lecter from *The Silence of the Lambs*.

Escobar stopped in front of a gated home slightly bigger than the others, set back from the street, and I realized it was probably a bed-and-breakfast. Orange solar lamps lit up the coral rock walls and terracotta roof tiles wrapped in tropical plants. Was this where Escobar was living during the shoot? I pulled over to the side of the road and turned off my headlights, watching through my binoculars.

Neither of them climbed out of the Hummer right away. Cannon was still talking to Escobar, and she seemed upset. Finally, he leaned over and kissed her lips. It was a quick kiss, maybe only a friendly good-bye, but my instincts voted otherwise. Finally, Cannon got out of the vehicle, fishing for her gate key in her purse. Escobar idled in the driveway while she let herself into the yard and waved good-bye.

Even once Cannon was gone, Escobar didn't move. He sat in his car, head bent down. He was probably reading my note, I guessed. Had I given him something to think about? I hoped so. Escobar made a sudden movement that looked as if he was pounding his palm against his dashboard, and I thought I could hear him shout a single word even from a block down the street: *"Mierda!"*

Gustavo Escobar was not a happy man.

"That's right, asshole," I murmured. "You are in deep shit."

"What?" Dad's voice said in my ear.

I'd forgotten that I still had my father on my cell phone. The Hummer suddenly lurched away from the curb, racing down the street, turning east. It was nine thirty.

"With any luck, we're about to have company," I said.

NINTEEN

DO YOU THINK you frighten me, *pinga?*" the killer said to the empty air. "Am I too stupid to see through your games?"

The familiar compulsion seized his body, every nerve and sinew itching as the moonlit night called to him, inviting him to dream. But he could not. Not now. The infestation of cheap *grillas* selling their diseases and perfumed lies would have to wait until his business was concluded with Mr. Vandamm.

The killer chuckled to himself. Didn't this fool know that he'd specialized in Hitchcock at Tisch, that he'd memorized every frame of *North by Northwest?* That, in fact, Hitchcock's sequence with the crop duster had deeply influenced his decision to use a prop plane instead of a raft for the escape at the end of *Nuestro Tío Fidel?*

Maybe he did know, but did he know the rest? He couldn't, or he would not dare toy with him.

He couldn't know that Papi had fought at Fidel's side in Santiago de Cuba in 1953, his gun thundering during the assault on Moncada Barracks. While others were only fantasizing about *la revolución*, his father had helped plant the seeds. And Papi had survived Fidel's betrayal and five endless years in his hellhole of a prison cell, hungry and sick, choosing to go naked rather than wear the blue uniform of a common criminal.

His father's courage lived in his name. He would not cower. He would not beg and offer to pay for silence. Like his father, he would fight.

Like his father, he also was not perfect. No man could grow up perfect in an imperfect world. Papi had returned from prison a changed man—quick to strike him and even his sister with a broom handle because he was so full of rage. He had not protected his frail son from neighborhood bullies, boys and girls alike, who beat him black and blue, calling his father a traitor and trash, *escoria*. He had not kept him and his sister away from his perverted *chulo* uncle, whose lessons were never gentle.

And Papi had not stood up to the hit squad that had stormed their house in the middle of the night, thrown him up against the wall, and shot him in the forehead. With only a few words, a few lies, Papi could have saved his own life, but he had been too stubborn to lie about his allegiances, even to spare his family from trauma. Even to spare his children the sight of his brain matter painting the living-room wall.

No, Papi had not been perfect, either in life or in death.

And his son had inherited imperfect traits. Self-indulgence, for one, as his girlfriend forever reminded him. He had been too arrogant and sloppy, and now he had brought himself a problem. He had invited his problem to his doorstep.

But every problem had a solution. Mami had taught him that. Mami's fist in the air as she sank into the ocean's embrace, her brave sacrifice, had taught him everything he needed to know to survive in a new land, a new life. As a new man.

"You think you frighten me?" he said. "You're nothing to me."

The killer's skin tightened across his face and chest, urging him to hunt again. The ocean waited. But he must postpone his duty and do away with the nuisance actor.

Unavoidable destiny had brought them together, not just his own act of hubris in seeking the actor out. After all, the actor's daughter looked just like Rosa—and behaved like Rosa, polluting the night with her empty beauty, a mockery of purity. He had never known that the actor had a daughter until he was introduced on the set.

Wasn't it destiny, then? How could Chela be a coincidence?

But he would not be lured into a simpleton's trap. He would need patience. Luckily, he knew the Fontainebleau and its perimeter well. He could call his boatman, who did as he was told without asking questions. He would need access to the hotel room. He would need a primary plan, a secondary plan, and an emergency plan.

So much to think about, so much to ponder.

But solving puzzles was his life's calling. He was a director, after all.

Escobar secured his own key for Phillip Vandamm's room. He had the good fortune of reaching a young actor on the hospitality staff who had scored him coke during the *Nuestro Tío Fidel* shoot. Good Colombian was hard to find, and the coke's purity was so distracting that Escobar was glad he did not have daily access. Roland mentioned that a key was already set aside in his name for that very room, which was unfortunate for him—if Escobar was able to carry out his plan, his name was already waiting for the police. But since he would never claim the key, he should have a degree of plausible deniability. Roland presented him with a card key that a careless housekeeper might have dropped—and a tiny vial of white powder, for old time's sake.

He would celebrate later. First, work.

As he did when he was directing, Escobar mulled over the actor's motivations. What was his end game? Did he truly expect to blackmail him, as he'd implied? Wouldn't he expect Escobar, a dangerous "predator," to come prepared?

Roland had told him that the man calling himself Vandamm had reserved the room earlier that evening, so his plan might have been a hasty one. If the actor was expecting Escobar to come to his room early in the morning, he might spend the night there. Escobar would have a great advantage if he surprised him. The ideal arrival time would be in the dead of night.

So instead of trolling for the filthy fallen, Escobar drove his Hummer aimlessly through Miami's streets to exhaust anyone who might be tailing him. He toured the glowing high-rises on Brickell, the astonishing murals in the Design District, wooded Old Cutler Road. Hour by hour, he drove, only stopping for gas. When he was bored, he imagined the urgent bubbles rising in the water from Maria's last breath.

But the memory had less and less power to transport and satisfy him. He had grown greedy in Miami. The pressures of the new film had awakened a demanding appetite, a need for more constant hunting. Memories no longer nourished him. He cursed the actor for interrupting his evening's plans. He was glad he did not see the night women strolling the streets, or he might not have been able to maintain his discipline.

At 2:00 A.M., Escobar finally made his way back toward South Beach.

It was nearly three by the time he walked to the lobby of the Fontainebleau from the public parking lot six blocks south. The lobby, mostly deserted, reminded him of an ancient royal catacomb, each room above him a gilded tomb.

A security guard he did not know glanced at him curiously as he walked toward the elevators, but Escobar held up his key to put him at ease. Would the rest be so easy? All of the elevators except one were closed for repairs, but the doors opened for him right away.

When the elevator deposited him on the tenth floor, Escobar realized that his heartbeat was racing in a nervous frenzy. *Fantástico.* When was the last time he had been truly nervous? Nervousness sharpened him, as it had on the raft and in those first bewildering days when a simple escalator had the power to stupefy him, a majestic mechanical beast with moving teeth.

Escobar listened at the door but heard nothing. No light streamed beneath the door. If the actor was in the room, he was probably sleeping.

Escobar never prayed since Mami's death, but he wished himself luck as he quietly inserted the key card in the lock and swiped it, igniting the desired green pinprick of light. The *click* when he opened the door was far too loud, but nothing in the room stirred, so Escobar breathed and let himself in.

His mother used to say he had the vision of a cat, and maybe she was right: Escobar could see the room clearly in the moonlight. Could see his *face*. The actor was in the queen-sized bed with his face toward the door, tucked beneath his blankets in a sleep of the dead.

Escobar's breath went shallow in his throat. For a short instant, he pondered the act he was about to commit, surprised by his hesitation. He had no fear of security cameras, because he was wearing the wig and disguise he usually reserved for hunting. What, then? What did he care about the life of a talentless actor?

The actor was no different from the street women, just another whore who had shamed himself for pay. He had earned his death sentence.

Escobar brought out the knife from the sheath on his belt. The nine-inch knife had a beautiful mother-of-pearl handle, but he had only used it once on his hunt, in Mexico, when he had found himself without a proper pool of water. At the time, he had judged the knife as too messy, with none of the gratification provided by drowning. But it would have to do.

Walking lightly, he approached the bed . . . and plunged. The knife slipped into the side of the actor's neck, where it would slice straight through his carotid artery and trachea—

But something was wrong. The actor's flesh offered little resistance, as if he were stuffed with cotton. Standing over the bed, Escobar saw the lie—the actor's head was one of the special-effects dummies. Escobar flung away the blanket and found a crude collection of pillows underneath. The phony head dropped away, the knife falling with it to the floor. He had been fooled by his own creation!

Suddenly, a door beside the bed flew open from an adjoining room, and a too-bright light assaulted his eyes.

"Don't move," a voice commanded. "Or I will shoot you dead."

The voice was low to the ground. Not the actor—someone else.

Escobar blinked to see past the powerful flashlight beam, and he made out a man sitting in a wheelchair. He saw the metallic gleam of a gun before he heard the chambered round.

"Don't test me, son," the voice said. "This bullet can run faster'n either one of us."

Was this a bad dream? Escobar felt dizzy. What was happening?

"Who are you?" Escobar whispered.

"Keep your mouth shut," the old man in the wheelchair said, his voice full of practiced command. Although he had never felt such a strong impulse to run, Escobar's limbs were rooted. Then the man's voice changed slightly, as if he were speaking to someone else. "Ten? I've got 'im."

Escobar heard a tiny voice, barely within his hearing, like a mosquito, or like the unlucky scientist at the end of *The Fly*, trapped in a spider's web. From a cell phone's ear bud.

"Hold tight, Dad," the tiny voice said. "Almost there!"

The man in the wheelchair was the actor's father.

"Be careful, *abuelo*," Escobar said in a soothing tone. He tested a step toward the door.

"*You* be careful, shithead," the old man said, raising the gun with a too-steady hand. "I just saw you try to kill my son. My warning shot's gonna be right between your eyes."

Escobar didn't doubt the old man's resolve. The wonder was that he hadn't fired already.

Es un arroz con mango, as Mami would have said. It was rice with mango, a complicated thing.

His first plan had failed.

On to the next.

a step toward the door.

"You be careful, shithead," the old man said, raising the gun with a too-steady hand. "Just saw you try to kill my son. My warning shot's gonna be right between your eyes."

Booker didn't doubt the old man's resolve. The wonder was that he hadn't fired already.

It's an error someday, as Mami would have said. Trova nice with mango, a complicated thing.

His first plan had failed.

On to the next.

TWENTY

I WAS SWEARING as I ran up the stairs.

Why hadn't Dad stuck to the plan? His job had been to monitor the video feed from the adjoining room and keep a record of Escobar's arrival. We had been in constant communication since Escobar first began his drive toward South Beach, when I was almost sure I'd roused Dad from sleep with my warning call. Dad knew Escobar's every movement, so he had been ready.

But I wasn't. In the hotel lobby, I'd caught bad luck.

I couldn't take Escobar's elevator car with him, and the others were delayed for overnight servicing. I waited for the elevator to return after it reached the tenth floor, but after a brief stop, it kept going up instead of coming back down. The main building only had fifteen floors, so I decided to wait it out. But then the elevator car's light got stuck on the fifteenth floor and seemed to stay forever. Somewhere above me, drunken revelers were deciding my future.

I started swearing.

"He's got a knife!" Dad whispered to me on his phone while I waited. He was so excited he sounded thirty years younger.

I ran for the stairs then. Escobar was already in my room, and

Dad sounded as if he was enjoying himself too much, reliving a stakeout from his youth.

"Just hold on," I said while I ran. "Wait for me. You hear me?"

But Dad hadn't waited. The next thing I'd heard was the commotion as he surprised Escobar in the hotel room. I braced for the sound of gunfire. My legs felt like jelly, not moving nearly fast enough. My heartbeat pounded my eardrums.

I'd known my luck was plummeting as soon as I got stuck in the lobby, a line of dominoes falling one by one. It would all go to hell somehow. I'd known it as soon as the elevator refused to come back.

Dad had thirty years of police experience before he retired, but he hadn't been in the field for years. He'd seen combat in Vietnam, but he might have forgotten some of the lessons he learned. And Escobar was no ordinary perpetrator—he might as well be an illusionist.

I ran up the stairs two at a time, my mind racing with the dangers. "Don't get too close to him," I told Dad. "Make him show you his hands. He might have another weapon."

"Show me your hands." Dad's voice came from my phone. Talking to Escobar.

I wished I hadn't given Dad the .22 I'd swiped from Raphael. I should have kept it. The gun had made Dad too bold, and now I didn't have one.

Eighth floor. Ninth floor. I panted, flinging myself up the stairs as fast as I could go.

"You'll shoot me in cold blood, *abuelo*?" I heard Escobar say faintly.

"Tell him to shut up!" I shouted to Dad. "Get him on the floor with his hands behind his back. I'm almost there!"

A beat later, I heard Dad repeat my instructions.

Tenth floor. I threw the door open and raced down the carpeted hallway, perspiration stinging my eyes. I pulled my card key out of my back pocket. One ear bud fell free, but I was close enough to see the room, so I let it go.

In slow motion, I swiped the card to let myself into the room. The light showed red. The door was still locked. Once it was on my trail, bad luck never let me go.

I swiped the card again, and this time the light was green.

I ran into the room, which was dark except for a bright flash-light beam strobing on Escobar's monstrous, distorted face near the doorway.

"Ten, watch out—" Dad said.

I've told the story a hundred times, but I'm still not clear on the sequence. A gunshot first? Then a loud *pop*, the hiss of spray, and fire in my eyes? Or did the fire in my eyes come first and then the gunshot?

I never saw exactly what happened. Even in my dreams, all I see is darkness.

I know now that the fire in my eyes was a six-ounce tear-gas grenade Escobar had hidden in his pocket. Thick, acidic smoke clogged my eyes, nose, and mouth in the confined room, stealing my breath. I was barely aware of the sound of a struggle, but I was calling my father's name when I heard the second gunshot.

I have no confusion about the second gunshot. The sound is crisp and vivid in my memory, just to the left of where I had fallen against the wall to catch my balance, almost close enough to touch. Impossibly loud, rattling my bones. A shot to end the world.

I heard Escobar running toward me for the doorway, and instinct made me try to block him, but he easily dodged me and pushed me out of his way because I couldn't see.

I heard my father groan and cough. *Thank God he's alive*, I thought.

"Dad?" I said.

"I'm . . . okay," my father said through his coughing.

I stumbled toward where I thought I'd heard my father, and my hand felt his wheelchair's armrest. I pushed the chair, trying to angle it back toward the open doorway and the adjoining room that wasn't shrouded in poisonous smoke. The tear gas followed us, but it wasn't as thick. I saw splashes of light. I closed the door behind me and stumbled toward the glass patio door, where I tugged and tried to flush the room with fresh air. Precious seconds passed while I tried to find the lock. All the while, my eyes screamed. The ocean gusts were a balm on my face.

I thought we were better off in the next room than we would be in the hall. We might be vulnerable to Escobar in the hall, and there was sure to be smoke in the hallway, too. Fresh air was best. I could already breathe better past my burning lungs.

"Rinse your . . . eyes," my father said.

I stumbled to the bathroom and flipped on the ceiling fan. I could still only see in sparks of light, but I grabbed a hand towel and drowned it in water. I brought the towel to my father and pressed it to his face. "You, too," I said. "Rinse."

"Forget about . . . me," Dad said. "Go get him, Ten."

I stood over the sink and splashed my face until my clothes were soaked. My shirt stung my skin, so I pulled it off. My first concerns were my father and my blindness. Thoughts of Gustavo Escobar were far away.

The next time I found my way to my father's chair, I smelled blood for the first time. That smell froze my world.

"Dad?" I said. "Were you hit?" Hadn't I asked him before?

"Flesh wound," Dad said. "Barely. You all right?"

I tugged at his clothing, trying to see his injury with my blurry vision. For a man in my father's condition, there was no such thing as a minor gunshot wound. A round from a .22 could do a lot of damage. "Where? Let me see."

No blood or entrance wound on his chest or his head. That was good.

"I'm . . . fine, Ten," Dad said, pushing me with surprising strength. "Go get that SOB."

"Where were you shot?"

"He's getting away," Dad said. "Do you want it to be for . . . nothing?" My father still had the gun. The nozzle was warm. He raised it to give it to me, his fevered eyes staring hard into mine. "Eight rounds left."

"Tell me," I said. Worry was turning into horror.

Reluctantly, my father took my hand and laid it across his stomach. His shirt was moist with blood. I knew what had happened: Escobar had tried to take the gun away from my father but couldn't. Instead, he'd forced my father to shoot himself in the stomach.

When I was a kid, Dad had told me that a gunshot wound to the stomach was one of the most painful ways to die. On his stakeout nights, I'd felt torn between hoping he would come home soon and praying that he wouldn't come home at all. That was where my father and I had started, before we traveled our mighty long way together.

I exhaled with a wounded sound I did not recognize. The room spun.

I fumbled around the room for a telephone and called the operator to say my father had been shot and needed medical attention. I gave the room number. Beside me, my father's breathing sounded heavier and heavier, each breath a labor. Maybe a part of me always knew.

"They're sending paramedics," I told him. "Don't worry."

"I'm all right," Dad said, his voice unsteady with the lie. "Go get him, Ten. Don't let him . . . get away."

I took the wet towel I'd given him for his eyes and pressed it to his belly instead.

"Pressure right there," I said. It was only something to say. Anything to do.

"Go, Ten," Dad said. "No matter what . . . I'm all right."

I hung my head, eyes closed tight. I wanted to pretend I couldn't hear him. I wanted to pretend the whole night away. He wasn't just asking me to go catch Esocbar; he was asking me to walk away.

I don't know if it was my life's bravest moment or the most cowardly. I kissed my father's forehead and took the gun from his hand. Still half-blind, I brought myself to my feet, wheezing to breathe past the embers in my lungs.

"I'll get him, Dad," I said.

I stumbled out into the smoky hallway and ran.

That hallway was empty except for curious residents poking their heads out of their rooms, coughing from tear-gas vapors. I hoped that Escobar had wasted time at the elevator. He might have as much as a ninety-second head start and probably the advantage of full vision. I ran straight for the stairs, flying down so fast that I don't know how I stayed upright.

Distantly, floors below me, I heard quickly tapping footsteps. Escobar could have exited the stairwell at any floor, but instead, he had chosen to run all the way down to the lobby. I ran on the balls of my feet, trying to minimize the sound. If he didn't hear me coming after him, he might slow down.

My first taste of luck. Escobar could have been long gone, but he wasn't.

The smell of my father's blood on my skin made my stomach lurch. Every other step, I wanted to turn back to be with him, but that would have been selfish. My father had never needed hand-holding; he needed something much more important from me that night.

He'll be all right, I told myself. One day, we would both share a laugh over how he'd called his gut shot a "flesh wound." The promise of future laughter kept me on my feet.

On the fifth floor, I nearly tripped over a prosthetic arm discarded on the steps. I didn't have the full picture yet, but I knew that the phony arm was part of the reason Escobar had been able to reach his tear gas while Dad held him at gunpoint. I'd thought I was clever to prop my prosthetic head in the bed, but Escobar had prepared for us, too.

We had underestimated him.

"Is that you I hear, *mijo*?" a voice called from below. My teeth locked, but I shoved my emotions away, trying to learn. He sounded as winded as I felt, and he hadn't just sucked in a lungful of tear gas after running up ten flights of stairs.

"I didn't mean for that to happen," he went on when I didn't answer. He sounded distraught. "He left me no choice, do you understand? Unlike you, he was a good man."

As long as he was monologuing, he wasn't running as fast as he could. I leaped down six stairs to the next landing, ignoring the hot pain that shot up my leg. I wished I could swoop down on him like Old Testament wrath.

"You can stop this now, Tennyson!" he went on, his voice bouncing against the concrete walls from everywhere. "Tend to your father. Don't force me to destroy you!"

At the next floor, I leaped down eight steps and felt my ankle twinge, nearly giving way. I had to balance myself against the wall before I could keep running. My palm smeared the wall with my father's blood.

Escobar must have heard my approach, because he went silent. A door opened below me with a cone of light. He had reached the lobby! If he got to the cab stand, he would melt in the wind. As I raced down the last three flights, I tried to remember what Escobar was wearing. With my vision so blurry, I would be lucky to see him. A lightweight dark boating jacket? I'd barely glanced at him in the dark before the tear-gas blast.

I reached the lobby, scanning as quickly as I could. Because of the lobby's size, Escobar had to run a distance before he could vanish from sight, my only chance. The blue-lighted floor of the bar glowed on one side, and the rest looked like a football field of white tiles.

Nothing and no one seemed to stir. I tried to slow my breathing so I could crane my ears, and I made out the clicking footsteps again, several yards to my right. My eyes swept the blur until I barely saw a dark spot moving across the floor, toward the exit.

Not the beach side. The cab side.

I could have stopped chasing Escobar then. Instead, I heard my father's voice in my head: *Go get him, Ten.*

"Escobar!" I shouted loudly enough to wake the dead. With that cry of rage, I ran across the massive lobby floor toward the doors.

I vaguely heard people trying to call to me, ordering me to halt, a couple of women screaming at the blood on me or maybe the gun in my hand. But I ran on. I burst through the doors into the cool night.

The air was thick with the scent of seawater. Sirens wailed their distant approach. The line of cabs waiting outside the hotel lobby was a blurred yellow snake.

I almost ran headlong into a bellman, suddenly in sharp focus. He was in his mid-twenties, small-boned, and hadn't lived long enough to deal with someone like me. I grabbed his shoulder hard enough to pinch nerves, the gun's muzzle planted at his chin. I would never terrorize a bystander that way, but I was someone else.

"Which way?" I said.

The speechless bellman shook his head as if to claim he didn't know what I was asking, but I saw his involuntary reflex as his eyes darted to the right.

Not the cabs, then. Toward the marina.

I let the bellman go and raced down the walkway toward the

white hulks that were the marina's resident yachts. The gate to the marina was wide open, my second piece of luck. Was the *Rosa* docked at the Fontainebleau? If so, Escobar would barely have time to board before I would catch him.

The marina was a maze of choices. Right or left? Which way?

Even the telltale footsteps were silent, and for a moment, I had to stop running, unsure. In that instant of stillness, fatigue and breathlessness made me feel lightheaded. Could I go on? My eyes were sheets of tears as they tried to wash away the poison.

A flock of seagulls squawked with annoyance just ahead of me, disturbed from their evening sleep. Escobar! I ran full speed toward the commotion. A cloud of gray-white wings and feathers flapped near my face as I tried to keep my feet on the wooden dock rather than straying to the water below. I heard the footsteps again, building speed, and I matched their fervor.

Sharp right turn. Then left. I could barely make out Escobar, but I saw him in flashes.

Where was he going? The yachts were behind us. As the skyline opened up, Escobar seemed to be running toward the bay itself.

Fine. If he planned to drown himself, I would give him all the help he needed.

Escobar suddenly leaped, and he was out of my sight. But there was no splash when he should have hit the water. Instead, I heard the zipping burr of a motorboat engine. *Dammit!* He had a boat ready for him. All alone, he'd planned to escape by water.

I was so fixated on trying to see Escobar that I nearly lost my footing at the end of the pier, waving my arms to keep my balance. He was the hazy gray form retreating at a good clip. I could hear him better than I could see him. I paced the pier with a cry of frustration, trying to wipe my eyes clear with my free palm.

No no no no no no

If I didn't stop Escobar, I had nothing except whatever grief was waiting for me back in my hotel room, the consequences of the choices I'd made. Already, I wanted to sink to my knees and beg God for a chance to live the night again.

Instead, I lay on my stomach flat on the pier and leaned over the edge to try to see if I could find another motorboat. My eyes were close to useless, but I made out a bright orange life vest only a few yards to my left.

A boat! The life vest lay on its bench. Two identical small boats lay within easy reach, tied side-by-side. They might have been the hotel's property, used for transporting residents.

I don't know much about boats. I'd operated motorboats maybe three times in twenty years, usually on vacation with clients. I didn't have a permit or real training, but I leaped down into the boat closest to the pier. The boat bobbed from my sudden weight, but I caught my balance on the fiberglass rim.

It was a simple outboard speedboat with seating for five. I didn't see an anchor line; the boat was only tied to the dock.

I could still hear Escobar's engine.

I pulled on the life jacket, figuring I would need it, and untied the boat with a few yanks of the rope. I saw a bright red flashlight nestled in a compartment, so I turned it on for much-needed light as I tried to start the engine. I vaguely remembered hasty lessons about connecting the fuel tank to the motor and how to set the throttle and drive selector. My efforts were far from textbook, but my hands took control from my brain.

The motor growled to life with my first yank of the starter cord. My journey away from the dock wasn't pretty—I came precariously close to plowing into two different yachts as I tried to master forward and reverse—but soon the wind was smacking my face as I rounded my way out of the marina's bay and headed out to open sea. Toward Escobar.

I could barely hear his engine over mine, but the whisper was enough.

I plunged ahead into the black night.

✦ ✦ ✦

I sped after Escobar's ghost on the ocean. The rough water flung my little craft around at will; sometimes I felt as if I wasn't moving forward, only up and down. I had never learned the rules about navigating choppy seas, much less memorized them. More than once, as the nose plunged down sharply, I expected to capsize. I bounced from my seat and landed hard on the cushion, barely keeping control of the boat as seawater sprayed my face.

But somehow I kept up my chase. The wind cleared the tears from my eyes, and my vision improved. Larger vessels appeared in the distance, backdrops to show me Escobar's progress as he blinked past their lights, changing direction to try to lose me. Sometimes I could see his foamy wake. His engine grew louder as I gained on him.

Then a boat appeared about sixty yards to the right of me. Starboard? Port? *Port* and *left* both have four letters. Starboard. It was dressed up in lights. It was the only cabin cruiser in sight, and I recognized it from a distance: *Rosa*. Escobar had planned to escape from the hotel, ride the speedboat out to sea, and meet his floating accomplice.

But his plans hadn't counted on me.

The *Rosa* would be a far easier target to follow than the near-invisible speedboat. As long as I didn't run out of gas, it was mine. I didn't know how fast my boat could go, but I doubted that the *Rosa* could travel much faster, especially since Escobar would need time to board.

I had swashbuckling visions straight out of *Captain Blood* as I drew closer to the larger boat, so at first I didn't notice that Escobar was racing too fast toward the *Rosa* without slowing. *He's going to*— I hadn't finished the thought before the bright golden flames appeared in a perfect fireball that melted into a shower of sparks and debris.

I shot to my feet, seething with rage. He had no right! I called Escobar every filthy name I could think of, shouting myself hoarse. Suicide was too good for him. He had no right.

Dad had told me to get Escobar. I could still hear his voice: *Go get him, Ten.*

Gustavo Escobar had robbed me of the chance to fulfill my father's dying wish.

TWENTY-ONE

I'D FORGOTTEN THAT I had an open cell-phone line to my father's phone, and no one had turned off the phone in my father's pocket. By the time I remembered my dangling ear bud as I approached the shore, strangers' voices were confirming what I already knew.

"... shock ... blood loss ..." a man's voice recited from my earpiece.

"Any next of kin?" a woman's dispassionate voice said.

They weren't in a hurry, trying to save a life. They were chronicling a death.

Richard Allen Hardwick was pronounced dead at 3:33 A.M. in room 1027 of the Fontainebleau Hilton Hotel in Miami Beach. He never made it to the hospital; at least he would have been glad of that. The bullet caused severe liver damage, and he suffered a cardiac arrest while he was bleeding to death. Paramedics tried to revive him at the scene, but Dad had chosen his time and place. With our phones to tether us, he had been with me until the end.

He died doing God's work.

The Coast Guard escorted me back to the pier, and the police and news vans were waiting in a pack. I recognized Detective

Hernandez in the uniformed crowd, but she didn't meet my eyes, or maybe I didn't notice if she did. Now she had her circus after all.

Marcela was sleeping, or she might have heard about Dad's death on the news.

But the main story, of course, was Gustavo Escobar.

I'd wanted to stop a serial killer. Be careful what you wish for.

I couldn't avoid a day in jail.

With a dead old man, an exploded speedboat, and a beloved director presumed dead, the police figured it was safest to keep me close. Very close. I was spared the perp walk, and I got a cell to myself, but after a three-hour interrogation, I was a guest of the South Beach Police for the next twelve.

Not that it mattered. The world had gone gray, surreal. Instead of racing, my mind was completely still, the kind of state I'd sought in meditation for years. My biggest sadness was informing Marcela and Chela by phone that Dad was gone. I don't remember what I said to either one of them or much of what they said to me. I had dropped out of my own life.

If I could have, I would have flown back to L.A. to be with Chela. But I was powerless against the bars of my six-by-eight-foot jail cell, and with powerlessness came peace. There was nothing more to do. Nothing more I could say.

I slept in my cell while the world outside buzzed about the death of Gustavo Escobar after a boat chase and when the shocking evidence of his secret life began to emerge. I did not dream. When food came, I didn't eat.

I couldn't even grieve, not yet. I slept deeply and soundly. In many ways, my time in lockup was a gift.

I knew I might never feel that kind of peace again.

✦ ✦ ✦

"So . . . how did you know?"

Sometimes it's a short journey from buffoon to sage. By the next night, my police interrogators had been replaced by special agents from the FBI field office in Miami and one profiler who had flown in from the Behavioral Analysis Unit in Quantico, Virginia. FBI agents had dealt with me before but never with such civility and respect. Special agents Manuel Perez, Gloria Dozier, and Jessica Jackson had all but laid out a red carpet for me.

Was I hungry? Did I need anything to drink? Was the temperature in the room all right?

The FBI had diverted many of its resources to antiterrorism since 9/11, but apparently a gift-wrapped serial killer still made the Bureau happy. The FBI could take its share of credit for unearthing Escobar's past without any fallout for the spectacle of his death. Once they decided I hadn't broken the law except for a minor concealed-weapons matter, I was Uncle Sam's best friend.

The three of them gathered around me, trying to learn from my wisdom.

"Why were you so sure?" Agent Perez said.

"I didn't know," I said. "I was investigating a lead. Following a hunch."

My mouth and lungs still burned from the tear gas, so I could barely speak above a whisper. By then, the blessed numbness had worn off. I was no longer in my jail cell, but I felt caged in the interrogation room. My grief over Dad's death had manifested as a migraine that easily overpowered the pain relievers I was popping like mints. The fluorescent bulbs were high-powered spotlights, every voice a shout. My muscles ached from chasing Escobar, and misery transformed the aches to pains. Back to reality.

Dad was gone. Had died in pain. Alone. Because of me.

"Well, you caught one of the really bad ones, Mr. Hardwick," Agent Perez said.

Information had been in short supply, but the FBI agents explained that they had found Escobar's trophy room on his boat, with more evidence on his laptop in the bed-and-breakfast suite he shared with Louise Cannon. Like many serial killers, he felt compelled to keep evidence so he could relive his crimes, and he had stored and printed digital photographs of Maria and four other prostitutes he had drowned in his short time in Miami.

But the killings hadn't started in Miami.

Escobar had at least twenty photographs of women, dating back a dozen years. All of them were Latina or black, most were unidentified—"No one might ever come forward to claim some of these girls," Agent Jackson said sadly—but the oldest photograph was of his own sister, Rosa Escobar, for whom there were few records. When she'd vanished from her Brooklyn apartment in 1998, no one had reported her missing.

Escobar had been bold enough to name his boat after his first victim.

On another hunch, I asked to see the photograph of Rosa Escobar. After a brief huddle, they agreed. Rosa looked exactly like Chela. Gustavo Escobar's skin was pale, but his sister was brown, with dark corkscrew curls like Chela's. She had been pretty in life, but in death, she was a bad dream. She was nude in the photo, splayed in a bathtub after an apparent struggle, her eyes wide with shocked betrayal. I could see dark handprints around her neck where her brother had strangled her and held her under the water.

And I had taken Chela straight to that man. Introduced her to him.

My empty stomach locked tight. I waved to let the agents know they could take the photo away. I couldn't have found my voice if I'd tried.

The agents, by contrast, looked energized. All three of them were perfectly coiffed and stylishly dressed, camera-ready, and it was probably no coincidence that they were all attractive and fit. They were a media team ready to try to tame the circus.

The agents explained that Escobar had been ruled missing and presumed dead after the boating accident. The Coast Guard was searching for his remains, but so far, only charred scraps of his clothing had been found. Rough seas might have swept him away, and the sharks might have done the rest, they surmised. No one would have to endure a trial.

I'd disclosed Chela's part in steering me toward the case, but they promised to protect her privacy as much as they could—which, as it turned out, was hardly at all. They advised me to say as little as possible to the media until they completed a more thorough investigation of Escobar's past.

"I need to be with my family," I finally said when I'd had enough.

They nodded with sympathy. Special Agent Jessica Jackson squeezed my shoulder as if she could leech away my pain.

"I know it doesn't feel like it now," she said, "but you're a bona fide hero, Mr. Hardwick. Your father died for a greater cause. Uncovering Gustavo Escobar will bring closure to a lot of parents, brothers, sisters, and children out there."

But who would bring closure to me?

All my life, I think I've lived as if acting in a Broadway play. A film. As a character in a book. I'd made a critical mistake. I'd thought this story was a mystery, and I was the hero.

I was wrong.

It was a tragedy, and I was the fool.

TWENTY-TWO

I'D ALWAYS BELIEVED that the LAPD took more from Dad than it gave him, but the department tried to make up for that on his burial day.

Four LAPD helicopters somberly followed our family's limousine from my doorstep at 5450 Gleason to First A.M.E. Church in downtown L.A. News helicopters circled behind them. The noise overhead beat across the limo's rooftop.

I saw Chela's tiny gloved hand on the seat beside me, so I held it. We avoided each other's eyes. I had never seen her wear lace, but Marcela had spent an hour getting her dressed, as if they were preparing for the church wedding my father never had. We'd had some conversation at breakfast over the episode of *Robot Chicken* Chela was playing from the DVR, but the ride in the limousine was silent, all distraction gone.

We couldn't be anywhere else. Do anything else. The day had come.

When we arrived at the church, two dozen police officers in formal dress waited in two regimented lines to create a passage to the church door past the crowd. Overhead, the helicopters split off in four directions in a "missing man" fly-over formation that had been carefully explained by the LAPD liaison from the chief's office.

I was ushered to my place beside the rosewood casket draped with an American flag. *This isn't my father*, I told the casket, just so I could hold on. *It's the body my father wore*. I was the only pallbearer who wasn't wearing LAPD colors. The casket was closed, the result of an argument I had won with Marcela; every detail had been a negotiation. Dad wouldn't have wanted his body on display. Instead, youthful photographs at the pulpit better captured his memory. In his US Army photo, he looked just like me.

Booming percussion and the trumpet solo from Aaron Copland's "Fanfare for the Common Man" pealed inside the church during the processional. Dad had told Marcela that he wanted the piece played when this day came, along with his beloved gospel music. The trumpet sounded like upward flight toward heaven, a proclamation. The music's majestic beauty made my teeth lock tight as I shouldered the casket's weight.

Dad had done two tours in Vietnam, but the LAPD claimed rights to him that day. Between his long police career and his affiliation with the church, Dad might as well have been the mayor. Nothing was spared in his honor. After the trumpet fanfare finished, the full men's gospel choir—clad all in black except for their kente-cloth vests—swayed with Dad's favorite hymn, "Precious Lord Take My Hand." Muted sobs broke free behind us. The swollen pews and beautiful voices were a testament to how much we had lost.

When I took my seat, Chela pushed close to me. "I can't do this," she whispered.

The same thing I was thinking.

"You're already doing it," I said to both of us.

Retired or not, Dad was a cop who had died in the course of his duty. It didn't matter that most of the police officers in that room hadn't called Dad to talk to him since his stroke, even men he'd known well. Or that Dad had waged vicious political battles with the sitting chief. The public nature of Dad's death had thrust the LAPD into a positive national light, and at his funeral, Dad was treated like one of the department's most valuable treasures.

If only Dad could see this, I thought. I wanted to believe he was watching us all from heaven, but I couldn't feel that certainty even when it would have mattered most. Marcela wore her faith like a warm cloak; when she crossed herself in careful gestures across her chest, it looked as if she were bundling against the cold.

Marcela was Catholic, and Dad was A.M.E., so the only clergy missing was a rabbi. From the list of speakers—the mayor, several council members, a federal judge, and the police chief—we might have been at a political rally instead of a funeral. Dad had saved lives, steered careers, brightened the world. Dad was Jimmy Stewart in *It's a Wonderful Life*, and L.A. was Bedford Falls.

Family addresses came last, after the choir got us on our feet with "Soon and Very Soon We Are Going to See the King." I listened for God peeking through in the music's promise.

Marcela's face streamed with tears, and she leaned on me while we walked to the pulpit, but she stayed on her feet and didn't trip on the steps. First, she read a statement Chela had asked her to read, a simply worded message of gratitude and second chances.

Then Marcela raised her eyes. She didn't need notes for what she wanted to say.

"My brother is a police officer. My father was a soldier," she said. "I know what it means to stay up nights worrying. But since Captain was retired and didn't like to walk far from his TV, I thought all of that was behind me." She smiled, inviting the congregation to laugh. I heard myself laugh, too. "As I like to say, *no hay miel sin hiel*, or 'you can't have the honey without the sting.' In other words, there's always a catch."

More laughter. For one instant, grief and anger dissolved from Marcela's face. But Marcela was silent for a long time, her emotions catching up to her. I laid my hand across the small of her back, and she found her voice again.

"Even when I first met him as a patient—when he could barely talk or move—he was concerned about others. How was the lady across the hall who yelled in such pain? Why didn't anyone ever come to visit the man in the bed next to his? Or he was telling jokes, trying to make me smile. His body ailed him, but his spirit was full of life. And oh, he was such a fighter! People would say, 'How could you fall in love with a man who was so much older?' But the question I had for them was, how could I *not* fall in love with Captain Richard Hardwick?"

Marcela and I had known two different versions of Dad while he healed in that facility. She had been the true family to him when I was just a visitor.

Marcela said a prayer in Spanish, and then she was finished.

Once I'd helped Marcela take a seat behind the pulpit, I realized with horror that it was my turn to speak. The silence in the massive church echoed as I reached into my jacket to try to find the index cards I'd stayed up half the night trying to fill with the right words. The only honest thing to say would have been *I got my father killed*.

Marcela knew it. Chela knew it. Everyone in that church knew it. Anyone who had heard the story of that night with Gustavo Escobar knew that Dad was dead because of me.

My hand shook, and the words blurred as if I still had tear gas in my eyes.

"All my life," I began with half a voice, "I wanted to make Dad half as proud to be my father as I am to be his son."

I gazed out at the sea of faces. The lights from the news cameras felt like an indictment. My eyes rested on Lieutenant Rodrick Nelson, Dad's protégé, one of his few colleagues who had visited him in the past year. Lieutenant Nelson had spoken about my father at length with easy elegance. In his dress uniform, he looked like the son Dad should have had.

"I love you, Dad. Miss you." My voice sounded muffled on the loudspeaker.

More words were scribbled on my cards, but I had nothing left to say.

Home life was excruciating in the days after Dad died. The spaces his absence left were filled with the silence of resentment from Marcela and Chela. They stopped just short of accusations, but I saw their questions in their eyes. My story wasn't enough to satisfy any of us.

Why had I encouraged Dad to work a case so late at night, so unprepared? How could I have left him to die instead of making sure the paramedics got to him quickly? After Chela did some internet research, she casually speculated that sustained pressure to the gunshot wound might have kept Dad alive long enough for life-saving medical treatment.

Marcela was planning to move out. She hadn't said so yet, but I felt it in her silence and her long afternoons away with friends. My house was no longer her home.

Death doesn't always bring families closer together. Maybe it never does.

Every day, new details surfaced about Escobar that showed me how foolish I had been. He had caused hilarity with a prosthetic arm at a Sundance party the previous year. He had been a professional magician as a teenager. In the *National Enquirer*, an email surfaced from Escobar to his agent where he joked about casting me for *Freaknik* "because it would be safer to have a detective on the set." He had hired me to amuse himself.

Escobar had planned out our collision from the beginning.

The new details only fed the feeding frenzy.

We didn't watch the news anymore, although the Gustavo

Escobar story was exactly the kind that would have kept Dad glued to CNN and HLN. Whether it was Escobar's Hollywood connection, his ties to Cuba's troubled political history, or the trail of dead women he had left behind, Gustavo Escobar was the Big Story. He was a Russian nesting doll, with fresh headlines every day.

I only took calls from my lawyer, and barely. Melanie Wilde was my public face, and I'd agreed to let her write a couple of vague public statements. I had done her family a favor a while back, and she repaid me with legal help whenever she could. She had been one of the first people to call me after Dad died and one of the few to get through to me.

"Brace yourself," Melanie said when she called the day after the funeral, as if I wasn't always bracing. "Sofia Maitlin is on a goodwill mission to set the record straight about her daughter's kidnapping. She's put out a press release, and she's about to do the morning-TV circuit. She says the FBI took credit, but it was really you. Your hero status is about to balloon to a new level."

The word *hero* gave me a pain in my abdomen. Maitlin was finally going to tell the truth about how I had nearly died rescuing her daughter. I cynically wondered if she was coming out of hibernation to promote a new movie, but she had enough secrets to make exposure risky.

"I'll ask her not to."

"Too late," Melanie said. "The press release is out there making the circuit. It's all over TMZ and the entertainment shows, and the networks won't be far behind. She says, and I quote, 'I'm not the least bit surprised that Tennyson Hardwick put an end to this monster's reign of evil. Without him, I never would have seen my daughter alive again.'"

Maitlin might have meant well, but I'd hoped to quietly drop out of the Escobar story after Dad's funeral. That wouldn't happen now. It was bad enough that Marcela was considering a ten-thousand-dollar offer to talk to *Star* magazine; she'd mentioned it at breakfast as if it was nothing. I was so tired of arguing I hadn't said a word. It was as if Marcela had transformed into the gold digger I'd always worried she was. I would meditate and try to let her grieve in her own way. I try not to judge people, but it was hard.

I thanked Melanie for the information. Sometimes there's nowhere else for bad to grow.

I stayed home despite the reporters camped out on my street. All of my career, I'd hovered close to the celebrity experience without truly tasting it. Now tabloid reporters were going through my garbage, in every possible way.

The sex-worker story had resurfaced. The only thing I didn't mind about Dad being gone was that he didn't have to hear the details. Former customers came forward, women whose careers had waned and who were desperate to be in the public eye. I never saw the story, but I hear there were six women in a roundup. One name shocked me, but if you didn't read it, I won't go into it now. The headline read: TENNYSON HARDWICK: SEX-CORT TO THE STARS!

I knew why Maitlin had stepped up in my defense. Outside, a war was raging about what to make of me, a larger version of the silent war in my house.

It was all a part of the bad dream that began the night my father died—one continuous dream, with no chance to wake. The world around me melted, and I didn't recognize my new world. In my new world, my father was gone, shot dead after I roused him from sleep and asked too much of him. I'd taken wild chances, just because I'd gotten away with it before.

That was enough ugly to fill up everything. The rest didn't matter.

I was tired all the time. I hated being awake. I hated trying to sleep.

I only opened my door that night because I recognized the face through the peephole. At least the paparazzi didn't ring my doorbell day and night. It's not true that there's no civility left.

Lieutenant Rodrick Nelson was on my front porch in my lamp-light, which I took as a bad sign on face value. We didn't like each other—sometimes the sentiment went deeper—and we both had loved the same man. He was so drunk I could see him swaying through the peephole. At least he was in civilian clothes. I hoped that meant he wasn't armed.

"Should I open this door?" I said.

"Depends on whether you're a man or not." Even drunk, Nelson didn't slur his words.

I wasn't in the mood to trade beatings, but maybe Nelson deserved his chance. I'd been craving some quality time with him for years. He was six-three and solid, with a passing resemblance to Richard Roundtree at his peak. He had to duck to walk into the house, since Alice had been petite and hadn't built her doorway to accommodate strangers.

"Better judgment told me not to come here," Nelson said. "But here I am. I have to know if it's true."

I almost laughed to myself. "Which part?"

"You knew he'd taken a gut shot, but you left him to chase Escobar."

In my head, I saw Dad's blood pooling on his shirt. Smelled it.

"I was following the orders of my CO," I said. "That's all you need to understand."

"So it's true," he said, his red eyes blazing with disbelief. "Preach always said you'd be the death of him."

I wondered if Nelson would be enough of an asshole to put me in jail for the fight he was starting at my house. "It's not a good idea for us to talk right now," I said.

"You're so right about that," Nelson said. "But I just couldn't go another minute without making sure you understood the big picture, Tennyson." His voice almost sounded warm when he said my name. "All that shit that's on TV now? Mr. Good Time? Gigolo to the stars? He knew all that. There was a whole file on you. That madam? It came right to his desk. And do you know what Preach Hardwick—the most upstanding cop I ever had the privilege to work with—did with that file?"

Nelson ground his fist on my coffee table. "He squashed it. All of it was wiped away. You, the madam, the whole case. He soiled himself for you. He made himself a hypocrite for you. Pissed away his career—because his enemies used it against him. All that stress and strain before he retired? His heart attack? Congratulate yourself. He did it for you."

I wished he'd hit me instead. Even if Nelson was exaggerating, it might not be by much. I'd suspected that Dad might have heard about my sex arrest in Hollywood as part of an ongoing sting, but I hadn't known for sure. We had both avoided the subject.

"Is that all?" My voice was a monotone.

"No," Nelson said. "Just so you know, I'm not the kind of prick who would come piss on somebody when they've just had a family tragedy. Not on an ordinary day. I'm sure you loved him in your own fucked-up way, and I respect that. But when I see you trying to capitalize on it, trotting out Sofia Maitlin to throw your name around—"

"I had nothing to do with that."

"It makes me sick," Nelson went on, as if I hadn't spoken. "Physically ill. All those sermons Preach gave me about how you'd turned out all right were a load of horseshit."

That time, Nelson missed his mark. I was glad to hear what Dad had said about me. That must have driven Nelson crazy.

"Get the fuck out of our house!"

My thoughts had come screaming to life but in Chela's voice.

Chela was standing on the stairs, dressed in the baggy UCLA sweatshirt she'd put on the night she came back from Raphael. Seeing the sweatshirt brought that night back to life.

Nelson was startled to see Chela. Maybe he'd thought she wasn't home, like Marcela, who was out shopping for clothes to wear on her interviews. For once, he was speechless.

"How dare you," Chela said, marching down the steps. Her face was bright red with rage. "His father—my grandfather—just died. I'm going to report you to the chief."

Nelson's lips fell apart. Chela had him there. One call to the chief's office would get him a formal tongue lashing and maybe worse.

"You remember Chela?" I said. "My daughter."

None of the tabloids had named her, but the *Enquirer* had mentioned the existence of "a teen prostitute runaway" I'd raised since she was fourteen. When April brought the story to us, Chela cried for two hours straight. She had been avoiding school, and as far as I knew, she was avoiding calls from her boyfriend, Bernard. Chela had lost her privacy, too. I wanted to help her navigate the wreckage, but I was mired in mine.

"I'm sorry you had to hear that, young lady," Nelson said. "You've been through—"

"You're not sorry," she said, continuing her march until she was toe-to-toe with him. "You didn't care who heard it. You had to be a jerk. Well, guess what—this sucks for everybody, not just you. So grow up and leave us alone."

I couldn't have said it better myself.

Nelson blinked, as if Chela had brought him back to sobriety. He gave me a long gaze. "I'm sorry, man," he said. "I saw that Maitlin thing . . ."

"Not a problem," I said.

Both of us might have been lying, or maybe not. We also both knew I wouldn't report him to the chief. Ours was a family matter.

Nelson went outside to call himself a cab. I checked the peephole from time to time to make sure he didn't try to climb into his car. I didn't want any more death on my conscience.

"Thanks for that," I told Chela. She was so upset she was shaking, but I didn't try to hug her. She hadn't come close enough for me to hug her since I told her Dad was dead.

"He's wrong," Chela said. "It's not your fault. It's mine."

"That's bull, Chela."

"I was the one who wanted to find out who killed Maria. I'm the one who went to that club. Maria's always been about the hustle, making a play. What else did I think she wanted?"

"She was your friend, Chela."

"I wish I had never seen her!" Chela said, screaming again. But screams were better than silence. Her stoic wall was crumbling.

"It's not Maria's fault," I said. "It's not your fault. It's Escobar's fault."

If I said it often enough, maybe I would believe it.

"But Ten, why?" she said. "Why didn't you stop the bleeding? You could have saved him. We don't understand."

The "we," I assumed, meant Marcela, who had studied enough medicine to know that Dad might as well have been dead when the bullet shredded his liver. But I hadn't known the extent of the damage before I left him.

"He was tired of being sick, Chela," I said. "Marcela might say she doesn't understand, but she doesn't want to accept it. He asked me to go. He knew what that meant."

Chela turned away from me. I heard her sob.

We needed a team of therapists. I wouldn't know where to begin.

"And now I have to talk to him," Chela said, still crying. "He keeps calling me."

"Who?" I said, right before I remembered Bernard.

I held Chela's shoulders, and she didn't pull away. She looked up at my face, and I saw my misery mirrored there, my twin. "This isn't how you pictured it," I said. "But this is what you wanted. You have your chance to tell the truth."

"And then what?" Chela said.

"And then you'll find out who Bernard really is."

Chela stepped away from me, flicking her shoulders as if my

touch itched. "Maybe it doesn't make sense, but I kind of hate you right now." Chela said it matter-of-factly. Nothing Lieutenant Nelson said could have hurt me more.

"I know," I said. *Join the club.*

"It's just a phase," she said. "The first stage of grief is anger—did you know that? I've been researching. It's so true. I want to kill all the fish in the tank and burn the house down."

"Just give us warning," I said.

I understood how being around others could feel like a chore. I'd barely spoken to April for five minutes since I'd been back in L.A.

"Is this really happening?" Chela said, the same question she'd asked me when I first called her with the terrible news.

"Yes," I said. "It's still really happening."

"It's no big deal if Marcela wants to do that interview," Chela said. "He wouldn't care. She likes telling everybody how great he was. So what if she gets paid?"

I didn't agree yet, but I was working on it. Chela sounded more sensible every day.

"I'm doing my best," I said.

"Me, too," Chela said. "So is Marcela. You should call April, by the way. She's totally into you, and you barely talked to her at the funeral."

"You call Bernard, I'll call April."

Chela didn't smile, but her crying had stopped.

At least for another night.

TWENTY-THREE

WITH THE REWIND button in her head, Chela changed everything.

She never sees Maria standing in the crowd behind the set of *Freaknik,* or hears her calling "Che-LAAA," because her voice gets lost in the noise. Maria gives up, thinking maybe it wasn't really her. With her daughter in mind, Maria vows again that she'll get her GED like she always said. She calls Mouse Girl and says she'll skip going out to Club Phoenixx that night.

And Gustavo Escobar never sees Maria. And she never goes after him.

And the Captain isn't dead.

And she has her life back.

As she stood in her jacket in the breezeway of the athletic center at Bernard's church, Chela could picture the Miami sunshine, the fat crewman with his belly flopping, Ten's ridiculous prop glasses. It could have happened the way she imagined it a hundred times over. There was no reason for the Captain to be dead.

Chela fiercely held her tears at bay while she stood in front of the wrestlers and their parents who filed out of the gym with oblivious contentment, grinning and laughing. She thought she could feel people glancing at her over their shoulders when they thought she was out of sight, wondering how she had the nerve to set foot on hallowed church grounds.

Chela had never understood the concept of wrestling at church. She played with a picture of a bearded Jesus pinning Judas down after a wicked throw, so funny it kept her tears away.

Bernard's parents weren't with him, as usual. Since Bernard had gotten his license to drive himself legally, his father had stopped coming to watch him wrestle at church youth-league tournaments. His father's new job required him to fly to New Jersey a week a month, and that had killed wrestling for them. Usually, you could hear Mr. Faison yelling all the way outside.

His dad would have been proud. The first match had been embarrassingly long and ineffective for both wrestlers, but Bernard had looked like the Undertaker in the last match. *Bam, bam, bam.* That other Jesus freak had never known what hit him.

Bernard was one of the last ones out, since he stayed behind to talk to the coach. Bernard was a kiss-ass in every arena. All of his teachers loved him, too. He worked it without trying.

Bernard was suddenly in front of her, standing in the lamplight. He looked as if he'd grown an inch since she went to Miami, but he smelled like sweat and a dirty mat. His mouth hung open with shock. That was why so many other kids thought he was a geek; he'd let his eyes bug out, no matter who was watching.

"You saw the whole thing?" Bernard said. She was glad he didn't start right off asking why she hadn't returned his calls and texts. Apparently, when people close to you died, everyone else gave you a lot of room. Her mother had given her a hell of a lot of room after Nana Bessie died.

"Yeah," Chela said. "That last match gives new meaning to the phrase 'What would Jesus do?'"

Bernard made a sour face. He didn't like jokes with the word *Jesus* in them, even if they were funny. "Is that some kind of atheist humor?"

"Agnostic," she corrected. Maybe she didn't believe in God the way church people did, but atheism sounded like its own religion. "Here's atheist humor: 'Life's a bitch, and then you die.' Get it?" Jokes made Chela feel better, even when no one laughed.

"Actually, I don't get it," Bernard said.

"Of course not," she said. She felt herself trying to start a fight. Bernard annoyed her, acting as if he floated on balloons all the time, basking in Jesus. It was so childish. So what if his father had been assistant pastor at the church all those years? *Think for yourself*, she thought.

"I'm really sorry about your grandfather," Bernard said. He stepped closer, but she noticed he didn't hug her in front of witnesses. The coaches were locking up.

"Yeah, I know." Chela didn't want to talk about the Captain, but the next conversation was almost as bad. "So . . . it's been crazy."

"I figured. Can I drive you somewhere? Oh, wait—dumb question. Like you could have walked from your house. I didn't know you knew the way here."

"I didn't," Chela said. "I drove around like a jerk for a half hour."

"We could grab some burgers, and I could bring you back."

Chela shrugged. "I'm not hungry. Besides, I can't leave my car in a church parking lot—you never know what kind of people are hanging out here."

He looked at her as if he was trying to decide if she was kidding.

He would never bring it up, she realized. He would stand there and pretend he hadn't heard anything, or that the *National Enquirer* wasn't talking shit about her. Anybody who'd ever met her knew that she was the whore in the story.

"You've got nothing to say?" Chela said. "Just 'Let's get a burger'?"

"I thought it would be better to talk there."

"Right, I want to bare my soul at Jack in the Box."

"Why are you mad at me?" Bernard said. His brows furrowed with annoyance.

"It's a stage," she said. "Anger is the first stage of mourning."

"Oh." Bernard nodded, satisfied. "I read that somewhere."

"It's anger, denial, bargaining, depression, acceptance," she recited. Researching death was her favorite pastime on the internet. Considering that everyone in human history had died, she had expected to find more information on the subject.

"Denial's next?"

"For me, maybe depression. That one seems to be the real bitch."

One of the coaches, the younger one, glanced at Chela from the doorway behind them. Bernard stepped in front of Chela as if to try to shield her from his sight. He put his hand gently on her upper arm, the way the Captain's doctors had when they had bad news. "I know where we can talk," Bernard said. She was glad he had come up with a plan.

They didn't walk much farther than around the corner of the building, but they were out of view of the gym and the parking lot. Suddenly, they were surrounded by squat, perfectly trimmed trees, midget trees that looked as if they'd been grown in an enchanted forest. Everything in the solar lamplight was green. Somewhere, water gurgled.

"This is our meditation garden," Bernard said. "It's Japanese, since we have a lot of Japanese members in our congregation. Makes you think of the Garden of Gethsemane, right?"

"Sure, whatever that is," Chela said. Bernard often lapsed into a foreign language. She had her own language, too, and he had never heard a word of it.

"This is my favorite part of the church," he said.

"Really? I thought it was sweaty mats."

"My second favorite place, then. It's easier to pray where it . . . looks like this."

"Pretty," Chela said.

"Exactly."

Despite its cement backdrop behind them, the little garden did seem to have a magical hold on her. It wasn't a long stretch of sparkling Miami beach, but it was a safe and quiet place.

"Ten meditates every day," Chela said.

"I know," Bernard said. "He told me."

Chela looked at him sidelong, surprised. Since when did Ten and Bernard hang out?

"Just conversation while I was waiting for you," Bernard said. "A long time ago. You know how parents are—trying to relate."

It was strange to hear Bernard call Ten her *parent*. But she didn't correct him. How could she? Even the *National Enquirer* knew he was the guy who had saved her ass.

"It's so crazy now," Chela said.

"Yeah, I can't imagine. How is Ten dealing with things?"

"Uh . . . like a robot," Chela said. "Nobody's having a lot of heart-to-hearts right now."

"That sucks."

"Actually, I like being left alone. It works well with my anger phase."

A silence came, made larger in the garden. Chela decided to say the first thing that popped into her head. "I know what people are saying about me. And before you ask me anything, yes, it's true."

She dared a glance at Bernard, and he looked startled. He'd never believed it was true. He had waited to hear her side. "Oh," he said.

"I wanted to tell you all along, but it was too gross. So think about all the highlights, and it's probably true. I was a ho. A harlot. A whore. Pick your name for it."

"I don't have a name for it," he said. "I guess . . . prostitute? But you were just a kid. I can't believe people would—that a madam would—"

Mother must be miserable these days, with her business out in the streets, Chela thought. The tabloid had even found a photo of her that must have been taken thirty years ago, when she had darker hair and a young woman's face. Mother was older than the Captain by now, she thought. Even tough old ladies got frail. Nana Bessie sure had.

"Bernard," Chela said, trying to sound patient. "It's an ugly world. She did me a favor."

"A favor?"

"Yeah, she probably kept me from getting killed like . . ."

She stopped. He knew the rest.

"You're so lucky Ten came along," Bernard said.

"It wasn't luck—she's the one who called him," Chela said. Mother wasn't stupid; she had probably known what Ten would do when he found her. He wouldn't have let Chela stay with her. Mother had arranged it for her.

"You sound like you're defending her," Bernard said.

"Life must be nice in Black-and-White Land, where you live."

They both knew they were veering into more treacherous terrain. They were silent again. She and Ten had learned to leave the subject of Mother alone, too.

"So . . . are you okay after that?" Bernard said.

"Okay?"

"Yeah—I mean, did you get sick? Do you need a doctor?" Bernard said.

"I don't have any diseases, if that's what you're asking."

"I didn't mean it like that. I'm just worried about you, Chela. You're my girlfriend. What do you expect?"

Chela hadn't expected the way her heart puffed up when Bernard said she was his girlfriend. They had been going steady for more than a year, and he'd said it first. He said it way more than she did. When her tears came, she didn't wipe them away.

He wasn't holding up a cross to repel her as if he thought she was a vampire. He was the same Bernard he always was. And although Raphael tried to come to her tongue, Chela realized she would have to leave one secret buried. Just one. She couldn't tell Bernard she'd had sex with another man when they'd been waiting so long. She had done it to find that sicko killer.

"I didn't get any diseases, thank God," Chela said. "But I'm not okay, really. I'm pretty messed up. I hate my life."

"Never say that," Bernard said, his voice hushed. He hugged her, and she enjoyed his warmth. He was still pumped up from the wrestling match, so he felt like a radiator. He definitely seemed taller since she'd been gone. "Never say you hate your life. You can't see it right now, but you're so lucky, Chela."

If Ten were talking to her much these days, he might have said something like that. Chela tried to laugh, but it came out as a sob.

"You don't hate me?" she whispered. A little girl's voice.

"I'm no one to cast stones, Chela. None of us are."

While Bernard held her, Chela felt lucky for the first time in years.

TWENTY-FOUR

AS A CLOSE protection specialist—what most people call a bodyguard—I knew how to dodge a tail. I wasn't sure paparazzi were following me, but it was worth taking precautions. I didn't want April dragged into the mess of my life.

I waited for her outside her back door, where her Dumpster met her rose bed. The backyard of the house she shared with a roommate was nearly nonexistent, pushed close to its rear neighbor's fence. It was a nice neighborhood but overcrowded, with too many yappy dogs. At least the roses made the garbage smell better.

Television news played through open windows. I heard my name mentioned by a star newscaster, like the sound of sizzling butter in a frying pan, a shock and then gone. Nothing stuck to me. She could have called me the president of the United States.

"Where are you?" April said, relieved to hear from me when I called her cell phone. "Right outside your back door."

Thirty seconds later, I was in her bright kitchen. April had changed out of work clothes, into a braless white tank top and athletic pants with fabric so thin it looked like her skin. Her shoulders had thinned, and her lost weight sharpened her cheekbones. She looked like a dancer. My eyes followed her every motion, drinking her up. I could have stared at April all night.

April stopped short of touching me, leaning against the kitchen counter, scooting away an overfed cat. She shook her head, eyes sad.

"Ten . . ." Whatever she'd planned to say must have been too big for words.

"He loved that cane you got him," I said brightly, as if I were the one trying to cheer her up. "Stylin' with it like Fred Astaire." I did a brief imitation soft-shoe to demonstrate, and April giggled despite her sadness. I got the smile I wanted.

April blinked back tears. "The funeral . . ."

"Too bad he missed it."

"He was there," April said. "I feel him right now."

I shrugged. I always felt Dad, too, when our last moment came back to haunt me.

"He asked me to leave him," I said. "I did what he asked me to do." I sounded as if I was pleading for forgiveness, and maybe I was.

April nodded fervently. "I know," she said. "That was so hard, Ten. I'm sorry."

Relief uncoiled my back muscles. April knew me, and she understood. April knew me better than anyone alive. Now that Dad was gone, she was the only one who did.

April saw the thoughts on my face, nodding to me, holding out her hand as if there were a river separating us across her kitchen linoleum. "I'm here, baby. I'm right here."

We kissed. We went back in time with our kiss and remade the future. Our kiss took us away from the funeral day, away from the new world. Finally—something I recognized.

I pushed aside a dish rack and hoisted myself to the edge of April's kitchen counter. I pulled April close to me, my fingers touching every part of her I saw.

"Nia?" I said, asking if her roommate was home. April's roommate never left the house.

April nodded. Nia was home, but April pulled off her tank top. I whipped off my shirt, too, dropping it into the dry, empty sink.

I pulled April close, our chests a sheet of warmth between us. I rested on the feeling of blending with her, stretching myself across her. Rubbing her skin across my face. The places where our skin touched seemed to pulse.

"I've missed you," I said. "Not just since Miami. Since Cape Town."

April blinked. Cape Town was a forbidden subject between us, but I took liberties.

"Me, too," she said.

"I'm sorry about those sex stories."

"That's not your fault," April said. She didn't say that her family had seen the stories and asked questions, but I saw it in her face. She looked pained.

"It's my fault there's anything to write about."

"You were a different man then, Ten." The line sounded well rehearsed. She might have made the same defense to Professor William Forrest and Gloria Forrest back home. April had been raised with Jack and Jill and high expectations. Her father had marched with Dr. King. She was fighting her own battle while I fought mine, but she spared me the details.

"If you want some distance, I'll understand," I said.

"Don't talk crazy," she said.

"I don't mean just the stories," I said. "The case. Escobar. The risks I took."

For a moment, I saw a glint in April's eye: *Remember how I said you were trying to die?*

"I just said I'm here," she said. "You're a cop without a uniform. I got it at the funeral, Ten. You've never seen the resemblance, but you're just like him."

We stopped talking. I gently chewed April's neck, lingering on her pleasure spot. When April went limp, her breasts stood on her chest like perfect scoops of ice cream. The smell of Dad's blood tried to find me, but I hid between April's breasts.

I tugged down on her pants, a high school boy on prom night.

"Someone's . . . going to . . ." April whispered. She forgot her thought.

Despite kitchen windows and nearby neighbors, neither of us could think of a reason to care if anyone heard or saw us. We never closed the blinds. We never turned off the light.

April and I made love.

Under different circumstances, I might have spent the night at April's or invited her to spend the night with me, but the timing didn't feel right to bring her to the house or spend a night away from home. The timing was rarely right for us. Instead, I drove back alone.

I smelled coppery blood, and the blood smell didn't go away when I shook my head to clear it. I touched my upper lip, and it was moist. I was bleeding.

I couldn't remember ever having a nosebleed before, but suddenly I was rushing to find something to plug my nostril before I dripped all over my car seat and clothes. I pulled over at a BP gas station on the corner of La Cienega while I held a rumpled hand towel to my nose. The flow was steady, but it wasn't heavy. Like Chela had said, I knew how to stop bleeding.

I sighed so hard my throat hurt. Nearly a week after the tear-gas incident, I was still having discomfort, and now my first nosebleed. Would I have to add a doctor to my problems?

"Fucking asshole!" I said to Escobar. He always seemed to be with me.

On top of everything else, I hadn't been able to let the bastard go.

I kept the towel held up to my nose while I pulled out my iPhone and dialed the Miami number. I didn't hang up even after I realized later that it was after midnight Miami time.

"Hernandez." She sounded alert when she answered.

"Are you at work?"

"Hardwick?"

"I forgot the time zone," I said. "You working late?"

Detective Hernandez sighed. "No. Actually, I was at home sleeping. In bed."

I checked the card again. She had given me her cell phone number. "Sorry. You don't turn your phone off when you go to bed?"

A pause. "Can I help you, Mr. Hardwick?"

"Yes you can, Detective Hernandez," I said, matching her formal tone. "Anything yet?"

Detective Hernandez of South Beach Homicide was probably sorry she had given me her card when she hustled me out of the police station. I called her at least once every day, and so far, she was still taking my calls. We both knew she owed me. Now that the FBI was finished with me, they'd forgotten my name.

"No," she said. "*Nada.* I said you'd be the first person I call."

"Okay, sorry to wake you—"

"Mr. Hardwick, I'm not a shrink, but can I make an observation?"

"Not if you're going to tell me I need a shrink."

"No," she said. "But it's a big ocean. Strong currents. His remains might have been eaten days ago. Finding him isn't the event that's going to make sense of everything for you. You're looking for closure in the wrong place."

She wasn't telling me anything I didn't know.

"Thank you," I said. "But you'll call me if you hear anything?"

"I'll call you *first* if I hear anything."

Detective Hernandez had never told me she was sorry about the way she and her colleagues had treated me when I came to them, but she tried to show it every day. She was going out of her way to be helpful, which is a cop's greatest gift.

"Let me ask you something," I said. "One last thing."

"No call tomorrow?" She exaggerated her disappointment.

"Maybe not," I said.

"Then ask me anything."

I closed my eyes and saw Escobar's speedboat blossom into flames against the night sky.

"Do you think he's dead?" I said.

"I saw the boat. I read the report. Yeah, I absolutely think he's dead."

I'd known what her answer would be, but it felt hollow. So hollow.

"And that's you talking?" I said. "Not the spin machine?"

"I'm not spinning you. I wish we'd fish out his corpse, because the missing body just makes people crazier with the legends and theories. But I think the guy is dead, thanks to you. You should get a medal. I don't care what all those piss-bags say about you."

I almost smiled. "You embarrass me when you get all warm and mushy, Detective."

"I won't make it a habit," Hernandez said. "Do you have a girl-friend?"

"Yes." Could she sense April on me through the telephone?

"*Bueno.* A girlfriend sounds like the best hobby for you right now. Take that as a little hint from a fellow crime fighter. Having a life helps."

I thanked her, pretended she'd shown me the light, and said good-bye. Neither of us had stated the obvious. When it came to Escobar, she had been wrong. I had been right.

Before I drove home, I checked my face in the rearview mirror, dabbing my lip.

Blood is never easy to clean away.

TWENTY-FIVE

THE NEXT DAY, I was glad I'd parked around the corner and that I'd rented a car for the week. Three photographers and one video cameraman were camped out across the street from the house I was visiting in Brentwood, more paparazzi than I'd had at my curb that morning.

The story was moving in another direction.

Usually, I would stop and take a close look at anyone milling around near me, but I didn't want to be photographed at that house. I'd never expected to visit the Brentwood house again, wading through the overgrown pathway of orange trees. The lawn needed watering, dotted with fragrant, rotting fruit. The gardener was a week late. Mother's house was purposely modest on the outside, but Mother had kept her yard meticulous; she would be horrified by its condition. To her neighbors, she had been the quiet old lady down the street, and now the ruse was real.

I wasn't surprised when a uniformed male nursing assistant in his late twenties answered her door. He looked as if he spent more time in a weight room than at a nursing station.

I realized I didn't know what to call Mother. Her favorite name from Dostoevsky's *Crime and Punishment*, Katerina Marmeladova? I wasn't sure how much he knew.

"Tennyson Hardwick," I said, keeping it simple.

His face soured with recognition, although he tried to mask it. He asked me to wait in the living room. I glanced around nervously before I stepped into the house.

"Where are her dogs?" I said.

I don't mess with Mother's poodles. That might sound funny, but Mother had standard-sized poodles the size of wolves, and she trained them to kill.

"In the room with her," the nursing assistant said.

Soon after he left to announce me, I heard Mother's cackle from down the hall. I was glad to hear her sounding healthy, but I wasn't sure the laugh was a good sign. My last visit, when I'd come for help on a case, she hadn't been happy to see me. She had far less reason to be happy now. Tabloids said the district attorney's office was considering an indictment.

As I thought about police knocking on Mother's door, the side of my mouth twitched. *Damn.* I'd been careful but not careful enough. I could have watched Mother go to prison without losing sleep—past sins catch up—but I hadn't planned to be the one to send her.

And Lieutenant Nelson was going to push for indictments, trying to clean up his old mentor's business. Melanie, my lawyer, thought any case against me would be weak, hardly worth their time. But Mother was a bigger fish. Reports were surfacing from Europe. Mother had lived a long life outside the law, years before I'd met her.

"She says she can't wait to talk to you," the nursing assistant said.

"Fine," I said. "But first, her dogs go outside."

"She won't like that," he said. "She loves those dogs."

"No dogs."

This time, Mother didn't receive the news well. She cursed in Serbian until she was wheezing. But a moment later, the nurse came back with the two huge identical white poodles on tight leashes. Both dogs were trussed in enough pink ribbons to march in a parade, but that was just Mother's inside joke. You had to judge Dunja and Dragona by their flashing eyes. One of the dogs growled as they walked closer to me.

"Thanks a lot," the nursing assistant said, gesturing to the hall while he walked the dogs to the door. "Now you put her in a pissy mood."

Mother was living in her bedroom now. She'd knocked out a wall to double the size of the master suite. Her home was much better kept than her yard. She might be aging, but she was still living elegantly. For now.

I saw her flaming red hair before I saw her face in the chair. Beneath her favorite wig, Mother's cheeks had shrunken the way Dad's had. Her face was pale. Mother was sick, not just older. She was sitting upright in her plush wingback chair, within two easy steps of her bed.

I wasn't expecting the oxygen tubes in her nose, tied to a tank beside her chair. But then again, she'd been smoking since she was twelve, she always said.

The look on her face reminded me that I should have had her patted down for weapons. She raised her finger to jab the air, angry. "Were you followed?"

"I took precautions."

"Like you took precautions with your father?"

Mother drew first blood.

"Next subject," I said.

She indicated her bedside table, which was stacked with more than two dozen tabloids and magazines. "I've been reading about you," she said. "You must be pleased. You always liked special attention."

"I haven't talked to a reporter or to the district attorney," I said. "My only statements have been through my lawyer. I've only talked about Escobar."

Mother's face darkened with a sour laugh. "I don't know what you're talking about," she recited. She squinted her eyes, and I knew she was paranoid that her house might be bugged. She also didn't believe me.

"I never wanted this for you," I said.

That terrible laugh again. "Then tell me why, at the age of eighty-three, I have attorneys on retainer on two continents. Did you plan to see me die in prison from your lies?"

We both knew I didn't have to lie. Mother was rehearsing her testimony.

"It's not coming from me," I said. "Believe it or don't."

Mother was trembling, maybe from anger, maybe from something else.

"If my lawyers finds out differently, I will see you rot in hell," Mother said. She said it like a woman with the confidence that she could have a man killed.

"Thought you didn't believe in hell."

"I live in hell now," she said. "So now I believe."

I noticed a neat row of prescription bottles on her table, but I didn't ask what else she was fighting. "It's not me. I've never had any bad wishes against you," I said. "That's the first thing I came to say."

"Go," Mother said. "Leave my house."

"She wants to see you. That's the second thing."

Mother's sagging jowls trembled. "I don't believe you," she said, blinking.

"She's right outside, in the car. She's waiting for me to come back and say you want to see her. She's cool with it if you don't."

"There is no length you won't go to?" Mother said. "The devil himself must have your beautiful face. You have no more conscience than to come to an old woman's house to try to trick her? To entrap her? And they say I'm the terrible one. All these lies."

She might be paranoid for good reason, but she was wasting her routine on me. "If you say you want to see her, you better be nice. Shit on me all you want, but not on her."

"*I* should be nice?" Mother said. "Four years pass without a word, and I am not nice?"

"Promise me, or I'll tell her you said no thanks. She'll live. She's tough." I almost said, *Thanks to you.*

Mother's lips curled, but she thought better against whatever she wanted to say. "Yes," she said. "Send her in. But only her. You, I never want to see again. And if this is all a lie, I will make a special example of you. I am owed many favors. Don't think I make idle threats."

"It's not like that, Mother," I said.

"Always the self-righteous one," Mother said. "So now I don't have only the cancer to worry about—now it is lawyers and extradition hearings and money, money, money. All because Tennyson Hardwick always needs his head patted and scratched."

"A killer is dead."

"Yes, and damn the cost," she said, voice trembling with the weight of our friendship. Once upon a time, Mother and I spent many hours laughing together. I'd made more than half a million dollars working for her; she would have anointed me as a business partner, if I'd agreed. "Send her in, Tennyson. I'm wasting air when I talk to you. My oxygen is expensive."

"Hope you feel better, Mother. Sorry about your cancer and your troubles."

"At least I'll be dead before the bastards can send me to prison."

"You've always got an angle, darlin'."

The aged madam chortled, forever a gangster. "Damn right I do. *Pozdrav*, Tennyson."

Serbian for *good-bye*. It could also mean *hello*, but not this time. "*Pozdrav*, Mother."

I leaned over and kissed her forehead. Her skin felt as thin as tissue. Just like Dad's.

My last visit went better than I thought, but I didn't like eyes watching me as I walked back to my rental car. I put on my sunglasses and lowered my head. I never looked back.

It was so strange to be back on her old street again, sitting at the curb beneath the jacaranda trees. Did Molly still live around the corner, three houses down? Chela and Molly used to skate up and down the street, the first time since Minnesota that Chela had a friend with a mother and father and brother without a story involving the police. Mother lectured Chela so often about the consequences of saying the wrong thing that Molly's parents thought Chela didn't speak English for a year. But this was the street where she'd been starting to feel like a normal kid on TV. She took out the garbage and got the mail and had her own room. She fed the dogs and did chores.

Mother's house looked almost the same, except that the trees were taller and the grass needed cutting. Even the beige paint color was the same. The mailbox was wooden, painted to look like a standard poodle, slightly more faded. Chela wondered how Dunja and Dragona were doing. She'd brought their favorite rawhide treats.

Finally, Ten got back. He knocked on the car window and beckoned her outside.

"She's sick, Chela," Ten told her in Mother's doorway, but she heard *You're sick, Chela.* Stereo effect. He spoke in a low voice so the man in white standing nearby wouldn't overhear. A male nurse, Chela noted. As if Mother would have any other kind.

"What's wrong with her?"

"She has cancer. I don't know what kind or what stage. She looks much older."

Had she expected to find Mother jogging around the block? Chela had told Mother she would get cancer if she didn't stop smoking three packs a day of that unfiltered European shit. But none of that made her feel better. Chela's visit to Mother was ruined already.

"If you can't handle it, I can make up an excuse," Ten said.

Chela shot him a look. Ten was the one who'd taken her away and told her not to call. "Thanks, you've already done plenty."

Ten was wearing his robot face, or more like Mr. Spock. Half the time, he didn't seem to hear a word she said. "I'll be waiting in the living room."

"You don't need to wait."

"I'm here. Might as well." He sounded like the Captain.

After Raphael, Ten might be afraid she'd never come out of Mother's house. After Raphael, she was still shocked he'd agreed to bring her.

But seeing Bernard had helped her realize how stupid it was to be afraid. She'd wanted to talk to Mother since the beginning, but Ten had never wanted to hear it. To him, Mother had amazing superpowers of mind control, so he'd put up an electric fence between them. Chela had expected him to try to talk her out of a visit, but he'd said he would come along. Maybe he'd needed to see her, too.

Chela was so surprised by the sight of Mother shrunken in an enormous chair that at first she didn't notice how much bigger the room was. Mother had knocked down the wall between their rooms and made them both her suite. Chela wondered how long Mother had waited for her.

Chela leaned over Mother's chair and hugged her. When Chela tried to stand up straight, Mother held on.

"You were always a beauty. But now!" Mother's eyes twinkled as she looked her up and down. "Chela, you are so lovely. I always knew you would be tall." When Chela smiled, Mother laid a dry, warm hand across her cheek. "So, so lovely. And school?"

"Graduated from high school with a B-plus average," Chela said. "Not bad for a lazy ass."

"You would never wake up for school. Always an excuse."

Ten's like a jail guard, Chela almost said, but jokes about Ten didn't feel right. He'd made her go to school. In contrast, Mother had taught her there was more to life than books. She wasn't sure either of them had been wrong.

"He wants to adopt me." Chela hadn't planned to tell Mother. "Legally."

Mother's face puckered. "He loves lawyers too much."

"He wanted to do it before I was eighteen, but it didn't work out. After that, I didn't see the point. I still don't."

"What was the problem before? Records?"

"My birth mother wouldn't give her consent. Bitch."

"Your . . . ?" Mother was surprised, leaning closer. She held her fingers to the tubes in her nose, keeping them in place. "Your mother was gone."

"He found her."

"How?"

"He's a detective. That's what he does."

Mother's face turned paler. "A police detective?"

Chela made a face. "Ten?" she said. "No way. His dad was a cop, but he was retired. Captain Hardwick."

Chela didn't realize that she'd said the wrong thing until it was too late. Mother blinked, her eyes suddenly as intense as a lizard's. "What did you say to Captain Hardwick, Chela?"

Chela had forgotten how paranoid Mother was and how much she had done. How could she think Chela would tell the Captain their secret?

"I never talked about you," Chela said. "He was retired, anyway."

Mother gave her a long gaze, trying to decide what she thought.

Chela's throat suddenly felt hot. She took a seat on Mother's ottoman. "He died."

"Yes, so I have been reading," Mother said. She picked up a magazine, waving it.

"That's not Ten's fault," Chela said. "I dragged him into it. I ran into a friend . . ."

Mother made a sound. She didn't want Chela to say the rest out loud. "It's done," she said. "We all lose everyone. Everything. We survive." She paused, a thin, humorless smile creasing her lips. "Until we don't."

Mother never had been the sentimental type. Mother had been younger than Chela when she lost her parents, and she had survived a hell of a lot.

Mother drew in a long breath through her nose. "My medicine makes me tired," she said.

"I don't have to stay."

"A while longer," Mother said. "I'll tell you when to go."

They were both quiet for a time. Chela heard Dunja and Dragona barking in the backyard. Mother's room smelled like talcum powder and urine. Chela tried not to notice the bedside potty hidden under her silk bathrobe. Nana Bessie had used a toilet just like it; Chela had emptied it, sometimes twice a day, sometimes more.

"If by accident you live too long, keep your mind sharp," Mother said. "Look at me—all the lies being told. It will take many months, maybe years, for me to be extradited, indicted, arraigned, so . . ." Mother shrugged, catching her breath. "I pay no attention. Let my lawyers worry. Make sure you have money at the end."

"Definitely," Chela said. Mother had opened Chela's first bank account with her, given her an ATM card when she was fourteen. Mother had changed her life. But so had Ten.

"Always have your own money no one but you can touch," Mother went on. "With money, you are ready for every circumstance."

"I remember," Chela said. She had six hundred dollars in cash in a box under her bed that Ten had no clue about, enough to buy a plane ticket anywhere. Old habit.

"What will you do now?" Mother said. "For money?"

"Maybe go to college. I'm not sure."

"Only go to a college with rich men," Mother said.

"I have a boyfriend."

"Everyone can fall in love," Mother said dismissively. "A beautiful woman should never go poor." Mother didn't ask questions about Bernard, and Chela didn't offer more. Bernard wasn't the kind of man Mother had in mind for her.

"I do not know everything," Mother said. "But I know these things." She sounded tired suddenly. For a moment, she sat in silence. "What about him?" Mother said. "Tennyson. Will you stay?"

"A while, I guess," Chela said. "Until I figure out what's next."

"He . . . has been a father to you?" The look in her eye made Chela wonder if Mother thought she was sleeping with Ten.

With good reason, probably. When Ten first brought her to his house, Chela had thought she could marry him one day—or at least get him in bed—but it was best to forget that.

"Yeah, he acts like a dad."

Chela didn't say, *Too bad for me*, as she would have once, but Mother seemed to know her thought. Mother clicked her teeth. "A nice face, that's all," she said. "He is too old for you, an old schoolgirl crush. If you must get a man, get a young man. But stand on your own."

Chela smiled. Mother's advice wasn't always perfect, but sometimes it was. And Chela could say anything to her. She'd missed that.

"I don't need anyone to adopt me," Chela said.

"Let him sign papers, if he wants," Mother said, shrugging. "What does it hurt?"

Chela had never expected to hear those words from Mother.

Patrice Sheryl McLawhorn, wherever she was, could go straight to whatever pit of hell was reserved for losers like her. Chela wished she hadn't agreed to let Ten ask her anything. Chela didn't need that woman to get permission; she had it from Mother now.

"It has been wonderful to see you," Mother said. "But stay away now. All right?" She used a voice like she might have used with a small puppy, artificially cheery, an octave higher.

Mother was sending her away. Chela felt a sting, but she could add it to her things to cry about later. The depression phase would be a monster.

Chela grabbed Mother's cool, nearly weightless hands the way she had Nana Bessie's.

"Thank you, Mother," Chela said. For four years, she had sifted through her memories, wondering if she'd ever spoken the simple words. "I would have died out there without you. Thank you for saving my life."

The rest was a different conversation. The rest didn't seem as important.

For the first time in Chela's memory, tears welled at the corners of Mother's eyes.

TWENTY-SIX

I WOKE UP in April's bed, although I had yet to invite her to spend the night in mine. I'd floated the idea at dinner the night before, and Chela and Marcela had both given me looks. Two weeks after my father was shot to death, they still wanted the house to themselves.

So I opened my eyes to mismatched furniture, a mound of clothes balanced on an exercise bicycle, and a collection of reporter's notebooks in need of either a file cabinet or a trash can. Her room looked like a college dorm. April's futon mattress felt lumpy, and she didn't know anything about bed sheets with a high thread count. What was I doing there?

Then I rolled over and found April sleeping nude beside me, and it all made sense.

My fingertip traced the lines across her back, following her shoulder blade to her spine. April's brown skin transfixed me, an ocean worthy of contemplation. I nestled my body behind hers and followed my fingertip's path with soft brushes from my lips. How did she always taste so sweet? Was it her skin itself?

April stirred with a quiet, throaty chuckle, pressing closer to me. Her curves were a perfect fit against my bare pelvis, firm and soft. I kissed the back of her neck and gently flicked my tongue against her earlobe. April made the humming sound I'd missed so much, the one that meant *Yes*. She reached behind her to pull my head closer, until our cheeks pressed together.

"I love you," I said.

"I love you, too, baby."

Her whisper swept through me like an electrical current, warming my body with a gently rising flame. Only April's words could stroke me like hands, igniting the parts of me no one else could touch. How had I lived apart from her so long?

Grief bubbled inside the pleasure; either bad memories or a premonition or both. Sadness cinched my arm around her more tightly as I cradled her warm, petite waist. I touched every part of her I could claim, vowing I would never let her go.

When April turned to face me, my body rejoiced so much that my toes curled. We held each other's scalps so tightly while we kissed that our faces had no beginning and no end. Our tongues spoke a secret language. Her hand roamed between my legs, sure and practiced, cradling me like treasure.

We both wanted to taste each other at once, our bodies sliding into place. April felt nearly weightless on top of me. We licked each other in concert. When her mouth swallowed me, I fell away from myself, my lips apart, my eyes closed. The pleasure was acute, as sharp as pain. When my mind returned to my body, I flipped over until April was beneath me, and my mouth was eager to return the sensation.

April's fingers clawed for her sheet, and she stiffened, trying to muffle her first orgasm.

We were both drenched in perspiration and each other's fluids when I nudged myself between her taut thighs and found her wet, welcoming embrace. April was as snug as a virgin. Our bodies joined slowly, her natural tightness parting for my size bit by bit with my careful probes. Every quarter of an inch filled us both, until our bodies were pressed tight. We rocked together, hissing and moaning our improvised song. When we couldn't keep our song's rhythm syrup-slow, we thrashed and bucked until I forgot my own name.

Making love was still a novelty to me. Afterward, gasping, I could only stare at the ceiling with wonder. I must have dozed off, because April's touch woke me.

"Baby?" April said, fingertips propping my chin. "Let me see your face."

"Hmmm?" I said, still fumbling for thoughts and speech.

"Your eyes look red all the time. Do you think that's from the tear gas?"

Back to reality. My eyes were red because they hurt like hell. I had started wearing my dark glasses indoors because light hurt my eyes. I also wasn't sleeping well, although I was always tired. My eyes could have been red from fatigue. I had my pick of ailments. I had lost ten pounds since Dad died. The smell of food often made me feel sick, and my appetite was zero. All of that was in my eyes, too.

"As long as I can see, they're still working," I said.

"Ten, you should make two appointments: an eye doctor and a therapist. For you and Chela. Maybe Marcela, too. You need to face this."

I rolled back to face the opposite wall, a pillow over my face. I was surprised at how angry I felt. I missed our old rules, suddenly. Conversation felt like a betrayal.

April seemed to take my silence as careful thought. "What happened was a big thing," April said quietly. "This is why police departments have therapists. Your father was murdered practically in front of you. I went to therapy, and there was nothing in my life like that."

"You?" I said. April's life had been close to idyllic, except for me. "When?"

"When I first got back from Cape Town." She sighed. "I was depressed."

We didn't talk about our last breakup often. A year before, I had cut my visit with her at a Stellenbosch bed-and-breakfast short after she told me we had to be friends. I might never have called Sofia Maitlin for the job if my relationship with April had turned a different way.

"You were sad," I said. "I was, too. That's natural, April."

"Not sad—something else," April said. "A feeling that wouldn't let me go, following me everywhere I went, making me doubt everything about myself. I never wanted to get out of bed, but I couldn't sleep. I ate junk food all day. I needed a therapist. I needed to talk it out."

"I'm sorry you went through that," I said, "but no therapist is going to relate to this."

"I already found one who would," she said, smiling. Her dimple melted my irritation away. *Damn*, April was cute. "He works out of Pasadena. Very well respected. He treats drug addiction, sex addiction, PTSD. He does more than you need. He's been on *Oprah*. My coworker whose brother was injured in Afghanistan told me about him."

Drug addiction, sex addiction, PTSD. If danger was a drug, he was tailor-made for me.

"How would that help Chela?" I said.

"He does family and individual counseling. You see him separately, sometimes you see him together. Therapy helped me—I know it can help you. It won't change what happened, or bring your dad back, but it helps make sense of things."

If therapy was how she'd gotten over me, she might need another dose, I thought. But I decided it was best not to say it.

"What did it help you make sense of?" I said.

"Remember that time we went to Little Ethiopia and I got that cane for your dad? You were looking for Sofia Maitlin's kid, just breezing through, working your case. But I couldn't stop thinking about you." For a brief moment, April had shadowed me while I interviewed a potential suspect in the Maitlin kidnapping. But I hadn't had room for April then.

"I had a phone."

"You didn't want to be friends," April said.

"It was hard for me to be around you, too."

The air was getting thick. Had we imagined we'd both just said *I love you?*

"Who's Marsha?" April said finally.

I closed my eyes. Shit. I didn't want to talk about Marsha.

"Are you in love with her?" April said.

"Hell, no," I said. I'd once thought Marsha reminded me of April, but that part of her was only an act. Marsha wasn't even her real name. Might as well call her Mata Hari.

"Chela mentioned her," April said. "Said she came to breakfast at your house that time?"

April's voice was neutral, but breakfast was a special occasion to her. I'd kept her and Chela at such a distance that it had always been a treat for April to eat breakfast at our table. Marsha had crashed my family breakfast only once, but it wasn't worth explaining.

"We were working the Maitlin case," I said. "I can't tell you much more."

April looked surprised. "Why not? We're just talking. You know I don't wear my reporter hat in bed. And I'm just a laid-off reporter now, anyway."

"You're starting that blog."

April's blog, "L.A. Tymes," was a mixture of police, political, and entertainment stories and had won hundreds of followers in a few days. April had impeccable inside information, whether or not she worked for the mainstream media.

"I'm not asking for my blog, Ten. And I'm not asking if you were sleeping together. We've both been dating. That's not my question."

I hadn't asked about men in her life and didn't want to. We were different that way.

"Is she a cop?" April went on.

"Something like that," Ten said. "April, I hate the way I sound right now, but I can't talk about Marsha. It has nothing to do with dating." I lowered my voice and spoke into her ear, as paranoid as Mother. The one most likely to keep me under surveillance was Marsha herself. "We worked together on the Maitlin case, and that's all I can say."

Covert ops? April mouthed at me. I stared at April, dumbfounded.

"Chela told me," she said. "And she said Marsha is really bad news in your life."

I had told Chela too much about what happened in Hong Kong, and she had put together some of the pieces on her own. Chela had unleashed April on Marsha.

"She was," I said. "But I couldn't have done the Maitlin case without her."

"And you did others."

I held up a single finger: *one.* Memories of Hong Kong were probably in my eyes, too.

"It's over?" April said.

"I don't want to talk to her, and she isn't calling. She disappears for a living."

"And then reappears," April said. What had Chela told her? April had drawn a line about what she could accept from me, and Marsha was on the other side of it. She wanted me to understand that right away.

"I don't want anything to do with her, and I'm not afraid to tell her. We're done."

"Will you call the therapist?" April said.

"Give me the number," I said. "I'll call today."

I wanted to be the man April wanted me to be. I didn't like the idea of telling a stranger my troubles, but I needed a therapist for Chela. I'd sent the adoption papers she signed to Melanie's office to examine, but Chela needed more than I could give her. Under the circumstances, the adoption felt anticlimactic.

"What about a doctor?" April said, nearly a whisper. "Please?"

That time, I shrugged and kissed her lips. My eyes felt as if they were scratched raw from the tear gas. It wasn't as bad as it had been at first, but it was a long way from better. "I'll see how I feel today. Then maybe tomorrow."

"You know I'm only bugging you because I love you, right?"

I smiled. "Always. I love you, too, April."

Once I started saying the words, I couldn't stop.

TWENTY-SEVEN

THE FIRST LETTER was waiting in my home mailbox that night, in a bright white envelope unmarked except for my name. Inside, a single sheet, a single line, three typewritten words.

Night-night, Mommy.

The note made the back of my neck flare. Whatever it was, it wasn't good news.

I could think of three or four possible sources of an anonymous note in my mailbox, maybe more: Marsha had first reached me through anonymous emails, and April might have conjured Marsha by calling her name. Maybe I'd been caught on tape somewhere, and Marsha wanted me to know. It was best not to try to guess Marsha's motives. She'd left a couple of *call me* messages since Dad's death, but I wasn't going to talk to Marsha. Period.

But Marsha was only the first possibility. It could be a random nut, a childish taunt from Lieutenant Nelson, even Chela's birth mother suddenly at our doorstep because she'd heard news of the impending adoption. That was my life. An anonymous note could have been from anyone.

But the flaring on the back of my neck—both hot and cold and stinging enough to make me wince—had nothing to do with Marsha, Nelson or Chela's ghost of a mother.

I looked up at the full moon, which seemed only slightly hazy to my tired eyes. I don't know what made me look up, but I could see Escobar's boat explode against the backdrop of the night sky. I remembered the falling debris, the shower of sparks. A boating accident was the perfect way to fake your death. Between the fire and the water, it was plausible for the police not to find a trace. What if Escobar had planned one last piece of movie magic?

If Escobar had faked his death, he would come after me. And he would put a bullshit note in my mailbox that said *Night-night, Mommy* just because it appealed to the twisted thing he called his mind. He would want me to know he was here.

I went into the house and fired up my computer to research security companies to better safeguard my home. I had an alarm, but no surveillance cameras covered my front door and driveway. Or my mailbox. What the hell had I been thinking?

I hadn't signed on to my computer in days. I had a string of emails from Len, my agent, but I didn't even read the subject lines. Instead, I went to Google to research cameras like the ones at Club Phoenixx. I didn't care about the cost. Maybe Mother's paranoia was contagious, or maybe it was clairvoyance.

I'd wasted too much time stumbling in a stupor, I realized. It didn't matter what Detective Hernandez said or what the FBI didn't say.

I didn't know the meaning of *Night-night, Mommy* then, although it would soon be painfully obvious. If I hadn't been so tired, I might have known on sight.

But the note in my mailbox only reminded me that I had no time to rest.

I stopped in mid-step when I saw Marcela at the dining-room table sorting through documents she'd pulled out of the oak filing cabinet my father had kept since I was a kid. One folder was marked *Eva,* my mother's name, unopened and cast to the side. I wanted to tell Marcela to take her hands off my daddy's stuff, just like I was eight years old again.

"What are you doing?" I said.

She looked up at me above her reading glasses. With her hair swept across her forehead and her face sagging with sadness, she had aged since Dad died. "You said I could find some of his articles."

Dad had kept careful records, cutting out every newspaper and magazine story that mentioned his name. Marcela was preparing for her interview. She thought the *Star* wanted to write Dad's biography.

"I would appreciate it," I said slowly, "if you wouldn't say anything about me."

"You're his son, Tennyson. Your name will come up."

"Do you mind if I ask what you plan to say?"

"You'll have to trust me," Marcela said.

I leaned on the doorframe for support, running my palm across my hair. Anger with nowhere to go made me tired. "So you're not trying to air out feelings about what happened. Feelings toward me."

Marcela's eyes flashed. "This interview isn't about you—it's about Richard. And his legacy. And his message. If you're so worried about my feelings, why don't you ask me how I feel? Don't hide behind my interview."

I heard the *pop* of gunfire. Smelled the tear gas. And blood, of course.

"All right," I said. "Tell me."

"You made a terrible mistake," she said. "Involving him. It was too much."

I couldn't argue with her. My head hung as if my neck had lost its strength.

We were quiet with that for a moment.

"I'm sorry." I said the only thing to say.

"I know you are," she said. "I'm sorry, too. I wanted more time with him."

I sighed. "Marcela, the problem is, if you say these things during your interview, they'll twist it around. They're not your friends. When they pay that kind of money, they're looking for something juicy."

"This isn't the interview," Marcela said. "And he would want me to do it."

I raised my eyebrow. "Dad? He liked making the papers, not the tabloids."

"He would have wanted me to do anything that made me feel . . ." She stopped, choosing her words. "Like I have something to look forward to. Not happy, but . . . less sad. Something exciting. Something different. I can take a cruise to the Mediterranean with that money."

"I have money," I said. "Dad has—" Dad had a savings account, and Marcela was his wife. I couldn't access the account, but he'd added her name months ago because they ran so many errands together. I'd never expected to get rich after Dad died, but unless he'd left a will, I might only get the hole in my life.

"I want to use my own money," Marcela said. "I don't want anyone to say I married him for the wrong reasons."

I pursed my lips. Marcela knew how long it had taken me to warm up to the idea of her.

"You're his wife," I said. "What's his is yours."

Marcela nodded. "I know."

"Did he leave a will?" I said.

"I don't think so," Marcela said. "The will was the one thing he wouldn't plan. He never wanted to talk about it. I asked him many times, but he was superstitious."

I had never encouraged Dad to write a will, which suddenly seemed absurd. Now Marcela could close out Dad's bank account, collect his checks, and move on. I had no legal control over Dad's estate, not even to try to set something aside for Chela.

Marcela and I might argue over the tiniest possessions, such as who would keep his antique rolltop desk, which he'd brought to my house when he moved in, salvaged from our old house, a symbol of my childhood. No wonder I'd had doubts about the wedding— if Marcela could have planned what happened, I would have felt jacked.

"We're family now, Tennyson," Marcela said gently. "We'll work out how to honor each other. But I want to pay for my own cruise, so I'm doing this interview. You don't want to talk about him to people outside, but I do. We each have a choice."

Dad might have said the same thing.

"Did you see anybody hanging around the house today?" I changed the subject.

Marcela shook her head. "No. Like who?"

"Like Gustavo Escobar."

Marcela stood up, took a step toward me. "Why would you say that? He's dead."

"Until his body shows up . . ." I shook my head.

"The police and the FBI investigated. They said he could not have survived the explosion."

"Yeah, well, I'm putting up cameras around the whole perimeter, as far as the street."

"What perimeter?"

"The house. The windows. The doors. Everything, Marcela."

Marcela studied me with concern in her brow. "Tennyson," Marcela said, "I'm worried about you—as a nurse, not just as your stepmother." She had never called herself my stepmother. I didn't mind the sound of it.

I'd avoided showing Marcela the *Night-night, Mommy* note because I didn't want to worry her needlessly. But the absence of the note made me sound like a nut. Maybe I was a nut.

"You don't need to worry about me," I said.

"Richard made me promise I'd take care of you," she said. "You're stuck with me now."

"Same here," I said.

"You're *mi familia*, Tennyson," Marcela said, pinching my cheek. "That's what I'm planning to say about you during the interview. Then I'll say how lucky I was to have known your father even for a short time. Agreed?"

I couldn't disapprove of that. I hugged Marcela, and for the first time in two weeks, the contact didn't feel forced or obligatory.

I set up an appointment with the security company and stored my anonymous note in a plastic baggie I kept in my bedroom drawer. Later, I invited April over to watch *Cadillac Records* on DVD. Chela finally agreed to invite Bernard. That night, April and I held hands on one end of the room, Chela held Bernard's on the other. I popped popcorn. The grown folks went through two six-packs of Coronas and stayed up late. We sang badly to the movie's blues and rock and roll. Once in a while, Chela laughed, and Marcela smiled.

Not a single one of us was related by blood.

Familia.

TWENTY-EIGHT

ANTONIJA OBRADOVIC, RAISED as Toni, self-named Louisa, Sara, Katerina, and other names that suited her—but in recent years mostly known as Mother—lifted her head from her pillow. Her bedroom television was at a low volume to keep her company, but she'd heard a sound that wasn't from the poker championship playing on ESPN.

It sounded like a baby's cry.

Mother had borne only one child, always sickly, so she had learned the sound well in the girl's short five months of life. She still heard the plaintive, helpless cry at the edge of sleep decades later, but this sound had been louder, sharper.

The whimper came again. Not a child and not a dream—it was Dragona! Mother knew her dogs, despite the way pain distorted Dragona's voice. What was wrong with her? Why had the dogs left her bedside? She'd heard them jump from the bed perhaps an hour before, but she'd thought they were only restless. Dragona sounded as if she was outside her door.

Mother whistled loudly, the whistle that usually brought her lovelies rushing to her side. She had been stern before she was kind, and her dogs were trained well. Mother prided herself on being an expert trainer of both dogs and people.

But neither dog came right away. When the whimpering was twinned—and Mother was sure Dunja was crying out, too—she felt alarm. Her dogs never cried. Why should they? Since her illness, she'd had the door installed for them in the kitchen so they could come and go without her. And the pain in their whimpers was palpable, mirroring the pain in her own cracked bones where her cancer was eating her.

"Dunja! Dragona!" she called sharply, and the dogs came toward her in the dark, moving slowly. Mother reached over to turn on her lamp at her bedside, but it only clicked. Was the bulb burned out again? She'd told those stupid boys that she needed her lamp working at all times, since it was the only one she could reach. The hallway light was out, too, so the only light in her room was the pale blue glow of her television.

Dragona's cold nose touched her wrist as the dog pushed her muzzle toward her. Dragona whimpered again, a sound to break a mother's heart. Mother rubbed the soft ball of fur at the top of the dog's head. She heard Dunja not far behind, but he didn't join his sister beside her. She heard his collar as he flopped to the floor.

"What's wrong, my sweet?" she said in Serbian. "What's happened?"

Then it came to her. Both of the dogs had been poisoned!

Mother forgot Dragona and reached under her pillow for her favorite .22 she had brought with her from Kosovo after she helped her husband, Bogdan, flee to Subotica during the Kosovo war. She had killed half a dozen men in her lifetime; her first had been the German soldier who tried to rape her during World War II, when killing still made her cry.

But her little gun was gone. How could that be?

No light. Her dogs poisoned. No gun.

Mother felt a stab of fear but also an excitement that had been absent for too long. This was something new. Unexpected.

A sound came from the hallway, a man's shoe scraping across her tile.

"Who's there?" she called to her doorway. "Who dares enter my house?"

She had collected many enemies. With all of the publicity and photos of her circulating because of that silly Tennyson, her visitor might be from Kosovo, Moscow, New York, Las Vegas, or someone in Los Angeles who felt cheated or wronged. Some of the girls who had worked for her had been too stupid to count their money properly and perhaps held grudges. Mother didn't know why someone hid in the shadows of her home, but she knew what it meant.

Where was that gun? She reached farther behind her pillow, surprised that her heart could still dance with such panic.

Her hand brushed something hard, but then a telltale *clank* told her that she'd knocked the gun behind her headboard to the floor. Her coordination was no longer reliable. Mother let out a sour laugh. Yes, this had always been her quarrel with God since the day the Germans killed her parents—God Almighty held a grudge against her and had never played fair for a day.

A man's voice said something beyond her doorway, so softly that she couldn't make out the hurried words, a kind of strange recitation. She could barely hear the voice over her dogs' unified suffering.

The man mumbled again.

"What?" Mother called.

That voice! Something about that voice . . .

Mother's heart withered in her frantic chest, more grief than fear. Could it be . . . ? Her medications played tricks on her ears, but she thought she heard him. Why was he back? How had she wronged him? Mother was not easily fooled, but he had fooled her.

Perhaps he had fooled everyone.

TWENTY-NINE

MY CELL PHONE rang at five in the morning. I'd gotten a new phone and number, so only a handful of people had it. The caller ID identified the caller as LAPD.

My heart jumped. Maybe Escobar's body had been found. Maybe another prostitute had been murdered. I was so anxious I nearly dropped the phone.

"This is Tennyson," I said.

"It's Nelson."

Nelson wouldn't call me so early about anything small. "What is it, Nelson? Escobar?"

April sat up beside me.

A long pause. I'd caught Nelson off guard. "What about Escobar?"

"If it's not Escobar, why are you calling me this early?"

"I need you to get to RHD," Nelson said. RHD was the department's Robbery-Homicide Division. "I need you here in one hour, by 6:00 A.M. If you're not here, I'll send a team to bring you in and get a search warrant, just like old times."

April turned on the lamp, which made me wince from the

light. She stared at me with concern, and I could only shrug. Four years ago, Nelson had torn up my house trying to build a case against me after a friend was murdered. The memory still pissed me off.

"What's going on?"

"I'm calling you as a courtesy," Nelson said. "The alternative is you get pulled out of your house in front of the cameras. Merry Christmas, you stupid SOB. I'm doing you a favor."

"At least tell me what it's about."

"Antonija Obradovic," Nelson said, pronouncing the name slowly. And badly.

"Who the hell is that?"

"Mother."

I closed my eyes. *Shit.* April put a concerned hand on my shoulder.

"Man, come on," I said. "If you have a case, why do you need me?"

Nelson didn't answer me.

"This is bullshit, Nelson. She's eighty-three. She has cancer. Why you wanna try to strong-arm me to testify against a sick old lady?"

"You don't need to testify against her," Nelson said. "She's dead."

I heard him, but my next word was a reflex. "What?"

Nelson's voice wound away in a long tunnel. "Six A.M. sharp, Hardwick," Nelson said. "Don't make me sorry I did it the polite way. I'm only doing it for Preach."

As my mind crept to wakefulness, I felt more nerves than grief. How had Mother died? I wouldn't be invited to RHD if Mother had succumbed to her cancer. I was tangled in it.

"What happened? I just saw her—"

"We know," Nelson said. "You argued with her, an eyewitness said. Take a shower, get dressed, and bring your ass to RHD. You'll be here a while."

"This is harassment, Nelson. Why would I kill Mother?"

"You tell me," Nelson said, and hung up.

I hadn't told April that I'd gone with Chela to see our old madam. I never planned to keep it from her, but I hadn't found the right moment to tell the story. As April walked with me up the steps to the Robbery-Homicide Division, I knew I'd put it off too long. She'd insisted on coming to the police station with me, but she was mad enough to avoid my eyes. Maybe she wanted to judge my new chaos up close before she cut me loose again. I was sad that Mother was dead, but April was a bigger worry.

"This is Nelson's vendetta," I told her. "There's no way he has evidence against me."

"Maybe you should have brought your lawyer, Tennyson."

"This is a dance he likes to do with me every couple of years. I'm not worried."

That's how simple I thought it was.

On April's advice, I had shaved for the first time in three days and found a suit to wear. I didn't look as if I'd been asleep the hour before, much less as if I'd spent my night killing anyone.

When Nelson met me in the hall, he gave April a scathing look, wondering why she didn't know better. April's father had been Nelson's college mentor at Florida A&M, I remembered, and he had tried to warn April away from me before. Small world.

"I'll be right here, baby," April said, and kissed me for the department to see.

"Jesus, leave that girl alone," Nelson said to me as he walked me down the hall. He didn't pull on me, but he walked closer than I liked.

Three detectives waited in the gray interrogation room. When the door closed behind Nelson and me, I felt as if I was in jail already.

"I have to Mirandize," Nelson said before I'd taken my seat. Handcuffs *clanked*.

"What?" I said. My thoughts crawled.

"You have the right to remain silent," Nelson began in a drone, and he recited my Miranda rights in a puff of breath. "Do you understand these rights?"

"I'm under arrest?" I said.

When Nelson grabbed my arm, I wanted to snatch it away, but I could only go limp. Four detectives were ready to subdue me. Cold metal was clamped around my wrist. Nelson sat me roughly in the chair and chained the handcuffs to the center ring under the tabletop.

"This is beneath you," I told Nelson.

"Shut your fucking mouth," said a burly detective, pushing his thick, square-jawed face in front of mine. Like every Bad Cop I'd ever met, he looked as if he wanted ten minutes alone with me. "What were you doing at Antonija Obradovic's house?"

None of the reasons I'd gone to Mother's house was any of their business.

"Are your ears working, Tennyson?" Nelson said.

"Just tell me what happened," I said to Nelson. "Why are you coming at me like this?"

"Answer my goddamned question," Bad Cop said.

Someone slid an eight-by-ten photo toward me, and I glanced down.

Mother's bedroom in full color. Mother was nude, a sack of bones bent face-first over a portable toilet near her bed. I flinched away from the photo. My stomach hurt suddenly. I felt sick. I tugged at my handcuffs, ready to go home. The photo reminded me that I had just talked to Mother and kissed her forehead. Her skin was still warm to me.

"God," I said.

"Back to my question," Bad Cop said.

"Holy God." Someone had murdered Mother savagely. I had assumed her killing had been execution-style, antiseptic, the way she herself might have done it. An old debt she owed someone. This was different. Worse.

"You do remember seeing her?" Nelson said. "Arguing with her?"

"I wasn't arguing," I said. "She was yelling at me. She blamed me for dragging her name into the press."

"And then you killed her . . . why?" Bad Cop said. "What were you protecting?"

"Did she threaten you?" A soft-spoken detective addressed me for the first time.

A second photo appeared beside the first; the two dogs were dead, too, splayed across Mother's carpeted bedroom floor, practically side-by-side.

"Our witness," Nelson said, "says you told him you hated Mother's dogs."

"Why'd you do her, Tennyson?" Bad Cop said. "And the dogs? Why all the anger?"

I looked away from the dead dogs. I had to remind myself I wasn't having a nightmare.

Nelson came closer to me. "Something to do with Chela?"

"Your little teenage girlfriend?" Bad Cop said. "We can haul her sweet little ass in here, too. Sit her down in cuffs. She was at Mother's with you." He gave a thin, hard smile. "I hear she might enjoy a nice cavity search."

Anger twitched my face. The room faded to white. "She's my daughter, asshole."

"That's Preach's granddaughter," Nelson cautioned his colleague. "Have some respect." I appreciated the gesture, but if Nelson was the Good Cop, I was in trouble.

"I'm guessing she has a colorful history with Mother," Bad Cop said to me. "A love-hate relationship, just like you. What do you think?"

For the first time, I remembered the note I'd found in my mailbox: *Night-night, Mommy.* Had someone deliberately left me that note to telegraph Mother's death? To show me that I was being set up as a suspect? It seemed too great a coincidence. The bulldozer that had destroyed my previous life was working on my new one, too. The room spun.

"I need to talk to my lawyer," I said.

The cops groaned theatrically, complaining among themselves, calling me names.

"Pussy."

"Bitch."

"Why do you need a lawyer, crybaby?" one said. "Guilty people need lawyers."

Nelson hushed his colleagues and opened the door to let them out. "Give me a minute with him," Nelson said.

False intimacy was Nelson's specialty. Whether or not anyone else was present, I was under surveillance from the adjoining room. I could see the red glow of the camera mounted on the wall. My heart pounded with everything I wanted to say.

"If you have evidence, lock me up," I said instead. "My lawyer is Melanie Wilde."

By law, that was supposed to be the end of our conversation. Yeah, right.

Nelson pulled a chair closer to mine. "Where's your poker face this morning, Tennyson?" Nelson said, staring me down. "You're a mess. You look like you want to puke. You look so bad I almost feel sorry for you."

My eyes hurt. I wanted to rub them, but I couldn't because of the handcuffs. I shook at the chains, frustrated. "Nelson, you know I didn't do this. Or Chela. We just buried my father—her grandfather. Leave her out."

"I can't leave anybody out," Nelson said. "I need a head on a stick."

My stomach gurgled loudly, and my throat tightened. I was going to throw up. "A bag," I said with a thin voice. "Now."

"Motherfu—" Nelson glanced around, surprised. He leaped from his seat, afraid of getting his Brooks Brothers suit sprayed. He ran for the trash can and pulled out a crumpled white plastic bag. As soon as the bag was in front of me, my stomach emptied. Luckily, I hadn't eaten breakfast, but the sickly sweet-sour scent of vomit floated above us in the room.

"That's it," Nelson said, as if I were in labor. He gently wiped the side of my mouth with a coffee-stained napkin that had fallen from the bag. "Get it out, Tennyson." I wanted to tell Nelson to back the hell away from me, but the idea of talking made me vomit again.

"Here's how it's going to be," Nelson said. "You're not going to lawyer up."

I glanced up at Nelson: *That's what you think.*

"And I'll tell you why," Nelson went on. "Because if you lawyer up, I'm going to call a press conference in time for the morning news cycle to announce that we're holding you. And then we're going to bring in Chela, look for whatever we can dig up on her, and see what she feels like telling us."

Chela would be shattered if she got dragged into Mother's homicide case. I still had no idea how I would tell her Mother was dead.

"What do you want from me?" I managed to say.

"Everything. Why you were there. What you said. If you killed her—tell me why."

"You think I killed an old lady?" I met his eyes, man to man. I'd made the mistake of trying to reach Lieutenant Rodrick Nelson's human side in the past, but I couldn't help it.

"Tennyson, I've been in this game a long time. All I believe is evidence."

"No cameras," I said. "Just us talking."

"No deal. You don't get to negotiate. Talk. Now."

"I didn't kill her, so you've got nothing on me."

"You sure about that?" His wild-eyed glint made me not sure at all. He did have something on me. Of course he did.

"If it's fingerprints, I told you I was there yesterday."

Nelson gave me an acid smirk. Then he pulled a laptop in front of me, where a grainy image was frozen on the screen, too dark to make out the details. A large, shadowy room.

"This was a very careful woman," Nelson said. "Security footage from the bedroom."

My heart thumped. Something was wrong. "It's pretty damn dark."

"Turns out sound is all we need," Nelson said. He rewound the footage and pressed play. "The dogs are whimpering at first, but listen for the voices."

Sure enough, I heard the pained simpering of the dogs. I guessed they had been poisoned to give the killer access to Mother. I'd never liked those dogs, but I wouldn't have wished a painful death on them.

"What?" Mother said suddenly, her voice crisp as life. She was a gray shadow in her bed. She might have been sitting up, but it was hard to see.

More whimpering. Then, beneath the whimpering, I heard a muffled man's voice. From the hall? I couldn't hear him clearly.

"Our techs will work on that," Nelson said. "Here comes my favorite part."

More whimpering. Then Mother raised her voice to call out: "Tennyson?"

And the screen went black.

My body turned to ice in the handcuffs.

"That's when the camera lost the feed," Nelson said. "Disabled by the killer."

The killer was technically savvy. He sounded more and more like me.

"That's bullshit," I said. "I'm being set up."

"Talk."

I didn't dare tell him about the anonymous note. If Escobar had sent the note and then killed Mother, he might be implicating me in other ways I didn't know yet. I had no witnesses to verify that I received the note anonymously rather than typing it myself. Escobar might have planted other phony evidence in Mother's room that would turn the note against me.

I forced myself to inhale, putting my meditation practice to work. I might have forgotten to breathe for nearly a minute. No wonder I'd been sick. My jabbing heartbeat slowed.

"What if Gustavo Escobar survived the explosion?" I said quietly.

Nelson stared at me blankly. "For your sake, I hope and pray that isn't your story."

"His body hasn't been recovered. That's a fact."

"What would that have to do with a Serbian madam?"

"Nothing," I said. "But it has everything to do with me. Because if Escobar's anything like me, he's real pissed off about our last night together."

"So he kills Mother why?" he said.

"To fuck with me," I said.

"And he told her to call out your name." He didn't hide his skepticism.

"I don't know how he did it, Nelson. I don't know if it's him— but it's not me."

"People only get framed in movies," Nelson said. "In twenty years, I've never seen it. But now I get why you asked about Escobar when I called you. That was the first thing out of your mouth. That's your story." He sounded dumbfounded. "You're really gonna make me do it, aren't you? You're finally gonna make me put you in prison."

His voice sounded as if he was my best friend. As if I had a gun to his head.

"South Beach Police didn't want to hear about Escobar, either," I said. "Hear me or not, but I wasn't at Mother's that night. I have alibis all night long. So if there's evidence against me, you'd better ask yourself where it's coming from . . . brother. The South Beach cops can tell you it hurts like hell to look like a fool. Again."

I didn't have to remind Nelson that my instincts had bested his in three major cases. Nelson stood up and went to the door. Our heart-to-heart was over, but I'd rattled him, too. A press conference might come back to haunt him, and he knew it.

"I'm bringing my guys back in," Nelson said. "Don't try to float that Escobar shit. Walk us through your visit to Mother's. No lawyer, or we go public. Cooperate, or we go public. After we hear what you have to say, you'll go home—or you won't."

I sighed and nodded. I would answer their questions about my relationship with Mother. And Chela's history with her. I might end up in jail no matter what I did.

One of Mother's last acts on earth had been to call out my name.

THIRTY

I SLOWED THE rental car when I got within a block of the house on Brentwood.

I'd traded my previous rental for a black Ford Explorer with windows tinted so dark that they should have been illegal. But even inside the cocoon, I felt exposed driving near Mother's house, especially with Chela and April with me. A black-and-white police cruiser parked at the corner made my heart jump.

After four hours of questioning and efforts to make me sweat in an empty room, Nelson had let me go. As usual, he tried to paint himself as my generous savior, although he made it clear that he would come back for me soon. I was lucky to be free, and I wanted to stay free. But I couldn't hide at home.

The press outside Mother's house was a horde, not just the tabloids anymore. The Hollywood Madam had just been murdered, another weird twist in the story that had begun with Gustavo Escobar. Three news vans were parked haphazardly across the road, an obstacle course for drivers. Most of the people crowded near Mother's lawn were in the media, although a few neighborhood teenagers coasted past on skateboards.

April and Chela, who trusted me most, were my only allies in the hunt for Escobar.

I drove by the house slowly, our vehicle hushed. Escobar could have been on that street, hidden in sight, his specialty. The frumpy videographer with a mountaineer's beard could be Escobar. Or the gray-haired man parked in a white van across the street. Escobar could have had plastic surgery, although he would have bruising and swelling from a nose job. But he might be hidden somewhere among the media spectators, basking in his cleverness.

I heard April snapping photos with the Pentax digital camera she'd saved all year for. She had started taking original photos for her blog, and her photography skills had taken a leap. "I'll just try to get everybody," she said. "We'll study them later."

While April photographed the observers, I studied Mother's house. Mother had no fencing in her front yard, although her windows were too high to reach from ground level. The backyard had eight-foot cyclone fencing. How had the killer gotten into the house?

"Did Mother keep the dogs out back at night?" I asked Chela.

Chela shook her head. She sat in the passenger seat beside me, staring out her window with her fingers lightly touching the glass. Her nose was red from crying, but her crying had stopped. My six-hour stay at the police station hadn't been nearly as bad as telling Chela that Mother was dead. And how. The sonofabitch had drowned her in her own piss.

Drowned. That was the important thing.

"No way," Chela said softly. "They slept in her bed. They were like her kids."

"What was her security besides the cameras on the front door and the bedroom?"

"The alarm," Chela said. "And she slept with her gun at night." She sniffled. "She said she always had, since she was living on the streets in Kosovo."

Even if Mother had still been sleeping with her gun, her re-flexes would have been slowed by age, sleep, and illness. She might have been a challenging target if she hadn't been so frail.

"So he had to override the alarm?" April said.

"Or just shut off the power," I said. "Or maybe the alarm wasn't set. We just know he got in somehow. He poisoned the dogs. He got to her room."

Escobar was good. And if Escobar had targeted Mother since my visit to her with Chela, he'd come up with his plan quickly. He'd devised his plan for his boat quickly, too. Escobar thought faster than I did. Or more deeply. The last time I'd raced him, I'd lost.

"Maybe one of the nurses saw something," Chela said.

Even finding the name of the nursing company Mother used would be a hassle. She might have hired her nurses privately. I was miles behind Escobar. I needed Dad. I needed Nelson. I needed someone else on my team.

I felt Escobar near me. He was at Mother's house, probably looking for me, too. I would have sworn to it in court.

"Too many eyes on us," I said, noticing a couple of photogra-phers stirring as they stared in our direction. "Time to go."

"'Bye, Mother," Chela whispered.

At my insistence, April had left her car parked in the Whole Foods lot instead of its usual spot in front of my house. I dreaded what I had to say to her, but I couldn't see another way. April and I couldn't find our way back together under the shadow of Gustavo Escobar.

"I'll walk you to your car," I said, idling the SUV in the space two rows from hers. I wasn't parked directly next to April's car, but I could still see Chela at all times as I walked with April toward her PT Cruiser.

No matter where April and I began, we always ended up in the same place. It dawned on me that I could never have her. Maybe I had always known it, just as Nelson knew.

"How are we going to do this if I don't park at your place?" she said. "We'll meet somewhere and you'll pick me up? What about tonight?"

One of us had to have good sense, I thought. I had seen the photographs of what Escobar had done to Mother and to his own sister. I wanted to send Chela with April, but Chela had told me she wasn't going anywhere. I had to work on Chela next.

"Oh," April said, reading my expression. "There is no tonight."

The sharp disappointment and sadness on her face, amplified in the bright sunlight, would haunt me.

"You're not safe around me, April. Maybe no one is. Let's get in your car."

If I was under surveillance from either the police or Escobar, I didn't want us to linger in plain view. We sat in her car, our old familiar middle ground. The interior smelled slightly sour, probably from old food wrappers. "You need to clean out this car," I said.

"I know, I know. I forgot you're such a neat freak."

For a moment, we both smiled. It was the best I'd felt all day. But it didn't last.

I took April's hand into mine, rubbing her lithe fingers one by one. "If I'm right about Escobar and what he's doing, I don't have much time," I said. "The police are processing the scene and evidence, and Nelson said I should expect an arrest warrant. Maybe this is Escobar's way of getting even—I tried to send him to jail, so he'll send me."

My lawyer, Melanie, had told me not to worry, but she didn't know Escobar the way I did.

"Ten, that's why I want to be with you," April said. "You need me now. If we're together, we're together through everything."

"Not this," I said. "Not Escobar. Please trust me. I'm not just bailing, I promise. I need you, April, but you have to stay away from me for a while. We'll use the phone. I'll call you."

"If you were just running away from me, would you know the difference?"

I gave a short sigh. "Maybe I'll learn that in therapy," I said. "But right now, I have to deal with this."

"You called the therapist?" April said, hopeful.

I wanted to please her so much I almost lied. "Not yet. I have the card on my desk. I'm trying, April. Give me a minute, baby. I'm scared." I rarely spoke about being afraid. I had faced killers and kidnappers before, but this time, I was weary and in the dark.

"I know," April said. "I'm scared, too."

I might be wrong about Escobar, but I didn't know any other way to explain how I'd been so closely tied to Mother's murder. If it wasn't Escobar, then who? How?

"If you have doubts about me and my involvement in this, I understand," I said.

"Please—I know you didn't kill Mother. And I know you care about me." April shrugged. "I guess that's enough for today."

"I can't take a chance on losing you like Dad," I said. "Not to him."

She nodded, hugging me. "Okay, Ten. It's fine."

But it wasn't okay or fine. Far from it.

Our kiss was over too soon. I missed April before I climbed out of her car.

"Clip. Safety," I told Chela, and I handed her my Glock. "You remember."

Chela and I hadn't been shooting in a couple of months, but we had gone to the range three times in the past year. Chela knew how to fire my 9mm.

"You hear anything you don't like, get into the safe room."

Before she died, Alice had built a hidden room adjacent to

her kitchen that had served as a pantry until I cleaned it out and equipped it for its given purpose. Over the years, I'd stocked the safe room with camping supplies, batteries, and canned foods. An empty wooden rack for wine bottles camouflaged the door from the outside, but I'd moved all but two bottles so Chela could open the door easily.

Marcela was already gone. With a little persuasion, Marcela had agreed to take her Mediterranean cruise early and repay me for her ticket. I'd considered moving with Chela to a hotel a few miles outside L.A. but quickly rejected the notion. Moving might spook the police and give them an excuse to move in faster. Arrest me, leaving Chela unprotected. If Escobar was following us, it wouldn't matter where we went. It was better to stay near my neighbors. We both knew my house best.

"Wish you could come with me," I said. I was on my way to see Louise Cannon. Cannon didn't want to see me, but I had told her I was coming.

"I don't want to be around her," Chela said.

Louise Cannon reportedly had dated Escobar for three years, and Chela was sure Cannon must have known or suspected what Escobar was. I wasn't as sure, but it was possible she knew something. And in case Escobar was keeping tabs on his former girl-friend, it was best to keep Chela far out of his sight.

"Keep your phone and gun with you at all times—even in the bathroom," I said.

"Got it," Chela said. "But I won't be following you around ev-erywhere, so get used to leaving me here." She paused. "Except at night."

"No," I said. "Not at night."

I couldn't remember the last time my house hadn't felt crowded. Now it was nearly empty. I'd had so much, and I'd barely noticed.

"What am I supposed to do if they arrest you for real?" Chela said.

"I'll bond out when I can. It might be a day or two. Might be less."

"What if you can't?"

It was hard to imagine a bond I wouldn't be willing to pay, but Chela was right: I might not have the choice. That was up to a judge. With no income, my savings account would go fast. I could live with Escobar hurting me, but I couldn't stand him hurting my little girl, too.

"If I do time, nothing has to change for you," I said. It was the first time I'd let myself imagine going to prison. "The house is paid for except for the taxes. Melanie can work out the bills if you keep expenses low. I want you to go to school."

Chela rolled her eyes. "B average, Ten. College is expensive."

"We'll figure it out. Start at a community college. Don't slow down because of me."

"Slow down?" Chela said. "I graduated five months ago. I'm not exactly racing."

"It's time to start, Chela. Pick a direction. Ask Bernard. He's good at planning."

"He's an alien. He'll be running that stupid studio before he's twenty-five."

"Do it for Mother, not me. She couldn't admit it, but this is what she wanted for you."

By the time I mentioned Mother, I was whispering. The weight of her softened my voice. Mother was a new tragedy, and we hadn't recovered from the last one.

Chela sobbed loudly, her forehead resting against my chest. I cradled the back of her head. We stood that way a long time while I held her tightly. Bringing up Mother that way was a dirty trick, but I had to fight for Chela with every weapon I had.

Chela let out a wail like I'd never heard from her. Her cry was so deep it seemed to vibrate the walls. She clung to me, nails digging.

"I hate him!" Chela screamed, her words nearly smothered by her sobs. "Please find him, Ten." Chela was trembling.

"I'm trying, sweetheart. I hate him, too."

I hadn't known I could loathe anyone as much as Escobar. He had killed my father. He had killed three people we cared about. Could I find him before I got mired in the snare he'd laid for me? Maybe not. I hated him for that most of all.

"I'll find him, Chela," I said. And then in another man's voice, "I'll kill him."

THIRTY-ONE

LOUISE CANNON HAD disappeared from the public eye after Escobar's double life was revealed. I might be the last person she wanted to see, but I couldn't help that.

Yeah, and don't be fooled. She might know more than the police think.

While a few paparazzi were still staking out the Studio City offices of Escobar's production company, Trabajando Films, I knew it wasn't likely that Cannon would show up there—although I drove past to see if I could spot Escobar haunting his old home. I saw two young employees go inside, one male and one female. No luck spotting Escobar. No Cannon.

But Elliot had told me how to track Cannon down. The guy had burst into tears as soon as he heard my voice on the phone, telling me how sorry he was about Dad, but I finally calmed him down. He was protective of Cannon, but he told me she was back in L.A., and he'd heard she was using an editing bay at Matinee Studios in West Hollywood. "Go easy with her, Tin Man," Elliot had said. "She's in shock."

Join the club, I thought. Cannon wasn't answering my calls, just as I wasn't answering most of mine, but I'd left a message on her cell phone to let her know I was coming to see her.

Matinee Studios, near Roscoe's Chicken N Waffles on Sunset and Gower, rented out its state-of-the-art editing facility in the western-themed shopping complex. Inside, the décor was heavy on mirrors, rubbed bronze panels, and odd sculptures from found objects like street signs and empty paint cans. It didn't feel warm or homey, but with the entrance in the rear, Matinee afforded privacy to its clients. As was typical, the studio had a wall dedicated to movie posters and framed photo stills from the projects that had come through its doors.

Nuestro Tío Fidel was one poster, signed by Escobar and the movie's star. Escobar's wildly scrawled signature reminded me that I was in the right place.

I called Cannon from the lobby, blending in with other clients milling in conferences. This time, she picked up her phone right away.

"Yes?" she said, already frazzled.

"Louise, it's Tennyson," I said. A long pause. "Please hear me out. I need to talk to you for ten minutes. It's urgent. I'm right here at Matinee."

"Here?" Louise said, distraught. I didn't have to wonder if she was at the studio.

"Please," I said. "We're both going through a terrible time, but—"

"I can't talk to you right now," she said. "I'm sorry about everything." Before the phone clicked off, I heard a toilet flush in the background. She was in or near a bathroom.

"Excuse me," I said to the twenty-somethings grazing near a vending machine at the edge of the lobby. "I need to find my girlfriend in the bathroom."

"Little girls' room is that way," said a woman, pointing down the hall. She'd roped her hair in Japanese-schoolgirl-style pigtails that made her look twelve instead of twenty-five. "Turn left for girls, right for boys."

I thanked her and sprinted down the hall. Since I seemed to know what I wanted and where I was going, the lobby guard barely glanced at me. The hallway was long, lined with closed doors to the editing bays. I sped up my pace.

I rounded another corner in time to see Louise Cannon walking briskly away from the swinging bathroom door, her hands shoved into her pockets, head low.

"Louise!" I called.

She stopped in mid-track, not looking back. I jogged up to face her, smiling as if she were my favorite sister.

Louise Cannon wasn't fooled into returning my smile, or maybe she wasn't capable. The tip of her nose was still sunburned and peeling from Miami, but the rest of her face was as pale as a powdered corpse from Elliot's makeup chair. Her hair was stringy and limp around her face, her eyes sunken deep. She wasn't sleeping well, either.

"People will see you," she whimpered.

"Where can we go?" I said. "I just need a few minutes, and I'll be gone."

Cannon walked around me, following her previous path like an ant on the march. "Come on," she said, resigned. "I wish you hadn't come here. This is the only place I have."

It's not my fault you have lousy taste in men, I thought, but I kept my expression pleasant. Louise Cannon wasn't the only one who had been fooled by Gustavo Escobar.

Cannon's editing bay looked like a second home; she'd brought in a large bean-bag chair and afghan in the corner for sleeping. The counter was lined with empty Coke Zero bottles and takeout containers. Cannon and April would be good roommates, I thought.

Cannon moved quickly to turn off her monitor, but not before I saw what she was editing: Brittany Summers in a full scream from the *Freaknik* footage. A bile-like flavor rose in my throat. Barely two weeks after Escobar had been revealed as a serial killer, Cannon was either obsessively watching the footage or trying to finish the film. I tried to keep the surprise from my face, but from Cannon's sheepish eyes, she knew what I was thinking.

For a long moment, neither of us knew what to say.

"I didn't know," Cannon said finally. "That's what you're wondering—what everyone is wondering. You're thinking, 'How could she *not* know?' But I didn't." She found a bottle of water hidden in the collection of empty Coke Zeros and took a long swig.

"I'm not thinking that," I said.

"I'm sorry about . . . your father." She could barely whisper the words.

"I'm sorry the boat crashed," I said, and that was true. I would have preferred to rip Escobar's trachea out of his throat with my own hands.

When I mentioned the boat, Cannon looked away as if I'd slapped her. She was mourning him. She folded her arms so tightly across her chest that I wondered how she could take a breath. She nodded. "Thank you. That's good of you to say. You didn't have to."

One question answered: Escobar had not been in touch with her. Her body language didn't seem to reveal a secret—she missed him.

"This is going to be a difficult question," I said. "Do you think he could be alive?"

Cannon looked at me, her eyes sweeping me like spotlights. I didn't read nervousness, guilt, or fear in her eyes, just naked hope. "What? Why are you asking that?"

"His body hasn't been found," I said.

"I've already told the FBI—"

"I'm not the feds or the police," I said. "We're just talking. I was there. I saw what happened. And I'm still not sure, that's all."

Cannon waited a long time before she answered me. "He was

very good in the water," she said quietly. "It's hard to imagine him drowning."

The word *drowning* froze our conversation for another half a minute. We both wanted to discover that Escobar was alive, but for very different reasons.

"What about . . . deep-sea diving?" I said.

Slowly, she nodded. A hint of triumph lifted the corner of her mouth. "He wanted to get scuba-certified."

"Wanted to?"

"Never did, as far as I know. He talked about it on vacations. In Maui. The Caymans. We always went snorkeling, even in Miami."

"But he could have gotten certified without your knowledge?"

After a pause, Cannon nodded again. "Obviously, he didn't tell me everything." Her voice was raw with too many emotions to decipher.

In the ensuing silence, I considered the scenario. If Escobar had equipped his boat with scuba gear beforehand—even just a tank—he could have found his way to safety. The water might have been as cool as sixty-five degrees, but it probably was closer to seventy, and neither temperature would have caused hypothermia right away. And we hadn't been that far from the shore. If he was a water buff, he might have made it even without certification.

I stared at Cannon. "And you haven't heard from him?"

Cannon tried to look indignant, but she couldn't pull it off. Her face seemed to fracture. "No," she said firmly. "I knew that was why you wanted to come. To ask me that."

"You're sure he hasn't tried to reach you?"

Cannon pursed her lips angrily. "I said no."

"Would you tell me if he had?"

This time, her eyes dropped away. No, she might not tell me—which meant I couldn't believe a word she said. "I wouldn't want him . . . to hurt anyone else. If he did those things . . ."

"You have doubts?"

Cannon sat down in the plush editor's chair, pushing herself away from me to a monitor farther down the counter. She looked up at me with red eyes. "I know you've been through an ordeal I can't imagine, but put yourself in my place. I knew that man for ten years, and for three of them, we talked about having a baby, raising a . . . family." She stopped herself from sobbing, pressing her fist to her mouth. "He had a temper. He yelled. He pushed me once—and we went to counseling. I never saw anything in him that matches what the FBI is saying."

"The evidence in his boat? His laptop?"

"I'm not saying he didn't do it," Cannon said. "I feel terrible for those women, for those families. For you. But if you had showed up here to try to convince me it was all a mistake, all lies, don't you think I could accept that a lot better? I knew a different man. I was hoping you . . ." She didn't finish, shaking her head. "Never mind. Are we done?"

"I understand that," I said, purposely not answering her question. "The stories don't match the man or the creative genius you knew." I hoped to keep her talking.

"And he was, you know—he was a genius," Cannon said. After hesitating, she rolled her chair back toward me to turn the monitor on so I could see Brittany's terrified face. "What he was doing with *Freaknik* had never done before . . ."

She rolled the film, and Brittany's scream filled the room as she backed herself against a Florida coral stone wall, genuinely terror-filled. If I hadn't been there, I wouldn't have known she was acting. A monster in khakis lurched after her with his mouth open wide, teeth drooling blood. It took me a moment to realize that the monster was me.

"I wouldn't try to release that." If she did, I would sue to try to prevent it.

"Of course not. It would be in terrible taste. But I'm going to finish it with the footage we have . . . and maybe one day, people will see . . ." She shrugged and sighed. "It's like what happened in Cuba. The walking dead? If Gus was that monster, he didn't start out that way. Castro turned him that way. Do you know he saw his father shot to death right in front of him? His mother drowned on a raft trying to escape with him? Castro was the true monster." Her voice shook.

I hadn't known about Escobar's mother. The biographies of Escobar floating on the internet had mentioned his father's political assassination but not the drowning.

"His mother drowned?" I said.

"Yes, she drowned off of the coast of Miami trying to save him and his sister during a storm," Cannon said. "The fiftieth anniversary of her death just passed. He was so distracted he could barely work."

My heart sped. Despite one guest shot on *Criminal Minds*, I wasn't an FBI profiler. But that did sound like a trigger for the accelerated pace of killings in Miami. "When was the anniversary?"

"About six weeks ago, on August 1. He cried in my arms like a little kid. He was very young when it happened, but he remembers. The idea that it was fifty years . . ."

"Was he in Miami on the anniversary?"

"Yes," Cannon said. "We were doing last-minute scouting—" She stopped, as if she'd revealed something she shouldn't have.

"You sound like you still want to protect him, Louise."

"Actually, I was imagining him making excuses, sneaking out of our room to drown those women . . ." She rubbed her arms. "Isn't that when the killings began?"

"It was."

"Well, then. Stop trying to read my mind."

I'd have cut off a finger to read her mind. Instead, I nodded. "Sorry."

"Tell me why you're really here."

"A woman I knew and worked with has been murdered," I said.

"Evidence on the scene is pointing to me, and I didn't do it. The only explanation I can think of is that someone very smart and very angry is trying to set me up. I only know one person that smart and angry, and there's no proof he's dead."

"The Hollywood Madam," Cannon said, realizing. "I heard. But I thought that was organized crime, some Russian connection." At least Nelson had stood by his promise to keep my name out of the investigation. Temporarily.

"Serbian," I corrected her. "It wasn't."

Unlike the police, Cannon didn't ask me why Escobar would target Mother. She understood right away. "That's horrible. But like I said, I haven't heard from him."

"I hope you'll let me know if you do. My family might be in danger. My daughter."

Cannon nodded, accepting. "Yes, they would be," she said. "He held grudges. If it's Gus . . . I don't have to tell you there's no end to his creativity. He was a practical joker, always surprising people. I would be very careful if I were you. You would never see him coming."

Her voice was so dispassionate that it chilled me, as much a threat as a warning. Her eyes didn't blink as she gazed at me. I saw a glimmer of madness.

I'd gained everything I could from Louise Cannon, the woman who might have known Gustavo Escobar best, so I thanked her and left her to the editing bay. After I closed the door, I heard Brittany Summers's frantic scream as Cannon edited Escobar's scene.

I usually pride myself on how well I read people. Cannon might not have known anything about Escobar's violent past or his whereabouts, or she could have been harboring him right under her desk.

For once, I had no idea.

THIRTY-TWO

BY SIX O'CLOCK, Chela was sorry she'd stayed at the house by herself. The sun was still bright through the windows, but the day's colors were shifting. The idea of night took Chela back to Miami Beach, flashing her images of Maria's smile and Escobar's horrible disguise.

Chela was ashamed of her panic, but she scurried from the doors to the windows to make sure they were locked. In the living room, she peeked through the blinds to see if the paparazzi vans were still outside, and she was disappointed to find the street empty. Ten had installed a new video camera to monitor the front door, but that wouldn't protect her from Escobar.

Chela moved away from the window. A loud *click* when she walked past the kitchen made her jump. Her hand brushed against the Glock's lump in the back of her jeans, ready to draw. She stood frozen in the hall until she remembered that the fridge was getting loud and cranky with age. When the fridge's familiar whirring began, she exhaled and felt silly for her pulse pattering in her neck.

For the third time in ninety minutes, Chela pulled out her cell phone to call Bernard. He was still at work at Lionsgate, where he had an internship, but maybe his schedule had changed.

"Are you sure you can't get off early?" she said when he answered, her voice hushed.

"What happened?" he said, instantly concerned.

I'm a loony jumping at my own shadow, she thought. "Nothing. I just . . ."

"Chela, I already told you—there's a meeting tonight. I might not get out until seven or seven thirty, and then there's the traffic from Santa Monica." He didn't sound irritated, exactly, but he'd told her he could get in trouble with his boss if she kept calling. "What about Ten?"

Her eyes swept the room for movement or shadows. Nothing stirred.

"He's still with Little Miss Innocent, that freak's girlfriend," she said, disgusted anew by the idea of Louise Cannon letting Escobar touch her and tell her God knows what. A bad taste furred her tongue. "Never mind. I'm sure he'll be back soon."

"You sure you're okay?" Bernard said. "Maybe you could call Ten's girlfriend or—"

Chela rolled her eyes. "Thanks, but I'll talk to you later," she said, and clicked off.

She felt her temper rising—that anger phase again—and she didn't want to take out her frustrations on Bernard. April wasn't all bad, but what could that clueless princess do to help her against Escobar?

It was as though Gustavo Escobar had been chasing her through her whole life. Chela remembered having vivid nightmares after her mother left, when she was alone with Nana Bessie and her grandmother got sicker and sicker, coughing through the night. Nana Bessie's wet coughs had sounded like death, growling to life in her room's dark corners as if to claim them both. Chela had dreamed about the coughing and the shadowy death for years after she left Minnesota—until she moved into Mother's.

Last night, for the first time in years, she'd had the dream again:

a shapeless mass spilling from the shadows, reaching out to touch her. Ten had called to tell her Mother was dead when she was barely awake, as if it were a part of her dream. No wonder she was spooked. Even the living room looked ominous to her, with its walls covered in old movie posters and a parade of dead stars. Everywhere she looked, she saw dead faces.

Everyone died. Everyone. Life was a lie. A joke.

Chela considered camping in the living room to watch TV, but a glance toward the Captain's half-open room door swamped her with sadness. She missed the sound of the news playing or the judge shows he'd liked so much. The living-room TV had been his, not hers. She could watch TV in her room with the door locked.

But as Chela walked toward the stairs, a sound above her froze her with her hand on the banister as soon as she clutched the polished wooden globe. It had sounded like a groan or a squeak, the sound of weight on wooden floorboards. Was someone upstairs?

Ten's house had seemed like the perfect playland in the beginning, with its hidden rooms and custom-built doorways that were too tall or too short, like a funhouse. Ten said that the actress who owned the house was eccentric and had built it a piece at a time whenever she got money. But now, all Chela could think about was how some of the walk-in closets upstairs had entrances on two sides and how much room there was to crouch and hide in the linen closet and the vast space in the unexplored attic upstairs. The house felt like a trap.

Screw it.

Chela rushed to the wine racks and pulled open the narrow door to the safe room. She'd promised herself she wouldn't be a baby and hide in there the whole time Ten was gone, especially since she'd been stuck in there for hours when she first met Ten because the cops searched his house. Cops always hassled Ten.

But they had never found her in the safe room, so Escobar might not, either. By the time Chela had locked the deadbolt, she was breathing fast, with tears in her eyes. She never used to cry, and now she cried all the time. Her whole face hurt. Everything hurt.

Was that a sound outside the door? Footsteps? Chela smothered a gasp in her throat.

Chela was about to dial Ten's number when her iPhone vibrated in her hand. The screen said PRIVATE NUMBER, but she knew it was Ten's new phone.

"What's wrong?" Ten said. He must have heard her tears in her breathing.

"I'm—" Chela stopped, struggling with the pain of a simple word. Her sudden sob sounded like a Chihuahua's pathetic bark. "I'm scared. I keep thinking I hear noises."

"I'm ten minutes away. Are you hidden?"

"Yes."

"Then stay that way. Don't worry, Chela. I'm almost there."

When Chela hung up, her sobs came harder and faster.

The depression stage had arrived, right on schedule.

THIRTY-THREE

WHEN I RETURNED home, an unmarked gray sedan was parked halfway down the block with two men inside pretending to read the newspaper. Classic stakeout pose. If I'd been tailed through the day, I'd missed the signs. I waved to the cops as I walked up my cactus-lined driveway, and the driver stuck his arm out the window to flip me his middle finger.

Fuck you, too, I thought in Mother's voice. The extra eyes meant I was still a suspect in her murder, but I was glad those cops were there, if only for Chela's sake. Until those detectives banged on my door to arrest me, I wasn't in a position to be picky.

While Chela cooked up frozen Chinese stir-fry, I sat on the living-room sofa and stared at the blank TV screen, a mirror for my empty head. I couldn't wait for Escobar's next move—I had to plan mine—but I didn't know where to begin. I've rarely felt paralysis like it.

I found myself thinking about one of my last outings with Alice, when she'd insisted on going whitewater rafting on the Rogue River outside of Portland. I didn't know it then, but the excursion was probably on her bucket list. She never told me she was sick.

We'd had separate rafts, following the river's powerful whims, and Alice had screamed with laughter at first. But as the afternoon wore on, each of us paddling furiously to steer clear of towering boulders while our guide shouted warnings, I noticed that Alice wasn't smiling anymore. Her screams came without laughter. She wasn't having fun, but there was no turning back. The river's current only ran one way.

"Almost done!" I'd called to her, and she'd nodded like a little girl.

I had never been rafting, but I kept paddling even through the unexpected jolts by the current. As I'd watched Alice's energy drain, I'd remembered how much older she was, and I'd wished I could paddle for her.

We turned one last bend, and the rushing water and bubbling white foam signaled strong currents ahead. I turned to glance beside my raft, and I'll never forget the defeated, helpless look on Alice's face. She'd pressed on with the promise of rest soon, but she hadn't expected such a challenge before the end. Instead of digging in for the fight, she'd stopped paddling.

I shouted encouragement, but Alice's raft whirled toward the first pair of large rocks as if she'd been tethered to them. By the time she started paddling with fervor, her raft had flipped.

One of the guides jumped in to help her before I could steer my raft anywhere close to her. The water was shallow, and we were wearing life preservers, so Alice only suffered plugged ears and a scraped elbow. But whatever lesson she'd hoped to learn on the rapids that day, the rocks had won the battle. The rocks had convinced her that she was too old, or that she wasn't strong enough, or some other unspoken message. I saw Alice only two or three times after that incident. She was never the same. Two years later, I heard she was dead.

Maybe we all meet a boulder with our name on it one day. I knew the name on mine.

As Chela filled my house with thin smoke from her overcooked stir-fry, I understood why Alice's shoulders had slumped and her face had lost its light. While Chela sat next to me on the sofa, flipping through TV channels, I dozed off, dreaming about the Rogue River rapids.

Dad was the person in the doomed raft beside me, so shrunken and frail.

Then Dad turned into April.

I woke up with a jolt. The room was dark except for the blue light from the TV screen showing a reality show I didn't recognize. Chela was still sitting next to me, head bent as she played Angry Birds on her iPad.

"What?" she said, not looking up.

I checked the old-fashioned, silenced grandfather clock Alice had left standing in the corner. It was eight thirty. I'd slept for nearly ninety minutes, my longest stretch of sleep in a while, but I felt more tired than before.

Had I asked April to call me when she got home? I couldn't remember. I hadn't heard from her since I dropped her off at her car at Whole Foods. I'd been so busy trying to track down Louise Cannon that I hadn't checked on April.

"Have you talked to April?" I asked Chela.

"Not since we dropped her off."

I sat up and grabbed my phone from the coffee table. My call to April's number went to voice mail without ringing. Her phone wasn't on; that wasn't like April at all. I told myself she was only on another call, probably for work, but I was considering other possibilities.

"It's me," I said to her voice mail. "Call me as soon as you get this."

My heart was pounding to life, and adrenaline drove sleep from my brain. Why had I sent her back home? Maybe I had been pushing her away.

I pulled my original cell phone out of the drawer where I'd buried it, plugging it in to charge. My voice mailbox had filled up two weeks before. My world had narrowed to only six people I wanted to hear from or talk to. I searched through the contacts on my old phone until I found the number for Nia, April's roommate.

I held my breath until Nia picked up the phone on the fourth ring.

"Is April around?"

"I thought she was with you. I was about to remind her she's supposed to give me a ride to work tomorrow," Nia said, already wary. "What's going on?"

I remembered racing up the stairs at the Fontainebleau. My heart pumped ice, but I kept my voice calm and told her to ask April to call me if she heard from her.

I went to my front stoop to check my mailbox, and I was relieved when I found only the usual junk. No cryptic message. I checked the video camera I'd mounted the day before to monitor the door and the the mailbox, and it had not been tampered with. Down the street, the unmarked car still spied on me.

I dialed April again. Nothing. I called her workplace extension, but that went to voice mail, too. April might be a dozen places. It wasn't even nine o'clock. She might have decided to see a movie or to go out to dinner with someone. *Chill, man,* I told myself.

But I couldn't.

"Come on," I called to Chela. "I have to go out." Cops outside or not, I wouldn't leave Chela in the house alone after dark.

"Where are we going?"

"April's house."

Chela didn't complain or ask me why. She looked up at me with perceptive eyes, grabbing her sweatshirt to face the cool night.

Chela usually commandeered the radio as soon as we climbed into any vehicle, breaking my Driver Is Deejay rule, but she made no move to turn on any music. I checked my rearview mirror; the gray sedan eased behind me, flipping on the headlights to follow at a leisurely distance. Chela turned to look over her shoulder, nervous when she noticed our tail.

"Cops," I told her. "It's not him."

Chela looked only slightly relieved, settling back in her seat. "Oh." She raised her knees to her chest in the oversized seat, wrapping her arms around herself.

I was careful about my speed and every turn signal, hoping I wouldn't get pulled over and hauled to lockup. Every detail leaped to bright vividness: the shimmering stoplights, the glowing neon at the strip malls, random words on painted signs. My mind was preparing for the worst. At the stoplight, I handed Chela my lawyer's business card.

"Anything comes up with those cops, call Melanie," I told Chela. "Stay with her."

"Thanks, but I'll call Bernard." Chela was ready to start taking care of herself.

After fifteen minutes of virtual silence while I drove, we pulled up in front of April's house. The driveway was empty, but April's street was busy even at night, with cars speeding past quiet homes while residents walked their dogs by lamplight. Still, April wasn't used to being vigilant, watching strangers' every move. April had grown up in Tallahassee, and she'd once told me that she occasionally forgot to lock her front door, and she rarely carried a key.

April wouldn't have been ready for Escobar. He could have worn a costume and grabbed her before anyone noticed.

Our police escort pulled up, parking a discreet distance away.

"Coming with me?" I asked Chela as the car idled. "Or hanging with the babysitters?"

"Yeah, right," Chela said, opening her door.

Nia flipped on her porch light and opened her front door before we had a chance to knock. She'd seen us through her window. Nia and April often left their front shutters half-open even after dark, a peep show to anyone who wanted to see them eating dinner or watching TV. I remembered my exposure with April as we'd made love in the kitchen, and I cursed myself again. How could I have been so stupid?

Nia was so thin that I'd once asked April if she ever ate. She was about Chela's height, with a severe jaw that looked masculine when she clenched it. Nia's polite smile for Chela died when she looked at me, arms folded. I didn't have to guess what Nia thought of me lately.

Nia didn't move to invite us in. "I don't like you showing up here like this."

"I'm a bodyguard. I can't help being careful. Did you get any strange mail today?"

She shrugged. "Bills. Flyers. Strange how?"

"An envelope with no return address? Weird message?"

Nia lowered her chin to change her stare, losing her patience. "What's up, Ten?"

"Can I take a peek in your mailbox?"

She gave a frustrated sigh, but she nodded. April's mailbox, like mine, was beside the front door. An engraved detail from the black paint jumped out at me as I opened it: a cherub blowing a trumpet. I reached inside and checked for loose paper. None. At the bottom, my fingertips brushed a spare key.

I almost cursed out loud. I fished out the key and gave it to her. "You two should know better," I said. "That's the first place some- one would look."

Nia sharpened her *you ain't my daddy* stare. Unlike April, who had been raised a hothouse flower, Nia was a foster kid who had fought her way from Compton to USC film school. Nia and I had gotten along fine once upon a time, but those days were gone.

I sighed. "Until I see a body, I'm not sure that bastard is dead," I said. "Feel me?"

The resentment in Nia's face melted away. She clutched the key in her fist. "Wait—you think he's still out there?"

I shrugged. "April said she was going home to work from here, and you say she hasn't shown up or called. It makes the back of my neck tingle, that's all. So keep your blinds closed, lock your door, and don't keep a key out like an invitation."

Nia nodded, contrite. She glanced toward Chela, hesitating before she went on. "There's no keeping April away from you, so don't string her along. Step up or step the hell off, Ten."

"I will," I said. "First, let's track her down. Tell her to call me."

I was planning to head to Whole Foods next, to make sure her car wasn't still in the parking lot where I'd left her. But as Chela and I turned to step off the front stoop, I noticed a bright white sliver beneath the welcome mat I'd missed without the porch light.

"Wait," I said before Nia could close the door. I pointed. "What's that?"

Nia and I bent low to examine it together: it looked like the edge of a standard envelope, nestled at the bottom center of the mat, hidden except for half an inch. Even less.

"Hadn't seen that—" Nia said, reaching down, but I gently blocked her wrist.

"Let me," I said.

I don't know how I kept my fingers from trembling as I lifted that welcome mat, hoping I was wrong about what I would find. The concrete under the mat was stained nearly black with mildew, but a fresh white envelope lay waiting.

My name was typed across the center, and nothing else.

"Oh, dear Jesus," I whispered, the truest prayer of my life. My heart pounded a flood of hot blood through my veins. *Please don't let her be dead.*

"Why is somebody leaving your mail here?" Nia said, but I barely heard her.

"Oh, God, Ten," Chela whimpered, pulling closer.

"Let's get inside," I said, lifting the envelope by its edges, trying to leave any fingerprints intact. It took all of my self-control not to rip it open on the porch, but I didn't want Escobar to see us. We filed inside quickly. As I slammed the door, I told Nia to close the blinds.

I laid the envelope on the cluttered dinette table, easing my unsteady fingertip to open the unsealed flap. This note was two lines:

A simple transaction—a life for a life. No police. No delays. Meet me at the tar pits at midnight. If you fail to follow these instructions, both a lover and a father will die for your sins.

My fragile new world spun. I read the note a second time, trying to will the words away. My unblinking eyes stung fire.

"What?" Nia said, anxious.

All actors are born liars. I folded the note with a shrug. "Some crazy fan."

Somehow, Nia couldn't hear my heartbeat or feel my stomach blister. She couldn't see my knees trying to fold beneath me. Until that moment, I'd thought that losing Dad would be the worst feeling of my life. I would have sacrificed half a dozen strangers on Hollywood Boulevard at high noon to keep April safe. Maybe more, and now it was too late.

Escobar might have bugged the room. I would have.

"What the hell?" Nia said. "Now crazies are dropping off your mail here?"

Before I could remember language, my phone rang in my pocket. Did he have my number, too? I wore my calm mask, but I reached for my phone with numb fingertips. LAPD, the phone display read. I closed my eyes for a second's rest. I was falling deeper into the hole. "Hardwick," I said.

Nelson's voice scolded me. "Haven't you found some place for Chela by now? I thought you'd have sense enough to know we aren't bullshitting."

I opened my mouth to speak, but silence was my only alternative. Everything I couldn't tell him roared in my mind. Nelson knew and admired April's father, so he might be on my side if I could tell him April was gone. But I didn't dare trust him.

Nia gave me a *what the hell* look as I moved to the kitchen doorway and peered through the jalousie windows above the countertop where April and I had made love. A black-and-white cruiser was pulling up a few yards beyond April's back door. I was trapped in the house.

If Escobar was watching, April might be dead already.

"What now, Nelson?" I could barely raise my voice to be heard.

"We got a copy of the will."

Standing in April's hallway, I pinned the phone to my shoulder while I folded the note from Escobar to stick it into my shoe. Then I grabbed a handful of twenties from my wallet and stashed them in the other shoe. I would be running soon. "Whose will? Mother's?"

"I need you to walk out the front door with your hands in plain sight," Nelson said. "Leave your kid and girlfriend inside. Then you're coming in the car with me."

"You're outside April's house?"

"Don't try to stall me, asshole. You heard me."

My mind nearly went blank, veering back to April. I tried to remember what I would ask him on an ordinary night. "What's the problem with the will?"

"Okay, I'll play along," Nelson said. "She left it all to you. Pretty big haul, if her accounts don't get seized. So, Sugar Pants ... you're going to come tell us the truth about the nature of your relationship with our vic. We can chat about it all night."

If I'd been capable of any more shock, the news about Mother's will would have done it. Nelson was probably bluffing, but he might not be. Anything was possible that night. The images from Escobar's death scenes tried to trample my thoughts. I almost spoke the words aloud: *Escobar has April.*

"I'm coming right now," I said instead. "Please don't make a scene and embarrass April at her home, man." It hurt to say April's name. My hand shook as I clicked off the phone.

Chela was on my heels as I walked toward the door. "Well?"

I gave Chela the keys to the rented SUV and the rest of my wad of twenties. In my rush, one of the bills fell to the floor. "It's LAPD. Call Melanie, have her investigator take you to Bernard's. I mean it. Don't go home under any circumstances. I'll call you when I can." I glanced back at Nia. "If you hear from April, let me know right away."

"The hell I will," Nia said with angry eyes that seemed to know everything. "You're the last person she needs to call."

The truth hurt enough to make me stumble on my way to the door.

"What about the note, Ten?" Chela said, still following me.

I gave her a lie of a smile, mostly for Nia's benefit. "I'll take care of it," I said, pinching her cheek. "Do exactly as I said. Call Melanie right now."

Chela stared up at my face with wide eyes. I let her see a private glimpse of my sorrow, dropping my mask. I didn't trust Nia to do what I asked, but Chela needed to be more careful than she'd ever been. With a whimper, Chela hugged me, and we held on tight. I kissed the springy curls on top of her head.

We both knew I might never see her again.

A small crowd of neighbors gathered at a safe distance to watch. A second unmarked Crown Victoria, this one blue, had joined the first, blocking my SUV near April's driveway. Nelson waited with his arms folded. The other two detectives stood on the sidewalk beyond the driveway. No guns drawn. No handcuffs.

God help me, I might still have a chance.

I walked with my arms akimbo at a pace that wouldn't worry anyone. "I didn't know about the will," I said to Nelson. "She never said anything. But what does it change?"

"Trained police look for something we call motive," Nelson said. Despite his sarcasm, there was no smirk on his face. He didn't look much happier than I felt. Maybe he'd never believed I killed Mother, and now his faith was shaken.

I stopped walking within six yards of Nelson. If I didn't spook him, I might be able to talk my way out. He had rank over the other two; on his word, they would let me go.

"Why would I be stupid enough to make it such an obvious murder?" I said quietly. "She was half-dead already. I could have made it look natural."

"You still had the problem of the dogs," Nelson said. "Rat poison and natural causes don't add up. I gotta frisk you, Tennyson. You know what to do."

I glanced back toward the house before I spread my hands across the car's warm hood. Nia and Chela were both peeking through the blinds, but I didn't have the luxury of shame.

"I would have made it look like suicide," I said. "She took the dogs with her."

Nelson's hands carefully patted me down, not gentle and not rough, pure regulation. He pulled out my wallet and cell phone, confiscating them.

"You're right," Nelson said. "You could have played it that way, but maybe you didn't. We're getting warrants on your house and the car, so we'll know more soon."

"You don't have enough for warrants."

"I was surprised myself, but the judge thinks differently."

I pursed my lips. I let Nelson see the sorrow I'd shown Chela, surrendering. "Don't cuff me here. Not in front of April and my kid. Let me drive myself."

Nelson glanced toward the gabled house, where he imagined

April stood watching near Chela. Even trained skeptics are wired to believe in fairy tales.

Nelson puffed out his cheeks, sighing. "Hell no, you can't drive yourself. You're not touching your car, Ten. But no cuffs. Just get in my car. Front seat."

I felt as if I'd been holding my breath since I saw the note from Escobar, and a thin band of oxygen finally wound into my lungs. Nelson was riding alone, and my hands would be free. My only options were terrible, but at least I still had options.

Nothing except death was going to keep me from finding April. And finishing my business with Escobar.

THIRTY-FOUR

NELSON TURNED BACK toward the Robbery-Homicide Division. The other two plainclothes cops had stayed behind with my car. Nelson was pushing the speed limit, only pausing at stop signs. Neither of us wanted the ride to last long. We both knew it would end badly for one of us, or maybe both of us.

"April has to come in to talk to us next," Nelson said.

"Why?"

"You said you had an alibi all night long," he said. "It's showtime, brother."

I leaned forward, head hanging. Sagging muscles would help me build rapport with Nelson, and it took less energy than pretending. Once, I would have thought April getting hauled in to talk to the police was a bad day all by itself. Escobar's note itched against the sole of my foot. I couldn't trust Nelson with April. Even if I could, I couldn't bet her life on it.

"I can't," I said. "I won't do that to her."

Nelson pursed his lips with a frustrated swing of his head. "You're back to no alibi."

My eyes fell shut. We had been in the car for ninety seconds, and I was still no closer to free. Once we hit smooth traffic flow or the freeway, my plan would get much more complicated. The green light ahead flipped to yellow.

As Nelson slowed, my heart sped.

"If April's the only way, then I don't have an alibi."

"Fuck you, Ten," Nelson said. "I'll bring her in without you. I need this closed. I knew this shit was coming one day. When you go down, you take everybody with you, huh?"

The light ahead turned red. The battered painting truck in front of Nelson's car hit the brake lights, and Nelson's foot shifted away from the accelerator. The car would be fully stopped in twenty seconds, close enough to stopped in ten.

My muscles tightened. I could bash Nelson's head against his window, which might kill him, or I could try to knock him out. Killing him would be easier than fighting him.

"Something's come up, Nelson," I heard myself say instead, my voice graveyard quiet. "You're a good cop. I know you hate this. Hate me. But we're damn near family, you and me. So I'm going to trust you more than you've ever trusted me." He was quiet, mouth a little open, as if too stunned to speak. "April's life is on the line. There's something I have to do, and I'm running out of time to do it. I swear to God that by tomorrow morning, it will all be over, and you can have what's left of me. But right now . . . I've got to go."

"What the fuck are you talking about?"

I unlocked my car door while he was still ten yards away from a full stop behind the truck. The car lurched, stopping as Nelson turned to me. His regulation Smith & Wesson was on me before my door was halfway open. He'd angled himself to keep his pistol low and close, out of my reach.

Behind us, a car screeched its brakes. I expected impact or a gunshot, but neither came.

"Close that goddamn door," Nelson said. "Hands on the dashboard. You're not this stupid, Ten."

I stared straight ahead into the lines of red brake lights. "You can shoot me—that's your choice. Follow your head or your heart. We're way past bullshit here."

"Do not test me, bruh. I'm counting to three. One . . ."

"All Preach's life, he tried to teach me. Trust him, one last time."

"Two . . ."

"She's my woman, Nelson. I have to do this."

"I will shoot you."

"She's worth dying for." I swung my right leg out of the car, my foot pressing against the asphalt. My feet dragged, waiting to hear the gun's report. When I didn't hear anything, I closed my car door behind me and walked past the stalled traffic in the next lane. My legs were asleep, slowly waking with each step.

Then I was running.

Nelson flung his car door open. He didn't want to shoot me, but he could tackle me from behind. Nelson's footsteps closed behind me, conditioned and quick. Nelson was fast; his breath huffed across the back of my neck as we ran between the crowded lanes. I darted to the shadowy sidewalk.

Nelson brushed my back as I changed direction, trying to grab a handful of my clothes. I pushed off from him, and he stumbled long enough for me to get out of his reach. An empty garbage can crashed behind me, tangling him.

"You're lying to me, I'll kill you myself. You're lying to me, your life is over, you sonofabitch!" Nelson shouted, his voice receding.

I ducked around a corner and was gone.

I left the *ampm* more than a mile from where I'd begun, with a new throwaway cell phone and enough minutes to last the rest of the night. Or my probable life span. Whichever ended first. I found a mom-

and-pop doughnut shop, took a booth in the rear, and kept my face away from the door and windows. A patrol car sped by with sirens fussing, but I paid no attention.

I hate to break a promise, but I dialed the number I'd sworn never to dial again. Once, we'd worked together to find a missing child because it felt like the right thing to do. But we'd lost track of right and wrong.

I expected to leave a message or have to wait for a return call. Instead, she picked up in the middle of the first ring. She had been waiting for me.

"Where you been, baby?"

Her voice was like tickling fingernails, unearthing buried images of her skin. I hesitated to call her Marsha out loud; her name was another of her lies. I had no name for her—no polite ones, anyway. I glanced around me to make sure no one was listening.

"He has April," I said.

Marsha didn't waste my time asking who had April. Working with Marsha was the closest I'd come to sharing a mind. "He made contact?"

"A note under her welcome mat. Says I have to exchange a life for a life. Police aren't an option. I got a note before the madam died, but I hadn't put it together. It says to meet him at the tar pits at midnight. No cops."

The shop manager came with the cup of coffee I'd asked for absently when I first skulked in. I waved him thanks.

"Why is this my business?" Marsha said.

"I said it's April."

"I heard you, precious. But L.A.'s nowhere in my job description."

I'd seen Marsha run two illegal domestic operations, so that excuse was feeble. My emotions were too dead for anger. I rested my head on my hand, blocking my face from the woman making her way toward the rear restroom. I pinched the room's light from my eyes. "I need help with this one," I said. "I wouldn't call if I had any other way."

Marsha didn't answer. I was lucky she hadn't hung up on me, considering the names I'd called her the last time we'd been in a room together. Her long silence made me nervous.

"What do you want from me?" I said. "Name it."

"The next time I call you, pick up the damn phone," Marsha said.

When I last worked with Marsha, she'd asked me to seduce a Hong Kong businessman's wife, learn family secrets in bed, and report everything I saw and heard. A woman had fallen in love with me, and her husband had hired a gang to kill me. I'd promised myself I would never owe Marsha another favor. But it was a brave new world.

"Tell me the truth," I said. "Do you think she's dead?"

I dreaded the answer, but I had to hear someone tell me, one way or the other.

"I'm not a profiler," Marsha said, "but I doubt it. Your madam ran prostitutes, so she's a bonus. Your dad . . . well, you know better than I do." So much for condolences.

Reluctantly, I took my mind back to the Fontainebleu's stairwell. Escobar had lost time when he stopped running to tell me he hadn't wanted to kill Dad. Almost an apology.

"He didn't seem to get off on it," I said.

"Killing civilians probably offends his self-image. April's not what he's looking for. From what I've seen, it goes back to his sister. The mother dies on the journey, his sister turns to prostitution, shames her parents' memory. Yada yada. He's not killing prostitutes just because they're convenient—he has a vendetta. They violate some kind of code. He has more leverage over you if April is alive, or you think she is. My money says she's probably not dead. Yet."

Marsha had been studying Escobar, apparently. Maybe that was what she had called to tell me. It sounded too good to believe, but if Marsha was stringing me along, I'd asked for it. My shirt stopped squeezing my chest.

"I need this," I said. "I love her."

I could almost see Marsha rolling her eyes.

"You stepped in it deep this time, Ten," she said. "Sometimes the cavalry doesn't ride in, lover. Sorry about your father. "

Hearing Marsha say she was sorry made Dad's death fresh, and I felt dizzy with images of Dad's bloodstained shirt, the faces of the women Escobar had killed in terror and pain, April's dimpled smile. Even if April wasn't dead, she was suffering. I remembered Escobar yanking Brittany's hair on the set, and I held the edge of my tabletop, resisting an urge to smash my coffee mug against the wall. If Marsha couldn't help me, April might be as good as dead. She had to know that, too.

"He's going to kill her, and he wants me to see it," I said, just in case she didn't understand. "He'll make me watch. Then he'll do his best to kill me, too."

Prostitution angle aside, Esocbar had killed Mother to get to me, not to punish her. Would it matter to Escobar that April had never sold her body?

"Not tonight, Ten. Some professional advice?" Marsha said. "I hope you're not set on dying for this girl. Needless to say, that would be a tragic waste. So think it over."

"There's nothing to think over."

"Get to your mail, and I'll send you files on your guy. That's all I can do. Keep that phone with you, and keep it charged." We conducted business through an encrypted email server. My phone was cheap. Since I couldn't go home or to April's, I would need an internet café with a computer to read her email.

"Files and phones don't help me," I said. "This is about to go down, and I need someone I can trust at my back."

During Marsha's pause, I thought I'd changed her mind.

"I'll send prayers," Marsha said.

"Prayers?" Talk of prayers was so unlike Marsha that I wondered if she was twisting the knife. Or speaking in code.

"Don't scratch up that pretty face," Marsha said, and clicked away.

The sudden silence emptied me, until thoughts of April's suffering filled me again.

I tried dialing April's cell-phone number. Again, it didn't ring before going to voice mail. She might have dropped her phone somewhere, or Escobar might have taken it. April might never hear her message, but I had to talk to her. Escobar might let her hear my voice.

"April, I'm coming, baby," I said. I closed my eyes, imagining the two of us on the summit of Table Mountain in Cape Town, staring down at the beautiful basin. I imagined holding her hands. I tried to paint our sanctuary with my voice. "Just hang on a while longer. I'm coming. I'm so sorry I wasn't there. But I'm coming now. I'll be there soon."

I wanted to say more, but I hadn't called only to talk to April. I breathed fast as the silent phone waited for my message to Escobar. My teeth hurt at the idea of him listening.

"Don't hurt her," I said. "I'm doing what you asked. I'm coming alone."

I had run out of lies.

I left too much money on the table and rose to my feet.

I walked into the cool night.

THIRTY-FIVE

GUSTAVO ESCOBAR COMPOSED himself, hands tight on his van's steering wheel. Anger had clouded his judgment, and he had almost killed the girl too soon. He had *seen* himself kill her, swinging his sledgehammer to her face once, twice, three times, a tantrum of killing.

Useless. Crude. Childish.

Thank goodness he had come to his senses before he pulled his van over to grab the hammer that lay across the seat beside him. His fingertips vibrated from the hammer's imaginary blows. He blew out his breath in slow, even streams to bring the night back into focus. He drove calmly past the predictable sequence of traffic lights. Stop, go, slow.

His plan was still intact. His perfect night awaited him.

The actor had not called in the police. At first, Escobar blamed himself for the police at the actor's house. The old whore runner's death so soon after the actor's visit had been bound to cast suspicion on him, and he had not corrected her when she called out Tennyson's name on tape. Ah, well. A small price to pay.

But when he heard the girl's address in the chatter on his police scanner, witnessed the sudden arrival of more police cars, Escobar had been certain the actor had disobeyed him. Ignored him. His anger had crested, and he'd looked for a side street so he could pull over, open the cage, and crush her poisoned skull. He would have rolled her faceless corpse into the street within a block of her front door, a bloody testament to how badly the actor had failed her.

But that waste had been averted.

The actor had been desperate enough to run from police custody. Escobar had seen the foot chase with his own eyes as he watched, invisible, from his van only yards behind them.

Escobar had bought the van for cash in New Orleans during the cross-country drive he'd spent eating gas-station food and listening to radio reports about his monstrosity. Escobar had painted the cartoon poodle with a happily lolling red tongue and a logo for a fake company called Pet Hotel so garish that no one noticed him. He dared the world to see him, and yet no one did. A van wasn't quite as useful as his *Rosa*, not nearly secluded enough. Still, a van did the job.

Escobar craned his ears. Had the girl moaned? For four hours, her head had been covered in a pillowcase, and she had been bound and gagged in the oversized livestock cage he had been saving for her.

No—for the whore, Chela. He actually had been saving the cage for Tennyson's teenage slut.

"Are you awake now?" he called to her, just loudly enough to be heard over the engine as they secretly glided on the streets. She had been sleeping, so this was his first chance to explain her circumstances. She deserved to understand.

Some of the women he had dreamed with were screamers and weepers who soaked through their gags. Others were stone silent. Still others veered between states of loud and quiet, frantic and frozen. This new one was mostly silent except for an occasional soft moan, as if she had awakened in slight pain. She was polite even in her captivity.

Politeness had made her so easy.

So easy for him to roll his wheelchair and follow her to the grocery store's coffee counter to stage his accidental "spill" when they bumped together. When he wouldn't take money for dry cleaning, she'd given him that lovely smile. So polite. She hadn't wanted to let him buy her a latte, but she'd agreed when he insisted. Upon prodding, she had even let him roll with her cup across the room to add a dash of cream and sugar from the condiments tray.

And he'd added a dash of the other thing, too, from his pocket. *Night-night.*

To her, he had been harmless, a charming old man who told stories of old Hollywood and pet owners who pampered their dogs to death. As in all good conversations, five minutes became ten, ten became twenty. They had still been talking when she followed him to his van, which was parked beside her car. The bright pink stood out from across the parking lot. What a coincidence, to both be moving in the same direction.

Then the gun. The look on her face. The rest was more or less the same with them all.

The girl stirred slightly, a tiny *clank* against the steel bars.

"I know what you're thinking," he said. "How can this have happened to you? You never expected it. You're still dizzy from it. That's how I felt when my mother drowned."

She made the moaning sound again, more softly. She was waking and afraid.

"I will not hurt you unnecessarily," he said. "That's a promise. But you must die."

The girl's moaning and her sounds of motion ceased. She was one of the stoic ones. But she would not stay reasonable. She would wait for her moment and then try to scream to raise the dead. Her script would be the same, eventually. *No. Please. Stop.*

"Perhaps you think this is a terrible dream, no?" he went on. "But the dream is mine, not yours. You're a passing face. We weren't supposed to meet here, this way. We could have exchanged thoughts on so many subjects. But what's done is done."

Her silence seemed to deepen. He could barely hear her breathing.

"I understand," he said. "You're gathering your wits. Trying to learn. That's a very smart thing to do. You're braver than most, so rare. I wish it could make a difference for you. But you won't survive this night. Tennyson should see that in your face—that his presence means nothing. He should see in your eyes how he left you alone, April. He left you for me."

She stirred with a nearly imperceptible whimper, valiantly fighting to keep her tears silent. She didn't want him to know she was crying.

"*Bueno,*" he said. "Release it. For you, it's a tragedy of misplaced trust. He kept his daughter close to him, but you he sent away. I'll tell your story one day, on film, how the unspoiled suffer. But as I promised, I won't celebrate your pain. I only ask that when your time comes to die, don't look at me with betrayed eyes like you did in the parking lot. Don't pretend I never told you what I would do."

That time, she couldn't hide the sound of her sob.

He visualized the scene to her music of misery. The actor arrives, helpless to save his true love. When she drowns, the actor begs him to spare the life of his daughter, only to be told that she will be next. And then the actor will die—slowly, so slowly. Flayed? Toothless? Castrated? Escobar would improvise on how to dispose of the man who had destroyed his life.

The daughter, Chela, would be a sweeter prize, but he would not come for her right away. He would savor the wait. Give her months, even years, of depraved dreams. Then he would climb out of those nightmares to take her. He would punish Chela and the actor both for the death of this innocent crying in his van.

"This may sound strange to you, but I'm very sorry for this, April," he said. "It is, as people say, a necessary evil."

The actor had stolen his life, but the Escobar name would live forever.

The memory of fear had followed April Forrest into the darkness, but then she had found a peaceful tunnel. She might have heard the engine's purr, felt the lulling starting and stopping of the vehicle, but she wasn't curious about anything during her deep, calm sleep.

Until she began to wonder: *Where am I?*

The question awakened a barrage of terrible realizations, and cascading terror built in her. She had lost consciousness. She felt groggy and confused. *How? When?*

She could not speak, even if she had the energy to try. Her mouth was snugly gagged with a bland fabric that stuck to her dry tongue. She fought the instincts to bite it or her throat's pulsing desire to expel it. The gag made her feel sick.

But it was worse than only that.

April pitched back to sleep, but a nagging feeling of urgency woke her quickly.

She was gagged in the dark. A chloroform-scented fabric lay draped lightly across her face, dense enough to warm her face from her breath. April spent long seconds telling herself to breathe and relax so she would not panic. It would be too easy to believe she couldn't breathe.

But she could. *In, out. In. Out.*

But she could not move, she realized. She was lying on her side on a hard surface barely softened by some kind of cushion, her wrists bound behind her, feet bare. The binds were tight. April heard herself moan. When she moved, she felt hard, ordered barriers against her arm. Tiny bars from a cage? *Sweet Jesus, please help me. Deliver me, Jesus. Deliver me.*

Praying and breathing helped her fight the panic. Ten thought it was easier to face the world with deep breaths; he meditated like a statue for twenty minutes each morning when he woke. Breathing. In, out. Breathing was a kind of prayer.

"Are you awake now?"

A man's voice. The clarity of the voice clawed through her confusion, helping her pinpoint his distance, something tangible she could hold on to. The voice might be six feet from her. They were both in a vehicle, she realized. Moving.

She'd been at the supermarket, she remembered. The funny old man in the wheelchair had thrust a gun into her stomach, nudging deeply, and hard. He had hurt her.

"I know what you're thinking . . ." the man's voice went on, but she lost her focus as she wondered who would do this to her. Why?

". . . when my mother drowned," the man went on, as if they were old friends talking, and April knew it was Gustavo Escobar. Ten had been right. Escobar was alive! The realization awed her, dimming her hearing. Escobar seemed to murmur.

". . . But you must die." Escobar's voice came back, as if from a nightmare.

April's heart forgot its rhythms, pounding too fast, too hard.

". . . He should see in your eyes how he left you alone, April. To *me*."

Jesus Lord, please please please hear me.

April's sob surprised her. She cursed herself, because she couldn't hear Escobar when she was crying. What if a show of fear would trigger him? But she couldn't stop the next sob, either, which wrenched her stomach. Ten hadn't been able to stop Escobar in time, and she had walked into his trap. They had let each other down so badly.

Escobar soothed her with his lying voice, and April clamped

her mouth tight. Maybe he would keep driving if she were quiet; at least then she could catch a thought. Her body trembled as if she were packed in ice, but April kept as quiet as she could.

"I hope you believe my sorrow for you is sincere," Escobar said.

If not for her gag, April would have told Escobar that if he were sorry, he should let her go. It wasn't too late, she would have said. April trembled so much that her cage *clank*ed against the side of the vehicle with her shivers.

"Don't waste your strength on knots and bars," Escobar said. "I've done this a time or two. My advice is to stay calm. You'll only be sleeping."

More ice water flushed April as she remembered how many women he had killed. Killing was a sport to him, a compulsion, and it came easily. The darkness paled. Was she slipping back to sleep again?

"You have a phone message," Escobar said, snapping her to alertness. "Both of us, actually. It's only fair that you hear it, since the first part is for you."

In the next instant, she heard Tennyson's recorded voice on her speaker phone over the engine's hum. "April, I'm coming, baby," he said. Tennyson's calm words and voice helped to slow her wild heart. His voice reminded her how much she loved him, and he loved her. His voice became her world. His voice and words rocking her like an infant in his arms. "I'm coming. I'm so sorry I wasn't there. But I'm coming now. I'll be there soon."

Yes, she thought. *He'll be here soon.* April sobbed with gratitude.

Tennyson's next words were for Escobar, not for her. All kindness left his voice.

"Don't hurt her," Tennyson told the killer. "I'm doing what you asked. I'm coming alone."

That time, Tennyson sounded like death. His voice had come, and then he was gone.

April sobbed for what she swore would be her last time. Her last indulgence.

"Such a tragic love story," Escobar said. "To die over something so senseless."

While April fought her tears and terror, Escobar drove on.

April came to full wakefulness when the van lurched to a stop.

Not a stoplight. Escobar changed gears. He was parking.

When Escobar stopped the engine, April held her breath. For the past hour, she'd told herself she would be fine as long as the van was moving. Until the van stopped, he could not touch her. He could not hurt her. At any moment, she might hear a siren. Rescue. Freedom.

But now Escobar opened his door. The van bounced from his weight as he hopped out. Footsteps fell on the pavement as he walked toward the van's rear door. He was in a hurry.

April's heartbeat matched the pace of his footsteps, outraced them. Her heartbeat filled her ears, mouth, and throat. Keys jingled, and the rear door gave a warning squeak as Escobar flung it open. April clenched her knees together, pulled her body into a ball. She swallowed back the whimpers trying to rise in her throat.

He probably gets off on scaring people. Don't give him the satisfaction.

Sound, defiant advice. But the whimpers tried to surface, humming from her voice box. Escobar liked to scare his *victims*. That was the true word for her. She had seen the women's faces in the tabloids and the news, their features blurred, their deaths irreparable.

More keys, and the door to her cage opened.

"I know you're awake, *negra*," Escobar said, so close to her, too close, and frozen feather tips traveled from her scalp to her toes. April instinctively moved away from his voice, trying to coil her body, bending her neck against the unyielding corner of the cage.

If he touched her, she would scream. She wouldn't be able to help herself.

"Yes, I understand," Escobar said, sighing. "I've felt helpless like you. My sister, Rosa . . ." He sighed. "My mother gave her life for us—her life. And when Rosa came here, she was always with the same friends, doing nothing, expecting me to give her money for clothes, for shoes, for trashy movies. She was my only sister, so I did it for love. She was beautiful, and I spoiled her too much." He paused and took a breath.

"And then I found her, April. With my own eyes, I saw her. She was standing on Atlantic Avenue selling herself to men, twitching her ass. A common street whore like the *grillas* in Havana. My father's blood, my mother's sacrifice, meant nothing to her. Pride and family name meant nothing. She had no decency in her, not like you and me."

He sighed so heavily that April felt his breath on her bare legs. She'd been wearing a skirt when she went to the police station with Ten, so professional, and she felt naked to Escobar's stare. Where were her shoes? Her shoes were gone.

April's whimpering grew louder. She wouldn't be able to control it soon.

"And do you know the true crime?" Escobar said softly. "For cleansing the streets of her filth, and the others, they call *me* a monster. What a world, no?"

April wished she could laugh. Ten had told April a story about how he'd tricked captors into removing his gag by pretending to laugh, because they wanted to know what was so funny. April wanted to tell Escobar how misunderstood he was, how she would never tell anyone she had seen him, how he knew in his heart that she didn't deserve to die.

But she couldn't laugh. She tried, but her throat was frozen with smothered screams.

A smooth, cool palm stroked April's calf. She bucked away, hitting her head on the side of the cage. One of her screams clawed free, made muffled and useless by her gag.

"Shhhh," Escobar said. "That was a loving touch, April. I promised not to hurt you unnecessarily, and I won't soil you—soil myself—that way. I'm not an animal. I'm sorry if touching upsets you."

April's breathing came in hitching gasps; she tried to calm herself and keep her thoughts clear. *He's calling you by name, humanizing you. Talk to him!* She struggled to form word sounds to follow Ten's example, to make Escobar curious enough to remove the gag, but she sounded as if she was hyperventilating. Maybe she was. The air in the pillowcase was hot and thick, with a new odor that clogged her nose.

The scent was like hot asphalt from a road construction site. But also a vague rot, like the Everglades swamp. Or a morgue.

This would be the killing place.

Esocbar grunted, and suddenly the cage pitched toward him. Another grunt, and the cage slid again. He was pulling her closer to the van door. He was strong.

"I'll let you out of this livestock pen," he said, "but you must walk. If you don't walk, if you struggle, I'll be forced to hurt you. You know what I can do."

April tried to say "Okay," hoping he could see her nodding. Walking meant open space and opportunities. If she could walk, maybe she could run. She didn't want to die in a cage.

Please don't let this be a trick, God.

"Be still. I'll put on your shoes," Escobar said.

April tried to be still, but she couldn't help flinching and trying to pull away when she felt Escobar's hand on her right ankle; he caught her and held on with his viselike grip. April had worn flats, not heels, so the shoe slid on easily. With her left foot, her leg gave another spasm as she tried to pull back, but he held her in place. His strength seemed effortless.

A quick *snap*, and he freed her ankles from their binds.

"Was that so bad?"

April shook her head. "Unh unh," she said, trying to tell him what he wanted to hear. But it *was* so bad. She fought back her gag reflex, sure she was about to vomit. If she threw up with her mouth covered, she might choke.

"*Tranquilo*," Escobar said. "Stay calm. The pillowcase comes off next."

April went still and silent again, rigid with combined fear and anticipation. *Yes!* The blindness was horrifying. If she could see, she would feel more in control. *Thank you, God.* Escobar might whisper sweet lies to her until the moment he killed her, but she was grateful for his lies. He had given her the shoes without hurting her. Untied her ankles. Maybe he would take off the pillowcase, too. Maybe the gag would be next.

Suddenly, the fabric whipped away, scratching the bridge of her nose, and her nostrils filled with unfiltered air. The odor was worse without the pillowcase, but the light and freshness of the air made up for that. April sucked in the air through her nostrils. Her throat unclamped itself, and the sick feeling passed.

Her face was turned away from Escobar's voice. She didn't have to see him yet.

"Better?" Escobar said.

April nodded, looking toward the van's empty passenger seat. She saw the thick wooden handle of some kind of large tool on the seat, so she looked at the floor of the van instead. Was that for her? She didn't want the sick feeling to come back.

"Now you're going to very slowly and carefully slide yourself out of the pen until you're standing beside me," Escobar said.

April nodded.

"Look at me." For the first time, the monster in him spoke to her. The anger in Escobar's voice was so thick and deep that April felt faint. She quickly brought her eyes to him.

Escobar's face filled her vision.

He was nothing to look at. His thick-framed round glasses were trendy, a film director's. His jowls weren't as tight as the rest of his face. He was in his fifties. He looked as if he hadn't shaved in a few days. The hair on his scalp was trimmed away except for dark fuzz. He didn't look big. He didn't look small. He looked like no one and nothing.

Escobar was still wearing the same blue sweater vest he'd worn when he was the old man in the wheelchair. April felt a wave of shame and sadness for how easily she'd been fooled—and after Ten had tried so hard to warn her! For the first time, April thought about her parents. Her brothers, Kevin and Jason. They would spend the rest of their lives haunted by what was happening to her. They would never recover.

"We both have to remember one thing, April," Escobar said to her, his monster growling at the edge of his voice. He stared earnestly, not blinking. "You chose him. You chose whoring filth. Maybe you felt sorry for him, thought you could change him. I tried the same path with Rosa. But you're responsible for this, so embrace it. Face it, *chica*. Give this night meaning."

April could only stare, frozen. Escobar's lip curled with his disappointment in her before he stepped back. "You look like the others, with those big cartoony eyes," he said. "All right, come out. Walk with me. Tennyson might already be here."

He smiled when he said Tennyson's name, and the monster seemed to be gone. She felt her face trying to mimic his smile, but April had lost her joy at the idea of Tennyson coming for her. That was what Escobar wanted.

If he would take off her gag, she would tell him she would do anything if he let her go. She would do anything if he would spare them.

"Move," the monster's voice said.

April scurried to back herself out of the cage; her legs were confused about how to support her, nearly crumpling her to the ground. Escobar caught her forearm to keep her standing, holding tight. This time, his grip had lost its patience. The first pain.

Escobar slammed the van door closed and pinned her to the rear door with a palm across her chest. Her arms, behind her, were pressed awkwardly against a hard door handle, but she couldn't move to relieve the pressure. He had no anger in his face, but he couldn't help hurting her. Of course he would hurt her. April did not cry out. She would not, she decided. She wouldn't let Escobar reduce her to a wreck for Ten to see. April tried to raise her neck to her full height, fighting the parts of her body that wanted to cower.

Even when she saw the gun, she stood tall. The muzzle was barely a foot from her, pointing toward her chin. Instead of the small handgun Escobar had used to capture her at the supermarket, he had a shotgun. April remembered the thick-handled tool she'd seen in the truck. Escobar had brought an arsenal for them.

"If you struggle, I shoot you," Escobar said. "If you make noise, I shoot you. If you run, I shoot you. *Punto.* If I have to shoot you, I disappear again, and my life goes on. I'll find Chela next. Shooting you makes no difference to me. Am I clear?"

April nodded. *Chela!* April had not thought about Chela, had not fathomed that Escobar would know her name. April wouldn't be able to yell out a warning to Tennyson, and Escobar would shoot Ten. Probably both of them. She was foolish not to try to run and get on with dying. That was better than pretending she believed she could survive. Or did she believe?

Ten was all they had. He was all *he* had.

"Come," Escobar said, tugging her arm. "Walk."

As April walked a pace in front of Escobar, feeling his gun at her back, the night came into bright focus. Neon shone through treetops. Garbage cans were marked HANCOCK PARK. The paved pathway where they walked was so well lighted that April was shocked at Escobar's boldness. Despite the trees, they were near a busy street, Wilshire Boulevard. She heard the steady, swishing burr of traffic. The street was close enough to hear music playing through an open car window, *boom-boom-boom*. Trees and shrubbery hid them from sight, but she guessed they couldn't be more than thirty or forty yards from witnesses.

Escobar would not take off her gag, then. He couldn't risk letting her scream.

Tears stung, but April blinked them back. She knew exactly where she was. She might have walked this path when her brother Jason dragged her to the museum when he came to visit two summers ago.

Suddenly, April understood the smell.

Understood all of it.

Escobar had chosen the tar pits for the theater value. An epic set piece.

He planned to bury them both.

THIRTY-SIX

MY FATHER TOOK me to the La Brea Tar Pits when I was a kid, maybe more than once. That irony crossed my mind while I was riding in the cab on Wilshire, staring out at the carnival of lights on Miracle Mile. Dad hadn't been one to think about field trips outside of our neighborhood library branch, but something about the tar pits and the remains scientists were unearthing there inspired him to want to bring me.

The La Brea Tar Pits are an excavation site in the most unlikely place—nestled in the urban heart of L.A., bordered by Hancock Park and one of its busiest streets on Museum Row. While time marched on, the tar pits remained, spitting up bygone creatures lulled to their deaths by the water above the deadly tar.

Saber-toothed tigers. Mastodons. A mammoth. The bones and stories were on display at the museum, dating back at least thirty thousand years. A place like that makes you feel small, like a blip in time. I remember standing beside my father while a tour guide explained that the only human remains researchers had found there had been a teenage girl discovered in 1914, buried and forgotten for ten thousand years. The story had scared me, and I'd tried to reach for my father's hand, but he pulled his hand away, telling me I was too old for that nonsense.

April might already be beneath the tar, history repeating. Drowned.

In that cab, I saw my dad like a vision, a man my age, in his forties, sun gleaming off his forehead, my own smile mirrored on his face. I could see him as if time had carried us back.

But I couldn't see April. Whenever my thoughts tried to drift to April, my stomach clenched, and my mind fled somewhere else. She was already becoming a dead hole to me, an awful discovery I was about to make.

If April was alive, it was only because Escobar wanted to use her to make me suffer. He was ready for me, and he would try to hurt her while I watched. I would have to do whatever I could to free her, which meant trying to bargain with Escobar for her life. But he probably would try to kill us both. He might do better than try.

The night ahead was a blur of waiting pain.

I had decided against trying to find a weapon. Escobar hadn't given me time, and I thought I might have a better chance of bargaining with him if I came unarmed, allowing him to have control. If Marsha was right, Escobar would feel conflicted about killing April. If I were lucky, I would be the only one of us to die.

I checked the time on my phone: ten minutes to midnight.

"Speed it up," I told the cabbie, dropping one of my twenties onto the front seat.

We had at least two miles to go, and he slowed for yellow lights instead of gunning through. We'd hit pockets of stalling traffic in the middle of the night, typical for L.A. I wanted to jump out of the cab and run on foot, but even a slow cab would get me there faster.

"Gotta follow the law, man," the cabbie said. "Can't get another ticket, or I'm done. I don't mess with CHP."

Even his Southern-tinged speech was languid; no part of him

was in a hurry. If I hadn't been so certain that April was already dead, I might have clocked him and thrown him from the moving car. I might have slit that stranger's throat to try to save her, if I believed I had to.

He turned on his radio, where a political news station played. All of the names were meaningless. The words were meaningless. I was floating above the world, waiting to crash back down.

"Where you from?" The cabbie might have asked me more than once, but I hadn't heard him the first time.

"Here. Born and raised."

"You're lucky, man. I'm from Georgia," he said. "I love it here, but I wish I'd stayed closer to grits and sweet tea. Just something special about home—know what I mean?"

I shook my head. "You live and you die. Nothing special about any of it."

He glanced at me in his rearview mirror, probably to judge if I was a robber or a lunatic. Then he looked back to the road. He gave up on talking to me.

I thought about a quick call to Chela, but we had said everything that needed saying. I had nothing left to do, except one last thing.

At the next red light, I couldn't sit still. It was ten minutes until midnight. We were at least half a mile from the tar pits, maybe more, but I needed motion to feel that I was doing anything for April. I dropped the rest of my money on the cabbie's seat before I climbed out of the car. "Wish me luck," I said. *Pray for me*, I wanted to say.

"God will make a way!" the cabbie called behind me. "What's your name?"

"Tennyson!" I called back.

I had someone's prayer, even if he was a stranger. He would speak my name.

I ran toward April with all my might.

✦ ✦ ✦

I wasn't the same man who'd raced after Escobar in the stairwell after he shot my father. I felt I'd aged decades in hours, was breathless by the time I reached the park entrance at the corner of Wilshire and Curson Avenue. The bands across my chest felt so tight I wondered if I was having a heart attack.

But I couldn't afford to care.

Where was he? Escobar might not be there—I'd find another note or some gruesome, bloody token. But after my eyes swept the deserted grounds, looking toward the museum and the parking lot first, a flicker of light caught my eye from my left side. The light was hardly brighter than a firefly's, but I saw it.

As always, Escobar was hidden in plain sight, maybe no more than twenty yards from me. I didn't see him in the shadows at first, but the light was an obvious signal. He was shrouded near the hulking figures of the park's signature mastodons.

Escobar had balls. We were barely a stone's throw from Wilshire Boulevard, and he had posted himself near the park's most recognized feature—the white concrete behemoths representing countless creatures that had sunk below the tar over the ages. The father stood mired helplessly in the tar, tusks high in a silent, terrified bellow, while two smaller ones—perhaps a mate and a child—watched from the shore. A family's moment of helplessness was perpetually captured for tourists from all over the world.

The exhibit was protected by a high black fence winding around a pit the size of a baseball diamond, but I walked toward the flickering light, watching for Escobar. The light was coming from *behind* the fence, close to the tar.

"Gus?" I called. My body flinched, expecting an answer from a gun.

The light flickered more persistently. A pen flashlight, I

guessed. I followed the paved path until the fence abruptly ended. A panel had been cut away, sagging inward.

My entry point.

The night stood still in the instant before I climbed over the broken fence, a moment of the unknown, of hope preserved. I was still alive. April might still be alive. The moon was full, casting a bluish hue over the black, silent tar. The creatures standing before me might have been real. Dad might have been beside me, holding my hand.

"Stop there, *compadre.*"

Escobar's voice came from the far side of the larger mastodon standing on solid ground. I still couldn't see him. Was he alone?

"Where's April?" I said.

A muffled sound might have been from her, close to Escobar. I leaned over slightly to try to see under the mastodon, and I thought I saw two pairs of legs, one clothed and one bare.

"April?" I said, taking another step forward.

"I said stop," Escobar said, and the new sound was definitely from my love, muffled pain. The sound sent pinpricks into my spinal cord. My knees turned to Jell-O.

"Don't hurt her," I said. "I'm here. I'm alone. That was our deal." I heard my own voice and wondered if I knew how foolish it was to try to bargain with a psychopath.

"Stay where you are," he said calmly. Unhurried. "Starting with your shirt, remove your clothes. Strip down. *Ahora.* Now."

I glanced around, expecting to find a crowd of tourists gawking with cameras, but the tourists had left with the sunlight. It was nearly one in the morning. Wilshire Boulevard's sparse traffic breezed past us, unaware. Any random jogger would have seen me, if anyone had been jogging. No security guard patrolled nearby. *Shit.* I considered trying to stall Escobar, but I didn't want to test his patience.

April made another sound, an attempt at communication. A

warning? She was obviously gagged, but she sounded like herself somehow. Escobar had not broken her.

"It's all right, baby," I lied, unbuttoning the dress shirt I had been wearing since my morning visit to Nelson's office. I suddenly wished I had confided in Nelson instead of fleeing his car. Had I been thinking straight? Anything had to be better than facing Escobar alone.

"The rest," Escobar said after I'd tossed my shirt to the ground. "Very slowly."

I unhooked my slacks and let them fall to my ankles. I had lost weight in the past couple of weeks; my clothes barely fit me. I stepped out of my pants, taking time with each foot.

"Satisfied?" I said, hoping I could keep my briefs on. "I'm unarmed. No wire."

"You're a good boy. You know how to take direction better than that, Tennyson," Escobar said. "*Todos.*"

He wanted me nude. Exposed. Vulnerable. I bent over slightly to tug down my briefs, keeping my eyes toward the voice. The morning air bit into my skin, but my shiver had nothing to do with the cold.

"*Bueno.* Now," Escobar said. "Step toward the small one. Walk slowly."

The baby mastodon stood in front of its mother, closer to the tar's edge. As I took careful steps, I saw two shadowed figures behind the larger beast.

April was bent over in front of Escobar, and a shotgun lay across her back, pointed straight at me. April was wearing the dress I'd seen her in earlier; Escobar hadn't stripped her. Maybe he hadn't raped her. The gun was pointed at me, not at her. So far, so good.

"Please," I said. "Let her go. April hasn't done anything. She isn't like the others."

"Or like you?" Escobar said.

"Or like me. She's nothing like me. You know that."

"Look in the shadow. See what I have left for you." When I hesitated, Escobar pumped his shotgun to chamber a round. I couldn't make out all of the gun's details, but it was a twelve-gauge. At this range, he could hit me without trying.

Confused, I did as he had asked and saw coiled there a pair of ankle cuffs, joined with eighteen inches of unbreakable plastic wire. Probably available at any sex-toy shop on Sunset Boulevard. I slipped the loops over my feet, desperation bubbling up like methane through tar.

But there was hope, too. If he was focused on me, he wasn't thinking about April.

"You're right," Escobar said, his voice tight. "She's not like you. But her judgment was poor, no? And now here we are. So you must watch her drown, Tennyson. That's her price for foolish choices. When I'm finished here, I'll come for Chela."

He must have done something to April—something outside of my vision—because she tried to suppress a sound of pain as he pushed her closer to the tar. A tide of rage stirred in me, but if I let myself hear April's pain, it would blot out that part of me that could save us.

"You only get one shot before this place is crawling with cops," I said. "You picked the wrong spot, Gus. You picked the wrong weapon." *You picked the wrong man.*

April let out a muted yell as Escobar forced her to take another step closer to the edge of the tar pit. April's hands were bound behind her back. Under Escobar's grip, she walked bent over, as if she carried an overwhelming weight on her back. But Escobar barely seemed to notice her.

"You're wrong, Tennyson," Escobar said. "The first shot will attract attention, *sí*. But I will aim low. And there you'll lie, screaming and helpless, while I force her head beneath the water. She will drown quickly. In panic, they always drown quickly. I shoot you a second time, this one in the head, and I will vanish—a phantom once again."

I forced a chuckle. "Sorry, man, but you don't know April. That girl doesn't panic."

Was April laughing, too? She made a sound remarkably like my chuckle, and I nearly smiled. *Good girl, April.* If we unnerved Escobar, we could knock him off his game.

Escobar made a sudden jerking movement. April's laugh, if that was what it had been, became a wounded animal's cry. I heard the wet *snap* of a breaking bone. April shuddered, nearly lurching off her feet, but Escobar pulled her close. April sobbed once but stopped midway through, as if from pure will. My whole body went cold to try to block out her pain.

"Laugh at me again," Escobar said, "and I'll break her other wrist. They're as fragile as a sparrow's wing. And you, April—*walk*, or see him castrated."

He pushed April another step closer to the tar.

Think think think think think think think think think

"Whatever happens to April, the same thing happens to Louise," I said.

Escobar barked a laugh. "You're truly desperate, Tennyson."

"You know she's been working night and day trying to finish your masterpiece," I said. "Don't try to tell me you haven't been spying on the woman who was supposed to be the mother of your child. When's the last time you saw her, Gus? You thought I came out here without a bargaining chip? You let April go—my people let Louise go."

"I care nothing for her," Escobar said.

But we were both lying. If he hadn't cared about Louise, he would have kept moving instead of stopping to deny his feelings. I heard it in his voice.

"Yes, you do. She's the closest you've found to someone who understands you. You care about Louise, and you care about that damn movie," I said. "My partner hunts and hurts people for a living. If she doesn't get good news from me in five minutes, we both lose somebody tonight."

My description of Marsha didn't sound that far off, if only she had agreed to help me. If Marsha had backed me up, by this time, Escobar would have been cooling meat.

Escobar hesitated. "*She?*" Good. He'd been listening.

"Yes," I said. "I know a lot of interesting women. Some of them aren't very nice." *Bingo.* The devil is in the details. A female was so unlikely in this context that I could see that he was struggling not to believe me.

"Always an actor, Tennyson—and not a very good one," he said, deciding I was lying. He dragged April closer to the muck.

I hadn't expected a threat against Louise to work. Even if Escobar cared about Louise, his mission would come first. But I had bought a few seconds to try to unsettle him, break his concentration, force a mistake. I only needed seconds. Escobar wouldn't want to fire his gun any sooner than he had to. As long as we were hidden, he could say or do anything; but the moment his gun fired, he might have three minutes or less to finish his work.

His sickness was hurting his logic; it was much harder to try to wound someone with a gun rather than simply firing at the center of mass. And the logistics of trying to drown April were complicated. Escobar couldn't outsmart his compulsion to follow his ritual.

Escobar pushed April forward another step, and suddenly, they were less than ten yards away from me, fully visible in the pale moonlight. April was gagged, but her eyes staring up at me hadn't changed. If she was crying, I couldn't see it. Despite the pain from her broken bone, all I saw in her eyes was defiance. And love. April looked more concerned about me than she was about herself.

"Don't you worry about a thing, baby girl," I said, as if we were alone. As if there were no gun riding across her back. "This will all be over soon."

"*Sí*," Escobar said, giving her a harsh push that nearly sent her to her knees at the edge of the water. "It will be over soon."

The water gurgled, and an odor like stale farts wafted from the pond. Timeless rot. The water looked as if it was boiling in slow motion. While Escobar glanced toward the ripples in the tar pit, I inched closer to him. With my brown skin against the night, he never saw me move. Despite the ankle cuffs, I would be close enough to leap at him if he gave me another chance. A shotgun was unwieldy; if I came at him from the right angle, he would never have the chance to aim.

My heartbeat sped. In the dark, it would be hard to recognize the right moment, and there would only be one.

Escobar chopped his knee behind April's so that she collapsed to the soil, her bare knees hitting the ground too hard. She looked like an impending execution, gagged, with her hands behind her. April cried out again, but only briefly, trying so hard not to. Her cry tried to pummel past my defenses, but I shut her pain away.

As much as I wished I could, I couldn't turn away from April's face. She needed my eyes to give her hope. I nodded to her: *I've got this. Just trust me.*

"Come, Tennyson," Escobar said. With an exaggerated wrenching movement, he grabbed a tight handful of April's hair with his free hand, yanking her head back the way he had pulled Brittany's on the set. April's hair was short, so he must have caught her by the roots. The sound April made this time was more indignation than pain.

Escobar grinned at me with déjà vu. "This," he said, "is how you take control. So now it's your turn. Come take her from me."

He waggled his shotgun at me, a beckoning finger. A Mossberg twelve-gauge. When I blinked, I thought I saw the barrel blaze.

The mass of pellets would travel faster than the speed of sound. I might not live to hear it.

"Better watch your aim," I said. "That's gonna rip me up."

"I can live with that if you can," Escobar said.

"But then April is wasted," I said. "You did all this for nothing. No purpose. Would this make *Mami* proud? For this she sacrificed herself?"

The anger on Escobar's face was nearly bright enough to glow, but he didn't speak. He glared at me with lips pursed tight, still hyperalert. He never looked away from me or loosened his expert grip on April. If I couldn't rattle him by mentioning his mother, rattling him might not be possible.

Escobar struck April with his knee again, and she fell flat to the soil with an *oof*. He planted his weight on her, driving her into the ground. Her face was inches from the black, oily water.

"You don't need April, Escobar," I said. "Let her go. You got me. Here I am. Look at me." My arms akimbo, I shuffled in a slow circle so Escobar could look me over at every angle. Every vulnerability.

"Come, Tennyson," Escobar urged. "If you love her, fight for her."

He would fire as soon as I took a step, and Escobar was deluded if he thought a shot at close range with a Mossberg would leave him a living toy to play with. I might be able to exchange my life for April's, but I couldn't trust Escobar to let her go after I was gone.

"We both know that's a losing game," I said. "The first move I make in that direction, I'm dead."

Escobar's gun never wavered, and April was too off-balance to resist him; her head flopped like a rag doll's under Escobar's death grip. He teased us both, bringing her face closer to the water, then away again. My adrenaline tapped out, leaving only a blind panic I wasn't sure I could shut away.

"You've surprised me, Tennyson," Escobar said with a resigned sigh. "I expected you to be more impulsive. More eager to play the hero. If this woman isn't worth it to you, *pues* . . . I understand." When he shrugged, the gun's aim shifted from my waist to my face. "Help will come sooner if I shoot you, but you'll live longer if I don't. That's your own decision. Truly, all that matters to me is that you watch this woman drown before I kill you."

A man of his word, Escobar plunged April's head into the tar.

THIRTY-SEVEN

APRIL HAD KNOWN she needed her own plan as soon as she saw Tennyson—especially after he stripped off his clothes and she realized he hadn't brought a weapon. Tennyson *was* a weapon, but a short-range one. He couldn't get past the shotgun and planned to sacrifice himself to try to save her. She could see it in his every motion, hear it in every word. His plan was in his eyes as he gazed at her.

It's up to me. She could jolt Escobar in some way, kick him, butt him with her head. She just had to find the right time, the right way; that was all Tennyson needed. She had to show him that she could fight with him, that he didn't have to die for her.

But Escobar wouldn't give her a chance to think. Every time she tried to map out a plan, he hurt her. Pain scattered April's thoughts.

She'd ignored the pain from having her arms twisted behind her back while Escobar walked her like a dog on a leash. But a sharp *crank* made her realize he would try to break her left wrist, and then hot, sharp pain flared when he finally did. Her wrist was a twig to him. While he distracted her with agony, he walked her closer to the water. More pain, and her knees were sinking into the damp, cold bank. He was moving too fast.

She inhaled, held it. Exhaled hard. Inhaled deeply. Packed the air down, compressing it in her lungs. Exhaled hard. Repeated.

You'll have to hold your breath. Pretend to struggle. Pretend to pass out. Hold your breath—

Then the world was gone. Only water, and something like sticky thin mud, everywhere.

Escobar's sudden motion took April by such surprise that she almost lost her breath. The water was so cold, the darkness so sudden and complete, that April forgot her plan. She forgot everything except the need to stay calm, as she appeared to be consumed with panic.

Instinct made her try to raise her head, but she couldn't move against Escobar's grip of stone. *Struggle, but don't burn up too much oxygen.* She let a trickle of bubbles escape her mouth. *He'll be watching for signs that you're losing control.*

Pretend to struggle. Pretend to drown.

Her writhing felt real, tiring her. The water was absurdly shallow over something the consistency of oatmeal. Only inches separated her from living or dying, and she tried to free her mouth and nose from the liquid cage. She felt the air on her shoulder, the back of her neck. Once, her ear broke the surface, and she heard Tennyson shout, "Don't do this!"—more a roar than a shout—with so much alarm in his voice that she knew he was on the verge of charging into Escobar's shotgun blast.

Go limp. Pretend to suffocate.

Even as her lungs screamed for air, April forced herself to flop forward, paralyzed. Her neck drooped, no longer pushing back against Escobar's palm. How many seconds had she been holding her breath since he'd pushed her in? Twenty? Thirty? How long would Escobar think she could last? Did he know she was a swimmer?

She had to take a chance. If he had contempt for women, he could easily underestimate her capacity. He had felt her struggle. Mightn't he believe she was exhausted, done?

April went limp.

One one-thousand, two one-thousand—

Escobar shook her, as if to test her, and she didn't move despite his claw grasping the hair on back of her head. As her face sank deeper into the pool, she felt the water's texture change, thickening. Her nostrils felt plugged with cold, oily asphalt. Her heartbeat sent tremors throughout her joints. Escobar would never believe she was unconscious if he felt her move.

April tried to lie perfectly still. *Seven one-thousand . . . eight . . .*

Escobar only had to loosen his grip for an instant. That was all she needed.

But could she wait long enough?

April was dying while I watched.

She had stopped fighting. Had she gotten a good breath? Was she drowning or playing possum? I'd seen the rush of bubbles. Water invading her lungs? Escobar kept his eyes on me, grinning. Only his clamped teeth showed his effort to hold her face beneath the water.

My muscles ached from being spring-loaded, ready to leap at him. But Escobar never stopped watching me. If I shifted my shoulders right or left, Escobar's gun followed me, waiting. Even in the dark, he saw every move I made, as if he knew my mind.

"You stand there and do nothing?" Escobar said. "You're so weak, Tennyson?"

The simplistic-minded confuse weakness and strength every day.

"Look at her, dammit!" I said, pointing. "You killed her!"

I'd seen April swim underwater from one end of a pool to the other without taking a breath, so I didn't believe she was dead, even if I was setting myself up for a nasty surprise. *Look over there!* was a child's game, a transparent ploy. But my words nearly choked me. I let Escobar hear my sorrow and resignation, allowing tears to run down my face. I swayed as if I might swoon, powerless hands posed on top of my head. For good measure, I pretended to sob.

And then . . . it wasn't entirely pretense.

Escobar's face softened to a kind of rapture as he studied me. My grief delighted him. His teeth unclenched as he loosened his grip on April. He shifted his weight slightly, easing his knee's pressure from her back. Escobar had kept too many photographs as trophies; I knew he wouldn't be able to resist a peek at a fresh kill. His eyes glanced away from me, toward April's submerged head. Would he pull her face out to check his work?

I never found out what Escobar might have done.

Because suddenly, my angel thrashed hard, bucking against Escobar with so much force that his gun wobbled an inch or two beyond me while he regained his balance.

I acted a millisecond later, flying at Escobar with maniac speed, but I dove instead of leaping high. Curled tightly, performed a shoulder roll, and came up from below. Praying it would take him a moment to adjust his aim.

Did I mention that I'm fast?

Before Escobar could get his shotgun in line, I was coming up, kicking from below, aiming at his groin and stomach, hoping I'd miss April. He lurched backward, but I got a grazing shot in and heard him gasp in pain. Then the three of us were a tangle of arms and legs and ankle cuffs and shotgun.

I wrapped one arm around Escobar's neck and tugged at his death grip on April with the other. She bucked again, struggling to free herself from his weight. Her head was still submerged, and then her face came free with a sucking sound, black with tar.

Escobar waved his shotgun, unable to find a way to contort his arm to hit a target. I didn't have an arm free to grab the gun, but I heaved hard away from April, and my weight landed on Escobar's shoulder with a *crunch*.

April's legs kicked at Escobar as she tried to curl herself away from the pit. I kicked, too, pushing Escobar's legs away from April's midsection to release her.

A heaving gasp came from her, followed by frantic choking and spitting up, the sound of a ferocious fight for life. April flopped herself away from the pit like a beached fish. April could win her battle to live as long as I kept Escobar away from her.

I wrestled Escobar for his weapon but he held on, and the barrel was too long to turn around on him the way he had turned the handgun on my father. He would shoot April out of spite if he could. I kneed Escobar in the thigh and, as he grimaced, found the leverage to twist and fling the shotgun out of his grip, sending it flying into the water with a near-silent splash ten feet from us, beneath the frozen mastodon's tusks.

But the price was steep: Escobar mule-kicked me with the soles of both shoes on my upper thigh, barely missing my groin. That would have finished me, but the pain still exploded a bomb in my gut.

Gustavo Escobar and I were a long way from finished. He knew how to fight, too.

My brain's messages to my muscles slowed, and Escobar wriggled away from me. Maybe I'd hoped he'd go after the shotgun. That little mistake would have mired him in the tar, and April and I could have sat on the bank and watched him become a paleontologist's wet dream.

But no, instead, he came at me. I'd gotten to my feet and instinctively tried to kick, ripping my own leg out from under me when I yanked on the ankle cuffs. *Damn!*

Tottering, I was a sitting duck as his shoulder slammed into me, going for a single-leg takedown that came right out of a college wrestling playbook.

"April, run!" I shouted.

"Help us . . ." I heard April try to shout, but it was little more than a hoarse whisper. She sounded as if she was still at ground level. She wasn't on her feet yet.

"April, *run!*" I yelled again.

I was down on my back in the shallow muck at the edge of the tar pit, and we were rolling, too close to disaster for either of us to gain advantage.

A few inches of water over a tarry abyss. With the water's oily texture, I could barely keep a grip on him. Escobar wriggled like an eel, adjusting easily to every grip and grapple. I sucked in two lungs full of air before he pinned me under the water.

Shit, I realized. *He's a wrestler.* Some scrap of information about his college wrestling scholarship had emerged in the tabloids, but I'd forgotten when it mattered most.

I've studied half a dozen different fighting arts, and every single one of them was pugilistic, dammit. At ground-and-pound range, in the slippery muck at the edge of a lethal tar pit, shackled by ankle chains, I was about as screwed as a guy could be without getting kissed first.

Another knee to my gut, and I coughed out my air. Some body responses are involuntary, even when they're deadly. I saw Escobar's pale face above me, the ancient mastodon above him. I saw his teeth when he smiled.

I'd only faced off with one true killer before Gustavo Escobar. The rest of the men I'd fought had been desperate; killing wasn't natural to them, even if they had killed others. My last dance with a death merchant had ended so improbably that I still didn't understand how I had walked away from Spider and his deadly knife.

And now Gustavo Escobar was killing me with his bare hands. Drowning me. Even when I heard Dad's voice—*Get him, Ten*—I couldn't catch my rhythm, couldn't break his advantage. The realization became clearer, the voice of defeat louder in my ears and my mind. *You're going to die tonight.*

He could catch April. He would go after Chela next. He would kill all of us. My last thoughts in the tar pit would be self-loathing and shame.

Escobar had slithered behind me as I thought of Chela, his arm slipping around my neck, as mine had once slipped around Spider's. I got my chin down and defeated the worst part of his naked strangle. He'd left me enough room to get my teeth into his forearm, and Lord, I bit him as if I were one of his movie undead.

He roared with pain, but I hadn't tracked, hadn't realized he'd gotten his left arm free, and he clubbed me on the side of the head so hard I saw stars, and then blackness.

Die. You're going to—

Like millions of creatures before me, I sank to sleep in the tar.

THIRTY-EIGHT

APRIL'S RIBS ACHED, but the terrible pressure on her back and the force behind her head—were gone. *Thank you, Lord.* April had pulled herself away from the water, hands clawing at the soil. *Thank you so much, Lord.* She coughed as if her lungs could split at the seams, but the oxygen massaged her insides, woke up her mind, slowed her galloping heart. For a single shining moment, April's horrific night had turned beautiful.

Then she clawed muddy tar from her face, blinked her eyes hard, and saw Tennyson and Escobar, and she realized the night could change again.

They were fighting like two cats in a sack, and she was still too wobbly to help. Any effort to move brought a fit of coughing. While her lungs spat out acrid water droplets, April looked around for a weapon, anything she could use to help him. Nothing came to sight.

She'd watched as the shotgun flew into the water, heard Tennyson's cry of pain as Escobar kicked him. Then Escobar smashed into him, taking him down at the edge of the pool, and they rolled savagely at the edge of the mire, flirting with prehistoric disaster. *Oh no oh no oh no oh no.*

"April, *run!*" If April hadn't seen for herself, she would have known from Tennyson's voice that they were far from free, and if she didn't run, they might never be. Escobar was a demon that had been loosed on them both. He didn't care about law, or love, or his own life. He was like nothing she had ever seen or known.

But April couldn't run. She tried to pull herself to her knees and collapsed back down. She tried to call for help—to scream at the top of her lungs—but her mouth barely made a sound. Would God spare her from the tar only to send her back again? To let this madman kill her and Tennyson?

"Run!" Tennyson shouted again as they rolled, slimed with water and tar and blood.

April rolled over, trying to summon strength back to her legs. She bumped her broken wrist and shrieked as the pain drained her again. How many times had she watched horror movies and complained when the heroine fell down, helpless? What was wrong with her?

You're in shock, a voice in her head explained. It might have been God's voice or her own. *Take a deep breath. Get on your feet. Get help.*

Help wasn't far. She didn't have to get to the van—only as far as the street, where she still heard traffic. She could wave down a car. It was all so simple, if only she could stand up.

With a grunt that was almost a scream, April brought herself to her knees again, pressing her throbbing, swollen wrist close to her back. Everything rocked, but the dizziness passed when she took a deep breath. Her coughing nearly knocked her over again, but determination kept her on her knees.

April didn't want to look, but she glanced at Tennyson and Escobar at the edge of the pit. She saw Tennyson pull Escobar into the water, felt her heart swell . . .

But like the demon he was, Escobar was on top. Escobar was riding Tennyson as if trying to rape him. Tennyson was down, unable to find footing, unable to gain purchase or find a moment to breathe. A human being cannot fight an ape, and Escobar's ferocity was simian, like a rabid baboon.

April flung herself to her unsteady feet. She swayed for balance, leaning against the baby mastodon's grooved concrete fur. She tried to gather power in her lungs. "Help us!" she called to the sky. "Somebody!"

Her voice was louder but not loud enough to reach Wilshire Boulevard.

April took one step, two steps, three steps toward the broken fence. Freedom. Help.

Before she could reach the fence, a shadow flew toward April in the night.

An angel? A phantom?

It was a dark-skinned woman dressed in skintight black. She moved like a leopard, leaping over the broken segment of fence. So swift and smooth was she that her feet seemed to float above the ground. She held a small, deadly automatic. But she wasn't a police officer; April knew that in a glance.

Did Escobar have a partner? April was so confused and distraught that she nearly sagged back to the ground.

The woman was running toward the water.

"Escobar!" she shouted. There was strength in her voice like nothing April had ever heard from a woman. Not cop-strong or army-strong. This was death. Her voice seemed to silence the night.

Escobar looked toward her, startled. "Who—"

"Your father was a hero," the woman said. "You don't deserve that patriot's name. This is for the girls you killed, you fucking pig."

"Wait—" Escobar said, holding up his palm as if to stop a bullet.

But she didn't wait. The gun flamed in the woman's hand with a *pop* that wasn't as loud as April expected. Escobar gasped, head jerking backward, eyes crossing as if each of them was trying to see the hole just above his nose. Escobar's bones melted, and he slid down into the water.

April expected Tennyson to rise next, but he didn't. The water was still and quiet except for a far-off gurgling sound, as if only the dead inhabited the tarry pond.

"Oh, shit on a stick," the woman said. "Ten?"

She ran to the water.

For the first time, April realized that the woman was Marsha.

"I knew you were about to do something stupid. Dead ain't sexy, precious."

I dreamed I heard Marsha's voice whispering just beyond my ear. My face twitched, and I tried to bat the voice away. Marsha's voice wasn't supposed to be in my ear. Only April's.

I blinked, and life turned loud and bright. I rolled over and spat what tasted like crude oil out of my mouth. When I coughed, my lungs bellowed for air. The ground felt hard and grainy against my back. I saw blades of grass, a tree trunk. Marsha was kneeling over me, water dripping from her mucky, matted hair.

I turned to my side as a dark liquid poured from my lips. I'll never forget that nasty taste.

"You stopped breathing, but you'll live," Marsha said. "Paramedics are on the way. I got to give you mouth-to-mouth, so I guess the night wasn't a total loss."

The tree trunk was actually a mastodon leg, I realized. The tar pit came back to me. Remembering my nakedness, I curled in a fetal position to hide myself. When I moved, my whole body screamed.

"Where's..." I tried to speak, but I couldn't finish my sentence because I was coughing.

Before I could try to sit up to look for April, I felt a hand around mine. "Ten? Just be still, baby. Everything's all right." April's voice was thin, but her coughing had stopped.

Sirens approached in a chorus.

Marsha stood up, wiping grass and debris from her damp black jeans. "Well, kids, this has been a blast, so to speak . . . but that's my cue. I've got no business here."

"Escobar?" I wheezed, gazing around. If he had escaped again, I might spend the rest of my life hunting him.

"They'll have to fish him out," Marsha said, nodding toward the water. "Or leave him in for twenty years and then open a new exhibit. *Cocksuckus gigantis,* commonly known as Los Angeles Man. It was hard enough getting you out of there. April's no weakling—not bad for a girl with only one good hand. That bastard broke her wrist, you know."

I had never seen April and Marsha side-by-side, although once they had seemed like two halves of my ideal woman. I'd often wished that Marsha had more of April's sweetness and that April had more of Marsha's daring. April was svelte and wonderfully athletic. But Marsha's mind and body were lethal. There is a difference. Marsha was like a knife, so sharp there was no place to hold it. That night, for an instant, they blended into one image. One woman.

Then I blinked. Marsha was standing above us, ready to float away with emotionless eyes, and April was beside me, squeezing my hand between hers like a mother. Later, on painkillers, I would wonder if Marsha ever had been there. At the hospital that night, it was hard to remember anything except April's miraculous, dimpled smile beaming down at me.

"Marsha shot him," April said. "She showed up out of nowhere and—"

"You mean that Good Samaritan shot him," Marsha said. "He shot Escobar and ran off. Said he recognized Escobar from TV. One less serial killer in the world, he said. Looked a little like

Brad Pitt. If you don't get your story straight, one of you is going to jail."

She wiped down her 9mm and tossed it into the water. A police siren wailed, getting closer.

I fought another coughing spell. "Thanks," I choked out. Talking felt like fire.

Marsha shrugged. "Your lady here would have handled it," she said. "But everyone can use a little backup now and then."

"No, really." April's lip quivered. "I could barely walk. You saved our lives."

Marsha blew us a kiss over her shoulder, stepping toward the gap in the fence. "Play safe," Marsha said. "See you around, Ten."

I coughed again. "Not if I see you first." I'd said it with more affection and gratitude than anything I'd ever said to her.

"Don't worry," she said. "You won't." She looked at April, who was holding me tight. "You take care of each other, you hear?"

April nodded, unable to speak.

I blinked, and Marsha was gone.

THIRTY-NINE

AT THE HOSPITAL the next day, during my battery of tests, a parade of grim-faced doctors came to my room to tell me how lucky I was to be alive. I'd heard the speech before, but my luck finally felt real.

I wasn't supposed to survive Gustavo Escobar. He was my boulder in the rapids, the end of my good fortune, and maybe I'd known that since the first time Chela mentioned a serial killer. An act of grace had saved April and me, not just Marsha's change of heart. I could barely hear the doctors because of the distraction of the bright, crisp sunlight through my window.

My first stolen morning after I cheated death.

I'd lied to the cabbie who drove me to the tar pits, I realized. Home does matter—and to me, home is the Southern California sun. My father always shared that sunshine with me, and it would take time to get used to the shadow he'd left behind, but it was the only home I had.

Escobar had gifted me with a groin injury called a testicular rupture. The name says it all. I'd had surgery overnight—without it, let's just say I would have had to get used to a change of scenery in the shower. The doctors planned to keep me in the hospital for a day to monitor my recovery and test results. I'm not usually a fan of painkillers, but I wanted to write a personal note of thanks to the pharmaceutical companies.

No wonder I'd nearly drowned. Or *did* drown, as Chela liked to point out.

"Did you see a white light?" Chela asked me from her chair beside my bed. She and Bernard had driven to the hospital as soon as they got the 2:00 A.M. call, and he was in the commissary fetching her breakfast. Instead of South Beach Chela, she had her hair in pigtails that made her look fifteen again; Bernard brought out the kid in her. I knew Chela would be fine without me, but we were both glad she didn't have to hurry to grow up.

"No white light," I said.

"There's this chemical your body produces at the time of death called dimethyltryptamine, right? They call it DMT, like a psychedelic. Did you feel a rush?" The girl had become a death scholar.

I shook my head. "Sorry."

April was at my window, peeking down at the crowd. I didn't have to turn on the television to know that the media had descended upon Good Samaritan Hospital to capture the latest twist in the Gustavo Escobar story. I could hear the helicopters beating overhead. The story never died. "Dimethyl . . . what?" April said. "Where'd you hear that?"

"The internet." Chela turned back to me. "Did you see the Captain? Your mother?"

I fought not to sigh. I understood Chela's new fascination with death—she'd lost a friend, her grandfather, a mother figure, and nearly me in what seemed like days—but I didn't have any happy endings to share with her. Except . . .

"I thought I heard my father's voice, maybe," I said. "I just wanted you and April to be safe. That's all I remember."

"His heart never stopped, Chela," April reminded her. "Just his breathing."

Chela looked disappointed. "Oh. Right."

Across the room, April mouthed a word at me, gesturing toward Chela: *Ther-a-py*.

I smiled and nodded. Smiles came easily. My agent, Len, had a romance with painkillers after his divorce; I made a mental note to toss away my prescription bottles before I got too cozy.

A knock sounded at the door, and Chela and April leaped to stand between me and the next visitor. Anyone who thinks a hospital is a good place to rest hasn't tried to rest in one.

The door cracked open, and April practically slammed it shut.

"Who is it?" April said.

"Um . . . Detective Lydia Hernandez," said a voice I had once known.

"Hell no," Chela said. "No cops."

Despite surgery, I'd spent ninety minutes giving RHD my statement at four in the morning, and April had finished her own interview separately. Every detective who heard our story knew our mysterious shooter was bullshit, that we were protecting someone, but they couldn't shake us. The dead body in the tar pit had been positively identified as Gustavo Escobar, which was the most important thing. At least they had a trophy.

But I recognized the voice at the door despite my narcotic haze. "Wait. Let her in."

Lieutenant Hernandez was wearing office attire in the colors of Miami, her dark hair loose over her shoulders. Her smile reminded me of everything I had once loved about Miami. The woman was twice as gorgeous as the vase of lilies she'd brought me. The last time I'd seen her, my father had been safe in his South Beach hotel room with his new bride.

"*Hola*, Tennyson," she said.

April had a jealous streak, and I glanced in her direction, ready to explain that I'd only met Detective Hernandez once during a dead end in my investigation. But April was the first one shaking her hand, guiding her inside, returning her smile, fawning over the flowers. After all, I'd nearly died trying to save April—and no pretty face could touch that.

"Hello, Detective," I said.

"Please," she said. "Call me Lydia, both of you. I'm so sorry about your ordeal. But at least he's gone now." She avoided mentioning Escobar by name, gazing at the cast on April's wrist. "I came to thank you. Again. I just wish I'd . . ." She sighed, shaking her head as she cast her head down. "*Nuestro Tío Fidel* meant so much to my parents. To so many people. I still don't understand how they were the same man."

"Art isn't the artist," April said quietly. "One day, maybe we'll all figure that out."

Not likely, I thought. When artists move us, we don't want to believe the worst about them, because we don't want to reject anything we love. How much longer would Escobar have stalked his victims if he hadn't made the mistake of hiring me for his film?

"When I came to you, I didn't give you much to go on," I told Hernandez. My voice was still slightly hoarse from the harshness of the tar pit. "Let it go, Lydia. I think you told me something like that once. Get a hobby?"

Lydia Hernandez gave me a grateful smile. We both knew she would have hesitated to interview Escobar even if I had come with fingerprints and a confession. But the past is the past.

"I hope it's all right, but I brought a date," Hernandez said. "The brass from LAPD who convinced me to talk to you wants to come pay his respects."

Before any of us could object, the door peeked open again, and Lieutenant Rodrick Nelson came in. He was wearing the dress uniform he'd worn to Dad's funeral, including his gloves, his face grim. I should have realized that Dad had called Nelson from Miami to clear my way with South Beach police.

"Hate to disappoint you, but he didn't kill me," I told Nelson.

Nelson didn't answer my joke. Instead, he reached over to

shake my hand. I admit I hesitated, but I gave him his handshake. He then turned to shake April's good hand and kissed her wrist like Prince Charming. One look at Chela told him not to bother trying with her, but he gave her a friendly nod.

"I won't stay long," Nelson said. His eyes were so tired he might have been up all night. "I owe you an apology. And it's not the first time." Nelson wasn't good at apologizing. His lips were so tight the words could barely squeeze out. It was painful to watch.

"Man, don't," I said. "If the chief sent you in here to kiss my ass—"

Nelson couldn't deny it. I saw the glimmer in his eyes. He sighed and checked behind him to make sure the door was closed. Then he tossed his black hat to the foot of my bed and yanked off his white gloves one by one. "You're right," he said. "This is bullshit. Excuse my language, ladies."

"Bullshit?" Chela said, but I raised my hand to shush her. I didn't want a fight to break out in my room and mess with my peaceful vibe. Who knew when I would find another one?

Nelson stepped closer to stand directly over me. "Yeah, Tennyson. Bullshit," he said. "Because I don't need the chief's office to tell me when to do what's right. I don't want to be here disturbing you and your family right now. But since I'm here, I'm gonna lay it out straight for you—not some damage control the chief's office cooked up so you won't talk shit to CNN."

He held out his hand for a shake again. I only stared, confused.

"From me," Nelson said. "I'm sorry."

This time, when I took Nelson's hand, he didn't let me go. He held on as he gazed at me. "You know I haven't liked some of your choices, especially when it came to Preach," he said, not blinking. "You're not always my kind of man, but you're definitely Preach's son. He was proud of you. And he was right; you'd make a hell of a cop, brother."

"Thanks." Until that moment, I hadn't realized he was the closest thing I'd ever have to a brother.

Nelson nodded and punched my shoulder, gently. "Get better, Tennyson," he said. "Your family's safe now. You shot that sonofabitch right between the eyes."

"Actually . . ." April began dutifully, remembering our script. "Ten didn't . . ."

Nelson grinned at me, winking. "Yeah," he said. "Right."

"Is this a signature from Sidney Poitier?" Gloria Forrest asked me, her mouth in a shocked O. "Bill, come look at this!"

April's parent hadn't made it beyond my foyer without gawking. I glanced at the space through their new eyes: lovely Mexican tiles on the floors and framed one-sheet and two-sheet movie posters from a bygone era. *A Raisin in the Sun. Guess Who's Coming to Dinner. In the Heat of the Night.*

I'd met April's parents briefly at the hospital, but I hadn't hosted them at my house until Marcela threw a dinner party the night I was released. I was in far from a party mood, but it seemed appropriate. They had flown to L.A. because of what had happened to April, so they might as well get to know their daughter's boyfriend. We were meeting her brothers for lunch the next day. April and I were in new territory.

"Oh, yeah, Mom, there's so much Hollywood history in here," April said. "Ten has an amazing collection. This house is a museum."

April gave me a coy smile while her parents marveled over the vintage movie posters. Of course, she hadn't mentioned that I had inherited much of the house's collection from a former client who had been old enough to be my grandmother. But the house had been mine for years. Alice's collection wasn't on display for anyone but me.

"Now, see here?" her father said, gesturing toward the *Raisin* poster. "Sidney Poitier! What a hero. There was nobody, you hear? He carried it all by himself. Seems like we've gone backward sometimes. I almost can't make myself go see a black movie anymore."

Dad and April's father could have had a long conversation about *that*.

"Yessir," I said. "My dad and I must have watched every Poitier movie ever made."

"It's good to meet a young man who cares about history, Tennyson," he said.

April was so excited she bit her lip. She took her mother by the hand, leading her into the living room. "Wait until you see his screening room," she said.

Marcela fixed *arroz con pollo* and fried plantains, so the house smelled too good to chat long before we sat to eat. Chela and Bernard sat beside the Forrests. When April's mother said it was time to say grace and said we should hold hands, we all bowed our heads. Dad had usually said grace, and a feeling of empty sadness so deep and wide came over me that I thought I would have to excuse myself from the table. But it rattled through me and moved on.

"Dear Lord," she said. "Thank you for bringing us all together and for the bravery of the young man at this table, who nearly died to help my child."

"Amen," Gloria Forrest and April said together.

"We don't like everything you've put before us on this path, Lord. We don't understand it all. But we trust in you and your will, and we will remember the lesson that tomorrow is not promised. Thank you for this meal prepared with love. Amen."

I wondered if her reference to not liking everything on her path meant our recent tragedies or just me. She avoided my eyes as she reached for the pitcher of water, so I guessed the latter. I'd thought I would have a harder time getting April's father to warm up to me, but her mother might be the challenge.

That was fine, though. We had time.

"So . . . Shelly?" April's mother said, fumbling with Chela's name. Chela corrected her. Mrs. Forrest looked embarrassed. "I'm sorry, Chela. What are your plans for the future?"

That was Chela's least favorite question, but it didn't show in her face. Her eyes stayed overly bright. "Well, this is an industry town, so I'll probably get an internship for a production company like my boyfriend," she said. "He's already making contacts for me."

That was news to me. I glanced up at Bernard, who could barely contain a smug smile. He had fought against Chela's defenses for a long time, and she had finally let him in. Maybe it was a Hardwick family trait.

"I see," April's father said. He looked troubled. "So you want to get straight into movies or television like Tennyson?"

"Oh, I don't think I want to act," Chela said. "I'm thinking the management track."

A crinkle at the edge of Mr. Forrest's mouth said that Chela had just jumped four notches on his esteem chart.

"But I haven't even chosen a major yet. I'm thinking law or economics." Another notch. Chela glanced at me as if to say, *How's that?*

"That reminds me," I told Chela. "You need to work on that application. We can go online and find one tonight. Maybe you can get in for the spring term."

Irritation flickered behind Chela's smile. "Sure . . . Dad. But don't forget, college is expensive. I won't have any scholarships or anything."

"You let me worry about that," I said.

I didn't know what the impact of Mother's legal issues would be on her estate, but it was hard to prosecute the dead. Melanie, my lawyer, had called to give me the details of Mother's will, and I definitely would have more than enough to put Chela through college. The inheritance was in my name, but Chela would have a good portion waiting for her when she turned twenty-one. I hadn't mentioned it yet. I was waiting for the right moment. The right leverage. Maybe it was time. Mother didn't have enough money to pay Chela for what she'd taken from her, but it would be a good start in life. *Pozdrav, Mother,* I thought.

"It's wonderful that you put a value on education," William Forrest said. "Don't forget about Florida A&M in Tallahassee. Bet you could get a scholarship there. And Gloria and I could keep an eye on you, make sure you don't get in trouble." He winked, but his wink wasn't entirely playful. He was a former judge who was the dean of the school's criminal justice department. The Forrests knew far too much about Chela.

Chela's phony smile faded. "Thanks, but I don't get into trouble." She sounded as if she was ready to spring claws. To her ears, he had accused her of plans to start streetwalking.

April gave her father an impatient look. "Dad . . ."

"Chela's a good girl," Marcela said. "She's been raised well."

"We trust her," I said. "But if she ends up in Florida, I'll be glad she has a place to go."

Mrs. Forrest quickly changed the subject to movies, and everyone relaxed again. April looked relieved. Until her mother's eyes came to me. Mrs. Forrest had been sipping from a glass of sangria, maybe to work up her nerve.

"Do you intend to keep doing your investigations, Tennyson?" Mrs. Forrest said.

April's eyes were heavy on me. She wondered, too.

"No, ma'am," I said. "But to be honest, I've said that before."

"Do you think you mean it this time?" April's mother probed.

I glanced up at the wondering, concerned eyes around the

table. I reached over for April's hand and held it, gently stroking the ridges of her knuckles with my thumb.

"Yes, ma'am," I said. "My father was a police officer, a good one, so there's a part of me that tried to be like him. Prove something to him, maybe. But ever since I was a kid, all I've ever wanted to be was an actor. I want to leave a legacy fifty years from now like Sidney Poitier. And I have a lot of work to do, so I'd better get started."

Everyone at the table was smiling. Especially April.

FORTY

MARCELA CAUGHT ME at the wine rack while I was trying to find the South African Riesling I'd promised April's father a taste of. As it turned out, he was a bit of a connoisseur, which gave us something else to talk about. It was already hard to believe that April had been so afraid to introduce me to her parents.

"How are you feeling?" Marcela said. She cast her eyes down toward my groin. "Is the swelling very bad?"

Marcela was a nurse, but my earlobes went hot. "Fine, thanks."

In truth, my last dose of painkillers was wearing off, and my walk had been stiffer and stiffer since the *tres leches* cake Marcela had served for dessert. I was glad April's parents were talking about calling a cab to go back to their hotel soon.

"Are you sure?" Marcela said. "I could take a look—"

I angled myself away from her, covering myself with my palm as if I were nude. "Don't get carried away with the stepmother thing."

"All right, but that's silly. I'm an RN. You don't have anything I haven't seen."

I was quiet, waiting for her to change the subject or move on. In the silence, I heard April, Chela, and April's mother laughing loudly from the living room. Maybe I had survived the party.

"I'm moving back to my old apartment," Marcela said. "Next week, I think."

"You don't have to do that."

Sadness shadowed her face. "Yes, I want to. I can't heal here. It's your house. Don't get me wrong: I'll still come see you. But now I have to see what's next for me."

I couldn't say I didn't understand. I gave Marcela a hug. "We'll miss you."

Marcela patted my shoulder to end the hug quickly, probably to keep her emotions at bay. "And I have a surprise for you," she said. "I was going to wait to give this to you, but then I thought maybe this was the perfect time. I was going through your father's things . . ."

"A will?" I didn't need money from my father, but I wished he'd left me something he had given thought to.

Marcela smiled. "No, but better, I think."

She reached into her pocket and pulled out a small silver-colored jewelry case. The finish was cracked from time, no longer shiny. *I've seen that before*, I thought, just before Marcela opened the case for me.

The ring appeared like déjà vu. It still had its luster—a gold band ringed by tiny diamonds, with one larger diamond glistening at the center, a bright sun.

"My mother's wedding ring?" I said, remembering.

Marcela grinned. "Yes. This was Eva's ring. And now it goes to you."

"Shouldn't it be yours?"

"No, Tennyson. Didn't Richard tell you? She wanted her new baby boy to have it. She told him to give it to you when it was time. He was saving it for you."

I remembered Dad showing me the ring once and telling me my mother's wishes, but I had been a very young man then, more of a boy, and I'd barely heard a word my father said in those days.

When Marcela slipped the ring case into my hand, I pursed my lips to ward off stinging eyes. Maybe it was the tear gas, maybe not.

"*Gracias*, Marcela," I said. "This is the perfect night."

The sky wasn't usually clear enough for me to see the Hollywood sign from my back deck, but that night, I could see it without Alice's telescope. I both loved and hated my town. Would I really have the chance to build a lasting legacy, or would I always be a trivia question associated with a kidnapped child or a serial killer? I didn't know. But I had to try.

April huddled beside me, finishing the last of her wine while we listened to Stevie Wonder's love songs drifting through my half-open glass sliding door. Chela and Bernard had gone to a late movie, April's parents were back at their hotel, and Marcela was in bed. For the first time since the tar pits, it seemed, April and I were alone.

Suddenly, my heart drilled my chest. It was as real a terror as any I'd ever felt. *You're on medication*, I reminded myself. *Maybe you should wait.* But I had already kept April waiting for years. Kept myself waiting. As April's mother had said at dinner, tomorrow was not promised.

And for the first time in my life, I knew exactly what I wanted.

"April?" I said. "It's time."

"Time for what?"

But I didn't have to answer. She knew from my eyes. The look on her face reminded me of Marcela's at her birthday party in Miami, blank with disbelief. "What?"

"I can't get down on one knee, but . . ." I opened the ring case for her. "This was my mother's ring. My father gave it to me. I'd like it to be yours."

April gazed at the sunshine in the ring case, then back up to me. My mother's diamond was gorgeous, but the sparkle in April's eyes dimmed it by comparison.

"Ten, you know I want to have kids," she said.

"One or two kids?" I said. "After Chela, how hard can that be?"

"And I'm a slob."

"And a pretty lousy cook," I said. "But we can work around that."

April studied my face for lies or uncertainty, shivering against me. She hushed her voice. "I saw you die that night, Ten," she said. "When you weren't breathing . . ."

I had made my first appointment to see the therapist April recommended the following week, but April behaved as if Escobar had not damaged her, too. Whenever I asked how afraid she'd been, she said she'd mostly been afraid for me. She couldn't stare it in the face yet. Gustavo Escobar would be with us for a long time, whether or not we were together.

But I hoped we would be. We would fight all of our demons better as a team.

"I thought I saw you die, too, April," I said, pulling her closer to me, absorbing her tremors. "And I'll spend the rest of my life trying to make sure you never go through anything like that again. Not even close. I can't promise you I'll be perfect—but I can promise to try to be the perfect man for you."

"Tennyson Hardwick," she said. "That's quite a proposition."

"It's not a proposition, sweetie," I said. "It's a proposal."

We kissed as if it were our last chance.

Acknowledgments

WE WOULD LIKE to thank all of the friends and family who have supported us through this special journey. Special thanks to our police source for helping us navigate the world of prostitution. Also, many thanks to our longtime editor, Atria Books Vice President and Senior Editor Malaika Adero, for her dedication, vision, and faith. Many thanks to Todd Hunter at Atria Books, as well as Atria publisher Judith Curr and publicist Yona Deshommes.

For Tennyson Hardwick series news and updates, "like" Tennyson's Facebook page at www.facebook.com/pages/Tennyson-Hardwick/35660298310.

You can also keep up with the coauthors on Twitter and Facebook.

Follow Blair Underwood on Twitter at www.twitter.com/blairunderwood (@BlairUnderwood), or "like" his Facebook page at www.facebook.com/BlairUnderwood.

Follow Tananarive Due on Twitter at www.twitter.com/tananarivedue (@TananariveDue), or "like" her Facebook page at www.facebook.com/pages/Tananarive-Due/15737779284. She also writes two blogs: *Tananarive Due's Reading Circle* at www.tananarivedue.blogspot.com and *Tananarive Due Writes*, a blog for writers and screenwriters at www.tananarivedue.blogspot.com. Her website is www.tananarivedue.com.

Visit Steven Barnes's website at www.diamondhour.com. Follow him on Twitter at www.twitter.com/StevenBarnes1. You can also send him a friend request on Facebook: www.facebook.com/steven.barnes.7127.